PRAISE FOR
THE SECRET HISTORY

"Stephanie Thornton's Theodora is tough and intelligent, spitting defiance against the cruel world of the Byzantine Empire. Her rise from street urchin to emperor's consort made me want to stand up and cheer. Her later years as empress are great fun to read, but it was her early struggle as an actress and courtesan that really had me roaring: either with rage at the misfortunes heaped on this poor girl or with delight as she once more picked herself up, with a steely glint in her eye, and kept on going."
—Kate Quinn, author of *Empress of the Seven Hills*

"*The Secret History* tells the tangled but very human story of Empress Theodora, from bawdy actress to reluctant whore to beloved empress. This remarkable woman, beloved wife of Emperor Justinian, mastered the intrigue and politics of sixth-century Byzantium while keeping dark personal secrets that could bring her death. Loss, ambition, and lust keep this rich story moving at top speed. Stephanie Thornton writes a remarkable first novel that brings a little-known woman to full, vibrant life again. A sprawling and irresistible story."
—Jeane Westin, author of *The Spymaster's Daughter*

"A fascinating and vivid account. . . . The life of the Empress Theodora leaps from the page, as colorful and complex as the woman herself."
—Michelle Diener, author of *The Emperor's Conspiracy*

THE SECRET HISTORY

A NOVEL OF EMPRESS THEODORA

STEPHANIE THORNTON

 NEW AMERICAN LIBRARY

New American Library
Published by the Penguin Group
Penguin Group (USA) Inc., 375 Hudson Street,
New York, New York 10014, USA

USA | Canada | UK | Ireland | Australia | New Zealand | India | South Africa | China

Penguin Books Ltd., Registered Offices: 80 Strand, London WC2R 0RL, England
For more information about the Penguin Group visit penguin.com.

First published by New American Library,
a division of Penguin Group (USA) Inc.

First Printing, July 2013

NA REGISTERED TRADEMARK—MARCA REGISTRADA

LIBRARY OF CONGRESS CATALOGING-IN-PUBLICATION DATA:

Thornton, Stephanie, 1980–
The secret history: a novel of Empress Theodora/Stephanie Thornton.
pages cm.
ISBN 978-0-451-41778-7
1. Theodora, Empress, consort of Justinian I, Emperor of the East, d. 548—Fiction.
2. Empresses—Fiction. 3. Byzantine Empire—History—Justinian I, 527–565—Fiction.
4. Biographical fiction. 5. Historical fiction. I. Title.
PS3620.H7847S43   2013
813'.6—dc23 2012045240

Printed in the United States of America
1   3   5   7   9   10   8   6   4   2

Set in Simoncini Garamond · Designed by Elke Sigal

ALWAYS LEARNING   PEARSON

To Stephen, for believing in me

THE SECRET
HISTORY

PART I

AD 517–527

I am She whom one honors and disdains.
I am the Saint and the prostitute.
I am the virgin and the wife.
I am knowledge and I am ignorance.
I am strength and I am fear.
I am Godless and I am the Greatness of God.

—FIFTH-CENTURY AD GNOSTIC HYMN
FROM NAG-HAMMADI, EGYPT

Chapter 1

My life began the night death visited our house.

I lay on the straw pallet with my sisters and listened to Comito grinding her teeth and Anastasia breathing evenly in the dark. An animal snorted in the distance—probably the scraggly new bear Father had acquired to train for the Greens, a beast scarcely fit for the spectacle of the Hippodrome. I scratched my stomach and poked Comito, none too gently. The fleas were bad tonight, and Constantinople's sticky heat made the stench of the nearby garbage heap especially pungent. I missed our old home in Cyprus, the salty smell of the Mediterranean, and the cicadas buzzing amidst the olive trees. Our ramshackle house near Constantinople's amphitheater could scarcely compare.

There was a shuffle in the dark—possibly a rat—but then my father grunted.

"Quiet, Acacius." My mother giggled. "You'll wake the girls."

She gave a little moan as I snuggled into Anastasia's bare back, hoping for more dreams like last night's fantasy of roasted goat with mint yogurt. Comito claimed I had made cow eyes at the butcher's son

3

when Mother sent us to collect our monthly grain ration earlier today, but in truth I was more impressed with the fresh leg of goat hanging from his stall than the cut of his calves under his tunica. It seemed like years since we'd had meat.

"Acacius." My mother's voice woke me, the same tone she used when my father came home after too much wine at the Boar's Eye. There was another sound, a thud like a sack of flour hitting the ground. "Acacius!"

"Mama?" I opened my eyes. My father was facedown on their pallet, arms crumpled like twigs under his bulk.

My mother struggled to move him. "Help me, Theodora."

The chipped mosaic blossoms scraped my knee as I helped shove him to his back. Anastasia whimpered in the moonlight.

Cold sweat covered my father's skin as he opened and closed his mouth like a mackerel freshly pulled from the Bosphorus, fingers plucking the neck of his tunica. My mother clutched his hand to her chest. "You stay right here, Acacius."

She rifled through a little cedar box with her free hand, the one with our scant supply of spices and medicines. Willow bark and chamomile filled my nose as Comito rubbed her eyes and Anastasia crawled into my lap, thumb in her mouth and her wooden doll tucked tight under her arm. It squinted at me through its charcoal smudge of an eye. My father looked from me to Mama to my sisters, and his tongue lurched in his mouth, as if he were trying to speak. Death has many sounds, the shrieks of men crushed by a chariot in the Hippodrome, the final rattle of ancient lungs, or the gentle sigh of a child ravaged by creeping sickness. My giant of a father only gurgled like an infant and then went still.

We sat in silence for a moment. Then my mother screamed and pummeled my father with tiny fists, dusting his chest with the yellow ash of crushed herbs. "No!" Tears streamed down her face. "No! Get up!"

4

She collapsed to his chest, golden curls covering him like a burial shroud as her body heaved with sobs. Departing this life in the throes of passion is as good a way to go as any, but I could not fathom my father greeting Saint Peter now. I clung to Anastasia as my tears fell into her hair.

"Don't be sad, Dora." She traced my cheeks with fingers still sticky from the honeyed *kopton* we'd eaten before bed, but her chin wobbled as my mother wailed louder. My little sister slid from my lap and touched Mama's shoulder, but she jerked back as Comito added her voice to the howls.

I pulled Anastasia to me and tucked us into the crook of my father's arm, savoring his fleeting warmth.

My father was dead.

Never again would he carry Anastasia on his shoulders to see the zebras before a show, or tease Comito until the tips of her ears turned red. He would never wrap me in an elephant hug that smelled of the wild rosemary he constantly chewed and the ever-present animal musk that clung to his skin, even after he'd just come home from the baths.

I don't know how long we listened to one another's tears, but his body grew stiff and clammy before I could rouse myself. He would have to be buried soon, before his flesh began to decay.

I touched my mother's back, but she jerked away as if stung, still draped over my father. "The sun will rise soon." I rubbed my eyes with the back of my hand. "We have to purify him."

She stumbled to her feet, hair veiling her eyes. "No. I won't." Her hands fluttered in the air. "I can't."

She slammed the door behind her, followed by a surly thump on our ceiling from the Syrian neighbors above. Raucous laughter from a nearby taverna floated to our apartment, the high trill of a woman and throaty baritone of the man who had likely paid for her services for the night. I stared at the shaft of silvery light that had swallowed my mother, torn between the urge to follow her or stay with my father's body.

"What should we do?" Comito wiped her puffy eyes. She was older than me by two years but looked far younger in the moonlight. Anastasia sucked her thumb and reached out to touch our father's cheek with her little hand. It was more than I could bear.

"Go. Gather flowers."

"It's dark out." Comito hated the dark—she still liked to fall asleep with an olive oil lamp burning, although she claimed it was for Anastasia.

I pressed a frayed basket to her hand as Anastasia whimpered. "The lion will eat us if we go outside," she said, her eyes big as plums.

I would have laughed—my father had been telling Anastasia myths from the Golden Age, most recently acting out the story of the Nemean Lion falling from the full moon—but instead I blinked hard and tweaked her nose. "Silly goose, Heracles slew the lion. You'll be perfectly safe." I bent down to whisper in her ear. "And you're much scarier than any lion when you growl."

She bared her teeth and made claws with her hands, her little mouth opening in an adorable roar. I swallowed hard and dropped a kiss on her head. "Help Comito pick a pretty posy. And find Uncle Asterius." My voice quavered as I spoke to Comito. "He needs to bring a priest."

They left and I was alone. I shouldn't have been alone—this was my mother's job. I didn't know how to prepare a body, how to purify my father so he could pass to the afterlife. But there was no one else.

My hands trembled as I struck the flame for our oil lamp and rummaged through our lone trunk, past my father's ivory backgammon set with its missing piece and the worn codex of Homer's *Song of Ilium*. I tossed out Mother's saffron wedding veil before I finally found what I was looking for—a single bottle of olive oil pressed from our own trees in Cyprus. I tried not to cry but had to set the bottle down to wipe the stream of snot and tears from my face. Once started, I couldn't seem to stop.

I didn't hear my mother return until she gathered me into her arms, the hot smell of wine on her breath as she pressed her lips to my forehead. Together we readied my father—she washed his body and redressed him in his green tunica, and my uneven stitches sewed him into his brown cloak until only his face and the splayed toes of his feet showed, the better to allow the angels to examine him and determine his fitness for paradise. He looked asleep, and I prayed that he might sit up and roar with laughter because we'd fallen for another of his jokes. Yet God was deaf to my prayers.

Myrrh choked the air and the sun had almost heaved itself over the horizon when Comito arrived with a priest and Uncle Asterius, Anastasia asleep in his arms with her thumb tucked in her mouth. He wasn't really our uncle, but our father's boss. As leader of the Green faction, he was also one of Constantinople's most powerful politicians. He draped an arm around my mother. "You have my deepest condolences, Zenobia." He crooned something in her ear that made her blanch white, but then she looked at us and gave a terse nod.

Uncle Asterius swept me into a hug that smelled of the lavender used to sweeten his linen. "Poor child," he said. "Everything is going to be all right."

Even then, I knew that to be a lie.

The funeral began in the thin morning light as Uncle Asterius' bleary-eyed slaves hefted the greenwood coffin onto their shoulders, my father's circus whip and pitchfork nestled beside him. Yawning shopkeepers crossed themselves as we made our way to the cedar-lined path that led to the cemetery outside the Gate of Charisios. The air stunk like rotting fish, compliments of the nearby *garos* factories, forced outside the city walls with their vats of fermenting fish sauce. The flowers my sisters had picked on the banks of the Lycus River— daisies, blue crocuses, violets, and scraggly yellow poppies—had already begun to wilt over the sides of the box, and the calm hymns of the lone priest battled with the mournful dirges sung by a professional mourner paid for by Uncle Asterius. We recited a truncated version of the Divine Liturgy and each kissed the rough wooden cross the priest held over the coffin before accepting a square of dry bread and a sip of *phouska*, the watery, sour wine only the poor would drink. My mother's hands trembled violently as she struggled to cut a lock of my father's hair, and the tears ran unchecked down her cheeks. I took the knife from her.

I stared at the blade and ran my thumb down its edge, transfixed by the pearl of blood that dropped onto my father's rough brown shroud. One swift cut and I could join him, free myself from grief's jagged teeth.

Two dark eyes stopped me. Anastasia wiped her nose on her sleeve and took my hand in her little one, kissing the tip of my thumb above the blood. "You hurt yourself, Dora. Are you going to die, too?"

I shook my head, the words tangled in my throat. It would be cowardly to abandon my family. I had many faults—Comito was always quick to point out my temper and snitch on me when I lied—but I wasn't a coward. Family was all we had.

I managed to cut a lock of my father's dark hair, identical to my own, and folded it into my palm, mingling my blood with the black strands. My mother fell to her knees and refused to rise long after the slaves tucked him into the red earth. We were alone in Constantinople—no money squirreled away under a pallet and no way to provide for ourselves.

I'd have promised God anything then to have our old lives back. Unfortunately, our new lives were just beginning.

The food in our cupboard finally ran out a week later. I'd picked the weevils from our bag of barley flour—it was still a quarter full and we were entitled to a free bread ration at one of the city's public bakeries, but Anastasia's stomach growled so I could hear it across the room and she cried for milk, now as much a luxury as pearls. I went to beg from one of our neighbors, an elderly widow who kept a brown and white nanny goat on the third floor.

"Your mam should go to the patriarchate," the woman said as she took the olive wood cup from my hand. "They'll give her bread tokens and some dried food, usually apricots. Sometimes they have blankets. Medicine, too." The warm milk squirted into the cup, and my stomach rumbled. "'Tisn't much, but it's something."

I couldn't tell the old woman that my mother's sometime habit of overindulging in her wine was now the norm and that the sickly sweet smell of poppy juice had become her new perfume. Yesterday I'd come home to find Anastasia crumpled on the floor, her face red as a radish with tears cutting swaths down her dirty cheeks. The poor thing had soiled herself while my mother lay on her pallet, arm flung over her face so I feared she was dead until I felt the dull throb of blood in her neck. I cursed her for abandoning us when we needed her most. I cursed the world; I cursed God.

I would have to get the food myself.

It took me half the afternoon to find the church, only to be told by the priest that my mother had to claim the monthly stipend allowed by the Widow's Battalion. That wasn't going to happen anytime soon.

I wove my way down the wide cobbles of the *Mese*—Middle Street—toward the main market, but I was forced to wait as a gilded sedan carried by eight bearded Lombard slaves lumbered down the street. The outline of a woman shone through delicate silk curtains— the *kyria* of some grand villa from the look of her, probably married to a senator and richer than God. I wanted to do more than see her—I wanted to *be* her. That little daydream abruptly ended as one of her slaves stomped a puddle of horse piss and who knew what else, splashing my sandals and tunica with filth.

Time to pull my head from the sky. We needed food.

At least a dozen languages swarmed around me as I entered the chaos of the food market—mostly Greek but a smattering of Latin in addition to what sounded like Coptic, Armenian, and possibly Syriac. A man wearing a string of cold sausages around his neck passed me, a pot of *garos* in his hand as he dipped and ate the meats, licking his greasy fingers. Under a rickety wooden stall two pigeons tussled over a bruised cabbage leaf, one I was tempted to swipe from them. My eyes roved over wheels of cheese wrapped in bristly pig skins, rainbows of spices in brown baskets, and crates of gossiping chickens to linger on a wooden cart with a charcoal brazier manned by a merchant with sweat dripping down his bare—and rather hairy—chest. Strips of lamb sizzled on the coals, and there was even a suckling pig roasting, probably preordered for some senator's feast after the chariot races tonight. My stomach rumbled, but I couldn't very well hide dripping hot meats down the front of my tunica.

My heart hammered up my spine. I'd never stolen anything in my life; I had never needed to. Theft was a sin, but I hoped God might look the other way if I stole our dinner this once. After all, it was his fault we were in this predicament.

The *kopton* stall beckoned, the flaky pastries drizzled with honey and almonds making my stomach groan with a vengeance, but I settled on a cart of plump *boukellaton* watched by a man with heavy eyes. The bread was sprinkled with sesame seeds and golden brown, not the cheap kind mixed with ash we were sometimes forced to buy. Anastasia liked the ring shapes—they made excellent bracelets—and bread was more practical to lift than most everything else.

I pretended to browse through a pile of apricots, sniffed one, and set it down. The *boukellaton* vendor was a slave with thick, dimpled arms dusted with flour. A woman dressed in a plain white tunica and accessorized by half a dozen children caught his attention as she swatted a boy out of her way and motioned to a small mountain of barley loaves piled on the ground. The slave turned his back to me. Sometimes God did work miracles.

I swiped two loaves and ran as if the cobbles were on fire. My heart pounded in my ears as I clutched the precious bread. I had done it.

The fabric at my shoulder tore as someone whipped me around so fast the loaves tumbled from my hands.

"I don't suppose you forgot to pay for those?" The slave towered over me—eyes wide-awake now—as his lips curled back in a sneer of perfectly straight teeth. His face was a map of pockmarked old scars and white flakes sprinkled his greasy hair.

"They're for my mother and sisters," I said, scrambling to pick up the bread. I wasn't fast enough—one golden ring was trampled under the crowd's feet and the other was snatched by a boy with nimbler fingers than mine. "My father died."

"I don't care if your whole family keeled over of the plague." He grabbed a handful of my hair and dragged me back toward his booth. I yelped and people stopped to stare, but they must have decided a tussle between a slave and a dirty pleb girl wasn't worth their time.

The man hauled me back to his stall and motioned to the vendor next to him. "Caught her," he said.

"Pretty little wench," the other man said. He gave a phlegmy cough as he stirred a giant pot of boiled cabbage. "Young though."

I tipped my chin, ready to argue that I'd seen thirteen years, but the slave's eyes roved over me. I'd add lying to my list of sins. "I've had eleven summers."

"Old enough to learn the ways of the world," the bread vendor said. He looked around for something but then unfastened the belt on his tunica. I struggled to get away, but he used the belt to tie my wrists tight behind me and looped the leather through one of the wheels on his cart. "Can't have you running away before I figure out what your punishment will be, now, can I?"

"My mother and sisters are waiting for me."

"Shut up," the slave said. "Females shouldn't speak unless spoken to."

I tried to kick him, but he stomped on my ankle. I decided to do as I was told for once.

It took the better part of an hour for the slave to sell the rest of his master's bread. The sky darkened around puffs of pink clouds, and a rainbow of glass lanterns lit the market as the Hippodrome beckoned the crowd like a pretty young whore on the docks. Finally the slave blew the crumbs from his cart and scowled as he untied me. He beckoned to his fat friend as he yanked me to my feet. "Annius, watch the cart for a minute."

"A minute's probably all you'll need." Annius laughed and waggled his bushy eyebrows at me.

I hadn't noticed the little alley behind the soup stall until the bread slave pushed me into its blackness, one of the spaces in the city cursed with permanent darkness. He fumbled with something as a rat scurried over my foot. I stepped back, thinking to run, but was greeted by a cold stone wall. The slave grabbed me by my hair. "You owe me, girl."

He was naked from the waist down, the thong that held his undergarments in place unstrapped beneath his *paludamentum*. I tried to shove him away, but he pulled my tunica with his free hand. Some of my hair came loose as I wrenched my head to the side and bit his hand, feeling the skin separate between my teeth and tasting the copper tang of his blood. He yowled and punched me to the ground, filling my skull with an explosion of white, followed by an eclipse of black as my tunica was shoved up around my waist. Something hard prodded between my legs.

I wrestled one hand free and shoved my fingers as far as I could down my throat. There wasn't much in my stomach, but what there was came up all over him.

"By the dog!" He loosened his hold enough that I managed to

twist away. I didn't look back but ran as fast as my legs could carry me. "You filthy, scabby slut!"

"Hang yourself on the cross!" I tore past the soup stall and kept running, dodging people as they shouted and shook their fists at me, a froth of laughter and sobs bubbling from my throat.

I found my way home, stopping only to wash myself in a public fountain, its water spewing from the mouth of a giant scowling fish. Two drunks whistled as I peeled my tunica from my skin to wash the vomit from my chest, but I focused on the cool clean water as it washed away the evidence of my stupidity. Tonight couldn't get any worse.

I was wrong, of course.

All hope of cajoling my mother from bed evaporated when I walked in the door. She was still on her pallet, but no longer surrounded by wine fumes or passed out in a fog of poppy juice. Instead, she was very much awake, legs wrapped tight around a naked man as he pounded into her, her nails digging into the bare flesh of his hairy back. I slammed the door and slid down the wall of our building, hiding my face in my knees. I had left quickly, but not so fast as to miss my mother's sharp glance or see the man, a complete stranger to me.

I stared at the dust, fingers plunged as far into my ears as I could make them go, yet not far enough to muffle all the sounds I didn't wish to hear. I would have left, but I didn't want my sisters to come home and stumble into what I'd just witnessed. The man emerged some time later, wiped his head, shiny and speckled like a plover's egg, and straightened his tunica. He was startled to see me. "You must be Theodora. I am Vitus."

As if that explained everything.

I wanted life to return to the way it was a month ago, when the ground under my feet had been solid. But time was not so obliging.

Vitus gave me an indecipherable look when I didn't speak, then turned and shuffled off, his step a little too jaunty for my liking.

"Theodora, come here."

My mother was dressed in her old tunica, staring at my father's scratched backgammon game on the table, her eyes empty pools of darkness. I stepped inside as she slammed the game to the floor, splintering the wood and scattering the ivory pieces like an army of drunken ants. One rolled to my toe and came to a stop. I almost stormed back out the door, but my fury got the better of me.

"How could you? Father would die another death if he could see you now."

She leveled a glare at me that could have frozen the fires of Gehenna. "Do you think I wanted to sleep with that filthy ox?"

"It certainly looked as if you were enjoying it."

She lunged from the table, her arm raised to slap me. I steeled myself for the blow, but her hand fell back to her side. "Of course that's how it looked. I have to keep a roof over our heads." She swallowed hard and walked back to the table, knocked the wax seal off an amphora of wine, and guzzled what little was left in it. Wiping her mouth with the back of her hand, she gave a dry chuckle. "Sometimes things don't work out quite the way you planned." She waved me forward and enveloped me in a hug I had to force myself not to pull away from. Her skin reeked of that filthy man. "Vitus is the new bear keeper for the Greens."

My father's job.

"So you're whoring for him?"

"In a manner of sorts. I married him."

The ground caught me as my knees buckled. It was then that I noticed the clump of saffron next to my mother's pallet. Her wedding veil.

"You'd marry him before the grass has a chance to grow on Father's grave? A man you don't even know?"

"This house belongs to Vitus now. I loved your father. Fiercely. But I can marry Vitus and keep our home and the grain dole, or I can refuse and we starve on the streets. Asterius was very clear about that the night your father died. Fortunately, Vitus was easy to persuade." Of course he was—my mother was at least half his age. "We women are the pawns of men, Theodora. The sooner you learn that, the better."

The ground beneath my feet wouldn't hold steady today. I wanted to cry and scream at the same time. "There has to be some other way—"

"There isn't." She slammed the terra-cotta jug on the table. "I'm too old for the tavernas, so unless you and Comito plan to take up a room—"

"Where is Comito?" I needed to steer the conversation to safer waters.

My mother's hand flitted in the air. "I can't be bothered to keep track of your sister. Anastasia is upstairs with the Syrians." She caressed my cheek. "I know this is hard, but your father would understand. We have to survive."

She passed me the remnants of their wedding meal. No boiled greens with *garos* sauce, *sphoungata* of eggs and cheese, or honey cakes, but a thick slice of crusty brown bread to symbolize their future prosperity. It was stale.

The bald man—Vitus—came home after I'd picked up Anastasia, and we'd swept up the backgammon set and dropped it in the trash heap behind our building. Vitus stunk of a taverna, although my mother's breath smelled more of wine than his. My new father's chin was soft, and one black hair curled around the outside of his nostril like a spider's leg. This man likely counted today a blessing. I still thought it a curse.

"I brought a gift for you and your sisters," he said. "It's not much, but I thought you might enjoy the treat." He handed me a dried mallow leaf envelope stuffed with almonds, spiced with garlic and pepper. My stomach growled.

I handed the gift to Anastasia. She shoveled several of the nuts into her mouth like a starving squirrel. Perhaps this man wasn't the devil, only one of his minions. "Thank you."

I covered my ears that night as Vitus grunted like a rutting pig on my mother's pallet. He took so long, I escaped with Anastasia outside to sleep in front of our door next to the half-full urn of urine for the fullers to collect in the morning. The air was still warm, and it was certainly more tolerable outside than in. Comito traipsed home in the middle of the night, smelling like cheap rose water and something else I couldn't place.

"Holy Mother of God," she said. "I almost stepped on you—I might have broken my neck."

"What a pity," I said, rolling over.

"What are you doing out here? It's not that hot." She moved to open the door, but her face contorted as she heard what I'd been trying to avoid. "Did I miss something?"

She had no idea.

Comito continued to disappear to God only knew where, and I learned to follow suit, spending my afternoons roaming the markets along the *Mese* and imagining I had the coins to buy gems from Asia, Persian silks and spices, and Baltic amber. More in our price range were the jars of leeches and senna and licorice root for constipation, both of which Mother sent me to fetch for Vitus. I spent countless hours in the engravers' market, curled up amongst its ever-present cats while I read Ovid and tried to make out Ptolemy's theories on the workings of the universe until my head hurt and the merchants realized I had no money and chased me away.

I watched men stop to stare at Comito as she dodged her way around the stalls. God had gifted my sister with my mother's thick mane of golden hair and blue eyes rimmed with lashes long as a camel's. Unfortunately, she had the brains of a rabbit—a not very intelligent rabbit.

"Theodora!" She grabbed my arm, her cheeks flushed. "I've been looking everywhere for you—Uncle Asterius turned us out."

"What?"

"He fired Vitus and hired a new Master of Bears. I don't know why."

I grabbed Comito's hand and pushed our way through the streets toward the Hippodrome and our building. A melon vendor shouted curses to make a whore blush as I shoved a customer with an overripe muskmelon out of my way, feeling the juice spatter my legs as the fruit crashed to the cobbles.

Comito was right. Our scant belongings had already been dumped outside our door by the time we got there. I opened my mouth to ask my mother what had happened, but two angry voices coming from the alley next to the Boar's Eye stopped me.

"Make sure I never see you again if you value your life."

"I won that job—you can't fire me!"

I crept closer to see Asterius and Vitus practically nose to nose, my stepfather's face red as a freshly stewed beet. Asterius pushed Vitus back with a finger on his chest. "You should have stayed content shoveling manure in the stables, but you've used this opportunity to spout that Monophysite drivel denying Christ's humanity to anyone who will listen. Everyone knows religion is bad for business."

"I'll report you to the consul."

Asterius gave a fearsome grin. "The consul and I are both of the opinion that Monophysites are heretics better suited to the fires of Gehenna than the sacred sands of the Hippodrome."

Vitus remained rooted to the spot, clenching and unclenching his fists. Then he stormed off in the opposite direction, his worn leather boots kicking up little puffs of dust. I wished him good riddance, except that without him we were back where we started.

"Uncle Asterius—" I shrugged my mother's hand off my shoulder and stepped from the shadows. "Our house—"

He whirled on me. "Belongs to the Greens. Find someone else to take up your charity case."

"You can't do that. We're not citizens yet. We won't even qualify for the grain ration without an address in the city!"

He kept walking. I kicked a crate of rotting fish heads and stubbed my toe. Hard.

I hobbled back to my family and hoisted Anastasia onto my hip— she was as heavy as a bag of turnips as she snuggled into my neck, her breath warm on my skin. "I'm hungry," she whimpered.

I looked at my mother crouched on the ground and Anastasia with her oily ringlets and thick tears welled in her eyes. Comito bit her lip, a sure sign she was about to turn on the waterworks.

I forced a smile for Anastasia, rubbing her nose with mine. "You're always hungry, silly goose."

I was at an utter loss. We had nothing to sell, no skills.

Vitus rejoined us. As a Monophysite, he was no better than a pagan. But he was all we had. "I'll take care of us." He sounded as sure of himself as the rest of us felt.

"How?" I asked.

"Don't be pert, girl. One of the stables will hire me. We'll just have to wait until morning."

My mother's lips were tight. "And where do we sleep tonight?"

No one answered.

"The Greens' stables," I said.

"You've lost your mind, girl," Vitus said. "If Asterius found us—"

"He won't." I stared him down, hands on my hips. I wished I were a little taller so I didn't have to look up his nose. "There are no games tonight, right?"

"No."

"Then he won't be there. And it's better than the public latrinas."

No one could argue with that.

Vitus did not find a job that day. Or the next. Or the day after that.

I mustered the courage to pinch a loaf of twice-baked barley bread one day—this time from a stall run by a woman—and Comito magically produced a ring of garlic sausages after one of her disappearances, but it wasn't enough. Mother grew ill-tempered when the wine ran out, and Anastasia whimpered through the days and even into her sleep. The sixth day she fell silent, a frightening lethargy settling into her limbs. Not even her one-eyed doll or a round of the Kingdoms game with her as Empress and Comito and me as her maids could rouse her. Something had to be done.

The four of us sat in the shade of the triumphal arch in the Forum of Theodosius, listening to the racket of squeals and men yelling at the nearby swine market. Vitus had already pawned everything we owned, even our sandals and my mother's saffron veil, and had gone back to the Blues to beg for a position, but none of us thought he'd return with good news. My mother's voice was scarcely a whisper, yet the sound of it made me jump.

"A laurel crown."

Emperors wore laurel crowns on parades through the city, but for a plebian to don the crown meant only one thing.

"No," I said. I had nothing left in this life, but to be reduced to begging left a bitter taste in my mouth. There were always piles of beggars outside the Hippodrome before big races—mothers with laps of filthy children, Ostrogoth soldiers missing limbs, and the occasional blind old man with no family or political connections to take care of him—all wearing bedraggled laurel crowns. It was a sort of pregame entertainment to spit at the beggars instead of dropping a copper *nummi* into their open palms. And today was the first of September, the start of the New Year and the celebration of Constantine's founding of Rome's new Eastern capital—known in ancient times as Byzantion—almost two hundred years ago. The Hippodrome would overflow its stands.

A lifetime of begging was not what I'd envisioned for my future. And yet . . .

I kissed my mother's cheek and gave Anastasia butterfly kisses, wishing she would giggle and gift me with one of her precious smiles. Instead, she lay as lifeless as her doll. "Comito and I will take care of everything," I said, not looking my mother in the eyes. "Meet us outside the Boar's Eye after the races tonight."

I'd save us or ruin us. God help us if I failed.

Chapter 2

We stunk like pigs.

No money meant we hadn't visited the public baths in more than a week, rendering us unfit for the society of even the most pungent swineherd. Comito and I scurried past a pagan shrine to Apollo, then skirted the walls of the Hippodrome near the Palace of Lausus. A eunuch in the court of Theodosius II, Lausus had owned his own miniature palace, but he had distributed much of his wealth to the poor. Too bad he'd been dead for fifty years.

The Baths of Zeuxippus were almost entirely deserted, just as I'd hoped. The majority of the city would be clustered around Constantine's massive porphyry pillar to sing hymns to the Emperor's gold statue, reputed to hold nails from Christ's cross in its spiked crown, before moving to the Hippodrome for the New Year's races before the sun set. A slave with dark stains at the armpits of his tunica stood at the entrance of the baths with the fee basket. By the dog—I hadn't thought of that.

"Aren't we going in?" Comito bit her bottom lip. Two men in snowy tunicas practically broke their necks to gawk at her on their way out of the gates.

"We don't have any money."

She grabbed my hand and pulled me around the walls. "Over here."

We strode past the slave at the entrance and skirted the high wall to the opposite end of the complex. A sycamore tree grew close, near enough we could climb it and jump over.

Comito hitched her tunica up so I could see her ankles, a sight many men would have paid good money to see. "Are you coming?"

She shimmied up the tree and I followed, careful not to drop the bundle tucked under my arm as the rough bark scraped my palms and an angry squirrel berated us. The jump looked much smaller from the ground. I climbed out as far as I could until I was almost over the wall, clamped the top of the cloth bag between my teeth, and lowered myself down over the branch. From there I let go, landing with a re-sounding crash, tail first in an obliging juniper bush. Comito was al-ready on the grass, looking as if she'd been waiting the entire time, not a golden hair out of place.

"You do this often?"

She brushed her tunica, blushing slightly at my raised eyebrows, but only turned and threaded her way through the maze of hedges.

The baths had been built upon an ancient temple of Zeus, and the colorful mosaic paths retold stories of familiar heroes from the Golden Age: Theseus wrestling the Minotaur, Heracles slaying the Hydra, and Perseus hoisting Medusa's head over her decapitated body. Marble statues marked as Plato and Virgil stared at me from a forest of figures long since dead, but I had eyes for only one man: Julius Caesar. Comito and I had never really gone to school—we spoke Greek and Latin, and we were lucky to attend a rare lesson at a church charity school—but my mother had helped us sketch our letters in the ashes of our cooking fire and taught us to read from her old codex of the *Tale of Ilium*, pawned by Vitus a few days ago. She also told us hearth tales of our history as we were growing up, stories passed down through the years by her mother and grandmothers. However, it was my father's retelling of Caesar's rise to power and his crossing the Rubicon that had been my favorite, although it inevitably sent my mother from the room and Comito to plugging her ears. I rarely got to hear the tale as Comito always begged for love stories, especially that of Cupid and Psyche. All the other myths of love ended in tragedy, perhaps cautionary tales for reality—but then, Comito had never been terribly concerned with reality.

We passed the exercise green with its dozing slaves and headed to the women's baths. The juniper brush had scraped my thigh, and I bent to inspect the scratch. "Go on," I said. "I'll catch up."

"Comito!" A young man with a mop of damp curls jogged across the green—Karas, the butcher's son. Comito glanced in my direction and picked up her pace, ignoring him, but he caught up to her and grasped her hand. I cursed myself for being too far away to hear their conversation and hurried over as Karas kissed her fingers. She flushed prettily and tucked a curl behind his ear before giving him a playful shove.

"Hello, Theodora." He grinned and swept a bow as he passed me.

I bumped Comito's hip with my own as we watched him jog away. The boy *did* have nice calves. "It seems you and Karas are getting along well these days." Realization dawned on me and my jaw fell. "You've been meeting him here, haven't you?"

Comito pinched my arm so hard I gasped. "You can't tell anyone. Promise you won't tell a soul."

I shook my arm free—there was sure to be a mark. "Of course I promise. You and he aren't—" I raised my eyebrows. "You know—"

Comito elbowed me in the ribs, scarlet from her cheeks to her hairline. "That's none of your business. I love him. We're going to get married and have a dozen babies, live in a room above the butcher shop—"

"You're as bad as an alley cat in heat." I grabbed my sister's hand

and yanked her to the women's changing room. "And you smell just as bad."

We hung our tunicas on the same hook and shivered our way to the *frigidarium*. Comito gasped as she stepped gingerly into the cold water, her nipples puckering as the water reached higher and higher up her body until it kissed the triangle of pale hair between her legs. Just as her blond curls were the height of fashion, Comito's curves were supple and soft, breasts like ripe pomegranates and skin so translucent the blue web of veins showed on her hips and chest. I, on the other hand, was all brown angles, better suited to being a charioteer than a woman. I plunged into the chill, making sure to splash her perfect hair.

"Do you really think this will work?" Comito chewed a damp strand of hair with chattering teeth. I had told her of my plan, and I was shocked when she'd agreed to help. Neither of us wanted to see our sister buried next to our father.

I shrugged. "I guess we'll find out, won't we?"

We stayed in the *frigidarium* until we couldn't take the cold anymore, then ran covered in goose pimples to the large pools of the *tepidarium*. A jowly matron turned her nose up and heaved herself out of the water as we entered. We quickly drained the cup of wine she'd left behind, both making sure to avoid the thick smear of henna on the rim.

No coins to pay for oil, or a slave to scour our backs, I scraped a borrowed bronze stirgil over Comito's skin a little harder than was necessary, but she returned the favor until my skin stung as if I'd been attacked by a nest of hornets.

We dried our hair and slipped back into our tunicas. Mine was mostly green, save the orange stain on the hem where Anastasia had dropped *garos* sauce during last year's feast of Saint Paul. Both our necklines and armpits were stained from too much wear, but hopefully no one would notice.

"Come; you can do my hair," Comito said.

It took two tries for me to plait my sister's hair to her satisfaction, but her fingers were deft as they tugged and pulled my dark hair into something presentable. She held me at arm's length and sighed. "I don't know how you manage to be such a heathen and still have a pretty face. It must be your eyes." She frowned. "Today they're hazel."

"And tomorrow they'll be brown," I said. "Like manure."

We giggled—it felt like the first time I'd laughed in ages—as another woman walked into the changing area. A Christian since my baptism, I still knew all the myths of Aphrodite, but this copper-haired woman could have beaten the goddess of love and beauty to win Paris' golden apple. Although she was past the first flush of youth, a blush like dainty rose petals bloomed on her high cheeks in the warmth of the baths and her bronze hair brushed an impossibly tiny waist. She held her arms out, and a slave unpinned her stola—an expensive one made from crimson silk with yellow butterflies embroidered on the hem—and whisked it to its own hook before the fabric touched the ground. The smell of musk perfume hung heavy in the air.

"The consul is waiting in the steam baths," the slave said. "He said to hurry—his wife expects him home before their guests arrive to break bread for the *krama*."

Men and women weren't supposed to mingle in bathhouses, but it appeared no one followed that rule any longer.

"It would do his waistline good to miss the afternoon meal." The woman winked at me. "I think I'll have a massage first."

Her voice had a lilting quality, like a harp. The woman was too well dressed to be one of the common *pornai*, the crass prostitutes who worked in the brothels and tavernas. Byzantine patricians kept their wives to have children and visited *pornai* to attend to their bodily needs, but few could afford to patronize a *scenica*, the most expensive sort of courtesan. No wonder this woman's skin shone and her silk gleamed as if it were worth a man's monthly salary. It probably was.

I looked to Comito, but she had eyes only for the silk. My elbow in her ribs earned me a fierce glare.

"We have to go," I said to her. "There's much to do before the races."

"Are you girls going to the Hippodrome tonight?" The courtesan stood completely naked—she could have put a statue of Helen of Troy to shame.

"Yes." I didn't meet her eyes. We weren't going as proper spectators, but no one needed to know that, especially not this *scenica*.

"Do you support the Blues or Greens?"

The Blues and the Greens went far beyond simple chariot factions to also oversee Constantinople's civic functions such as controlling guilds and maintaining the militia. The Blues were the party of the patricians and old landowners. Greens tended to support industry, trade, and the civil service. Comito gestured to our tunicas. "Greens."

The woman's nose wrinkled, but even that didn't mar her allure. "I cheer for the Blues," she said, "even if my patron that evening prefers the Greens."

"We'll see you on the opposite side then." I linked my arm through Comito's and hauled her out of the bathhouse to the sound of the courtesan's silvery laughter. "Poor things," I heard her say to her slave. "I think I scared them away."

The sun was already sinking, and the butterflies in my stomach threatened to declare war with one another. This had to work.

For the final touch to our costumes, Comito and I lingered to decorate each other with cornflowers and lilies scrumped from the bath gardens, garlands in our hair and pinned to our shoulders, posies of violets clutched in our hands. Comito made me wear the daisies. They were pretty but smelled awful.

We were jostled into the rush of people as soon as we stepped into the street, but we managed to wait until the Hippodrome's gates swallowed most of the crowd. A group of children sat outside the amphitheater entrance with wilted laurel wreaths on their heads and their hands outstretched. One boy displayed hands with nubs instead of fingers, the thumbs completely missing, while a little girl only a few years older than Anastasia had her greasy hair pinned back in an elaborate twist, the better to show the ragged scars where her ears should have been. Families with too many mouths to feed often sent their children to beg, but it was more profitable if the child was mutilated first. I watched a man in an ebony litter drop a coin to a black-haired boy with holes of waxy flesh where his eyes should have been. That could be us.

"I don't think I can do this," Comito whispered.

I gave her hand a reassuring squeeze, holding tight in case she tried to bolt. "Everything's going to be fine." A thief and a liar—next I'd be swindling my own mother.

The four prancing bronze horses guarding the Black Gate stared down at us, their patina long since green with age. Most of the crowd climbed the stairs to take their seats under the sky, but we passed a group of men placing bets on charioteers as we followed the path to the arena floor. We'd visited the Hippodrome before, but always with Father while he trained the bears. Then it had been silent, the wooden benches empty except for the occasional crust of stale bread or empty wineskin.

"You girls interested in some pregame entertainment?" One of the gamblers waggled his hips at us while his friends laughed.

"Not with you." I pulled Comito along, but her feet dragged.

"They'd probably pay us," she said.

"No," I said. "We haven't sunk that low."

At least not yet.

I gasped as we passed through the entrance arch and the walls opened up. The Kathisma, the loge shrouded in purple for the Emperor, was vacant, but the Hippodrome was a hive crawling with a hundred thousand people, the loud hum of their voices crowding out my thoughts. The floor of sand stretched before us with the Blue administration on one side and the Greens on the other, while the consul

27

sat directly across from us, a fat man in a snug white tunica clutching the consular scepter with its golden eagle. On the floor, the bronze charioteer statues of the *spina* stood frozen in a line stretching from the twisted Delphi Column, its three gilded snakeheads balancing the golden bowl looted from the famed Temple of Apollo. Next to it, the pink granite of the towering Egyptian obelisk pierced the night sky. The Mediterranean had seemed too vast to cross when we'd left Cyprus. Tonight the Hippodrome's floor seemed even larger.

A slave at the consul's elbow held the red and purple prize *mappa* that would signal the start of the games. Our chance would be lost once he took that cloth.

"It's now or never," I said to Comito.

We started to walk. The crowd seemed to quiet, but that was likely a trick of my ears. I couldn't hear anything; I couldn't see anything other than the dais filled with Greens to my right. Asterius sat in the middle, dressed in a white tunica edged with emerald satin, a merry grin on his face as he laughed at some joke and tore a chunk of meat off a chicken bone. I hoped he'd choke on it.

We tossed flower petals as we passed bronze statues of horses and charioteers, festooning the ground with white and purple as sand scratched my bare feet. Asterius saw us as we ran out of flowers. If looks could have killed, Comito and I would have been smitten to dust in that moment. The fool should have known this was coming—custom dictated private quarrels be settled publicly. Just not this publicly.

My smile worsened his glare. I gave Comito a tiny nod, and we recited the words we'd practiced on the way to the bathhouse earlier, hoping our voices would carry to the rest of the crowd.

"Life, health, and prosperity to you, valiant Greens, O noble men," we shouted in unison as the stands quieted. "Our father who served you was taken to God, and we bow to your Christian mercy."

It was the Greens' turn to acknowledge us. Asterius made us wait until the crowd began to murmur.

Now the show truly began. Our life had to be more dramatic than any show on the stage of the Kynêgion if we were to sway the crowd and persuade the Greens. We clutched each other and fell to our knees amidst the strewn flower petals, cheeks pressed together. "Our father is dead, our mother defenseless, our family homeless and destitute. We, the daughters of Acacius, Keeper of the Bears, seek your infinite mercy. To you Christian gentlemen, this is our plea."

I spared a glance for the spectators behind the Green administrators, almost entirely men. Most of the observers wore faces of pity. That was a good sign.

The cluster of men shrouded in green on either side of Asterius remained seated, arms crossed in front of their chests. Not a good sign.

Asterius glowered at us as he rose. We were only daughters of a bear trainer, and he knew it. He said not a word, indicating our petition was not even worthy of his breath. Instead, he turned his back on us.

I had been stupid. Our last hope was obliterated, shattered by this man simply because he wouldn't be bested by two girls. We would be forced to beg in the streets, and the city would mock us for our humiliation.

The crowd erupted into a cacophony of hissing. I had to hold Comito up as she sobbed into my shoulder, but my eyes were dry. I spat at the sand in front of Asterius and helped Comito stumble to the entrance arch.

We would have to beg. I couldn't return to my mother emptyhanded or watch Anastasia wither and die. I tried to squeeze away the thorns in my eyes as darkness swallowed us.

"Wait!" A man dressed in blue grabbed my arm. "You have to come back."

"No. We have to go—our sister—"

"Listen to them, Theodora." Comito's nails dug into my other arm as the man dragged us back toward the arena. She wiped her eyes as I saw the men on the Blue dais, standing and singing.

The consul banged his eagle scepter as the voices of the Blues rang out across the floor, rich and low in timbre. My heart nearly stopped at their words.

"Gentle and most Christian daughters of Acacius, fear not the heartless, unchristian Greens. We Blues have seen your valor and shall answer your pleas."

This was an unexpected bit of drama. Their response was probably only a way to best the Greens before tonight's tournament had even begun, but they could steal *kopton* from babies for all I cared. The Blues would be our salvation.

Asterius' face was a vibrant shade of red, his giant hands clenched into fists on the top of the arena wall. I blew him a kiss, much to the crowd's delight, and pulled Comito toward the Blues. They were smiling, motioning us forward with their arms much as I imagined the Sirens had beckoned Odysseus and his men.

"What do we say?" Comito asked in a terrified whisper.

"Don't worry," I said. The response already tumbled through my head. We stopped before the Blues, and I waited for the crowd to quiet enough so I could speak, no mean task as most stomped and cheered. "Noble and Christian Blues, the daughters of Acacius thank you for your mercy. Your hearts are warm, and thus, over the Greens you shall rule!"

The crowd erupted into laughter and furious cheers. Some hurled things toward the Greens—a rotten cabbage and the head of a mackerel hit Asterius in the chest. The leader of the Blues, an elderly man with a shiny scalp and an ornamental sword at his hip, gave me a gentle smile, but my eyes strayed to the *scenica* seated next to him. Her copper hair flouted the customary veil and was instead piled high upon her head to accentuate pink pearls the size of cherries hanging from her ears. She was the woman from the bathhouse this morning. She wore a blue stola that matched the color of the sky at dusk, layered with a delicate blue and lavender *paludamentum* pinned at the shoulder with a gold brooch like a flaming sun. The city's wives were relegated to stand in the top tiers, but a handful of courtesans draped themselves across the other Blues. Yet the copper-haired woman was so radiant that men stopped to stare when she moved. Women like her had power, power I wanted.

The chants of the crowd changed from "Long live the Blues" to the name of one of the charioteers, our plight already forgotten. The Blues waved us onto their dais as eight chariots took the track—four decorated with green ribbons and charioteers dressed in green tunicas, and four blue—their horses prancing with high steps on the way to their boxes.

The *scenica* turned in her seat as we settled in. "You did well tonight." Her hand caressed the back of her patron's neck. "Begging before these men was daring."

I searched for malice in her face but found none. "Better than begging on the street."

"Extremely pragmatic for one so young." Her eyes twinkled as the consul gave a great yell and tossed the red and purple *mappa* into the air. The mechanical gates to the starting boxes swung open, and the chariots bolted onto the track amid cheers so loud the courtesan had to yell to be heard. "My name is Macedonia."

I knew the name—Macedonia was Constantinople's greatest *scenica*, but she had started as a dancer in the Kynêgion. They said she knew tricks only the devil could have taught her.

"I'm Theodora," I said. "And this is Comito." My sister shrank back—apparently she wasn't keen on the idea of befriending a known whore. I had no such scruples.

"And your mother?"

"Is with our sister."

Macedonia raised an elegantly penciled brow. "With her new husband?"

I didn't know how this woman knew Vitus even existed.

She must have guessed my thoughts. "Asterius made a bit of a gaffe when he installed his paymaster as the Greens' Master of Bears." She glanced at the first heat. A blue chariot had overturned on this side of the Egyptian obelisk, its driver impaled through the ribs by one of the shafts—quite messy.

A man behind us cursed and launched a handful of roasted almonds toward the track, landing several in my lap. I helped myself and handed one to Comito. "I'm afraid I don't understand why the Blues would take us on."

"The Blues' bear master recently made an unfortunate miscalculation." Macedonia shivered. "They recovered most of him after the bear was finished. The Blues will take your new father as their bear trainer. At least then you'll have a roof over your head."

"How do you know all that?"

She smiled. "Men like to talk. I prefer to listen."

A giant cage of gray parrots was released as the first chariot crossed the finish. I was happy to note its horses were festooned with blue ribbons. The birds would be captured later, but now they squawked as they flew over the spectators toward false freedom.

Macedonia smiled and turned her attention to her patron. "Good luck, girls. I hope everything works out for you."

We didn't have a coin to our names, but we'd had plenty of luck tonight.

Unfortunately, luck never lasts.

Chapter 3

I yawned into my hand as we approached the Boar's Eye. Comito and I had stayed at the Hippodrome until after the last race was won, enjoying our new celebrity. A man old enough to be our father's father—or possibly even his father—had offered three goats for Comito's hand in marriage. She refused him, but I thought it a rather generous offer.

I wished I'd had at least a few coins to bet—the Blues won seven of the ten heats, and then there were the wrestlers and tightrope walkers to cheer. I'd gritted my teeth until they threatened to crack when the Greens paraded out their bear to finish, the same flea-infested beast my father had trained.

Oil lamps flickered outside the taverna, illuminating the flaked painting of a fat brown pig with one enormous eye like a Cyclops. Drunken laughter spilled onto the steps. Inside, the open room stunk of stale barley water and unwashed male bodies. Several curvaceous women sat on the laps of grinning patrons before the tiny hearth. Its oversized pot hung from a giant chain suspended over the smoking fire. The fug of boiling onions and carrots reminded me that I hadn't eaten all day, save for the few almonds. Decades of fires in the hearth had blackened the walls, and a dull haze hung low in the air. The Boar's Eye was a good place for trading secrets, but I had none to tell, not now that the entire city knew my story.

"I don't see them," Comito said. There was no sign of my mother or Anastasia. Or Vitus.

He might have abandoned us, cut his losses, and run. Then we'd be in the gutter again, no position with the Blues, no address of residence. No bread.

"We should try the rooms upstairs," Comito said. "There are usually one or two empty ones the owner rents out." Yet another discovery my sister had likely learned from the butcher's son.

Catcalls followed us as we made our way up the narrow staircase, the well-trod boards creaking underfoot. Only halfway up I heard the screams, like someone being tortured. The voice was familiar.

I took the steps two at a time, and I shoved open the first door so hard it bounced back at me. A tiny bench was cut into the wall and on it was a *pornai* riding a brown-haired youth in a position God never intended.

"Come to join us, love?" The girl's grin revealed two missing teeth. Another cry ripped the air.

"This one." Comito pushed open the next door.

Inside, my mother sported a fresh gash on her cheek, and the start of a black bruise blossomed over her eye. She held a dirty bandage—one that matched the hem of her green tunica—to the sides of Anastasia's head as my little sister gulped for air. Tears cut swaths down her cheeks.

"What happened?" I yelled. Vitus stood at the only table in the room and wiped a bloody knife on an old rag. On the table were two knobby lumps of pink flesh.

Ears. Two tiny ears with blood on the edges where they'd been sawed off.

I screamed and lunged at Vitus, but he turned the rusted blade on me.

"Stay back, you little vermin, or I'll cut your ears off, too." He waved the blade between Comito and me. "It's your fault I had to do this—you who eat my food and sleep under my roof, but don't bring home a single *nummi* to pay for any of it."

"You slimy piece of offal!" I screamed. "We were out begging for your position while you butchered my sister." I collapsed next to Anastasia and kissed her sweaty forehead as she sobbed, thumb in her mouth. I wanted to fix her, make her whole again, but there was nothing I could do. I should have told my mother my plan before we left for the baths, or we should have come straight home before the races—then none of this would have happened. This was all my fault.

Vitus picked up his bear whip, and I steeled myself for the blow; instead, he stormed from the room, slamming the door behind him.

"I tried to stop him." My mother's eyes were dead. "He said Anastasia would bring in more than both of you."

She peeled the filthy bandage from the holes where Anastasia's ears should have been, prompting a fresh gush of bright red blood and another scream from my sister. "We have to stop the bleeding."

Comito ran out without a word. I wanted to lob curses at her retreating back, but Anastasia's fresh cries stopped me as blood soaked through the dirty linens. I crooned to her, songs my father used to sing, hoping they might soothe her and trying to think what to do. I tucked the stained blanket to her chin, ignoring the cloud of dust that billowed up from it. She settled into intermittent sobs and hiccups, but clutched my hand tight as she clasped her one-eyed doll to her chest.

I had done this. And there was nothing I could do to fix it.

Comito returned in the pitch of night with an apothecary's bottle and fresh linens. She doused the linens—the brown liquid smelled like urine—and pressed them to the bloody wounds of Anastasia's ears as I rocked her. I was so thankful for the supplies I didn't bother to ask where she'd gotten them.

"The saint said we need to keep the wounds clean," Comito said. "He told me he'd pray for her."

I sent my own prayers to God, not trusting the word of some brown-robed apothecary. I offered God whatever he wanted to heal my sister, to save us all. And if that wouldn't work, I'd start praying to every demon in the underworld.

It became apparent a week later that our prayers hadn't been enough. Vitus had abandoned us, but Comito had managed to persuade the owner of the taverna to let us keep the room so we at least had the bread dole. My older sister was never around anymore, but I'd seen her talking to Mother, and later I'd heard her voice in one of the upstairs rooms, followed by the grunts of the owner. I didn't ask questions.

I awoke in the middle of the night to Anastasia's convulsing. It was cool in the room, but she was burning up. She whimpered as Mother lit an olive oil lamp, illuminating the wall frescoes of men and women in various compromising positions. A line of drool slipped from the corner of my sister's mouth to her chin as her muscles twitched in a terrifying dance.

My mother poured a clay cup of watered wine and held it to Anastasia's lips, but she wouldn't open her mouth. "Sweet pea, this will make you feel better. Please open up."

My sister only cried, her jaw locked tight. We were up all night, and the spasms became so strong my mother feared Anastasia's arm had broken, the bone on her upper arm bent at a painful angle as my little sister screamed through clenched teeth. The muscles in her back moved of their own accord, and she arched into my mother as she lost control of her bowels, the stench of blood and feces filling the room.

"A demon has possessed her," my mother said. "There's nothing I can do."

Comito returned with the first light of dawn, blanched at the scene before her, and pressed a kiss onto our sister's forehead. "I'll fetch the saint."

My mother muttered prayers as I took Anastasia, her hot little body bent like a bow as her birdlike hands fluttered on my lap, her eyes closed as I sang over her gasps, a jumble of hymns and taverna songs. Her eyes rolled back into her head, only the eerie whites staring unseeing, and her lips pulled back in a horrible grimace, her tiny teeth bared like a dog's. Then she was still.

"Anastasia?" I hoped she had gone to sleep, but there was no slump of relaxation, no even breathing. There was no breathing at all.

My mother tried to take her from me. "Anastasia?"

She shook my little sister, but it was no use. She was gone. The saint Comito brought to save Anastasia said her last rites instead, anointing her forehead with cooking oil from the taverna's hearth below as we stitched her stiff body into a moth-eaten blanket.

We had no money for a coffin and nothing to tuck next to her body since I had hidden her one-eyed doll under my pallet, wanting to keep something she had touched. Through her tears, Comito plaited Anastasia's hair like a patrician's daughter, looping the braids around the mottled flesh where her ears should have been. We buried her close to our father the next morning in the churchyard outside the city walls and piled her grave high with wildflowers, the stench of fermenting fish still permeating the air.

That night I slept with Anastasia's doll tucked under my chin, the mattress soaked through with my tears. I wished I could take her place—it was my fault Vitus had attacked her, my fault my little sister was cold in the ground while I lay warm in her bed.

Vitus had the decency not to show himself again. I prayed the devil found new ways to torture him.

. . .

None of us wanted to face the next day, but the keeper of the taverna called on us before the sun had risen. "I need this room for paying customers," he said, avoiding our eyes as he wiped his hands on his stained tunica. "You'll have to leave by this evening."

"Tonight?" I asked.

He opened his mouth to answer, but Comito pushed me out of the way. "We'll be gone tonight," she said, slamming the door in his face.

"Where are we going to go?" I gestured to our filthy room with its stone bench and risqué frescoes. Pigs lived better. "Without this we won't even have the bread dole."

"I'll be back in an hour," Comito said. She pinched her cheeks and slipped out the door before any of us could say anything. I wanted to follow, but she was already gone. Mother and I sat in silence while we waited for her return—there seemed to be nothing left to say that wouldn't remind us of Father or Anastasia.

Comito's promised hour stretched into two and almost three by the time she returned. "Did you find us somewhere to stay?" I asked.

"No." Comito stood still for a moment, her chin trembling. Then she threw herself onto the bench and sobbed into our mother's lap.

Christ's blood. We were about to be turned out again, and now we had to deal with Comito's theatrics? I yanked her up by her arm. "What happened?"

"Karas told me he loved me—we had talked about getting married." She wiped her eyes with her sleeve. "I thought he would help us, but he told me he couldn't see me anymore—that I'd disgraced myself." At this she dissolved into tears.

I sat next to her, patting her leg awkwardly as my mother stroked her hair. "He doesn't deserve you then," I said. "We didn't disgrace ourselves by begging—"

"Not by begging." Comito's blotchy face was truly unattractive, but now probably wasn't the best time to mention that. "He found out about the other men."

"What men?" I had my suspicions.

"The apothecary across from the butcher." She blubbered into her sleeve. "When Anastasia was hurt. And the taverna owner—"

"Karas is a fool." My mother pulled Comito to her chest. "You did what you had to."

"I love him," Comito sobbed. My sister was a fool, too. But I stopped myself from saying so.

"I thought he would marry me and we'd be happy the rest of our days. I'm tired of being so poor we can't count on having bread on the table or a roof over our heads."

That made two of us.

Comito sniffed, her face mottled as a freshly plucked chicken. "I could work here. The owner offered me this room, but I turned him down."

"No. That's a life sentence," my mother said. We sat in silence for a moment, and then she heaved a long-suffering sigh. "You girls must take to the stage. I've tried to protect you from it, but that's the only way."

Comito and I stared dumbstruck at her. Being an actress was only one step up from a *pornai*.

"I'm terrified of performing," Comito said. "And Theodora is too young."

I'd had my moon bloods for several months now—I could do all that was expected of me as an actress, including any offstage duties that would be required in a room like the one we sat in now. I just wasn't sure I wanted to.

"I was an actress before I met your father," my mother said.

"What?" I forced my jaw closed. Comito looked just as stunned.

"How do you think we met? Your father trained animals and I danced. I was good, too." She stood and pushed the ragged curls from her face, revealing new streaks of white at her temples. "There are only two options open to our type of women: the stage or a man's bed. I'm too old for the stage, and neither of you has a chance at making a decent marriage. You'll both go to the Kynêgion today and do whatever it takes to get on that stage. Unless either of you has any better ideas."

There was nothing to say to that—she was right. Men would love to see Comito prancing around the stage, especially clad only in the girdle the law required. I had to admit she had a decent singing voice. And she could dance.

I, on the other hand, would likely be as successful as a goat on-stage. This became painfully obvious as we practiced with our mother that afternoon.

"This isn't going to work," I said, after stomping on Comito's foot for the third time. "No Master of the Stage in his right mind would hire me as an actress."

"Stop complaining," my mother said. "Follow Comito's lead."

But Comito sat on the bench, nursing her flattened toes. "Theodora's right. But I'll still need her help."

"On the stage?" I asked.

She laughed so hard her eyes watered. "No, goose. As my servant."

"No."

She shook her head, instantly sober. "If I'm to do this, I'm going to do it right. All the actresses have pretty slaves to help dress them, carry their chairs. We can't afford to buy a slave. You'd be perfect."

I'd be a candidate for sainthood if I had to be Comito's servant. Unless I killed her first, which was a distinct possibility.

"Both you and Theodora will ask the Blues for a position on the boards," my mother said. "Your sister earns no money if she only assists you."

I had never been so thankful for my mother in all my life.

Comito glared at me, then swept her hand over her head and curtsied with a flourish. "All of Constantinople will bow at my feet."

Provided she actually managed to squeak out her lines once she was before the audience. "Everyone will bow except the clerics and priests and monks and all the others who believe actresses consort with the devil," I said.

Comito ignored me, but then I doubted she'd ever paid much attention to the men outside the Kynêgion, damning the women within to Gehenna's flames. "I'll find a patrician to be my patron," she said. "We'll wear silk and eat eel and lamb every day." She gave a sigh fit for the stage and collapsed onto the bench. "Then Karas will realize his mistake and come crawling back to me."

We borrowed tunicas from the *pornai* I'd interrupted the night Vitus had cut off Anastasia's ears—the girl had heard what happened to our sister and was happy to help—and Mother bid us good-bye with a kiss to our foreheads. "May God be with you," she said. I wished she could come with us, but it was unseemly for a woman to attend the theater, unless she was on the stage. Actresses were tolerated because they made the wretched populace happy. And many of the actresses made the theater patrons *very* happy once they were off the stage.

We stepped around the foul-smelling carcass of a donkey that had expired in the street outside the Boar's Eye and skirted the walls of the Hippodrome to climb the hill to the Kynêgion. There were shouts from within and the clang of swords, but the smallest dwarf I'd ever seen barred the entrance under a granite arch.

"Show isn't until after sundown," he said, arms crossed in front of his chest. "Come back later."

"Aren't you adorable?" Comito bent down so close their noses almost touched. "Although if you jumped out of a trash heap at night, you'd certainly give me quite a scare. Go get the Master of the Stage— tell him he has two new actresses to interview."

I had no idea who had replaced my sister, but I rather liked this new girl. Even more startling was the fact that the dwarf actually obeyed her, although his eyes did linger on her breasts as he shuffled off. "Just what Hilarion needs—two more tarts," I heard him mutter under his breath.

The Master of the Stage wiped his mouth on the sleeve of his tunica when he emerged, smelling of onions and digging between his teeth with a bone pick. He didn't even look at us. "We don't need new girls. Come back in a few months."

"You wouldn't have come to see us if you weren't interested," Comito said.

I was sure the man was going to berate her, but he stared at her for a moment—no doubt taking in every curve she owned—and chuckled. "Quite right," he said. "You'd make a lovely dancer."

Because dancers wore the least number of clothes.

"Unfortunately, I hired another dancer this morning." He wiped his bulbous nose, one that resembled a lumpy clove of garlic. "Try back in two weeks—it's the best I can do."

In two weeks we'd starve to death on the streets. The man's tunica was piped with blue—it was worth a chance.

"The Blues sent us," I called after him. "Macedonia promised you would take care of us."

Hilarion stopped and stroked his beard. "Now there's a name I haven't heard in a while." He looked to Comito. "I suppose we can find a position in the chorus for you—the crowd always enjoys a pretty face."

"I can sing as well," Comito said.

The Master of the Stage ignored that. "The show tonight is at dusk, but they're rehearsing now. Ask Antonina for your costume."

Comito glanced at me. "And my sister?"

Hilarion gave an exasperated sigh as he shook his head at me. "Nobody will pay to watch a girl with a chest as flat as a board."

"But she's good—"

"Take it or leave it," Hilarion said. "I haven't got all day."

"We'll take it," I said. "Thank you."

Hilarion stared at me for a moment, grunted, and hurried off.

"If you hadn't interrupted, I'm sure I could have worn him down," Comito said.

"It's fine." I gritted my teeth. "It looks like you've got yourself a new servant."

I expected her to grin, but instead her face fell. "What if I trip? Or forget my lines?"

"Then you'll stand up and laugh with the crowd," I said. "They're going to love you." But only if I didn't throttle her first.

We missed the rehearsal. The wardrobe keeper—Antonina—was nowhere to be found, not that I would have known her if I saw her. A slave finally helped me locate the costumes—she scurried like a mouse when I told her it was for Antonina. Comito slipped into a stola the color of sapphires, one with slits from the hem all the way to her hips.

"There's a *pornai* somewhere who's missing her dress tonight," I said.

"You're only jealous that I'm a proper actress now." Comito straightened the neckline of the boy's tunica I'd filched from the bottom of an obliging chest and handed me a little three-legged wooden stool. "Make sure you keep this with you."

I cocked an eyebrow at her, hands on my hips. "Why?"

"In case I get tired and need to sit," she said. "All proper actresses have one."

My foot would serve her pampered backside just as well.

"We all know I'm seeing green, but in case you've forgotten, you're only a chorus girl." I stepped over a fresh pile of dung from one of the horses used in the show and scattered several flies, probably the same ones that had taken up residence in my sister's empty skull. "You've only got a bit part."

Comito's role in the chorus was barely a step up from the troupe of foot soldiers, but at least she wasn't one of the comedy mimics, the lowest sort of actresses. "That's more than you'll ever have," she said.

She paused before the dung, hands on hips. "Are you going to clean up this mess, or do I have to go onstage with filth on my hem?"

"Walk around it."

She gave an exasperated sigh and walked regally around the pile. I grabbed Comito's hand. "You're going to miss your own debut if you don't hurry. Then I'll take your place."

The threat seemed to imbue my sister with a speed she'd never before possessed. I actually had to work to keep up with her. We were ushered underground into the dark passageways along the interior of the amphitheater, but the dull hum of the crowd droned above us. The place was a madhouse, filled with actors and dancers muttering lines and limbering up before the show. Some were half naked or entirely nude, between costume changes. This wasn't a place where anyone seemed to notice a naked body.

"I don't know when to go on." Comito bit her lip.

"Just follow the rest of the chorus," I said. Tonight's performance was that of Perseus and Medusa played by a hefty-looking man with rippling biceps and a handsome woman wearing a mask topped with snakes. The man pinched the woman's rear, and she grabbed his groin. Then they kissed, the type of kiss my mother and father had often shared.

Two girls scarcely older than Comito reclined on hard benches as their slaves rushed to and fro with makeup palettes and snake wigs. Medusa's sisters. A cluster of troupe girls stood to the side, fluttering about one another. They were without masks and dressed as my sister in simple blue stolas. None of them could compare with my sister's golden hair and milky skin.

Comito still looked worried, so I hugged her and flashed a bright smile. "At least you won't have snakes for hair."

Medusa stalked over to her sisters. I didn't catch the conversation, but things weren't going well for one of the lesser gorgons. Her face turned the same color as bread dough, except for two red spots painted on her cheeks, but she blanched an even paler shade of white when Medusa started screaming at her.

"And you thought you'd keep it?" Medusa yelled as her gaze fell on Comito. She stormed over to us and stopped before she plowed my sister over.

She scrutinized Comito like a donkey in the market. I waited for her to pull up my sister's lips to inspect her teeth, but unfortunately, things didn't go that far. Finally, she nodded. "You're the right size. Pretty enough, but not too pretty."

Her own hair poked out from under the wig at her temples, a violent shade of red. The snakes were far more attractive.

Hilarion chose that moment to emerge from what smelled like the latrina, wiping his hands on the rear of his tunica. My sister flinched as Medusa snapped her fingers at him.

"This one will take Antonina's place." Medusa glared at one of her sisters. "Perhaps permanently."

Antonina had been mysteriously absent when we were trying to find Comito's costume—I wondered what she'd been doing instead to incur the wrath of the Kynêgion's star actress. The man seemed unperturbed by Medusa's rage. "May I remind you, Petronia, I make the casting decisions in my own theater. Would you mind telling me why Antonina is unable to perform?"

"Because the little slut lost her voice last night cheering at the races at the Hippodrome." Petronia's mouth puckered as if she'd been sucking rancid prunes.

Hilarion looked at my sister. "Do you know the lines?"

Fear fluttered across Comito's face. Of course she didn't know the lines, but we knew the story and with any luck Hilarion hadn't noticed we'd missed the rehearsal. Comito would likely only need to screech when Medusa died. Even my sister could manage that.

"Of course she does," I said. "We've seen this plenty of times."

Hilarion looked me over, certainly remembering his earlier dismissal of me. "Fine," he said to Comito. "Don't miss your cue."

Petronia stalked away, but the other two actresses watched us like starving hawks. They were scrawny, probably country girls sold by their parents to pay the family's taxes and eliminate another mouth to feed.

"Where are you going?" Comito asked as I walked toward the girls.

"To take care of your lines," I said. One girl walked away, laughing and flipping her snakes over her shoulder. The other was pretty—beautiful even—or she would have been without the ghastly red spots painted on her cheeks and the tiny gap between her front teeth. "Are you Antonina?"

She spat at my feet. I took that as a yes.

"Your sister doesn't look smart enough to handle the lines." Antonina's voice didn't waver—I didn't know what she'd done to tick off Petronia, but she hadn't lost her voice at the Hippodrome.

No one else could make fun of my sister. Comito was my personal property to mock.

"Much like you," I said.

Antonina choked and looked about to throttle me.

"Tell me the lines and I'll split my sister's earnings with you. Eighty-twenty."

That got her attention. "Fifty-fifty."

"Seventy-thirty."

"Fine." She hissed the lines at me—there were two whopping sentences—and I sauntered back to Comito. "A gift for you, Sister." I recited the lines. "Perseus will slay Medusa, and you'll be a star. Don't forget us little people when all of Constantinople is at your feet."

Normally Comito would have laughed or at least rolled her eyes. She did neither but looked blankly at the mimic actresses. I forced her to sit, pulled her stola down to expose a little more cleavage, and pinched her cheeks. Horns blared to herald the start of the show.

Perseus and Petronia moved under the arch that opened to the amphi-theater floor.

"It's time." I pulled my sister to her feet. "I'll be right here waiting for you."

When the show started, I could only hold my breath and hope Comito wouldn't fall flat on her face, something I normally would have paid to see.

The audience loved her, even when she managed to forget one of her two lines. A pretty face goes a long way.

Afterward, Hilarion escorted Comito to greet the line of her new admirers before I could even congratulate her. She broke away, rosy cheeked, and pressed a small gold coin into my palm. A *tremissis*—enough to feed us for a week.

"Make sure Mother doesn't spend it all on wine," she said. "I'll be home later."

"Where are you going?"

"With the man who gave me this—that tall one with the perfect curls. He was the highest bidder." She kissed me on the cheek as the man in question gestured impatiently for her. "I've saved us, Theodora."

I watched her saunter off, hips swinging. My sister had just become a whore.

So why was I jealous?

Chapter 4

Even dressed as a cow, my sister moved the audience to its feet. I listened to the crowd above me—stomping and cheering at Comito's performance as Io. They hailed her as a goddess; but her breath was still sour in the morning, and she still had to piss like the rest of us. I made it my duty to remind her of those shortcomings on a daily basis.

I sat on Comito's stool, peeling an orange as the water organ above announced the start of tonight's show. Night seemed as morning to us now—we stayed late at the theater and tripped back to our rooms at the Boar's Eye as the last of the men were stumbling from the *pornai*'s rooms. Comito's new wages had persuaded the owner of the taverna to let us stay on, at least until we found better rooms elsewhere. My belly was rarely empty, thanks to Comito, and while that was a pleasant new sensation, I didn't relish being entirely useless.

"The crowd loves your sister." Antonina looked down at me, arms crossed in front of her ample chest as I dropped the orange rind to the floor.

"Everyone always does." I took a bite of the fruit and licked a drop of juice from my hand before it fell onto my tunica. I'd taken to remembering a particular proverb from the Old Testament: *A sound heart is life to the body, but envy is rottenness to the bones.* I didn't want to be jealous of Comito, yet I was.

Antonina tapped her foot. "I believe you owe me."

Christ above, but everyone wanted something these days. I pulled the coins from the purse at my hip. "Eighty-twenty," I said.

"Seventy-thirty," Antonina said. Her tone could have sliced bronze.

"Eighty-twenty."

She looked about to tear me to pieces, but she thrust out her hand and counted the coins. "This is only for one day," she said.

"That was the deal."

"No, the deal was for all the nights your sister took my place. Hilarion's only letting me back tonight."

"Cry me a river. Take it or leave it."

"Where's the rest? Your sister made more with all her after-hour customers," Antonina said. "Hand it over."

"The deal was for Comito's stage earnings, not her other income."

"I never would have agreed to that!"

My eyes narrowed. "Don't tell me Petronia won't let you tread the boards either." Her grimace told me I'd hit the truth. Antonina would quickly be destitute if Hilarion wasn't arranging men for her. "What in God's name did you do?"

"That's none of your business." She turned on her heel and stormed away.

How the mighty had fallen. I'd best make sure Comito stayed on Petronia's good side. I shook out a lemon-colored silk stola with orange ribbons on the sleeves, a gift from the senator Comito had bedded the night before, one with more hair on his back than on his head. She complained Hilarion worked her like a rented mule, but I knew she adored all the attention. My sister was busy all night, every night, but so far no man had come forward to proclaim himself her patron. An African ivory merchant had already booked her attentions tonight.

I'd be a liar to claim I didn't envy Comito her new silks and baubles, but what I really begrudged was the new company she kept. While I waited for her in alleys, she dined in sumptuous villas with imperial magistrates, merchants from foreign lands, and Constantinople's politicians. Men who had power. Yet all she ever recounted was the type of snails on the menu or what position the man preferred in bed.

"Not as many curves as her sister."

I almost dropped the yellow stola. Two male slaves in identical blue tunicas had snuck up behind me and now eyeballed me like a slave in the market. The one who'd spoken was broad shouldered and tall, not unpleasant on the eyes.

"They say her sister will take it any way you like." His friend wore a boy's tunica with short sleeves like mine. "I'll bet this one would, too." His upper lip had a hint of fuzz, but it was the wart on his chin that was most memorable, one with a thick black hair in the middle standing at attention.

"I take it all sorts of ways. If you can pay." I pulled myself to my full, nonimpressive height and gave them an imperious stare. "Which I know you can't."

"How much?" The one with the wart looked me up and down. I could see his reaction under the tent of his tunica.

"A *tremissis*." The outrageous sum ensured they'd leave me alone.

"Deal."

I laughed. "You must take me for a fool. You're slaves."

"And you're a theater tart." There was a flash of gold as his friend pulled the coin from the purse at his hip. "My master won't notice his donation to a good cause."

I really needed to learn to keep my mouth shut. Yet here was a man offering me the same coin Comito made. I couldn't go onstage, but there was nothing to keep me from earning a wage as my sister did, with the added benefit of choosing my own johns. If Comito could do it—

I swallowed, hard. "The performance ends soon. You'd best be quick."

It burned like the fires of Gehenna when the tall one entered me, and his whole body stiffened when he passed my maidenhead. I cried out, but his mouth devoured the sound as he pressed me into the cold wall. The scrapes on my back would sting the next morning as if I'd been scalded, but it probably could have been worse. The crowd above erupted into cheers as I wiped my blood and their seed from my legs as best I could, sore and filthy as Wart retied the belt that held his undergarments. His friend had kept his back to us, but he turned now and tossed me the *tremissis*. I almost dropped it when he tossed me another coin the size of my fingernail. Tarnished bronze to add to the gold.

"What's this for?"

He cocked an eyebrow at me. "Something extra for your first."

My cheeks flared with shame. The battered flesh between my legs throbbed, and I wanted to scrub my skin raw, rid myself of the smell of sex. I could never undo what I'd just done, but I desperately wanted to. I'd sold myself for two grimy coins.

The slaves were scarcely gone when I heard a cackle of laughter and Antonina sauntered toward me, her eyebrows touching her hairline. I made a show of smoothing my tunica, despising the heat that spread across my cheeks and the sting in my eyes.

"A true alley cat, aren't you?" Antonina chuckled. "It takes a special sort of tart to please the lowest of the low, but I'm so happy to see you've found your niche."

"Better than yours at least." I crossed my arms in front of my chest, digging my fingers into my own flesh to keep from crying. "How is it for a dried-up old *pornai* like yourself? I notice you don't have many customers these days."

I danced away as she lunged at me, varnished nails flashing. She managed to grab a fist of hair and yanked my head back so hard that white spots danced before my eyes. "You filthy viper—you don't know what I've been through."

I landed on my backside and grabbed her ankle. "You're the viper." But then I bit into the back of her leg, rather enjoying her howl of pain. I skittered away as the actors emerged from the stage, ignoring Comito's raised eyebrow.

"Get that filthy pagan out of here," Petronia screeched. "I thought I told you not to come back!"

I hadn't realized Antonina had added worship of the old gods to her long list of sins. She flicked imaginary dust from her tunica and sniffed as she passed me. "I hope you burn for eternity in the fires of Gehenna."

"I'll see you there."

I got drunk that night. Filthy, stinking drunk.

Comito stayed late with her ivory merchant, and I planned to collapse on my pallet once I got to the Boar's Eye, but an amphora of wine held the blissful promise of making me forget what I'd done, at least for the night.

And so I drank. I spent the entire bronze coin on two amphorae, drinking them unwatered.

"You'd best take it slow, little bird," the taverna owner said, his brows arching as I guzzled straight from the second bottle.

"I'm fine." My words slurred together, and the warm room spun on its axis. Yet I no longer cared so much that I'd lost my virtue. I laughed aloud at that, ignoring the looks from the other girls and their patrons. How were you supposed to keep your virtue when life trod all over you?

"It's time you came upstairs, Theodora." I vaguely registered my mother's voice as someone pulled me from my chair. The room lurched and I fell to my knees, vomiting the liquid contents of my stomach all over the floor and my hands.

"I'll come back and clean it up, Falkon," my mother said from somewhere far away. "Stupid, foolish girl," she said, dragging me up the stairs. "Whatever you've done, this isn't the solution." She stopped and forced my chin up. Somehow she had multiplied, so three of her frowned at me, then reached up to brush my stinking hair back from my face. "You don't want to end up like me, do you?"

I didn't have time to think on that. The world went black.

I was in the corner of the Kynêgion's dressing room, my tunica hiked up with a fuller behind me, his hands in my hair, a beneficial position since he stunk of the urine he'd stood in all day before seeking me out halfway through a production of *Saint Agnes of Rome*. I'd have preferred a silversmith or even a butcher, but it wasn't as if I had men waiting in line for me.

I'd sworn off wine, deciding the momentary respite from reality wasn't worth the pounding head and curdled stomach the next day. I was determined not to end up like my mother, but I was desperate to get out of this life. Unfortunately, a rumor started that I excelled at all sorts of depravities—no doubt a gift from Antonina—and none of the men in the past week was as generous as the first. I had to get onstage. Any pleb could flop on the ground and hike up her tunica, but only an actress could become a *scenica*. And I had no chance of getting onstage on my own, not with my flat chest and feet like an elephant. For the first time in my life, I found myself wishing to be like Comito.

That didn't last long.

"Theodora, we can't find the fake breasts, and I need them for the next act." I didn't hear Comito over the din of the water organ until it was too late. "What in the name of—" She screeched and covered her eyes as I struggled away from the fuller. He righted himself in a hurry and scuttled off, sending the flames of the torches shuddering in his wake.

"Get back here," I yelled. "You haven't paid me yet!"

I'd have chased after him, but Comito's hand on my shoulder stopped me.

"I'd ask what you were doing, but I think that much was obvious." Her lip curled with distaste. "How long has this been going on?"

"Does it really matter?" I rubbed my scalp where he'd pulled my hair too hard.

Comito glared at me. "Yes, it matters. I'm not doing this for fun. I'd rather be married to Karas, fat with his babies in a cozy room above the butchery. I'm trying to find a patron, but that's going to be awfully difficult if word gets out that my sister will spread her legs for anything that walks in the door." She looked in the direction the man had fled. "For free, no less. Always collect the coins before he takes off his belt."

I ignored her helpful advice. "This wouldn't be an issue if you'd get me onstage."

"Absolutely not."

"Why?"

"Because you can't act! You don't play the *lyra*, and your dancing is so poor you'd never make it on the lineup."

"You just don't want any more competition!"

She laughed. I picked up Saint Agnes' fake breasts with their flaked red nipples and threw them at her before storming outside.

I stomped down dark alleys, winding my way toward the open expanse of the harbor. Raindrops pattered down on the waters of the Golden Horn's narrow inlet, and my breath made tiny white clouds in the night air. The drops were cold and clean on my tongue, despite the smell of brine. Two grain ships from Egypt sat at anchor, painted black and gold eyes staring at me from their prows. Fishermen were still bringing in their haul of tunny, mackerel, and even a massive bloodied tuna almost as tall as me. A wizened old man sat at the edge of his dinghy before a tiny cooking fire, the remnants of today's catch cleaned and laid out for purchase next to a pile of day-old loaves on the benches of the boat. I parted with two *nummi* and groaned aloud as the sea bass melted in my mouth between the crusty bread. I could have eaten at least two more and washed them down with a cold cup of pickle juice, but the rain began in earnest, so I had to jump puddles on my way back to the Boar's Eye. My wool *paludamentum* smelled like wet goat as I peeled it from my shoulders, shaking rain from my drenched hair. Inside, logs popped as the fire roared and rosy-cheeked barmaids hustled trays of wine and stuffed grape leaves while still managing to giggle and bat their lashes as drunken patrons pinched their backsides.

"Evenin', Theodora." A *pornai* from the room across from us stood at the bottom of the stairs, hanging on a man who barely seemed able to stay upright. Chrysomallo was younger than me, perhaps ten or eleven, but a bronze amulet hung between her breasts—what there was of them anyway—and was engraved with a man mounting a woman dog-style to advertise her particular specialty.

"Busy night?" I walked sideways to avoid the man—he was pleasant enough on the eyes with a mop of sandy hair and a deep cleft in his chin, but he looked ready to void his stomach at any moment.

"I hear you're treading the boards down at the Kynêgion—when are you going to join us?" Just what I needed—a tart next door with a big mouth. "Someone's waiting for you upstairs," she said. Her man clapped his hand over his mouth and lurched toward the door, but he didn't quite make it. "By the dog, John! I told you that would happen." She looked toward the ceiling and sighed. "If that one upstairs isn't yours, feel free to send him my way."

John—although certainly not his real name, but the most common alias the men in the taverna gave—staggered out the door as Chrysomallo fiddled with the emblem around her neck. It seemed odd that the girls who worked here would brazenly advertise their occupation while their patrons took such pains to hide their identity. Not for the first time I wondered at the lack of fairness in God's world.

I climbed the stairs slowly, unsure who might be waiting outside my door. I never told men at the Kynêgion much about myself, usually not even my name, much less where I lived.

A well-made young man leaned against the wall by our room, a posy of daisies in one hand. I'd have known those shaggy curls anywhere.

"And here I thought I had a surprise visitor," I said, glaring at Karas. "I should have known it was for Comito."

His smile faltered. It wasn't my fault he'd scorned my sister and she now warmed the beds of Constantinople's elite.

"It's good to see you, Theodora," he said, running his hands through his mop of curls as he looked past me. He smelled like a slaughter room. "Is your sister downstairs?"

"She's still out—" I felt a momentary flicker of pity for the butcher's son. "With the other actresses." And my mother was on the other side of the door, either listening to all this or passed out after drinking too much wine. I folded my soggy *paludamentum* over my arm. "I know I look a fright, but I'd be happy to share a mug of barley water with you."

Karas showed off two rows of perfectly straight teeth. He and Comito would have made beautiful babies, but it was too late for that now.

He saw me settled at a table near the fire and ordered us two clay cups of barley water with mint and honey. I was halfway done with mine, having chattered about the recent races at the Hippodrome, the latest crop of pears, and the general state of the Empire while he stared at his cup. Finally, I faked a yawn into my hand. "It was lovely visiting with you, Karas, and I'll tell Comito you stopped by—"

"I made a mistake." He grabbed my hand. "I want Comito back."

We sat that way across the table, his hand over mine, probably stared at by half the people in the Boar's Eye. A butcher's son would never help our fortunes, not like a prefect or one of the other patricians my sister now entertained. And after my sister's little performance tonight, I wasn't about to saddle poor Karas with her. A patron was what she wanted, and a patron was what she'd get. "Comito has moved on," I finally said.

"I know she did things she shouldn't have, when Anastasia was sick. I should have helped her, but I was too jealous. My mother told me I should find a better girl, one with virtue. But I don't want another girl. I just want Comito." His face crumbled. "She's found someone else now, hasn't she?"

"A merchant." Several of them. And a senator.

I slipped my hand from under his. "I'm sorry, Karas." He still sat there as I looked down from the top of the stairs, so forlorn as he stared into his cup, the posy of wilting daisies on the table, that I almost went back and told him my sister would marry him the next morning. But she had been so awful to me tonight—I knew she rather enjoyed keeping me in the gutter. I forced myself to turn around and open the door to our room, glad for the robust moans that seeped through the walls to muffle the creak of the hinges as I tried not to wake my mother.

Now I had to make sure Comito never found out what I'd done.

Comito prodded me awake with her foot as autumn sunshine weaseled its way through the shutters of our only window the next morning.

"Late night?" My mother kissed the top of Comito's head, her eyes puffy and her breath still sour from last night's wine. "I'll see what's downstairs for breakfast—probably more eggs and boiled cabbage."

Comito let her stola fall at her feet and stretched out naked on our pallet as Mother shut the door. I rolled to the other side to give her my back, but she dangled a thick gold coin before my nose, a *solidus* bearing Emperor Anastasius' profile, sans his one green and one blue eye. I'd be lucky to earn so much in two months at this rate. "I still have to give Hilarion his cut," she said, "but Mother should find us better rooms today. I think this might be the one—a prefect in the

Emperor's court. He has a villa in Hieron—we could go there for the sea breezes in the summer—"

I let my sister's words go in one ear and out the other until she jabbed me in the ribs.

"I asked Hilarion on my way out if he thought you could go onstage yet. He said to talk to him this afternoon."

I was a Judas. I deserved to hang and have my bowels burst asunder, just as he had.

I opened my mouth to tell Comito of Karas, but she prattled on about her prefect and all the silks she was going to have embroidered, a new stola for every day of the month, with different wardrobes for each season. Perhaps things were better this way.

Comito might have a patron, and I might have a place onstage. Things were starting to look up, instead of simply skimming the horizon.

Never had a morning seemed so long. I scrubbed my skin until it shone at the baths and even let the slaves polish my nails, my heart skittering at the thought of my upcoming debut. Comito whined when I dragged her to rehearsal early, but Hilarion only laughed when I asked for my lines.

"Dark as a sewer rat and still flat as a slab of marble." He clapped me on the back. "At least you have a sense of humor. Come back and talk to me when you've grown breasts like your sister's."

I spent the night drawing his face in the ashes of the hearth and poking his eyes out with a rather sharp stick.

Winter would close the theater in another month and with it any hope I had of avoiding being a common *pornai* for the rest of my life. Comito was no help. Her prefect hadn't called on her, and she was desperate for some patron to claim her before the cool weather set in. She might be asked to entertain at a private villa during the dark months, but she would otherwise spend her winter huddled with

Mother and me in our new room above a silk shop. Our new home was almost the same size as the room at the Boar's Eye, but it was clean. And quiet.

It had taken me weeks to concoct tonight's scheme. It was a huge gamble but worth the risk.

I'd be an old crone if I waited around for Hilarion to decide to put me in the chorus. The dark face that looked back at me in the Kynêgion's bronze prop mirror made me cringe, but I licked my lips and pinched my cheeks. The costume I'd borrowed was too big in the bust, but it was short enough to show most of my legs, my best feature. It would have to do.

The oil torches of the subterranean corridor flickered as I passed, casting trembling webs of shadows on the rock walls. I traveled half the circle of the theater, my stomach twisting itself into a tighter knot with each step. An empty animal cage sat at the stage entrance, the same one that had most recently held a toothless lion slaughtered in a performance of Heracles and the Nemean Lion. My fate might not be much different.

The audience roared, and pebbles fell from the ceiling from thousands of stomping feet. I took a deep breath to keep my stomach from revolting and stepped through the cluster of dancers onstage as Perseus pulled Medusa's head out of a burlap sack, the final act of the play. He held the head midair as I strode to center stage. A hush fell over the amphitheater. This hadn't been covered in rehearsals.

Comito was supposed to hiss and spit at Perseus for slaying her mortal sister, but my sister looked like a red snapper freshly pulled from the Bosphorus, crimson faced and slack jawed. Antonina had managed to swindle her way into the role of Medusa for the night—Petronia was mysteriously absent—and was supposed to be dead, sprawled on the stage with her head hidden under a red wool blanket of blood, but she peeked from underneath and shot me such a glare it might actually have been possible to turn me to stone.

I took the gorgon head from Perseus, one with peeling paint on the eyes and thick braids of green woolen yarn for the snakes. The actor playing Perseus shook his head as he circled me. "This is a pleasant bit of improvisation," he said under his breath.

Hilarion didn't seem to agree—he looked ready to feed me to the bears from his seat in the lower stands, those reserved for the theater's special guests. Seated next to him was a woman with copper hair I hadn't seen since the night at the Hippodrome. Macedonia smiled and leaned back in her seat, motioning with an elegant turn of her wrist for me to continue.

The silence stretched too long as I gathered my thoughts. I should have had a better plan. The Kynêgion rarely performed antic shows for laughs, but as I could neither dance nor sing, I had a rather small repertoire to choose from.

I sniffed the head and gestured with it toward Antonina's prone form. "In the name of God, it really does resemble her," I said loud enough so all could hear, looking the gorgon head in its chipped eyes. "An improvement, actually."

The crowd roared as Antonina came to life and lunged after me, but I chucked the head at her and ran, pulling Perseus before me as a makeshift shield. He shook loose as Antonina twirled the head by its snakes and lobbed the thing at me. It knocked me sideways, and the audience roared with laughter. I scrambled to my feet, and I laughed with the audience, despite the lump I would find above my ear tomorrow. Antonina looked ready to throw something else at me, but I pulled Perseus' dagger from his belt. Perseus chuckled, and his arms floated up from his sides in surrender.

I meandered toward Antonina and gave a dramatic sigh. "Medusa here is so ugly, men would wish for death if it meant never having to see her face again. And her breasts are more wrinkled than the Fates'."

The audience laughed. Antonina's eyes flared; behind her, Comito pantomimed slicing her neck. I tossed Perseus his blade and bowed to the crowd before sauntering away, my heart slamming up my spine. I didn't make it far.

Antonina grabbed the back of my tunica and yanked it, hard. The threadbare fabric ripped, exposing my breasts to the thousands of people packed into the tiers. I wanted to run but forced my feet to stay planted instead. From the catcalls, it didn't sound like anyone wanted me to run offstage. I forced myself to release my tunica and let my breasts remain bare.

"Mine may be wrinkled as the Fates'," she hollered, "but yours are so small most men would miss them entirely!"

By the dog, I wanted to cut her tongue out.

I turned and smiled, pulling the rope around my waist and hoping no one would notice my fingers tremble. The fabric fell to the ground. "Jealousy doesn't become you." My fingers reached to the dark sky, and I turned so the entire audience could see all of me as butterflies— more like angry sparrows at this point—pummeled my stomach. Thank goodness I wore the girdle the law required; otherwise the city Patriarch might have me thrown into Blachernae prison tomorrow morning. I waited for the shouts of disappointment, but instead a golden burst of laughter and applause filled my ears.

My eyes fell on Macedonia—the *scenica* smiled and slowly clapped.

Antonina stepped toward me, but I wasn't taking any more chances. I saluted the audience, yanked my tunica up from my ankles, and made for the exit as fast as my feet could run, carrying the audience's cheers with me.

Nearly naked as I was, I was faster than Antonina in her full Medusa getup, at least until I barreled straight into Hilarion. *Damn.*

"What in the name of God was that?" His giant nose seemed to splay wider as he took a deep breath and held up a hand to stop Antonina from crashing into me. "How dare you—a pleb—ruin my production? I should have you whipped!"

"She didn't ruin it." Macedonia smiled from behind him. Overhead the steps of thousands of feet pounded into the night, hopefully carrying the story of my debut to every taverna in Constantinople. Macedonia's arm was hooked through a rather portly fellow's arm, but the golden chain at his neck proclaimed to the world he was an adviser to Emperor Anastasius. "The audience loved her. Count the coins after the slaves clean the floor—I'm sure she pulled in a tidy profit for you."

Hilarion opened his mouth to protest but shut it. "Fine. I won't have you whipped. This time. But there hadn't better be a next time."

"There won't be a next time if you put me on the stage."

He looked me over, then laughed. "You, a theater tart? You're still a child."

"Were you at a different show than I was?" Macedonia shook her head, and I caught the musky scent of her perfume. "She's definitely a woman."

I cursed the heat that flooded my cheeks, but Macedonia winked at me as her patron led her into the night.

"You can't honestly mean to promote her." Antonina looked ready to spit daggers. "After the stunt she just pulled?"

Hilarion ignored her and thrust a pudgy finger at my nose. "Only as a trooper in the chorus."

He half dragged me to the makeshift desk in his office, despite Antonina's rather colorful protestations, and scrawled the deal on a scrap of parchment, one with some other girl's contract on the other side. "If you can't write your name, just mark it with the sign of the cross."

He raised an eyebrow as I dipped the stylus in the inkpot and signed my name. "I'll start tomorrow," I said. He dismissed me in a hurry, presumably in a rush to count the take from the night.

"You'd better be glad he only made you a trooper." Antonina's breath smelled of mint leaves. "Because that's all you're ever going to amount to."

I was saved from responding by the gaggle of actresses that

swarmed us, praising my performance. Suddenly I was a star. Comito appeared and pulled me away after some minutes of trying to follow the girls' excited chatter. I could guess from the twist of her lips that we weren't going to celebrate with fish sandwiches and a jug of wine.

"Watch it, will you," I said. "You're going to pull my arm off."

She stopped and shook her head, releasing my arm as if I were some sort of insect. "I suppose you got what you wanted, didn't you?"

She was right. I had.

Chapter 5

God was generous this time. My life as a trooper in the chorus introduced me to a new sphere of men who were happy to pay for my attentions. There was also my cut of the coins showered onto the stage each night. Comito grudgingly taught me all she knew, how to pleasure a man and make him beg for more. It was my first taste of power.

I enjoyed it for exactly nineteen days.

"It's no use. I can barely breathe." I tried to pull the stola back over my head, but the cursed thing got stuck on my breasts and Comito had to untangle me.

"For a late bloomer, you're not wasting any time." Comito's lips twisted to one side as she studied me. "I'd swear your breasts are almost as big as mine."

"I hope they stop soon. I'm tired of them aching all the time." I rummaged for a larger stola in the costume box and straightened to find Comito scrutinizing me in earnest now. "What? Do I have *garos* on my face?"

"When did you last wear your cloth and girdle?" She almost

yanked my arm from its socket as she pulled me from the room. "When did you last bleed?"

"What do you mean? You don't think—?"

"When?"

I counted back and groaned. "Over two months ago." The wall was cold on my back as I slid to the floor, but Comito hauled me to my feet.

"Didn't you take anything in the mornings?"

Of course—I wasn't that big a fool. "I have a pessary of crocodile dung. From the market."

"You can't be serious." Her mouth fell open. "You are serious."

"I heard Antonina tell another girl. It's an old Egyptian trick."

"Did she know you were listening?"

My fingers curled into fists. "I'm going to kill her."

Already the amphitheater was filled with spectators' voices—there was to be a bearbaiting after our performance, the last of the season before winter shut down the theater. "What am I going to do?"

Comito tapped my head with her knuckles. "What else would you do? Get dressed and give such a performance that Hilarion can't help hiring you back into the chorus next season."

I don't recall if I followed her directions or fell on my face that night. I was the last person in the Empire who should be procreating, and the very thought of childbirth made me cower in terror. My mother had almost died delivering Anastasia, and I'd seen too many biers of women laid out with their dead infants. I might soon join them.

I sat outside after the performance and cursed myself under my breath. No man would want me once my belly swelled. And then there would be a baby to take care of. The entire situation was hopeless.

My tears had dried by the time Comito emerged, swathed in a shaggy fur coat made from at least a hundred dead squirrels. I dashed the sleeve of my tunica across my eyes before she could see my blotchy face.

"I was beginning to think you'd gotten lost." I eyed the package under her arm. "What's that?"

"Herbs. They might help, but it won't be pretty." She stopped and brushed an imaginary hair back from her eyes. "I'm assuming you want to get rid of it."

This from my sister, who wanted nothing more than a lap full of babies.

"Do I have a choice?"

She shrugged. "I've some coins saved, but not enough for the winter. And in your condition—"

I'd be a charity case. Worse, I might have to expose the child after giving birth. Many of the other troopers from the chorus had already done that several times. Better to do it now than be forced to choose between that or watching my baby die of starvation.

I took the package from her. "Will you help me?"

She nodded. "And Mother, too."

We walked in silence in the night until my curiosity got the better of me. "Where did you get the herbs?"

"Antonina."

I almost dropped the package. "I'm going to die."

Comito sighed and kept walking. "She thinks they're for me."

I watched my sister, dumbstruck, then hurried to catch her hand. "Thank you."

She gave me a watery smile. "That's what sisters are for."

Wine fumes greeted us as we let ourselves into our room—Mother was slumped at the table, an empty amphora on the ground and her fingers still loosely clasped around another. So much for my mother helping me.

Comito pulled vials from the linen package. "If this works, you won't be able to get up tomorrow."

I uncorked a cloudy bottle and promptly gagged on the smell. "What is that?"

"Tooth of a Cyclops and a virgin's blood." Comito rolled her eyes. "Tansy and pennyroyal. Antonina was quite proud that it was mixed by a Manichaean magician who can trace his lineage all the way back to the prophet Mani."

I supposed that was quite an honor, but it smelled like cat urine and rotten eggs. "I already want to die."

She chuckled. "If you drink more than half, you might get your wish." She pushed a terra-cotta basin to me. "For later. And you might want to plug your nose to get that all down."

I did as I was told and drained half of the tincture. It almost came back up, but I managed to swallow. "Now what?"

"We wait." Comito rewrapped the bottles in the linen. "I hope you've learned your lesson. From now on you'll use a pessary of pennyroyal, arum root, and fenugreek." She poured herself a glass of wine—one that smelled more like vinegar—and sat down next to me. "Let's hope this works."

She was right—when the tincture began its work, I prayed God would kill me. The need for the basin became clear when I vomited, but then my insides turned to water. I shook on my pallet and Comito mostly left me alone, but occasionally I felt her hand on my back. "Not yet," she said more than once.

Afternoon sunshine streamed down on me when I awoke to Comito's snores. I tried to move, but it felt as if I'd been run over by a chariot. And then stomped on by the horse.

There was a different noise, some sort of animal groan. It took me a moment to realize the sound was coming from my mouth, but then soft hands were on my back and a cool cloth on my forehead. My vision cleared enough to make out the outline of my mother beside me. "My poor, stupid girl," she said.

I closed my eyes. "Must have been something I ate."

She massaged my scalp, pulling the damp strands from my face. "I might be a drunk, but I'm no fool. Children are a hazard in your line of work."

I cringed at the mess of vomit on the floor. It would be easier for us to move than to clean it. "Did it work?"

She shook her head. "No sign of it."

"No." That couldn't be right.

I heard Comito stir. "Sometimes it works; sometimes it doesn't." She squinted out the window. "I have to go—there's a silk merchant who wants me before his wife returns from taking the waters at Bithynia." She touched my shoulder. "Do you want to come to the baths with me?"

The thought of moving made me want to be ill.

"I'll take care of her." My mother released a heavy sigh. Comito must have given her a look. "I'm her mother, for Mary's sake."

"All right," I heard Comito say. "I'll pick you up a nice vintage on the way home."

"There's a good girl," Mother said. The wet cloth on my head was heaven. "Now what are we going to do with you, Theodora?"

If only I knew.

Things went from bad to worse.

That winter I grew larger than an Egyptian hippo, becoming a virtual Penelope as I embroidered the same tiny smock and tore out the seams, unsure what to do with the child I carried. I swallowed my envy as Comito went back to the Kynêgion when the almond trees unfurled their pink blossoms. My sister supported both Mother and me without complaint, but our cupboards were more empty than not and soon there would be a baby, too. If the child and I survived the birth, that was.

I spent most of my time praying to God for guidance, for protection, for a sign—anything—but received no answer. A precious coin paid to the pagan augur in the market only told me I was going nowhere, all because I'd dreamed of putting on shoes. I began to think she was onto something.

I stretched my back and rubbed my swollen belly—today was an especially itchy day, and Mother had already rubbed my stomach with olive oil twice before she went out to pick up fresh fish for our evening meal—when Comito burst through the door, her face covered with strawberry blotches. She stopped, seemingly transfixed by my colossal stomach. Then she collapsed next to me and burst into tears.

The front of my tunica was soaked through by the time I could make sense of my sister's garbled mess of words.

"Married," Comito bawled. "He's married."

I wiped the tears from her cheeks with the end of my sleeve. "Who?"

"Karas!" She dissolved into another fit, during which I poured wine. I wanted the whole amphora, but cut mine heavily with water and filled the other to the top. This was my fault.

"He married the fuller's daughter." Comito sniffled. "I saw them today in the market—she already looks gone with child."

"Perhaps she's just plump," I said.

Comito ignored me, curling to a ball on her pallet. "That was supposed to be my baby, but instead I'm a whore."

"No, you're one of Constantinople's greatest actresses. She stinks of sausage and pig blood while you dress in silk stolas, dine on milk-stuffed suckling lambs, and drink wine out of gold goblets."

She looked at me as if she'd never seen me before. "Is that really what you think of me? I'd trade every stola I own for a baby and a husband who loved me." Her lower lip trembled. "I thought Karas would want me back if he saw how popular I'd become, that he'd realize how much he wanted me. Instead, I ruined everything." She swiped at her eyes with one hand, clenching the clay cup of wine with the other so tightly I thought it might crack.

I could either swallow the lie I'd told or tell Comito the truth. I owed her that after what I'd done.

"It's my fault," I said. "Not yours. He came looking for you at the Boar's Eye, but I told him you were with someone else. Which, might I point out, wasn't entirely false." Her expression changed as my words sunk in. "I shouldn't have done it."

She stared at me with unseeing eyes, then hurled her wine cup at me, followed by the other cup and the amphora. I dodged the amphora but wasn't so lucky with the cups. "You filthy, lying viper!"

I held my hands in front of me and backed toward the door as she searched for more projectiles. "I thought you wanted a patron. I didn't know you still loved him."

She paused, a bottle of olive oil with my name on it poised over her head. "And that meant you could decide my life for me?"

"I was angry. I thought you wouldn't help me."

She set the bottle down, slowly. "I've lost my only chance at true happiness. All because of you."

I took a tentative step forward, reaching out my hand. "I'm sorry, Comito. So, so sorry."

Her eyes were empty when she looked at me, and she stepped back as if I might contaminate her. "Get out."

"What? Now?"

Her voice was as hollow as her gaze. "I never want to see you again."

"But the baby—"

"I don't care about the baby!" Her face crumpled. "I said get out!"

I stumbled into the streets, drenched and smelling like a vat of wine. People stopped to stare—a woman as far gone as I was with child should have been locked from view—but then turned their noses up and continued on their way.

I'd lost my father, and then Anastasia. Now I'd lost Comito, too.

And it was all my fault.

Chapter 6

I gasped and grit my teeth. The pain around my stomach cre-scendoed even as I crouched on the ground like some sort of wild animal. I'd had pains over the last week as I begged for bread and slept wherever I could, including one night spent in the public latrina I'd rather forget. Yet I couldn't bring myself to beg my sister to take me back. Instead, I'd gone to Communion and worn out my knees praying to God for help. At least the churches didn't turn me away.

The stones of the city wall were cold against my forehead, my mid-night dig through a taverna's trash heap momentarily forgotten. The pain passed, and I leaned over the garbage again, but a sudden gush of warm water between my legs stopped me.

"Not now!" I hit the wall and cursed again at the haze of blood on my knuckles. I could scarcely see through my tears. The wall held me upright as I panted through more waves of agony and pushed my palms against the pain. At some point I became vaguely aware of a woman's drunken laughter.

"Once an alley cat, always an alley cat, eh, Theodora?"

Antonina. The Almighty had a twisted sense of humor.

"Lord in heaven, you're not having the cursed thing out here, are you?"

I was hallucinating. It almost sounded as if Antonina cared. My glare was cut short as I groaned and curled into the pain. Once it passed, I slumped against a crate, one filled with fish, judging from its briny smell.

"How long have you been at it?"

I didn't look at her—it cost me dear enough to answer. "I don't know." The moon had moved, so now it perched atop one of the buildings, possibly the last moon I'd ever see. A fierce desire to fight through this torture surged through me. "Long enough."

Someone cleared his throat—I hadn't noticed the man in the shadows. There was a low murmur of voices and then footsteps retreating into the darkness. I should have known she wouldn't stick around. Time's edges blurred as my pains bled into one another. Then something cold rummaged between my legs. I yelped.

"Relax," Antonina said. "It's not as if I'm the first to be in your skirts." I tried to push her hand away but had as much effect as a drunken baboon. "I need to see how far the baby's dropped." She pushed a chipped cup into my hand. "Drink this."

I must have glared, because she rolled her eyes. "It's only willow bark. It'll take the edge off the pains."

I'd drink nails if she promised it would make this easier. "Get it out of me."

"All in good time," Antonina said. "And not much time from the look of it." She peered down the alley, hands on hips. "The only midwife I know is on the other side of the city. It looks like it's you and me."

"Why in Christ's name would you help me? You hate me."

"I do. But somehow I doubt anyone else is going to come along and deliver you."

She had a point.

"I still hope you choke on a pomegranate one day."

Antonina laughed. "Right back at you, darling."

Another pain gripped me—either the willow bark didn't help or my pains were stronger—but this time Antonina helped me sit on the crate and rubbed my back. The rest of the night was a blur. Death hovered near, yet I fought for life. For my life and my child's.

"I'm sorry," I sobbed to Antonina from all fours. My legs and arms could no longer hold me, and I pressed my forehead to the dirt. "I can't do this."

She didn't move from her station next to me. "Yes, you can. And you will."

"I'm sorry for all the noise I'm making."

Antonina let out an exasperated sigh. "Stop apologizing and push!"

Sometime before dawn broke, I screamed. I hadn't screamed all night, but now I let fly the wail of pain I'd held inside. A weight fell from my womb into Antonina's waiting arms.

My daughter.

I clutched the flailing little thing as Antonina lifted her stola to retrieve a tiny knife from her boot. It flashed in the moonlight as she cut the umbilical cord with one swift motion. My daughter rooted at my breast, her eyes pools of darkness and a black whorl of hair on her scalp still tangled with the debris of birth. "What do you want to do with her?"

I hadn't exactly plotted out a future for myself and a baby on the streets of Constantinople. "I don't know."

Antonina set to work again as the afterbirth came. My mother had planted the placentas from her children back in Cyprus' rich soil. Mine would be left in the garbage heap of a taverna.

Ripping her *paludamentum* down the middle, Antonina wrapped my daughter in one piece and handed me the other to staunch the flow of blood between my legs. She seemed to look everywhere but at the child. "You could leave her under the elephants of the Golden Gate. Someone might take care of her."

"And if no one does?"

Antonina's face was a mask. "You'll never know. Or there are the bathhouse drains. She wouldn't be the first child to be dumped there." She shrugged when I didn't answer. "Children of whores usually die young anyway."

The baby whimpered, denied the breast she sought. Antonina watched me for a moment, then wiped her hands on the back of her tunica. "You'd best feed her then. Nothing worse than a crying baby."

I let the baby suck, awestruck at the little fingers splayed across my breast with their tiny fingernails. I ruined almost everything I touched, but somehow, despite everything, I had managed to create this perfect little person. And yet, because of me, there was no one I loved here to see her. I gave a strangled little sob and clutched my baby to me. It shocked me how much I wanted to keep her, to see her safe.

I looked up to see Antonina watching, lit by the moon. She blinked a few times and went back to cleaning her hands. "What will you name her?"

Yet another thing I hadn't let myself think of. "I'm not sure. Perhaps after my sister." Many daughters carried their mother's names. I kissed the baby's head. "Theodora Anastasia."

Antonina rolled her eyes. "I've had enough Theodoras to last a lifetime. But I like Anastasia—you could call her Tasia for short."

I knew to hold my tongue, but the next question jumped from my lips before I could even think. "How did you know what to do?"

Antonina busied herself with scrubbing her fingernails. "When you've done this as long as I have, you've seen plenty of babes born."

Perhaps she'd even gone to a bathhouse or left one at the Golden Gate herself. Antonina didn't have any children, at least none I knew of.

"I owe you."

She stood and wiped her fingers on the ripped costume. "I suppose you don't have anywhere to stay, now, do you?"

I didn't answer.

"I heard Comito threw you out. Really it was only a matter of time before you did something to tick her off, too."

I glared at her. Tasia had fallen off my breast, eyes closed, and I could feel her warm breath on my skin, the brush of a butterfly wing. "We'll manage."

Antonina heaved an exasperated sigh and squatted next to me, looping her arm under mine. "Come on."

"With you?"

"We might kill each other, but the alternative is to leave you out here to expire on your own." Antonina grunted as she hoisted me to my feet. "I didn't give up a roll with Timothy the Weasel for nothing, you know."

"With a name like that, he must be quite a catch." We looked at each other and exploded into giggles, mine more than a little hysterical. I leaned heavily on her while I maneuvered Tasia as best I could. A glaring alley cat suckled its kitten and hissed as we passed. I stumbled, light-headed.

"Brace up," Antonina said. "My flat is outside the city walls, and you're too blasted heavy to carry." She gestured to Tasia. "Give me the baby. The last thing I need is you dying on me and leaving me to deal with a crumb snatcher."

I almost protested, but Tasia felt like a giant watermelon and all I wanted to do was sleep. The rest of the way was quiet except for my labored breathing. Antonina stopped in front of a steep stairway shoved into the end of a three-story building, each level precariously stacked upon the others so it resembled a child's mud paddy before it collapsed. A red-painted phoenix graced the wall, but it might have been mistaken for a harpy had it not been for the faded flames tickling its feet.

"Let me guess," I said. "The top, right?" The top rooms were always the cheapest.

"The one with the view. Only the best."

Once we reached the door, I waited only long enough for her to point at a pallet on the floor before I sank into sleep.

Water splashed from one of the clay jugs I carried as my sandal caught on the rough plank of the stair and Tasia thumped against my back. A tanner had just sloshed the stale urine from his pot onto the step in front of me, soaking my sandals. I held my breath, praying Tasia wouldn't wake and start screaming again, but there was only silence. Miracle of miracles.

"By the dog," I cursed at him. "What do you think you're doing?"

His lip curled to reveal several brown teeth. "Dumping filth where it belongs."

"How dare you—"

"You Jews deserve worse than a little urine."

"I'm not a Jew."

"Likely story—this whole building is stuffed full of the dim-witted fools." With that, he hefted his pot onto his shoulder and stomped off. Somehow I doubted the tanner had seen the inside of Antonina's room—she was at least one tenant who didn't cling to the old faith.

The line at the water distribution center had snaked all the way to the aqueduct and sapped what little strength I'd recovered in the past week. I was determined not to leech off Antonina any more than I had to, but I had no money and wouldn't be deemed clean enough to entertain any men until Tasia's baptism. Right now I could only offer Antonina my share of the meager chores around her room, trying to keep Tasia quiet while Antonina slept through the afternoons. I had been startled to learn that Antonina did more than dabble in herbs and potions—the woman's room was a shrine to every god known to man since the days of the book of Genesis, and she'd introduced me to all of them. A painted statue of Bes welcomed visitors with a garish red smile, Isis stood festooned with a wreath of dried flowers, and Athena's wooden owl looked down from where he had been hung on the ceiling, an olive branch clutched in the one talon that hadn't been broken off. There was even a pile of white ash next to a cloudy beaker of water and an oil lamp for the Persian fire gods. Yet Antonina still wore a wooden cross around her neck.

"I like to spread my luck around," she had said when I asked about the necklace. "My father's father was a charioteer in Rome before the city fell. He had to flee when the Vandals sacked it, prayed to all the gods to save him as he fled here to the Eastern capital. I figure if I honor all the gods, then none will single me out for smiting."

"I'm not sure that's quite how it works." I'd bit my lip. "I don't think I've ever met a pagan before."

She'd smiled and handed me a clay cup of tea, a concoction with anise and fennel to help stop my bleeding and keep my milk flowing. "You have now."

I took the rest of the stairs slowly, one wet foot joining the other on each step, and wanting nothing more than to cuddle with my daughter until the sun set.

"It's about damn time you showed up."

I almost fell backward. My mother sat on my pallet, a cup of wine already accessorizing her black stola, one that somehow managed to enhance her sheet of blond hair, loose around her shoulders. She was in mourning.

Comito—

"You never told me what a barrel of laughter your mother is." Antonina kept her voice down, but it was too late—Tasia blinked her eyes and screamed as if she'd been dropped on her head. The tenants downstairs were likely cursing me to the fires of Gehenna and back. Antonina rubbed her temples. "Especially this early in the morning."

"Hello, Mother." I undid the shoulder of my tunica to free my breast and rubbed the nipple—cracked and raw though it was—on Tasia's pink gums, but she still howled like a red-faced demon's minion.

My mother set down her cup and took Tasia from me, hopped from one foot to the other, and thumped Tasia on the back, a little too hard for my taste. "What's her name?"

I moved to take my daughter back, but her eyes started to droop. "Anastasia. We call her Tasia." I gestured to my mother. I didn't want to ask, but I had to. "Why are you in mourning?"

Antonina took a swig from the wine jug. "I believe you ladies have some things to talk about"—I followed her eyes to a cedar chest by the door, the same one that had held my mother's belongings from Cyprus—"so I'm going to make myself scarce."

I ran my hands through my hair as Mother sat, letting Tasia use her saggy breasts as a pillow. "How'd you manage that?" I asked. "She slept like an angel for the first few days, and now she's a demon."

"You were the same way." Mother pointed to her wine, and I handed her the cup. "I almost sold you to a passing slave caravan before I discovered that thumping trick." She glanced around the tiny room with its stain of black mold trailing down the wall and the sagging ceiling. "Mother of Christ. What have you gotten yourself into?"

"Life."

"You're an idiot. Some women have brains but are plain as mud. Others—like your sister—are beautiful but dumb as rocks. You were blessed with both brains and beauty. Those gifts are your weapons, but you certainly don't use them."

I ignored her, stripped out of my stola, and almost tossed it on the table, an ancient old thing with carved lion's legs. The lion appeared to have lost a fight—one leg was mangled as if a dog had used it as a chew toy.

"I see having this little mite has filled you out a bit."

"Perhaps." I eyed the cedar box as I slipped into an old tunica. "What's going on, Mother? Why are you here? And why are you in mourning?"

"Vitus is dead."

I sat down on the pallet. Hard. "Really? Devoured by wild dogs? Covered with leeches until they sucked him dry?"

The grin she flashed me reminded me of when I was young and we'd hide from my father, only to jump out and scare the breath from him. "Nothing so exotic, unfortunately. Stabbed in the back after a horse bet went bad."

My little sister would sit with the angels while Vitus burned for eternity. "May the man who did the deed be sainted by God."

My mother raised her cup to me. "Amen."

"And Comito?" I held my breath.

"Your sister would be happy to have your head on a pike within the city walls. Or anywhere, really." My mother looked entirely nonchalant. "You really should be ashamed for what you did to her."

As if I needed reminding.

The silence expanded around us. "You didn't come all this way, with a trunk, to tell me about Vitus."

My mother sighed and tried to shift in her seat, but she gave up when Tasia stirred. "No, I did not. I'm moving in with you."

"What? Here?" I gestured to the room, so small Antonina and I could scarcely lie head to head without our feet touching the walls. We'd tried it.

"Your sister has a patron now, some Tyrian dye merchant." My mother shrugged. "There's not exactly room for me in his villa."

My proud, passionate mother. This was not the life she'd envisioned for herself, for any of us. "I don't know—it's not my room. Antonina's gone most nights, and I'm going to find a position as soon as I'm clean."

"I'll take care of Tasia while you two are out—God knows she'll need someone to make sure she doesn't end up like you. You won't even know I'm here."

"Right. It'll be like sharing a room with a fury."

She made a noise in the back of her throat, half laugh, half snort. "Sometimes I think I should have drowned you at birth."

Ah yes. It was so lovely to have my mother back.

Chapter 7

I hugged my sleeping bundle as Antonina and I crested the city's tallest hill and approached the domes of the Church of the Holy Apostles. Laid out like a crucifix, the white and gray basilica held the remains of our Emperors all the way back to Constantine, but it looked like a haggard old woman with its crumbling façade and chipped mosaics. The dank and gloomy interior reminded me more of a cave than a sanctified house of God.

Under the largest dome, mothers with ragged hair and dark smudges under their eyes held squalling and sleeping infants. A pigeon had made its nest on a niche above the altar, and a waterfall of white and black droppings obscured the face of Saint Peter on a fresco of Jesus surrounded by the twelve apostles. Despite the shabbiness of the church that held our Caesars, I rather liked the idea of Tasia being baptized there. I wished Comito could see this, but it was still too soon to go begging my way back into my sister's good graces. Mother was absent, too, sleeping off a bout of too much wine. Old habits died hard, or not at all.

Tasia woke as the priest finished the baptism service, ending with the usual verse in Latin from the Gospel of Matthew. "'Then little children were brought to Jesus for him to place his hands on them and pray for them,'" he said. "'But the disciples rebuked those who brought them. Jesus said, "Let the little children come to me, and do not hinder them, for the kingdom of heaven belongs to such as these."'"

I expected Tasia to cry as the red-robed priest took her from me and gingerly undid the mostly clean blanket Antonina had wrapped her in, but she only watched him with curious eyes. Of course, she screamed as if whipped when he dunked her in the holy water and handed her to her new godmother.

"The least they could do is warm the water," Antonina murmured, earning the glare of the priest as both she and I struggled to wrap my daughter again. "She's only a baby."

"I think they're more concerned with her immortal soul than her earthly comfort." I unpinned the stola Antonina had let me borrow so Tasia could nurse. She gave one last howl of protest and latched onto the nipple so hard I winced.

The Communion bread was dry on my tongue and the wine bitter after the confession, but I felt clean again, prepared for a fresh start. We followed the other families into the light, keeping close to the stone buildings to avoid the sun on our skin. A kaleidoscope of colored silk banners fluttered on the balconies of patrician villas, a stark contrast to the dirty *mappae* and stained tunicas hung from our lone window.

"Thank you," I said to Antonina.

"For what? For coming today?"

"For that." I kicked a rock on the path. "And for everything."

She glanced at me. "Don't mention it. I kind of like this little thing." She kissed the top of Tasia's head. "And you're not as bad as I thought."

"Thanks."

We walked on in silence, but then Antonina gave a sigh worthy of the stage. I ignored her, but she repeated the performance.

"Something on your mind?"

She flagged down a farmer's cart pulled by a decrepit mule and bought a couple of bruised apricots, along with a bundle of ferns, fennel, and beans, presumably for our supper tonight. She brushed one of the apricots on her sleeve and handed it to me. "That perfect girl is going to end up just like us."

"I won't let that happen."

Antonina gave a little bark of laughter. "What else will she do? Be a maid for some patrician?"

I bit into the apricot and slurped the juice to keep it from spilling down my chin. "Perhaps."

"Then she'll whore for the master."

"No," I said. "She won't."

"Then you need to do something."

"Oh really? And I suppose you're going to tell me exactly what that is."

She bit into her apricot and rolled her eyes. "I don't know—how about make more money? You can't live with me forever." I opened my mouth to tell her we'd leave tonight, but she frowned and shook her head. "That's not what I mean. You can stay as long as you like. You're like a canker I've grown accustomed to."

"Thanks."

"The point is, you've got to get her out of here." Antonina stroked Tasia's little fingers. "I don't want to see this little thing on the boards one day."

Tasia finished on one breast, so I moved her to the other, inhaling the baby smell I adored so much. My little piglet gave a contented sigh and closed her eyes.

I knew what I needed, much as I didn't want to admit to sounding like my sister or every other *pornai* in the Empire. Love was a luxury I could ill afford, but I needed a bronze wedding belt around my waist. A rich patron was the only way to pluck myself from the gutters, but only if I could convince him to marry me so I could protect my daughter.

We passed through the crumbling walls Constantine had built hundreds of years ago, no longer needed as the city spilled from its gates and Theodosius surrounded the new city with thicker, taller walls. Constantinople's fifth hill was directly before us, and somewhere carved into its slopes was one of the city's smaller theaters. I might as well get on with my life today.

Tasia nestled against my chest, her mouth open and cheeks pink with sleep. I could smell my milk on her breath. "Take her for me, will you?" I murmured to Antonina. "I'll meet you back home, but find her some goat milk if I'm late."

She slipped out of her gray *paludamentum* embroidered with black and white fish swimming up the front, and tied it over my now rather ample breasts. "My bloods started today, so take as much time as you'd like—I'm looking forward to a few days off. Good luck."

I watched them go, then ducked into one of the corner shops to ask where I might find the closest theater.

"An actress, eh?" The man grinned, revealing carcasses of brown teeth. "Follow the aqueduct to the Cistern of Aetius. The Seneca's on the other side, but don't blink or you might miss it."

"Thank you." I did as he said, stopping to wash my hands and face in a fountain spewing water from a lion's mouth. A couple of women with hennaed hair and garish turquoise stolas pushed past me, close enough so that I gagged at their cloud of cheap perfume. The façade they'd just come from leaned precariously against the hillside, hiding what must have been the world's tiniest stage. I'd slit my wrists if I couldn't get hired here, but between my pregnancy and Comito, I knew I wasn't welcome at the Kynêgion any longer.

A man I presumed to be the Master of the Stage stood under the façade's arch and whistled at another departing actress. His eyes flicked over me. "You here for a position?"

I gave my most becoming smile. "You guessed right."

"You clean?" He rubbed one side of his face as he studied me. "No scabby tarts for the fine patrons of the Seneca."

"Clean as the day I was born."

"That's what they all say." He bit his fingernail and spit a piece at my feet. "The best I got might be a trooper in the chorus."

Right back where I was at the Kynêgion. "Fine," I said.

His bushy caterpillar of an eyebrow arched. "You sing?"

"A little." It wouldn't do to lie—I wouldn't miraculously become a songbird overnight.

He gestured with one hand for me to show him, and I managed to squawk out the first line of a popular *troparion* often sung in church.

" 'O Gladsome Light of the Holy Glory of the Immortal Father, Heavenly, Holy, Blessed Jesus Christ!' "

He rubbed a finger in his ear, rolled the yellow smear of wax between his fingers, and wiped it on his tunica. "Dance?"

"Some."

"Instruments?"

"No, but I'm good for a laugh."

"No trooper then," he said. "But maybe a mimic."

I wouldn't even wear a mask if I became a mimic. In fact, I'd never wear much of anything. But something was better than nothing.

He opened a thin book with broken seams, one full of contracts from what I could see, most marked with a cross at the bottom. "You got experience?"

I wasn't sure if the truth would harm me or help me, but it probably couldn't hurt. "I played at the Kynêgion for the Blues."

"Name?"

"Theodora."

"Daughter of Acacius?" He shut the book. "I don't hire crazy."

"What?"

"We Masters of the Stage talk. I don't hire girls who aren't dependable"—he mimicked a pregnant belly—"and who like the bottle too much." I sputtered at the lie, but he shook his head. "Sorry, sweet. Don't let the door hit your pretty little arse on the way out."

I'd strangle Comito next time I saw her. I didn't know what other tales she'd told Hilarion, but she'd definitely found her revenge. I watched the Master of the Stage walk away. "Just one question," I said, thanking God when he turned around. "I suppose Hilarion told all the stage masters in the city about me?"

"Prob'ly a few outside, too. No one goes against Hilarion, not if we want to keep our stages open." He gave me a grandfatherly smile. "Maybe try a taverna?"

I wouldn't resort to a taverna—patricians rarely frequented the filthy houses, and I didn't want the average pleb. I wandered a bit longer before heading in the direction of the Kynêgion. None of the other stage masters would hire me, but perhaps if I was lucky—

My breasts were engorged by the time I reached the huge theater and pushed the limits of my neckline to their breaking point. Uncomfortable, but I could use all the help I could get.

"Theodora!" I turned to see Chrysomallo, the little *pornai* from the Boar's Eye, run toward me, decked out in a sleeveless blue trooper's costume. What there was of it anyway. "What are you doing here?"

"When did you become an actress?" I wanted to be happy for her for escaping that pit, but it was hard when that same pit might be my only way to earn a living.

"Just this season," she said. "There was a position open as a trooper in the chorus."

My position. I cringed, but she didn't notice.

"I'm so glad to be out of the Boar's Eye." She clapped her hands over her smile and squealed. "Did you come to apply for a position, too?"

"In a manner of speaking." I'd formulated a proposition almost impossible for Hilarion to reject. Almost. "Is Hilarion here?"

"Somewhere—he and one of the girls went to his office, but they're probably done by now. We're preparing for the opening show of *Antigone* tonight." Chrysomallo smiled. "I'll tell him you're here."

I grabbed her hand. "Perhaps I should go to him. Since he's so busy." It would be harder for him to throw me out if I wasn't already on the street.

"Right." She rolled her eyes and giggled. "Hilarion's always telling me I have the brain of a naiad."

We passed through the curious, and sometimes hostile, stares of some of the other actresses. Hilarion was in the trenches with the chorus as Antigone and Ismene rehearsed some of their early scenes. Chrysomallo ran off to join the rest of the troopers while I waited on one of the Senate's marble benches on the floor. I searched for Comito but didn't spy her anywhere. Hopefully that patron of hers kept her locked in a villa outside the city walls. Hilarion strode over to me as soon as the performers took a break.

"I don't care who sent you this time or which *scenicae* can vouch for you." He chewed his perpetual toothpick and carried two mismatched practice swords, pointing the short one at me. "Your sister left me in the lurch for that Tyrian merchant of hers, and I have no intention of ever letting either of you back on my stage."

I breathed a sigh of relief that Comito wasn't here any longer. Now there was no reason Hilarion wouldn't accept my offer.

"Nice to see you, too, Hilarion." I crossed one leg over the other and leaned toward him. It really was a shameless display, but it got his attention. "I've actually come with a proposition."

"Because no one else will hire you?" He almost smiled but waved the sword toward the exit. "Out."

"I have something you want. Badly."

He laughed. "The only thing you've got is that little body of yours.

It's sweet, but not that tempting. I've got plenty of girls to keep me happy."

He turned and walked off toward his office, but I followed him. "I'm not leaving until you hear me out." I didn't wait for him to protest but gave him the condensed version of what I'd planned.

Hilarion turned, his jaw slack and the bone toothpick he'd been gnawing stuck to his lip. "You want to do what?"

"You heard me." I closed his mouth and wiped my fingertips on my stola. "It can be the opening act tonight."

"Absolutely not. The Patriarch would shut us down for vulgarity, obscenity, lewd and immodest behavior—"

"You couldn't pay for better advertising," I added. "Think of it— standing room only."

He scowled, but I could practically hear his mind making the calculations—the stands would be full for the premiere tonight and word would spread. He'd have a full house every night for the month if he agreed to my little performance. He smacked his lips and grinned. "I'll get the bird—you can go on tonight."

I flashed him my most becoming smile. "And what do I get in return?"

His grin was replaced with a shrewd scowl. "Name your price."

"Forty percent of sales." It was obscene and I knew it.

Hilarion choked—he might have made a fine actor himself. "Five percent and not a *nummi* more."

"You must be addled. You're going to be rich after this. Thirty percent and not a *nummi* less."

He chewed his toothpick, pretending to consider it. "I'll give you ten percent. That's more than all the other girls make combined."

"But I'm not just one of the girls, now, am I?" I crossed my arms. "Twenty percent. And the rest of the girls still get paid."

"Fifteen and the girls get their usual wage. Final offer."

"Done."

"I would have taken five," I called over my shoulder. I'd have done it for free if it meant making a name for myself. One day I would be a *kyria*. And I wouldn't look back.

Hilarion's chuckle followed me out. "I'd have paid you forty."

The girls grumbled that night when Hilarion told them the playbill had been changed.

"I hate *Leda*," Chrysomallo whined. "The Zeus costume is ridiculous. The feathers make me itch for hours afterward."

"You won't need the costume tonight," Hilarion said. "Theodora's mostly the only one onstage."

"What?"

I took one long gulp of wine, thankful it wasn't watered, as most of the girls glared at me.

I walked onstage alone as the name of the play was announced— *Leda and the Swan*—glad for the warmth of the wine that soothed at least a few of my nerves. The crowd jeered—I wore far too many clothes in my white stola, hair swept up to show off the pair of fake pearl eardrops that dangled to my collarbone. I smiled and held up a finger to silence them. Taking my place in the direct center of the stage, I pulled the tie at my shoulder and let my stola fall in a heap. My stomach felt as if something inside it were alive, and I willed myself not to vomit.

The crowd went wild.

Hilarion crouched in the shadows of the *vomitorium*, clutching a burlap bag. It lurched as if trying to run from him, spewing the occasional feather.

I walked the full circle of the amphitheater, clothed only in a snowy ribbon tied to cover my most private parts, making my movements as slow and sensual as I could while my hands shook. There were catcalls from the audience, but then a hush fell as Chrysomallo and a few of the other girls pranced onstage with little silk bags clutched in their hands. I lay on the center of the stage, one ankle crossed over my knee. The evening air was warm, but the cool lime-stone on my back made my nipples pucker.

The girls sprinkled trails of grain across the floor and over my naked body. Then they danced off, and Hilarion released his bag.

I wanted to throttle him. In the myth, Leda had been seduced by Zeus in the form of a regal swan and then gave birth to Helen of Troy, the world's most beautiful woman. I was supposed to be bedded by a graceful swan, but instead three brown geese waddled toward me, much to the audience's delight. The birds squawked indignantly until they found the trails of grain.

This would certainly make a name for me—the girl who slept with geese.

The largest of the geese hesitated as he got close, but his stomach overrode any qualms he may have had about eating off a naked girl. He smelled like dirt, and his peck on my leg was less than gentle; but I moaned, arching my back as he honked and jumped back, showering me with downy feathers. The other two joined in the fun, plucking at the grains on my arms, breasts, and my mons veneris. I thrust my pelvis and acted out the pleasure of my solo bedding. The geese wandered off once their dinner was gone, but I wasn't done yet. The theater was silent—Constantinople could not ignore me now.

Chrysomallo flounced across the stage, strewing flower petals and scattering the geese. "From this blessed union, Helen was born!"

My face burned and my hair tumbled down my back as Chrys-omallo removed the pins to symbolize my transformation from Leda to Helen. Senators waved me to them as I wove my way through the first of their fourteen marble sections, noting with satisfaction many tunicas tented with excitement. Some reached out to grab my buttocks or stroke my breasts, and I let them, clenching my teeth and closing my eyes to lean into their hands, lips parted as I moaned. Tonight they could all indulge in the fantasy of touching a goddess. And tomorrow I would be all they could talk about.

My heart pounded as I held my breath and sauntered back to the *vomitorium*, refusing to glance behind me. My feet touched the shadows of the arch just as the audience burst into applause so loud I feared the roof would crumble.

The only two ways out of this profession were from the top or the bottom. I preferred the top.

Chapter 8

The ropes burned my wrists.

"The fires of Gehenna will burn worse, my child." The black-robed Patriarch gave me a patronizing smile as I picked at the rough cords. "I act with the authority of God and his vassal on earth, Emperor Anastasius. You have defied the sanctity of the very body God has given you with your lewd display here at the Kynêgion. Such vulgarity cannot be tolerated."

I stifled the urge to roll my eyes and gave Hilarion a pointed look instead.

He cleared his throat. "Perhaps we could reach some sort of agreement? Negotiate a deal that would be mutually beneficial to all parties?"

"My role as shepherd of the Empire cannot be compromised." The Patriarch snapped his fingers, and two slaves came forward to lead me away. We were almost out the door when Hilarion stopped us.

"Perhaps a cut of the profits?" He sounded as if he were merely bargaining for a cut of veal in the market, but I knew he must be desperate to make such an offer.

The Patriarch paused, then shook his head. "Coins cannot sway me. The girl shall remain in prison until I have deemed she has fully repented her evil ways. This is as God wills."

I wouldn't be led away to rot in prison, locked away from my daughter. I'd seen the way the man's eyes lingered over the swell of my breasts under my stola. "Perhaps a cut of the profits and a private viewing of Leda?" I asked. "Free of charge?"

The Patriarch stopped and nodded to his slaves. They dropped the ropes and left Hilarion's office. He waited until the door shut to speak. "A *very* private show." He spoke to my breasts. "And fifteen percent of the show's profits."

Hilarion choked, but he relented after the glare I shot him. "Fine. But we get to finish out the season with *Leda*." He spat on his hand and offered it to the Patriarch, but he received only a cold stare in return.

The Patriarch's fingers were gentle as he untied me. "When may I expect that private viewing?"

I rubbed my wrists and gave him a peck on the cheek. "I'll go change right now."

"I know I'm going to trip and fall on my face." Chrysomallo clutched my hand.

"Careful." I shook her off and rubbed my wrist, the skin still pink despite all the olive oil I'd rubbed into the evidence of the Patriarch's ropes.

"Still sore?"

More than my wrists were sore, but I shrugged. "Could be worse."

"I've never been to a *kyria*'s house before." Chrysomallo gaped as we passed under the pink marble arch to the villa of General Flavius Justinus, now commander of Emperor Anastasius' palace guard. The Empire had always been a place where an ambitious military man might be promoted, but the fall of the Western capital to the Vandals meant even more opportunities for men in Constantinople. Justin had been a Thracian swineherd in his youth, and he had risen high in his old age, at least high enough to install two gaudy gold statues of Heracles and Theseus—both in all their naked glory—to glower at his guests as they entered his villa. Our troupe was to play a sedate number for the wives during a dinner for the senators and other illustrious guests. I'd have tangled with a demon to perform for the men instead, but I would take what I could get. Hilarion had tried his best to exclude me, claiming he wanted me to perform exclusively on his stage, and only after I'd thrown a bust of Sophocles at his head and threatened to take Leda to another theater did he relent.

Chrysomallo gawked at a mother-of-pearl table with its gold reliquary case and cross, then glanced at me. "Your sister would love this. Do you think she'll come back to the Kynêgion now that her patron threw her out?"

That was news to me—last I'd heard Comito had been happily ensconced in the villa of her Tyrian dye merchant. I missed my sister, but her return would make things thorny.

I didn't have to answer. A beardless man in a delectable white and gold tunica herded us through the atrium. His lips were plump, and his skin looked soft as rose petals, his elongated fingers delicate as bird wings. My suspicions were confirmed when I heard him speak to Hilarion, his singsong voice high and unbroken. He was a *castrato*, likely once the child of a poor family eager to place its son in a patrician's villa to entertain his guests with his sweet singing voice.

We followed the eunuch through a lavish garden surrounded by bushes trimmed to resemble various animals, a short giraffe stalked by a leafy lion and a rhinoceros with a bird on its rump. Another slave stood over a pretty little pond in the middle of a cluster of roses. He rang a tiny silver bell as we passed, and several red fish—mullets from the look of them—kissed the surface as he hummed and leaned down to caress them. This truly was another world.

A freshly scrubbed mosaic gleamed under our feet as we passed the kitchens, a domestic scene of sparkling children playing with fluffy black dogs. A peacock and peahen with matching pearl collars strolled over to us from the garden, and a heavy green curtain edged with gold thread muffled the low hum of women's conversation from the *gynaeceum*, a reminder that we might visit this world, yet never truly belong.

My stomach growled as slaves paraded past with platters of purple sea urchins split open to show their orange guts atop tureens of creamy soup with garlic croutons, parrots dressed in their feathers and smeared with brown gravy, and a whole roast lamb stuffed with black olives and goat cheese. Chrysomallo groaned as a giant bowl of steaming stewed chicken and liver patties went by, so large two slaves struggled to carry it. "This is torture," she said. "I should have eaten before I came."

"Me, too," I said. "But then we wouldn't fit into our costumes."

She pulled a face at our proper stolas, worn tonight out of respect for our patrician audience, although these women rarely showed so much wrist or ankle.

The eunuch slipped through the curtain and cleared his throat. "They are ready for you."

Hilarion remained behind as we entered the *gynaeceum*, its walls the creamy color of soft parchment and painted with delicate floral frescoes to match the buttery silk couches. The *kyrias* of Constantinople's noble families resembled an artist's palette in their rainbow of silks, gemstones, and pearls glittering at their throats, ears, and wrists as they lounged on couches and nibbled their food. Every nose possessed a noble sweep, their oiled hair twisted into elaborate knots and curls to rival any Gordian knot. They were all I wanted to be.

One well-preserved lady with a face like that of a woodpecker outmatched all the others with the sheer number of jewels—all rubies—attached to her tiny frame. General Justin's wife, Lupicina. No wonder she dripped with jewels—the woman had been a slave before Justin married her. Worse, she'd actually been a barbarian prostitute until the General took a liking to her. Perhaps there was hope for us all.

I bowed my head. "We are honored to perform for such an illustrious group of Constantinople's most revered wives and mothers."

The ruby *kyria* managed a tight smile that didn't reach her eyes. "You may begin."

The show for the women was a sedate affair—the very proper marriage of Abraham and Sarah—and I had only a bit part since I wasn't interested in fighting for the role of the elderly church matriarch. The *kyria* yawned into their hands and returned to their gossip before we'd even finished our bows.

Our troupe moved back to the waiting area behind the curtain to don our cloaks while Hilarion waited for the eunuch to return with the coin purse. Chrysomallo and the other actresses drooled over the rich mosaics and gilded furniture, but I didn't care a whit for the anemone flowers in the wall fresco or the gold capitals topping the marble columns. From the other side of another green curtain came the low hum of voices, the conversation of some of the Empire's richest and most powerful men. They were men I wanted to meet, but we were going home.

My earring caught my *paludamentum* as I threw the cloak over my shoulder, ready to leave, but the eunuch emerged from the curtain and touched his palms together.

"The General begs another performance," he said, his girlish tone more command than request. "He and his guests await in the *triclinium.*"

There was a titter of excitement as we shrugged off our cloaks and girls rearranged their cleavage and pinched one another's cheeks. The men's dining room was smaller than I expected, made smaller yet by the jet ceiling and red and black rectangular frescoes that stretched from ceiling to floor, surrounding a central fresco depicting a boar hunt and naked hunters armed with spears and bronze shields. Men in white tunicas, many wearing a red senatorial sash tied around their waist, lounged together on saffron *lecti* as they finished their meals, the tiny bird bones and feathers discarded on the mosaic floor. Dregs of wine already spattered one crimson wall panel, and several toppled redware goblets revealed humorous paintings of men and women in rather inventive positions. This promised to be quite the evening.

"Leda!" A patrician with curls the color of sand and a dimpled chin waved to me with his wine cup—one that had probably been refilled a few too many times. He looked vaguely familiar, but I couldn't quite place him. "You cruel goddess, come to steal my heart again!" All the room laughed save a man at his elbow. He was scarcely older than me, but a scar cut from the base of his nose to his upper lip. His black hair was cropped close to his head, and his shoulders resembled a slave's in a marble quarry. Yet no slave glowered like that.

A beast of a man in the center of the room crooked a finger at us. He might have been a goose amongst swans in his plain brown tunica with solid leather sandals, a cloud of unruly white curls on his head that matched the sparse hairs peeking over his neckline, and the largest ears I'd ever seen. I liked him immediately.

"My guests have requested a display of dancing," he said, waving his goblet to the twenty or so men on the couches. "And as I am old and fat, I thought they might prefer a number performed by the fairer sex."

"My ladies are happy to oblige, General." Hilarion was all smiles and bows, but I hurried to take a place at the back of the circle. I wasn't likely to run into most of these men—or their fortunes—again, and none of them would rush to claim me once they realized I danced like an elephant. A clumsy elephant.

Thanks be to Christ they didn't expect us to sing, too. General Justin clapped a hasty beat, and the rest of the men joined in, singing one bawdy song after another. Chrysomallo gave me a wide berth as we danced, castanets snapping and the room turning warm until sweat pearled on our skin and I flung my hands in the air. "Enough!" I laughed, panting and fanning myself with my hand. "We won't have any energy for the rest of the night if we keep this up."

"And what do you plan to do that takes so much energy?" The sandy-haired man who'd called to me earlier waggled his brows.

One of the men punched his arm. "We all know what you want to do with her, John."

John.

Now I recognized him, the same man who'd hung on Chrys-omallo's arm the night I'd met Karas at the Boar's Eye. I wondered if he remembered spewing his dinner over the ground before stumbling into the night. Probably not—he'd likely woken up in an alley the next morning.

I sidestepped a few of the other girls, hiked up my stola, and perched on the arm of his *lectus*, tapping my chin as if searching for an answer. He might have been mistaken for Apollo with his soft skin and pale hair. I leaned down as if to whisper in his ear. "If you have to ask what takes so much energy," I said, tracing the dimple in his chin and speaking loud enough so all could hear, "you should probably go home before the big boys start to play."

He laughed with the rest of them, even as his ears turned red as the wall behind him. The waters of the Mediterranean couldn't have been warmer than the attention of all these men's eyes on me. Not everyone smiled though. John's black-haired friend crossed his arms against his chest and watched me with his original scowl. There was no mistaking which god of old he resembled: Ares, god of war.

"So, young lady." General Justin shifted on his *lectus*, waving away the flurry of slaves. "If we are not to have the pleasure of watching you dance, what do you propose for our entertainment?"

The way the men devoured us with their eyes, I knew what answer they expected. "A *skolion*," I said. There was a collective groan, but I waved them down. "The winning poet shall receive a kiss"—I grinned and shook my hips—"and maybe more—from whichever girl he chooses, free of charge!"

That got their attention. Chrysomallo looked at me with wide eyes. "Lord, Theodora. Are you sure you aren't a pimp?"

"A poor one if she's offering our services for free," one of the other girls hissed under her breath.

I gestured to the foot of the general's couch. "May I?" The rest of the troupe followed my lead, most finding their places lying between two men on the couches. Hilarion rolled his eyes at me and disappeared into the shadows of the doorway, there to remain unless there was any trouble.

Justin moved his legs. "Only so long as no one tells my wife."

I thought for a rhyme. "My lips are sealed, as I value your life."

There was a ripple of laughter. The *skolion*—a competition to see who could make the most bawdy rhyme—had begun.

The black-haired man stood and gave a little bow in my direction, an unpleasant smile hovering on his lips. "'For reasonable men I prepare only three *kraters* of wine: the first for health, the second for love and pleasure, and the third for sleep.'"

It was one of Dionysus' lines from a play by Eubolus, but spoken in an accent I couldn't quite place. The ancient Greeks had used giant *kraters* to mix their water and wine at symposiums like this.

Justin chuckled. "Quite a difficult challenge, Hecebolus. Rather ungentlemanly of you."

The man only raised his brows. "I never claimed to be a gentleman."

My mind skipped ahead as the crowd murmured. I wouldn't let this bear of a man outdo me. "And God had gifted women with such *craters* as well: one for health"—I pointed to my mouth—"and the second for pleasure with a baser sort of man." I gave a waggle of my seat before I rose and straddled Hecebolus. I pressed my breasts to his chest and startled at the hardness of his desire between my legs. "And the third"—anyone with half a brain could see the lust in his eyes as I tipped my head and brushed his lips with mine—"for sleep."

The entire symposium roared with laughter, everyone in the crowd stomping his feet and clapping. Hecebolus gave a perfunctory clap and shifted me from his lap. John saluted me with his glass, sloshing red wine over the rim. "If only God had graced you with a fourth crater, Theodora, so that we poor souls might enjoy you more."

I laughed and sauntered past Hecebolus with his black hair and blacker scowl to sit next to John, cupping my breasts in both his hands. "With a fourth like these, a man might forget I'm a whore."

"Two golden apples to rival the one given to Paris. With a face to outshine Helen's!" He kissed the swell of my breasts and clutched my hand to his heart, pulling me almost to his lap. Hecebolus moved away as if burned, a slight I pretended not to notice.

"You know," I said to John, "I met you before I played Leda."

"No." John blinked. "Surely I'd remember meeting such a goddess."

"It was at the Boar's Eye. You were visiting my friend Chrysomallo over there."

John glanced at Chrysomallo, cheeks flushed as he shrugged. "She's a pretty tart, but nothing compared to you." He shot me a wicked grin and wrapped his arm around my shoulder, giving himself a fuller view of my breasts. "However, the girls at the Boar's Eye taught me a thing or two over the years. Perhaps I could demonstrate them for you tonight?"

I laughed. "Perhaps."

"Please, Leda—I'll go mad with desire if I can't have one night with you."

I chuckled as my friends were claimed—Chrysomallo giggled when General Justin pulled her to his lap. "The whole night? You can't afford me."

He grinned, his bronze face lighting up. "Try me."

I shrugged, ignoring the strap of my stola as it slid from my shoulder. I should send him to Hilarion, but I preferred to negotiate my own wage.

"Ten *solidi.*"

If he was shocked, he didn't show it. Ten *solidi* could keep a regiment in bread and beer for a week or feed a pleb family for months. If I was lucky, he'd end up paying much more than that.

"I may starve if my creditors find out," he said, "but such a price would be worth one night with a goddess."

He tasted of wine and the cloves and almonds from the stewed chicken as he slipped an arm around my waist and tried to stand. Unsuccessfully. We tumbled to the floor in a tangle of limbs.

I looped one of his arms over my shoulder and held his waist with my free arm, wiping away a trickle of wine from the dimple in his chin. For ten *solidi* I could help the man to his sedan. God's blood, for ten *solidi* I'd strip naked and run down the *Mese* if he asked me.

I helped him from the *triclinium*, the men's catcalls accompanying us into the darkness until he pulled me into an empty room. He made quick work of the clasps at my shoulders and buried his face in my bare breasts, my hands in his sandy hair. My skin prickled with gooseflesh as he tugged my stola over my hips, then dug his fingers into my backside to pull me closer.

"I like this spot." His tongue flicked the mole under my left breast before moving up to the nipple. "And this one."

Someone cleared his throat. Hecebolus leaned against the door, arms crossed in front of his massive chest. Heat spread through more than my cheeks as I stepped out of John's arms and righted my stola, hoping no one else could hear the pounding of my heart.

"I'd like to counter your offer," he said. "Ten *solidi* for tonight, and maybe more nights after that. Let the lady choose."

It was my turn to almost fall over. It didn't matter that his offer was higher—for the first time I found myself actually wanting a man.

John took one look at me, groaned, and banged his head against the wall. "Tell me you're not going to choose him. Tell me I didn't just lose my night with Aphrodite."

Hecebolus brushed his tunica, a wolfish smile spreading across his face. The cut of his cloth and the weave of his calfskin boots reeked of money, sweeter than any perfume he might have worn. "Keep your pagan sentiments to yourself, John. This goddess is mine."

I raised my brows at John, still wobbly on his feet. "Care to raise your friend's offer?"

"Friend?" John shook his head, a loose grin still on his face. "Not after tonight. Alas, my purse is full of cobwebs." He pulled himself from the wall and punched the other man's arm. Hard. "Enjoy her for me. God knows I'll only have myself to scratch my chickpea tonight." I kissed the poor boy's cheek, but he turned so his lips brushed mine, and he gave me a jaunty smile. "You're missing out, Leda." Then he turned and sauntered into the night.

Hecebolus snapped his fingers, and a pretty young slave dressed in a red tunica appeared from the shadows of the hall. The eunuch counted five gold coins from his silk purse and dropped them into my palm, careful not to touch me. "The remainder shall be paid after services have been rendered." He sniffed.

I slipped the *solidi* into the hidden pocket sewn into my bodice and was about to comment that he could deposit the rest there later, but Hecebolus picked me up and flung me over his shoulder.

My initial instinct was to squawk and thwack him over the head. Instead, I wrapped my legs around him and lowered my lips to his, inhaling the spicy smell of his perfume. I didn't know if I wanted to wait until we made it to his villa.

We didn't get that far, barely managing to close the silk curtains before Hecebolus had me on the floor of his sedan. Several times. I moaned and arched into him, my fingernails digging into his back as unexpected waves of pleasure crashed over me. My limbs still tingled as I rearranged myself on the seat opposite him and smoothed the now-rumpled folds of my stola as he opened the curtains. The oil lamps along the *Mese* sputtered as we passed and then turned down a moonlit street so quiet that the bearers' footsteps echoed off the buildings.

I knew well how to satisfy a man, but this was the first time I hadn't had to pretend my own pleasure. This man was either a saint, or a demon.

Hecebolus watched me, and I had to force myself to sit still. I leaned back on the cushions and lazily traced the clover pattern on the curtains. "You don't wear the red stripe like most of Justin's other friends tonight," I said.

"I'm not a senator. Politicians would double-cross their own mothers if given the opportunity; yet they scorn the merchants they depend upon."

"Then why were you there?"

"John the Cappadocian asked me—he's particularly adept at maneuvering around the Emperor's import taxes."

Interesting. Poor John played with money; yet he had none of his own. Either he was terribly honest or incredibly stupid.

"So you're a merchant."

Hecebolus nodded, then tugged me to my knees before him. My finger traced the rope under his tunica—I was shocked to find he was ready for me again. My lips traced a line up the silk of his leg. "And what do you import?"

"Imperial dye." I drew back as if slapped. His accent—

"Purple dye? From Tyre?"

"How did you know?"

"And you recently patronized another actress?" I pulled myself back to my seat, sitting on my hands to stop their trembling. "Named Comito?"

"Until recently, yes." His face grew hard. "I wouldn't have pegged you as the jealous type."

I snatched the coins from my cleavage and flung them on my seat, not caring when they spilled all over the floor we had just enjoyed. "Consider that one complimentary." I unlatched the door and jumped from the moving sedan, then tripped and felt the seam of my stola rip as I caught myself with my palms. Hilarion would charge me for that.

"What in the name of Christ?" Hecebolus stuck his head out the window, the curtains framing him like a halo in a mosaic. His expression looked more like a demon than any Christian saint. "Get back here!"

I didn't look at him as I pressed my palms to my lips, tasting the copper tang of blood. "I'd rather walk."

All the way to the fires of Gehenna.

Comito was going to kill me.

Antonina barely managed to speak as she laughed, great heaving sobs as she clutched her ribs and blinked back tears. "Everything you touch turns to ash, Theodora."

"This is why I wasn't going to tell you." I scowled at her and dandled Tasia on my lap, feeding her goat milk through a turquoise glass baby feeder Mother had found at the market. The ingenious invention looked like a vase with a spout coming out the side, and Tasia sucked it dry. Sometimes Mother took her to Esther to feed her, a Jewish girl below us who was still breastfeeding her own infant, but I hated the smell of another woman on my daughter. I wanted to cling to her, the only thing that was pure in this world. Unfortunately, things weren't looking hopeful for either of our futures. I'd squandered the only chance with a patrician I was likely to get for some time.

"Maybe you could convince Hecebolus to take Comito back." Antonina wiped her cheeks. "I'm sure he'd be happy to keep you both, especially if it meant having you at the same time."

"Somehow I doubt Comito would appreciate that."

"Your sister was always a prude," Mother said. She had already had too much wine this afternoon, but apparently not enough to tie her tongue.

"And a snob," Antonina said. "She needs to lower her standards."

"Like you?" I glanced at her through the corner of my eyes. "How is Timothy the Weasel these days?"

"Infatuated, as always," she said.

"He's a kind man," Mother said, shaking a finger at me. "You'd do well to find someone like him."

I used a knife to break the wax seal on a fresh amphora of wine and pushed the jug toward her. "I don't understand why you don't take up with him," I said to Antonina. "Or go back to the stage."

"Back to the snake pit? Never." Antonina flopped into a chair, sending a puff of brown feathers out of its lone cushion as she dug through a box of perfumes and unguents. "You know I was in the same boat as you that first day you met me. Only Petronia made sure I didn't have the baby."

I remembered the lead actress screaming at Antonina that first day, the garish red hair poking out from under her snakes.

"What? Why did she care?"

She shrugged and rubbed rose oil into her hands. "I fooled around with Perseus, made the mistake of letting myself fall in love with him. Petronia found out the day you and Comito showed up at the Kynêgion."

I thought back to the lusty kiss between Perseus and Petronia. I'd always wondered what Antonina had really done. Now I knew.

"Then she had to take care of her own similar problem. That was why I took her place the night you stole my starring role." She pulled a tiny ivory spoon out of the box and stuck it in her ear, then wiped the yellow wax on a rag. "Now I've taken enough potions I'm quite sure the gods won't allow me any more babies."

So that was why she treated Tasia like her own.

"The Weasel's not terribly easy on the eyes," I said. That man wasn't named for a rodent for nothing. "But well off."

"Enough at least." Antonina gave a little smile. "And he's gone much of the time. That certainly recommends him."

If only I were so lucky.

I was right. Comito did almost kill me.

Antonina had met me at the Kynêgion to take Tasia home before she went out for the evening with the Weasel. "I like the graffito on the wall outside," Antonina said. "Did you know you have delicious breasts?"

I didn't have a chance to answer.

"You filthy little whore!" Comito barged into the room. Fortunately, Tasia was happily drooling on Antonina's shoulder, so she wasn't in the way when my sister flew at me. With a knife.

It was more sewing needle than a knife, really, but sharp all the same.

Tiny though the weapon was, I didn't relish the thought of being stabbed. Loving sister that she was, Comito went for my throat. Good thing her aim was bad—she missed by a pace.

I pushed her away and expected her to make a second attempt, but she only stared at me. The knife clattered to the floor and she followed, collapsed into a puddle of blue silk. "I can't believe you'd do this to me. Everyone is laughing at me—cast off by my patron so he could have my sister!"

"Let's get this straight right now—I didn't sleep with Hecebolus until after he'd thrown you out."

Comito looked ready to lunge, but Antonina cleared her throat as Tasia whimpered and held her chubby arms out to me. "Ladies, perhaps another time would be better suited for you to maim each other?"

"I'm going to pick up my daughter," I said to Comito. "I'd appreciate it if you didn't try to stab me while I'm holding her."

"You kept her?" Comito looked at me as if I'd gone mad. I was getting sorely tired of everyone looking at me that way.

"Of course I kept her," I said. "How could I not?"

Antonina tweaked Tasia's nose. "Theodora here is a regular saint."

Comito sniffed, but the scowl she threw me was full of malice. "You've always been selfish. I hope he casts you off and makes you into an even greater laughingstock than you've made me."

"He won't get a chance to cast me off. I'm not going to see him again."

"Really?" Comito's jaw hung limp. "You swear you'll leave him alone?"

"If it would make you happy and keep you from trying to stab me, yes, I swear." It wasn't as if the man would offer to be my patron anyway. "I didn't even know who he was until it was too late."

"Good." She flounced out the door, not bothering to shut it behind her. The hallway was full of eyes—the other actors and troopers had heard it all. Comito might get her wish—I was well on my way to becoming a laughingstock.

"Don't say a word." I shot Antonina a warning look and gave Tasia a peck on the cheek. She gurgled and grabbed a fistful of my hair.

"Not a word," Antonina said. "Although I'm quite convinced the Kynêgion would sell out if we performed your life story on the stage."

That evening I managed a fat senator who stunk of fish and garlic and pinched my breasts at his release. I cursed myself for going with Hecebolus the night after Justin's party, for letting desire get the best of me.

I'd never make that mistake again.

Chapter 9

Spring wilted under an angry sun so hot not even *Leda and the Swan* could draw a full house. Hilarion called us onstage one afternoon, mopping his shiny forehead despite the canvas cover stretched over the roof. Something slithered down the back of my neck, but my hand only came away with sweat.

"I've canceled the rest of the shows for the month." Hilarion held his hands up at the collective groan. "It's hotter than Hades, and we're hemorrhaging money with all the empty seats. We'll reopen on the New Year."

It was only July, almost two months until the New Year on the first of September. I did the calculations in my head. My meager savings wouldn't last half that long.

Most of the other troopers clustered by the entrance arch, fanning themselves with their hands. Chrysomallo waved me over. "Come have a drink with us at the Boar's Eye, Theodora."

Drowning my worries in wine didn't sound terribly appealing. "Thanks, but I'm going home to Tasia."

"Suit yourself." She fingered the tangled mess of gaudy ivory birds clipped to her ears. "What will you do until September?"

I bit my lip. "Your guess is as good as mine."

I awoke the next morning to women wailing in the street and black banners fluttering over every church and balcony in the city, as if night had draped itself over the city.

"Emperor Anastasius is dead." Antonina closed the door behind her, the mahogany tips of her hair poking out from under a black veil of mourning.

I crossed myself and shifted on my pallet, careful not to wake Tasia. "May God rest his soul." I yawned. "How did he die?"

"The official story says he was called to God in his sleep, but who knows if that's true." She stripped off the veil and her stola, and stretched out naked on her pallet. My mother snored from the corner, whether deep in sleep or in a fog of poppy juice, I wasn't sure. Probably both.

"I wonder who will wear the purple next." All I knew was that Anastasius had been almost ninety, and he had earned the nickname Dicorus from his mismatched eyes, one green and one blue. Like so many Emperors, he had no sons, although he did have a nephew. "Hypatius?"

"They say he's in Antioch right now—he'll never make it back in time." Antonina rolled to her stomach, head on her folded arms. "And old Dicorus never named him heir. It should be interesting at the Hippodrome today."

"The Hippodrome?" Tasia gurgled and grabbed a fistful of my hair. I rubbed my nose to hers and earned a gummy smile.

"The Patriarch will name the new Emperor there today." Antonina yawned. "Timothy asked me to go, but I'm exhausted. I'll watch Tasia if you want."

I had nothing better to do. It wasn't every day I got to see history being made.

The Hippodrome was a hot swarm of too many bodies packed under the glare of the sun. Bread and fruit vendors jostled amongst the crowd, but there wasn't enough to go around, adding rumbling stomachs to the volatile mix. People placed bets on which man would walk away with the eagle scepter and muttered as they waited for the Patriarch to emerge from the Sacred Palace onto the balcony of the Kathisma. Men called out to me—to Leda—but I ignored them. More than one heated debate ended in blows, one man losing a few teeth and another almost getting his eye gouged out near my vantage point. If the Patriarch didn't hurry, he'd end up with a riot on his hands.

Morning stretched into afternoon. The Blues and Greens hurled insults at each other across the arena, growing bolder as the hours ticked by. The heat saturated everything, so searing I wished I could strip down to my girdle. Unfortunately, that sort of behavior would probably get me into trouble here.

The crowd around me roared and jumped to its feet when the senators filed into their marble seats below the Kathisma. A familiar black-robed figure emerged on the balcony from the Sacred Palace as rows of Excubitor guards marched onto the floor of the Hippodrome, the bosses on their shields glaring at us like bronze eyes.

The crowd's roar dulled to a low rumble and finally, to silence when the Patriarch held up his hands. "Good people of Constantinople," he said, "it is my great honor to stand before you as God's mouthpiece to proclaim the new Emperor of the Roman Empire. I put forth *illustris* John."

For a moment I feared he might have referred to the Cappadocian and that I might have turned down a night with the future Emperor, but the imperial guards on the balcony lifted a slight old man on their shields—not John the Cappadocian—as the people in the stands bowed their heads.

A cry went up from the Blues. "Down with John! We'd sooner see a demon on the throne!"

They launched half-eaten apples and peach pits at the Kathisma, but then their voices began to chant, one word in unison—a name.

"Theocritus! Theocritus!" A beefy man—apparently Theocritus— was pushed from the crowd toward the Kathisma, dressed in the red uniform of the imperial bodyguards stationed at the Sacred Palace.

The Greens tried to drown out the Blues with a cry of their own. "John! John! John!"

I scarcely noticed as someone slipped next to me until his breath tickled my ear.

"Exciting, isn't it?"

Hecebolus.

I ignored him, but it was difficult with the sudden heat of his leg against mine. I tried to move away, but the ragged pleb next to me bared his teeth when I stepped on his foot.

"Who shall it be?" Hecebolus crossed his arms before him, a lazy smile on his face, as if he were bored with the proceedings. "The ancient *illustris* or the imperial sodomite who sleeps with Anastasius' chamberlain? Or perhaps someone else entirely?"

"As if you would know," I said. Problem was, he looked as though he might. "John, of course. He's a politician—he probably bribed the Senate."

"But Theocritus procured a rather large loan a few days ago, five silver coins for each Excubitor guard." He stared at the stage, but then his eyes flicked to me. "He asked one of your friends to distribute it for him."

"Not you?" Hecebolus was most certainly not my friend.

"No, not I." I swear he almost smiled. "Flavius Justinus. General Justin."

The uniformed Excubitors on the floor formed a shimmering bronze phalanx around the base of the Egyptian obelisk, pounding their swords against their shields until the noise reached the deafening crescendo of a thunderclap. The Patriarch held up his hands again, but the crowd ignored him.

A giant of a man stepped from the front line, his crown of white hair marking him amongst his men. Even from here I could make out his massive ears. Justin, general of the Excubitor guards.

He carried no sword or shield as he addressed the Patriarch, his strong voice quelling the entire arena. "Most esteemed Patriarch, the Excubitors would put forth their choice for Emperor, if they may."

The Patriarch's shoulders relaxed. I had guessed wrong—the Excubitors, the only troops in the city, would throw their weight behind Theocritus since he was a soldier, and make the decision. The Patriarch's voice was stronger this time. "And who have the Excubitors chosen, General?"

Justin tilted his chin up toward the Patriarch. "Me."

The soldiers pounded their shields again, and the Patriarch turned the color of parchment. "That is not possible," he said, his voice thin as a reed. "There are already two candidates."

Justin stared straight at the Kathisma balcony. "You'll have to tell that to my men."

The very men who would choose the next Emperor. Justin was no fool. I wondered how long he'd been planning this.

The Patriarch pulled at his collar, then motioned to the cluster of white-haired and egg-bald men seated below him. "The Senate must decide the matter."

More than one senator cast wary glances as the front line of Excubitors drew their swords and started to advance toward the Kathisma. A steady trickle of pragmatic citizens made its way to the exits. During Anastasius' reign, the Greens had massacred three thousand Blues in the Hippodrome with stones and daggers concealed in baskets of fruit, and the history of the Empire tended to be even more bloody when the throne changed hands. I turned to leave, but Hecebolus caught my hand.

"Stay. Things are about to get interesting."

I tried to ignore the feel of his thumb as it brushed my wrist, glad for the heat of the sun already warming my cheeks.

The Senate decided quickly.

A man with the belly of a pregnant mare stood amongst the senators, and silence blanketed the Hippodrome. "We, the chosen senators of this Empire, do hereby support General Flavius Justinus as the successor of Anastasius. Justin is acceptable to the Excubitors and both parties. He may not be the perfect candidate for the throne, but he is old and moderate."

Meaning if he didn't work out as planned, at least he'd be dead in a few years.

Below me, Theocritus silently exited, ostensibly to pack his valuables and exile himself to some pleasant island in the Aegean. John quickly followed suit.

The Patriarch wiped his face with a plain white *mappa*. "It is God's wish that General Flavius Justinus serve the Empire as Anastasius' heir."

The Excubitors beat their feet upon the ground, and the crowd joined the noise with raucous cheers. Justin was hoisted high on their shields and carried up the stairs to the Kathisma, where he was deposited on the eagle throne and draped with a heavy gold chain. People started to leave, the show over.

"Exactly as I anticipated." Hecebolus guided me by the elbow toward Deadman's Gate.

I rolled my eyes. "You're a regular oracle. You should set up shop in the market."

"I've bigger fish to catch." His hand slipped to the small of my back. "And anyway, civil unrest is bad for business. Justin traveled from Vederiana to Constantinople with only the cloak on his back and a bag of twice-baked bread to become a military man like Vespasian, Titus, and Constantine. He earned the support of his men long ago."

I knew little about Roman military history outside Caesar's crossing the Rubicon and Constantine's famous dream to mark the sign of the cross on his men's shields before the Battle of Milvian Bridge, but I recognized the names of some of our most successful Emperors.

"Justin will be a decent Emperor," Hecebolus said. "Uninspiring but safe."

"Unless someone manages to slip a blade between his ribs between now and his coronation."

"They'll have to move quickly—he's to be crowned tomorrow."

I raised an eyebrow. "He's not wasting any time."

"The old man would have preferred today, but his wife wanted time to arrange a proper ceremony."

A coronation full of the Empire's richest patricians. And I was without work for another two months. "And I assume you heard this from our new Emperor himself?"

He smiled. "What makes you think I have Justin's ear?"

"Who else might have promised Theocritus all that silver? And then delivered it to Justin instead?"

Hecebolus kept his expression hooded, but there was a smile in his dark eyes as he pushed a grubby old man from my side. Several more men hollered for Leda, but I pretended not to hear. "I'm only a merchant, not a politician." Hecebolus shrugged. "Justin promised a higher return rate."

"And once he wears the purple, you'll receive another token of his appreciation, perhaps an imperial monopoly on your purple dye?"

Hecebolus smiled. "I'd be a fool to say no if he offered."

We were almost outside, back into the shocking glare of the sun and the real world.

I grabbed his hand and pulled him into a shadowy alcove, ignoring the chattering plebs that streamed past us. "You're going to take me to that coronation."

He stepped back, arms in front of him as he surveyed me like a charioteer choosing a horse before a race. "And why would I do that?"

"Because you owe me." I pressed my body to his and let my fingers trail down his leg. "And I'll make it worth your while." I'd promised Comito I wouldn't see Hecebolus again, but it was too late for that now. I had to be at that coronation to land another patrician, no matter the cost.

His hand slipped to the nape of my neck to tip my head back. His lips hovered over mine, and I resisted the urge to touch the scar on his lip. "I owe you, do I?"

"Nothing in life is ever free." I ran the tip of my tongue over my lips. "What do you have to lose?"

His lips curled into a smile, one that made my flesh prickle. "The real question," he said, his fingers tracing my neckline and then dipping lower, "is what do I have to gain?"

And then he walked away.

Chapter 10

My hair still wet from the baths, I lay on the floor with Tasia the next morning and brushed soggy bread crumbs from her chubby cheeks as she alternated between gnawing a crust of brown bread and sucking her toes. Anastasia's old one-eyed doll lay on the floor, its face damp where Tasia had chewed it. My little sister would have been almost seven now—I liked to think she would have adored Tasia as much as I did.

Tasia had the cutest fat rolls on her little legs—I couldn't help but nibble and blow on them until she giggled. Unfortunately, I'd taken her *mappa* off, and a stream of urine sprayed onto the floor as someone knocked. I mopped up the mess as Mother opened the door to Hecebolus' pretty eunuch, dressed in red again.

His regal nose wrinkled, and he heaved a huge sigh at me. "Hecebolus of Tyre requests your attendance at the coronation of Emperor Justin." The slave snapped his fingers, and a woman so old I wondered how she had made it up the stairs stepped into our apartment. A waterfall of orange silk cascaded from her arms—the most exquisite stola I had ever laid eyes on.

It seemed Hecebolus had decided there was something for him to gain.

Mother gasped and reached out to touch it, but she pulled her fingers back. "This must have cost a fortune."

The slave sniffed. "Hecebolus' sedan will be here in an hour." Then he turned on his heel and left, the woman scurrying behind him. An hour was hardly enough time to prepare—it was a good thing I'd just come from the baths.

I fingered the burnt orange shot through with gold. I'd never seen samite before, but even I recognized the rare form of silk woven with real gold.

Mother looked at me as if she'd never seen me before. "Orange— you'll be a butterfly amongst moths."

"I might as well drape myself in imperial purple." I could look forward to being a head shorter if I wore the imperial color. "Or go naked."

Mother blinked, then laughed. "That would certainly get everyone's attention." She draped the fabric reverently across my chest. The color would warm my skin and set off the highlights of my dark hair. It would have been perfect had it not been from Hecebolus.

Mother strummed her fingers on her chin. "I'm not sure you need anyone else's attention. You seem to have caught Hecebolus' eye."

"He's a means to an end. The coronation is my best chance to find a patron."

She gave an exasperated sigh and picked up her amphora of wine, then made a face at it when she realized it was empty. "I didn't raise you to be a fool."

"I promised Comito—"

My mother stomped her foot. "Comito be damned. She's preening in some marble villa with slaves to shave the calluses off her feet while we huddle in this hovel."

"What?"

"Your sister already managed to catch some new patrician. Don't be a fool." My mother shook her empty jug at me. "It's not every day you have a man with more money than God practically begging to take you to bed."

I held up my hands to stop her rant. "Are you going to help me, or do I have to get dressed on my own?"

Mother threatened to beat me if I wrinkled the samite as she twisted my hair into an elaborate knot at the nape of my neck. I'd wear it uncovered, the better to stand out.

"You'd be a fool to reject him," she muttered, an amber brooch clamped between her teeth.

"Pull your head out of the sky, Mother. Hecebolus isn't about to become my patron."

She struggled to pin the clasp and stabbed me in the shoulder. I had a feeling it wasn't by accident. "This man wants you because he thinks you're the goddess every man wants in his bed, not the loud-mouthed chit we all know and love." She waggled a finger at me as I shoved my feet into the slippers Hecebolus had sent—they pinched like a mousetrap. "A shut mouth gathers no foot. Don't ruin this with that tongue of yours."

"I happen to have a very talented tongue." I gave her an impish grin that made her throw her hands in the air.

"You need a patron for that little girl of yours."

That sobered me like a bucket of cold water. "I'll get one, Mother. I promise."

It just wouldn't be Hecebolus.

An elegant sedan carried by eight barefoot slaves rescued me. Eight was terribly pretentious, but I rather liked it.

I ducked my head and took the seat opposite Hecebolus, feeling the tips of my ears flush at the thought of the last time I'd been in this litter. Hecebolus looked akin to some barbarian Emperor, his shoulders filling out his navy stola stitched with gold and his head freshly shaved. He rubbed his jaw and shifted in his seat. "I see the stola fits."

"It will do." I forced a smile. "I'll make sure you have it back to-night."

He raised an eyebrow, but I didn't say anything, preferring to let him imagine what that might mean.

The streets to the church were lined with Justin's ecstatic subjects, extra bread tokens tucked in their hands and drunk on the free wine that would flow down the cobbles of the *Mese* all day. The entire city smelled of pine and rosemary, the streets sprinkled with the crushed herbs to herald the imperial procession.

Justin had chosen the moldering Church of the Holy Apostles for his coronation, and Excubitor guards held back the boisterous crowd. Hecebolus closed his fingers around mine as we walked up the steps into the dark interior of the church. It seemed the full Senate was here to witness the historic occasion—mostly *illustres*, but with a few others thrown in from the middle class and provinces. The men all wore ankle-length white tunicas, the narrow sleeves edged in purple and all tied around the waist with a red sash, the formal dress of proper pa-trician men. Many of the white-hairs stared at me, although they looked the other way when I caught their eyes. I overheard many dis-cussing the Patriarch of Antioch whom Justin had just banished, a Monophysite named Severus. Beady-eyed patrician women adorned their husbands in their elegant stolas of green, red, and blue. No one else wore a flagrant color like orange.

Hecebolus led me toward the main nave of the presbytery. "I see they've cleaned out the pigeons," I said. The droppings covering Saint Peter's face had been scrubbed clean as well.

"I hadn't noticed," Hecebolus said.

The Patriarch's head was bent in discussion with another priest at the altar, but both stopped when they saw me. I inclined my head in their direction and rubbed my wrists. I had no intention of drawing attention to myself while the Patriarch was around—one private show of Leda had been more than enough. Hecebolus tucked a hand around my waist and scowled in their direction.

Heralds in pristine white tunicas and bay wreaths entered and lined the aisle, raised their golden horns to their lips, and trumpeted in unison.

"His Most Christian Sovereign, Augustus Basileus Flavius Justinus! Her Royal Majesty, Lupicina Eusebestati Euphemia!"

A figure swathed in imperial purple stepped into the atrium. Tall as he was, Justin appeared more grandfatherly than imposing, his white hair barely tamed to cover his donkey ears under his gold laurel crown. Lupicina scarcely came up to her husband's shoulder, even with her silver-gray hair swept up in a nest on her head. Strands of pearls and rubies from her crown fell midway down her back and blended into the seed pearls gleaming on her stola. I hoped for her sake no magpies happened overhead when she left the church, searching for something shiny to add to their nests.

The Patriarch bowed to them, and they proceeded to the main altar, imperial red sandals and white silk socks poking from under their robes.

"Not bad for a swineherd and a barbarian whore, eh?" Hecebolus nodded to a dark-haired man at the Emperor's side. "And a peasant from Tauresium."

I couldn't see the other man's face well, but even still, he bore a striking resemblance to Justin with his stocky shoulders and thick shock of curls. "Flavius Petrus Sabbatius Justinianus," Hecebolus said. "Justinian will be our next Emperor."

"Isn't it a bit early to be predicting the next heir?"

Hecebolus gave a wry grin. "Never."

"Who is he?"

"Justin's nephew. He's a rather ambitious sort. Justin recently adopted him, actually."

The Emperor and his wife knelt on the altar—it took Justin some time to force his long legs to bend—and bowed their heads. The Patriarch's Latin chant swelled throughout the nave. We all bowed our heads to pray for blessings upon the royal couple, the people, and the entire Empire while a choir of *castrati* sang a series of haunting hymns from the balconies. Then Justin's forehead was anointed with the oil of the sick, and the Patriarch offered him a codex of the Gospels thickly studded with diamonds and rubies. Too bad I'd never been a good thief—that book could have kept Antonina, Mother, Tasia, and me in a seaside villa for the rest of our lives. I also didn't wish to risk God smiting me in front of the entire patrician class of Constantinople.

"May God bless the rule of Emperor Justin and his consort, Lupicina," the Patriarch said. "May they be fair and just in all their rulings."

The patricians stomped their feet, but Justin held his hands up and silence reigned again.

"Good people of Constantinople," he began, "it is my most sincere honor to stand before you and receive the most heavy crown in all the world. I swear to guide this most holy nation, to protect her from without and enrich her from within. I have loved this city from my youth when I fled the barbarian invasions and found solace within her walls. I shall spend the rest of my life repaying her for loving me so well."

The crowd erupted into cheering, so loud that some of the whitehairs across the way covered their ears.

"Impressive for an illiterate Emperor, eh?" Hecebolus didn't look at me as he spoke, but he continued politely clapping as Justin and Lupicina left the church.

I had hoped for a chance to mingle, to bat my lashes at some of the unaccompanied men, but Hecebolus guided me to follow the rest of the patricians who were drawn toward the royal couple like a hive pulled to its queen.

The sedan ride back down the *Mese* was uneventful, although the revelry had progressed since we'd been in the church. Off-key taverna songs were being sung down the streets, old tunes with new lyrics praising Justin's virility in bed with Lupicina. Somehow I doubted the Empress would approve.

We passed the dark Kynêgion on our way to the Hippodrome—Justin had invited the entire populace of the city to the racetrack and financed a huge gala of games to supplement the free bread and wine. The stadium was already full—many of the plebs had likely claimed their seats before the sun rose, and many more would still be turned away. Men outside hawked ivory chips with seat numbers to the highest bidders.

Situated in front of the Black Gate before the Tripod of Plataea was a new addition to the *spina* of the Hippodrome—a squat wooden scaffold covered with clean straw and a block in the middle.

Dread unfurled down my spine. "What is that?"

Hecebolus' hand on the small of my back guided me forward. "It's the opening for the games. Theocritus knew it was a dangerous game he played when he gambled for the throne." Hecebolus led me to seats under the Kathisma. There were several familiar faces from the *skolion* and a number of senators, including the one with the mare's belly from yesterday. No one would doubt Justin favored Hecebolus now.

The stands filled, and people jammed the floor of the racetrack. Some might be lucky enough to walk away with a souvenir from the execution—a spatter of blood or chunk of hair. Theocritus had only seized an opportunity and been bested at his own game. By the man next to me.

Drums beat out at a pace quicker than a heartbeat as Excubitor guards marched from under the *vomitorium* arch. Justin emerged onto the Kathisma balcony, the heavy gold diadem in his white curls and with Lupicina at his side, both still drenched in the imperial purple, but now accompanied by a pack of greyhounds wearing pearl collars.

The Emperor's gaze flicked to the execution block, and I wondered for a moment if Justin thought how easy it might have been for him to be on that platform. He had paid the Excubitors five silver coins each to purchase their loyalty, but everyone assumed the money was from his own pocket. Perhaps no one cared if the throne had been bought.

Theocritus emerged from the circle of guards in a ragged tunica and stumbled up the stairs before he smashed face-first into the platform. The crowd around me jeered and hissed as the guards yanked him to his feet.

"Theocritus' assets and property have been seized," Hecebolus said. "His widow is forced to beg from her family. Fortunately, they had no children to suffer Justin's wrath."

Thank God for small blessings.

Theocritus met his fate boldly, accepting a priest's final blessing and bowing over the platform without a sound.

The executioner hoisted the ax above his head. I knew before it met its target that it wouldn't take. Theocritus had a neck like a bull, and the executioner was a small man even under his loose black tunica. The ax bounced back, almost taking the executioner with it. The woman next to me cheered, but someone nearby moaned. It took me a moment to realize the sound came from my own throat. The inept butcher tried four more times before he finally wrenched Theocritus' head free and held it up by its thin hair, streaming blood like a pagan sacrifice. The face was twisted in frozen agony, the mouth hanging limp.

I stood to leave, but Hecebolus' hand clamped my wrist tighter than the Patriarch's ropes. "Sit down and cheer."

"I will not."

"You will. Justin is watching you."

The damnable man was right. Justin's eyes were on me, one eyebrow almost to his retreating hairline. On the floor, a cluster of slaves hauled off the headless corpse, and the platform was disassembled, its straw taken to feed some unlucky horse. Trainers for the Greens and Blues emerged with wooden crates and let loose a handful of wild ostrich. Bored, the birds pecked the sand until two larger crates were dragged to the base of the Egyptian obelisk and four lionesses roared out. More blood sprayed the arena floor as the birds were ripped apart.

One of Justin's slaves beckoned Hecebolus halfway through the first heat of chariot races.

"Don't go anywhere." His hand was tight on my knee.

"Where else would I go?"

People turned to stare at me as Hecebolus mounted the stairs to the imperial balcony. I'd come to the coronation to land a rich patron, not realizing I'd accompanied one of the Emperor's new favorites.

He remained next to Emperor Justin through the chariot races while people around me screamed, *"Nika!"* to spur their favorite charioteer to victory. My eyes flicked to the Kathisma now and again, but each time Justin and Hecebolus seemed engrossed in conversation while the Excubitors stared straight ahead. Lupicina looked down at me, and I thought I saw a flicker of a smile pass her lips while she scratched behind the ears of the greyhound at her feet. I would have liked to be a flea on that mongrel. I'd have made sure to bite both men next to her.

Hecebolus returned during the bearbaiting. The black beast my father had trained had blood streaming from his ear, his mangled left eye dangling from its nerve, a tasty treat for the Blues' brown bear. The Greens were going to need a new bear.

"It's time to go." Hecebolus offered me his hand.

"So soon?" Things were not proceeding according to plan. The woman next to me glared as I stopped in front of her, blocking her view as I tried to slow Hecebolus.

"The *Naiad* sails with the tide."

I turned around on the stairs to face him. "The tide?"

"The Emperor just made me a patrician. And granted me the governorship of Pentapolis." He held a piece of purple parchment before me. Two lead seals dangled from the bottom, and the top was stamped with four gold letters. *LEGI. I have read.*

Hecebolus folded the paper and replaced it in his tunica. "The Emperor's stamp. He claims he's not about to learn to write his name after all these years getting by without it."

Pentapolis: five cities on the coast of Africa. The end of the world. "Couldn't he have found somewhere farther than Africa?"

"You'd hurl me off the edge of the map if you could." He gave me a wicked grin. "Your life is about to become painfully dull."

"I'm sure I'll survive." Somehow. Unfortunately, I wasn't on a first-name basis with any other patricians at the moment.

We walked out of the Hippodrome as the brown bear ripped the rest of the face from the black, a stringy mass of quivering pink muscle and blue veins. The ravaged bear roared one final time before collapsing to the ground.

Hecebolus helped me up into his litter but didn't let go of my hand. "Come with me, Theodora."

I tripped on the stair and whirled around. "What?"

"Come with me to Pentapolis. There's nothing for you here."

"Why in Christ's name would you want me to come with you?"

"You're the most famous *scenica* in the city, in the Empire for that matter." He straightened and scowled, as if insulted by my question. "I only want the best."

It was difficult to be a *scenica* when your usual customers included tanners and fullers, but I wasn't going to mention that. "I can't leave my daughter."

He dropped my hand, then stepped back. "I didn't know you had a daughter."

"There's a lot you don't know about me."

"I know you're just like me—scheming, conniving, and ambitious. And I know you have a sweet little body every man in the city wants, but that body's going to be in my bed all night, every night, all the way to Pentapolis."

His mouth was on mine, making it impossible to think. I pushed him back. "I promised you tonight, but nothing more."

"Leave your daughter here and come with me. I'll be gone only six months, a year at most, before I manage a position in the capital." His finger traced my jaw, his eyes delving into mine. "What do you have to lose?"

Nothing, except Tasia. It was a high price to pay, yet Hecebolus might wish to keep me when he returned to the capital. Or perhaps, if I played this right, I might wear his bronze marriage belt and the red sandals of a patrician by then. Tasia's future would be secure.

He stepped into the sedan and pulled me onto his hardness, his hands on my backside as he crushed my lips to his. It seemed we were never destined to make it to a bed. He brought me to the edge of ecstasy several times before pushing me over; it was a savage bout of lovemaking, but I matched him until he shuddered his release and collapsed onto my chest.

Afterward, his finger traced lazy circles on my breasts. His slaves carrying the sedan had circled the city walls at least three times, but I didn't care if they managed a few more. A perfect lethargy seeped into my bones, but it fled as his teeth teased my nipples. "We were made for each other, Theodora. Pentapolis will never be dull."

"I still haven't decided if I'm coming with you." I taunted him to readiness as I recognized the crumbling building with its hideous phoenix outside. It wouldn't hurt to leave him wanting more.

I managed to pin back my rumpled stola for the neighbors' benefit, despite his best attempts to keep me indecent, and dropped a kiss on his lip just below his scar. "I'll meet you on the dock tomorrow."

Only I still had to make up my mind if I was going.

Chapter 11

"Six months?" Mother clutched Tasia while I made a final sweep of the room. Antonina sat at the lion-legged table and stifled a yawn.

"Perhaps a year. At least that's what Hecebolus says."

"Of course he does. I must have dropped you on your head when you were young."

"You're getting senile, Mother. It was Comito you dropped." I narrowed my eyes at her. "And you were the one who told me not to reject Hecebolus."

"I didn't think he'd drag you to the edge of the Empire!"

Antonina rose from her rickety throne to take a swig from Mother's amphora and envelop me in a loose hug. "Your mother's going to miss you," she whispered. "She's scared for you."

That made two of us.

I looked to the ceiling to ease the needles in my eyes—the water stain had gotten worse, and the cloud of black mold seemed to be spreading down the wall. "She's only scared she's going to have to cut back on her wine."

"I heard that." Mother stomped her foot. "This is absurd. I forbid you to go."

Part of me wanted to obey like a little girl, unpack my things, and return to the Kynêgion in September. I could live my life in this dingy room, selling myself every night, but I couldn't do that to my daughter. I squeezed my eyes shut, barely managing to speak. "Please don't make this harder than it already is."

Tasia gurgled a string of babble and held out her arms for me. I dropped my bag, struggling to swallow my sobs. I loved her baby smell, her tiny hands with their pudgy fingers, and her beautiful brown eyes. And I was leaving it all behind.

"You'll be back so soon Tasia won't even notice you were gone." Antonina's hand was warm on my back. "You do what you have to. For her."

I swallowed hard and looked at Tasia, her cheeks still rosy from sleep. It tore my heart to think of leaving her, but it was only for her that I could even contemplate going with Hecebolus.

I wrapped my arms around my family for a damp hug, breathing in the scent of my daughter to carry with me. "I love you all so much."

Antonina's hand on my shoulder pulled me away from Tasia. "The ship will sail without you."

I dashed the tears from my eyes. "Take care of her."

"We will," Antonina said. "I promise."

My mother sighed and kissed my cheeks, her lips cool. "We do what we have to, I suppose."

Antonina hefted my bag onto her shoulder. "I'll walk you down."

My arms were empty, and my chest felt hollow. My life now amounted to three stolas—including the burnt orange I hadn't returned to Hecebolus—a string of cheap turquoise beads that only looked real onstage, and two bronze hair combs. I'd given my mother everything else, including the few coins I'd saved and Anastasia's old doll, for Tasia.

"Good luck," Antonina said, handing me the linen bag. A woman emptied her night soil bucket from the window of the gray building across the street, earning her a spew of curses from the wizened men below playing dice on a board scratched in the dirt. "Don't forget us when you come back a *kyria* dripping in pearls and gold."

I hugged her, but she laughed me off. "Gods, it's not as if you'll be gone long. Enjoy yourself." She waggled her eyebrows at me. "And enjoy that magnificent body of his."

I wiped my eyes. "You would say that."

She shrugged. "Life is short. God knows you've never really lived."

I detoured outside the city gates to visit Father's and Anastasia's graves one last time, both unmarked and long since covered with tall grass. I passed a dusty family on the way back, the man pushing a cart laden with pots, several crates, and a birdcage with a half-dead blue and black starling. The woman carried a baby on her hip and led a little boy with his thumb in his mouth.

"Excuse me," the man said, his accent so thick I could scarcely understand his Greek. "Where can I find a place to stay?"

I gestured to the city walls, the domed churches and great towers looming overhead. *"Is tin boli."*

In the city.

Everything was in the city; yet I would leave it all behind when I went with Hecebolus.

The long walk from the graveyard gave me time to compose myself, but my feet felt as if they were bleeding in my new slippers—the only decent ones I owned—by the time I smelled the docks, the heavy treacle of fish and brine. I wished for thunder and lightning to match my mood, but the sun danced on the waters of the Bosphorus, a sparkling mosaic of beveled turquoise glass, and only soaring pelicans marred the sky. A newly varnished ship gleamed in the sun, its crew already at the oars. I hurried as fast as my cursed shoes would let me, but the oars moved like giant dragonfly wings and its curved prow cut into the waters. I dropped my bag and broke into a run. "No! Wait!"

But the ship didn't stop. The sun caught the letters painted in gold on its side. *Greyhound.* The Emperor's private yacht.

I was an idiot.

Behind it groaned a boat bleached almost white by the sun, gulls pecking at the cracked and weathered masthead. Faded letters on its hull spelled its name in Greek—*Naiad.*

Hecebolus' ship.

"Jesus, Joseph, and Mary." The thing looked like a leaky bathing tub. "That boat will sink before we make it past the Golden Horn."

Hundreds of terra-cotta amphorae were being hoisted on board, a dozen or so the height of a man pulled by rope on deck while slaves carried smaller ones on their backs. Several paused to gawk at my approach, and one missed his cue as the next slave in line tossed one of the pots onto his back. It teetered for a moment, then tumbled to the ground and shattered. Thick red sauce speckled with green oozed onto the planks of the dock like blood.

But it wasn't blood. It was *garos.*

"By the dog!" I jumped and stepped back. It wasn't the mess of fish sauce I cursed, but the slave who'd dropped the amphora, the same one now being thrashed about the ears for his incompetence. I recognized the wart on his chin with its thick black hair I could see even from where I stood. The last thing I needed was one of my first customers on the ship with my new patron. I promised God my eternal obedience if Wart stayed behind once the ship set sail.

"Going to Pentapolis with us, miss?" A slave with more than a few teeth missing stepped out of my way as I walked up the tiny gangplank like one of the Hippodrome's tightrope walkers.

I took a moment to answer—I could still change my mind, run

back to the room across from the Gate of Charisios, return to Leda and the Swan. And resign my daughter to a life of the same.

I gave the slave my sunniest smile. "I am."

A red tunica passed behind the slave. And sniffed. "The governor has been expecting you."

"I don't believe we've been properly introduced."

He looked at me as if I were a snake. "Your cabin is below deck. Last on the right." Then he walked away.

I thumbed my fist at his retreating back and winked at the gap-toothed slave. He winked back. "Libanius is a nasty snob, almost as bad as the governor," he said. "I'll show you to your cabin."

The smell of fish grew perversely stronger below deck, but I couldn't tell if that was the slave's natural odor or the actual stink of the ship. The entire boat needed to be doused with vinegar.

My cabin was little more than a closet, empty save for a rope hammock and a metal bucket. Two silk pouches dangled from the hammock, one blue and one red. The first was full of dried herbs, ones that smelled familiar, but I couldn't quite place them. Perhaps a posy to ward off seasickness. Or poison if Hecebolus tired of me.

The second pouch held two lumps the size of small grapes. Two perfectly matched pink pearls on gold hooks fell into my hands.

I'd traded my daughter for eardrops.

I stuffed them back in the silk and followed my nose out of my cabin to a rickety wooden ladder leading farther into the bowels of the ship. I kicked off my slippers and climbed down. Water slapping walls echoed up at me, not the rush of the ocean outside, but the splash inside the hull as we swayed with the sea. My toes touched water on the next rung. We were sinking.

I scrambled back up, hearing my hem rip as I stepped on my stola. Libanius stood outside Hecebolus' closed door—at least I managed to surprise him coming up from the hull.

"There's water below!"

"Of course there's water below." He said it as if commenting on the presence of clouds in the sky. "The *Naiad* is a fish transport."

"What?"

The man actually rolled his eyes at me. "The governor is carrying live fish from the Black Sea to Antioch."

"Antioch doesn't have its own fish?"

"Parrotfish are a delicacy found only in the Black Sea, and the Patriarch of Antioch likes them fresh. The *Naiad* is equipped with a special pump to filter fresh seawater into the hull to keep them alive on the journey."

Wonders never cease. I eyed the door behind Libanius. "Is Hecebolus in?"

"The governor is above deck."

"Until?"

No answer—this slave was insufferable.

I kissed him on the cheek, relishing his look of horror at my honeyed smile. "Thank you for all your help, Libanius. I'm truly sorry I get to have Hecebolus and you don't."

A feral glare followed the flash of shock in his eyes. I'd hit the mark.

There was a terrible grating noise, and the beast of a ship shuddered. I took the stairs two at a time into the blue sky to find the dock had been emptied of the last amphorae and the gangplank hoisted off. It was time.

I clenched my teeth as the slaves threw off the ship's riggings and we slipped fully into the turquoise embrace of the Golden Horn, beards of algae drifting past. There was no going back now.

The massive wooden roof of the Hagia Sophia watched us depart, and the city walls melted into the buildings clustered like cowering giants on the seven hills. I entertained ideas of jumping overboard and swimming back to shore just as three shiny gray fins surfaced in our wake. Dolphins, racing our boat, with only me to watch.

Tasia would have loved them; she would have laughed and gurgled as they surged ahead and dove deep into the water.

I turned my back on the city to face the wild expanse of blue. Even when my entire family had been green and retching on our move from Cyprus, I had loved the feel of the waves and the endless stretch of the sea. I needed it to soothe me now.

I stayed above deck with the benches of rowers at my back, feeling the sea spray on my face and licking the taste of salt from my lips until the air turned chill and sent me shivering below. I was bored by counting the irregularities in the wooden panels of my cabin walls and wary of the dark stain I'd discovered in the corner. It felt like hours before I finally heard Hecebolus' voice next door. If I was going to do this, I was going to do it right.

A surprise up the sleeve of my *paludamentum*, I knocked on his door and was greeted with a loud grunt. Hecebolus sat next to a washbasin, his chin cocked to allow Libanius to shave the stubble from his neck. Unlike my cabin, his actually had a pallet on the floor. My heart skittered for a moment—Hecebolus might have been a sarcastic lout, but I couldn't wait to have him between my legs again. I held out my hand for the blade.

"Come to slit my throat?" The vein in his neck pulsed as he motioned a scowling Libanius away. The door slammed behind him.

"Not this time. I prefer the element of surprise." I dipped the metal into the basin and massaged a little olive oil into the coarse hairs on his neck. "This is quite a ship."

He arched an eyebrow at me.

"I've seen the fish."

"I make money while I sail." He turned his chin so I could finish scraping his neck. "The fish below are as precious as purple dye."

I bent over the basin, and my *paludamentum* slipped from my shoulder to expose the pale swell of my breast. His finger traced my collarbone down to my nipple, then flicked open the clasp of my pin. The cloak puddled at my feet and I stood naked before him.

"Surprise," I said.

His brow arched and a slow smile spread across his lips to crinkle his scar. "I think I'm going to enjoy this voyage."

I woke the next morning to the glow of an oil lamp. And Libanius' big nose.

I grimaced. "Didn't your mother ever teach you it's rude to wake someone?" I'd retired to my cabin after Hecebolus had me, but my room had no windows—the moon or the sun might have been up for all I knew.

Libanius ignored me. "I took the liberty of brewing this for you." He thrust a clay cup at my face.

I sat up and slipped my arms into my *paludamentum* as he averted his eyes, but not before I saw the revulsion there. The cup's curling steam smelled like a spice market, the same as the herbs in the blue pouch left for me. I knew better than to believe this man had discovered a sudden affinity for me. "What is this?"

"The governor cannot afford any bastard brats birthed by a nefarious prostitute."

"Nefarious?" Normally I'd enjoy the new accolade, but I could scarcely think through my fury. I shoved the cup back at him. "No slave is going to tell me what to do."

His lips curved into a frown. "My apologies—"

"Are not enough." My only real security with Hecebolus would come once he married me. And he'd almost certainly marry me if I gave birth to his son, ensuring his financial support even if he tired of me. Libanius knew that. I was sick of this half man.

Hecebolus was stretched on a bench above deck in the morning sunshine, reading a codex. He scarcely looked up as I stormed past the rowers. The wart-chinned slave sat at the end of one of the benches, watching me from hooded eyes. *Christ's blood*. I'd worry about him later.

Hecebolus peered over his reading as I skidded to a halt before him, chest heaving. "Your slave is a fool."

"I've heard Libanius called many things"—Hecebolus closed the codex and looked at me, crossing his muscled legs under his tunica—"but never a fool. What brings this about?"

"I brought her the tonic you requested, sir." I hadn't noticed the slave follow me, but now he stood behind me, hands clasped around the foul cup with the serene expression of an ascetic.

"What?" I whirled on Hecebolus. "You asked him—"

I felt the eyes of all the rowers on our little scene, a scene I had caused. Hecebolus clasped my hand. "Theodora, I plan to be promoted and return to Constantinople." His voice dropped. "A child could scarcely help my cause with the Emperor. Or the Senate."

He meant a child by me. And he was right.

"You're young." He patted my hand. "There's plenty of time for children."

Hope. I knew it was foolish, but I clung to it.

I took the cup from Libanius and tipped the contents down my throat, then leaned down, my dark hair hanging over my breasts as Hecebolus' eyes slipped under my cloak. "And this means we have plenty of time to enjoy ourselves."

He stood and picked me up like that first night at Justin's banquet. "Make sure we're not disturbed," he said to Libanius.

I smiled at the eunuch, but he didn't return the gesture.

I closed the door to my cabin behind me and almost yelped in surprise to see the slave with the wart on his chin leaning against the wall of the narrow hallway.

He chewed a sliver of wood, then spat at my feet. "You've risen high."

"Pardon me?"

"Sleeping with the governor." His voice was too loud. "That sure beats mounting slaves in the alleys behind the Kynêgion."

I grabbed his tunica and yanked him into my cabin, shutting the door. "What do you want?"

He sat on my hammock, looking far too comfortable for my liking. "I wonder if the governor might be interested to know the quality of the woman he's financing. Not a *scenica* like he thinks, but only a common *pornai*."

Hecebolus had brought me along only because he believed I was a high-class *scenica*, the perfect adornment for any patrician. He might sing another tune if he knew of my early career. I couldn't take that chance.

"What's your price?"

Wart rubbed his chin, the black hair waggling at me. "I doubt anyone would notice if those bronze combs of yours went missing."

I yanked them from my hair and threw them at him. "Now get out."

They disappeared into his pockets, but he made no attempt to leave. I opened the door. "I said get out."

He stepped closer and pushed the door shut. I was a caged animal, a helpless one at that. "It's a long journey to Pentapolis. And no women on the *Naiad*. Except you."

"I'm not sleeping with you."

"I'd rather not end up feeding the fishes. You know as well as I there are other ways to buy my silence."

"No."

He shrugged. "You'd gamble that the governor won't care about all the slaves you had, the filthy ways you serviced them before you became the city's little darling?"

Such were the rumors Antonina had spread. I'd be lucky if Hecebolus dropped me in the first port we came to. More likely it would be me feeding the fishes.

Control over my new life was slipping through my fingers like sand. This warty rat could destroy everything I'd worked for with a single word to Hecebolus. I hated him for possessing that power over me, but I couldn't let that happen, no matter what I had to sacrifice. I stepped closer and yanked up his tunica, hands fumbling with the rope beneath. My cheeks burned with shame.

"Hecebolus can never know of this," I said.

"You keep me happy and we'll see what happens."

He moaned as he sprang into my hand, hard and ready. "No noise." I muffled his mouth with my free hand before sinking to my knees, my eyes crushed shut. The taste of his sweat and filth mingled with the bitter tang of desperation. I felt dirtier than I ever had before, grimy and used, like one of the foul old whores at Constantinople's docks. I'd always been able to choose my men, but now I'd lost even that.

Yet another price to pay. I was beginning to think perhaps the cost was too high.

I dined with Hecebolus every night, drinking more and more wine after each secret meeting with Wart. The filthy slave seemed to know exactly when Hecebolus was otherwise occupied, and he would rap four times on my door to signal that he wanted me. I tried ignoring him once, but he only banged louder. I was cornered, and we both knew it.

I found myself waiting to hear Hecebolus' voice on the other side of the wall, not just for relief from Wart, but because it was getting more and more difficult to get the damn Tyrian out of my mind. His accent alone made me want to tear his tunica off, not to mention the heft of his massive shoulders. I felt safe in his arms, a new feeling I could grow accustomed to. I knew I was losing my head over him but couldn't think why it should matter.

One night Hecebolus brought an ebony chest full of codices to dinner. I smothered a smile as he winced and straightened—I happened to know that his back bore fresh scratches from my fingernails.

I picked up a copy of Ovid's *Amores* and flipped through it, reading the first verse my eyes fell on. "'Every lover is a soldier.'"

Hecebolus poured two cups of wine and added the spices himself, not bothering to dilute them with water. "Don't tell me you read, too."

"You prefer your women dumb and stupid?"

"It does make things easier." He ignored the not-so-gentle poke with my toe. "Most actresses I've met could scarcely write their name."

I thought back to Hilarion's stack of contracts marked with the sign of the cross. "I'm not your average actress."

He gave me a strange look. "No. You're not."

I took a long draft of wine. The waves outside were placid; yet the ship listed from the cups I'd already drunk. I couldn't seem to get the taste of Wart from my mouth—another drink couldn't hurt. "And do you believe that?" I asked.

"Believe what?"

"Every lover is a soldier?"

He narrowed his eyes at me and returned to his copy of *The Republic*. "I don't know."

"No pompous advice? That's a first."

"Perhaps I don't care for the subject."

"Well, I don't believe it. Love isn't a battlefield." I set aside Ovid and added the copy of *The Republic* on top, settling myself between Hecebolus' legs to toy with the rope at his waist. I smiled. "It's not so difficult loving you."

I wanted to grab the words and yank them back into my stupid, wine-sotted mouth as soon as I saw his grimace. I was here to secure a marriage belt by playing Aphrodite, not dull, simpering Hestia.

A shut mouth gathers no foot. Mother would wring my neck if she could see me now.

Hecebolus gently removed my hands and stood up. "It's been a long day. Perhaps we should both retire for the night."

There was nothing more I could do without further humiliating myself. I managed a dignified walk out of his cabin, waiting until Hecebolus had shut the door behind me before knocking my forehead against the wall.

Perhaps love really was a battlefield.

Chapter 12

Finally, on our twenty-second day at sea, one of the slaves made the cry for land. The scent of rich earth mixed with the ever-present smell of salt. I raced to the prow and there, far off on the horizon, was the brown smudge of Africa.

Our new home.

This frontier was at the ends of the earth, scarcely part of the Empire's thousand cities. It was here that my fortune would be made and, in less than a year, Hecebolus and I would depart these shores as man and wife. He hadn't mentioned my comments about love that night in his cabin, and I pretended I had never spoken them. I hadn't touched a drop of wine since then.

Our little kingdom was a dusty sprawl that cascaded from low hills, interspersed with rare patches of green cypress trees.

Apollonia.

Farther into the heathen continent spread the other four cities that made up Pentapolis: Teuchira, Ptolemais, Cyrene, and Barka. This was my new world, and I planned to rule it, and Hecebolus, well.

The magister cleared Hecebolus' ship, and we disembarked among curious stares and bows once the plebs realized they were in the presence of their new governor. The wart-faced sailor stared at the ground as I walked past him for what I hoped was the last time. Libanius ran ahead to fetch the governor's sedan—I'd caught the slave studying the schematics of the town and the new villa he would oversee. The governor's mansion squatted atop the town like a pale rooster over its flock.

The sedan was carved of ebony, but I scarcely noted the tasseled cushions or shiny gilding as we swayed down Apollonia's main street, too busy watching the scene out the windows. We wove in silence through a meager market filled with veiled women and barefoot children, some with red sores on their filthy legs. I loved the attention as much as I had on the stage—the stares and whispers.

Let them talk.

I wrinkled my nose as we jostled our way through the gates of the largest villa in town, the Palace of the Dux, sitting atop the highest hill. It lacked the terraced grace of Constantinople's Sacred Palace and was only a fraction of the size, but its stones were the color of a lion's mane, with columns on the portico like the great temples of old. A garden spilled over high walls, an oasis of green spiked with the scent of jasmine and honeysuckle.

Slaves poured from the entrance, at least forty identically dressed in reed sandals and pristine white tunicas edged with blue trim.

"I am Hecebolus, your new master and governor of Pentapolis." My future husband stepped down from his litter and surveyed his gift from the Emperor, obviously pleased with all his bribe had purchased. "I expect perfect obedience and order from each of you. Nothing less will be tolerated.

"I require a bath and tray of food in my chambers." Hecebolus gave orders for the remainder of his household and started toward the front door. I cleared my throat. Loudly.

Hecebolus glanced back at me—I swore he smiled. "This is one of the new maids, Theodora," Hecebolus said. "Install her in one of the garden rooms."

Filthy louse on a goat.

I wanted to lunge at him, grab him by the ear, and make him take it back, but then he strode off.

The swell of the sea still swayed beneath my feet as I stood in the front drive of a governor's villa in the midst of slaves who likely couldn't wait to tell this tale to everyone in the five cities who would listen.

I smoothed my crumpled curls from my face and gave what I hoped was a becoming smile. "To the garden room then?"

Libanius sniffed at me as if I were yesterday's garbage, then stepped forward and gestured toward a separate wing of the house. "This way."

He deposited me in a tiny box of a room, empty save for a pallet on the floor and the smell of old straw.

I wasn't going to stay cooped up in here, or worse, wait for someone to summon the governor's new maid to do a list of chores. I hadn't come all this way to empty buckets of night soil or scrub floors.

The governor's villa likely had its own baths, but I needed to stretch my legs and clear my mind. Even this ramshackle frontier town had to have a decent bathhouse. I retraced my steps to the entrance and passed the harbor, empty except for the *Naiad* floating lazily at the docks. Near the gutting tables, a massive stone slab like a sacrificial table was ringed with Latin. *All fish longer than the markings on this marble shall be given to the magistrates and governor, up to and including the fins.*

At least we could look forward to eating well. Or getting heartily sick of fish.

Apollonia might not compare to Constantinople, but it did possess a certain rugged beauty. The azure sea mingled with the blue sky and puffs of clouds. I wondered if the town had a theater as well—I wouldn't mind watching a show or two. Had Hecebolus presented me as a proper *kyria*, that would be out of the question, but since the imbecile had only introduced me as a maid, I was still free to enjoy myself. And I intended to.

I almost missed the baths, and I had to backtrack to a white-domed building with a sprawling view of the inner harbor. On the ground before the door was a diminutive mosaic with two sandals, three strigils, and the words *Salvom Lavisse. A bath is healthy for you.*

Mismatched Corinthian columns filled the courtyard, but the house itself was tiny and was laid out like a private residence with its peristyle garden court. The gap-toothed slave on the *Naiad* had warned me that a great wave had destroyed much of the town ages ago. From what I could tell, it hadn't been rebuilt, just rearranged.

A man stumbled down the steps and passed me with a lurid look. Then his hand squeezed my backside. I gave a startled shriek and kicked him in the shin as hard as I could.

"Don't mind Apasios," the slave at the entrance said. "He doesn't know how to go home from the baths sober."

But my cheeks flushed anyway. I was finished with that sort of behavior from men. Yet they didn't seem finished with me. I wondered if there was something wrong with me, something that drew them to me and told them I was easy prey.

I paid the slave with a coin I'd filched from Hecebolus a few weeks back and forced myself not to run through the courtyard. Few people lounged about the bathhouse—most were probably sleeping away the heat of the afternoon on their roofs or in the shade of their gardens. A handful of pretty young men twisted and lunged their sweaty bodies across the grass of the little exercise yard. I felt their eyes on me until I ducked into the dark warmth of the *tepidarium*.

The bath was decadent torture.

"You'll have to come back every day this week to be properly scrubbed." A brawny slave slapped rose-scented oil onto my heels. The flesh between her brows was so creased it joined the penciled lines above her eyes, a rather fearful sight as she glared at my feet. She had finished with my brows; they felt as if someone had jabbed bone needles into them. The entertainment finished with a scraping from a strigil that looked as though it could have shaved Medusa.

Finally clean and with my nails varnished as an extra treat, I picked up the hem of my stola and skirted the fresh carcass of a dead dog, its brown eyes glazed over and already covered with opportunistic flies. My stola had seen better days—I'd have to burn it to get rid of the *Naiad*'s fish stench.

The smell of fresh straw greeted me in my room—the pallet had been exchanged, and a new silk stola the rich shade of pomegranates hung from a peg by the window. It felt like a cool river as I slipped it over my head.

"Where have you been?"

I startled to feel Hecebolus' lips trail down my neck, but I smiled and turned in his arms. He was freshly bathed, his cheeks shaved smooth. My heart tripped a little at the musky scent of his pomade. I kissed the scar on his lip and caressed the back of his neck, feeling the damp still clinging to his hair.

"At the baths."

"I didn't see you there. I'd have liked to ravage you in the steam."

"I went to the baths in town." I nibbled his lips, but he pulled away, his expression as thunderous as Zeus of old.

"Unescorted?"

"Why would I need an escort?" I stepped back, arms akimbo. "Maids don't require escorts to baths."

"Because it's expected they'll spread their legs for any man who wants them. Only whores go about the streets unescorted."

I gestured to my waist. "There's no marriage belt here, so I suppose I'm still a whore."

He stared at me, then threw his head back and laughed. "You poor, misguided little fool. Did you honestly think I'd marry you?

Women like you are good for a lay, but that's all you'll ever be. No patrician in his right mind would marry trash."

Fury and terror slurred my thoughts. "You knew what I was before you agreed to bring me here!" All of Apollonia could probably hear me, but I didn't care.

Hecebolus looked at me as if I were a cockroach. Or worse. "I thought you were a *scenica*. The skinny slave with the wart on the *Naiad* disabused me of that notion. Turns out you're nothing but a common *pornai*."

Wart. The double-crossing piece of offal deserved a soft cock the next time he paid for a woman.

My plans were in shambles, but there had to be a way to get myself out of this. Frantic, I prayed Wart hadn't told him about what I'd done to keep his mouth shut.

You were blessed with both brains and beauty.

I flipped my hair behind my shoulder, making sure Hecebolus could see a fair way down my stola. "Don't tell me you're jealous."

He clenched and unclenched his fists, leaning so close I could smell the spiced wine on his breath. "You honestly think I'm jealous of all the men at the parties your pimp took you to? The men you lay with and their filthy slaves, thirty in one night?"

I laughed, shocked. "I'd be a rich woman if I could take thirty in one night."

There was a flash of white as his fist crashed into my cheek, an explosion of pain and spots of green and red dancing in my vision. I staggered back, scraping my elbow on the wall as I tripped to the floor. Hecebolus leaned over me, his face a blur. "If I'd known what you really were, I'd have left you in Constantinople to rot.

"You have two choices, Theodora," he growled. "You stay here and do exactly as I say, when I say it."

I didn't much like the sound of that. "Or?"

"Or you go back to the streets."

I'd come too far and given up too much to turn back now. I'd go mad in this prison, but I had nowhere else to go, no way to get back to Tasia if I left.

There was only one power I held over Hecebolus. I caressed his crotch and felt his reaction in my hand.

"I'll stay," I whispered in his ear. "But only because you're a good lay, too."

A villa with one hundred rooms shouldn't feel like a prison. Yet it did.

I woke the next morning to another new stola, this one a pale orange that melted into pink, reminding me of the skin of a peach. It was a nice change, considering how well the violent purple bruise on my eye matched the pomegranate stola. I touched my brow and winced. I felt a moment's remorse, worried that this really was my fault for allowing Hecebolus to believe I was a *scenica*. I should be thankful Wart hadn't spilled word of all our secret meetings to Hecebolus, or I'd be lucky to sport only a black eye. But I wasn't thankful. I was livid.

The slaves avoided me, not that I could blame them. Utterly alone, I made quick work exploring the gardens, the tiny library, even the aviary with its clipped doves. The little town I had scoffed at suddenly held adventures and excitement I could only dream of. Apollonia housed three basilicas, but I had to make my prayers in the villa's tiny chapel to an ancient priest who reeked of cedar, no doubt to keep away the moths that had already helped themselves to the fabric of his black tunica. I began to imagine cedar as the smell of death, which was fitting since I would probably only leave my prison when the same priest came to say my funeral rites.

And yet I slept on silk sheets carried from Serinda to the Empire on the Silk Road, dined on roast eel and more beef than the Emperor, and bathed in rose petal oil every afternoon. At night Hecebolus would have me with only the emeralds at my neck or the pearls threaded through my hair, leaving bruises on my pale skin. This was my price as a whore.

The sun warmed the saffron curtains in my room as I wrote a letter for Tasia one morning. I had a stash of five *solidi* to include, although I still wasn't sure how I'd manage to send the letter, because I didn't want Hecebolus to realize why his purse was always short. I hadn't had any letters from Mother or Antonina, but I told myself it was too early to worry.

My empty breakfast tray sat at my elbow, one bite of bayberry pork sausage and a handful of olive pits left over. I popped the sausage into my mouth, but my stylus jumped across the page as Hecebolus barged in, dressed in a navy tunica that swept the top of his feet. I slipped the letter into the stack of blank parchment.

Wordlessly, Hecebolus relieved me of my robe and pushed me onto my pallet. I endured until he gave his final thrust. What had once left me breathless and trembling had now become yet another performance. I was growing weary of the same feeling I'd always had with Wart, the feeling of being dirty and used.

"I won't need you tonight," he said, kissing an old bruise on my collarbone, one faded enough to be mistaken for a shadow. "I have to meet with the mayor of Cyrene."

I didn't care if he had to meet with a demon. A night without him was a gift from God.

"I'll count the minutes until tomorrow night." I didn't breathe easy until the door closed and I was alone again.

A whole day of freedom.

I addressed Tasia's letter to the district of the fifth hill of Constantinople and added it to the secret stash under my pallet, then whiled away the last hours of the afternoon at the villa's tiny baths. Bored out of my skull after my evening meal of boiled eggs with pine nut sauce, I decided to invade Hecebolus' study. I'd devoured *The Clouds* and was eager for more of Aristophanes' work. Perhaps Hecebolus had a copy of *Lysistrata*, although I doubted he would enjoy a story about women with minds of their own. Too bad I couldn't win my own war by denying Hecebolus my bed.

The study was across from Hecebolus' bedchamber, a small room with ceilings so low I could almost touch them if I stretched my arms above me; but the woodwork shone, and one of the tall tables sported a bronze mask with staring, vacant eyes, colored linen streamers dangling limply from its pointed helmet topped with a griffin's crest. It was probably a soldier's mask from some sort of parade during the Golden Age. Next to it sat a limestone figure of Bes, but the ancient Egyptian god was so well-endowed as to be laughable. Several other oddities collected dust—a golden icon of the soldier saints Sergius and Bacchus, a carved ostrich egg with a filigreed elephant on its front, and a mummified monkey, among others. Hecebolus was quite the collector. He'd even managed to collect me.

A tinkle of laughter came from the other side of the door, followed by a man's voice. There was a slap and another giggle. Hecebolus was definitely not meeting with the mayor of Cyrene, not unless the mayor had an extremely feminine laugh and enjoyed being spanked.

I could have kept walking and retreated to my room with a codex tucked under my arm, but something pushed me forward. My eyes took a moment to adjust as I opened the door—the room was black as ink except for the feeble flicker of an oil lamp. Hecebolus straddled a woman with flame-colored hair, her huge breasts splayed almost to her armpits.

"Theodora?" Hecebolus growled, but made no attempt to move. "I thought I told you to entertain yourself tonight."

"I don't recall Cyrene's mayor being so well-endowed." I stepped closer. "Who's your friend?"

His teeth glinted in the dark. "Flacilla is the best actress in Apollonia."

The orange-haired wench waggled her fingers at me. "Care to join us?"

"Some other time." I turned and shut the door behind me, ignoring their laughter from the other side. My nails bit into my palms. Hecebolus thought I was some sort of mouse, scurrying back to my hole to cower when threatened. He was dead wrong.

A large terra-cotta oil lamp shaped like a lion burned on a table down the hall, the flame flickering from the beast's mouth. I almost tripped on the edge of the exquisite silk rug as I carried the lamp back to Hecebolus' room and kicked the door open again.

"What in Christ's name—" Hecebolus had to crane his neck from his new position behind Flacilla. "I thought I told you—"

The lion's flame arched as I hurled it onto the bed, waiting only long enough to see the fire and oil spill onto the silks. Flames engulfed the fortune of tasseled hangings and threatened to consume the entire bed. The smell of burning feathers from the mattress filled the air.

Flacilla screamed and floundered to escape the inferno. The last I saw, her hair had caught fire, but I didn't stay to watch the show. Now she really did have flame-colored hair. I laughed as I raced down the corridors, but the sound was strangled.

I only had time to stuff my pearl eardrops, a gold bracelet, and an amber necklace into the pocket of my stola before Hecebolus exploded into my room, his face smudged with soot and the smell of smoke and fury rolling off him like a storm. He knocked me to the floor with a single punch. I threw myself at him and managed to rake my nails down his face before he slammed me into the floor again.

I curled into myself, trying to save my ribs as his fists pummeled me. I had to get out of here with the treasures stuffed between my breasts. His foot crashed into my skull, scarcely missing my eye. After that I lost track of where the blows landed.

Finally the barrage stopped. The inside of my mouth tasted like a copper *nummi*, and something wet trailed down my chin. Blood smeared my fingertips. One eye felt sewn shut.

"Get her out of here."

Someone yanked me up and dragged me through the villa, past the smell of baking bread and the latrina. The front gates groaned open, and something slammed into me.

The ground.

I lay there for some time—it felt like hours or even days, but it was surely much less—before uncurling from my cocoon of battered flesh. I wondered if this was how a butterfly felt before embarking on a new life. But then butterflies live only a matter of days.

You were blessed with both brains and beauty. Those gifts are your weapons, but you're certainly not using them.

God knew I hadn't used my brains these past months.

"Stupid idiot." I wanted to cry, but tears were a luxury I could ill afford. I managed to pull myself up to sit, thankful I hadn't hit the pile of goat dung to my left. A shiny black beetle used its back legs to roll a perfect sphere of the stuff away from me.

An inspection of my pockets revealed I'd lost the amber necklace and gold bracelet in the fight. The five *solidi* were still tucked in the straw of my pallet, along with my letters to Tasia. Two pearls shone softly in my hand, all I had left in the world.

To my right lay the path I knew led to the theater, and in front of me stood the baths and the Central Basilica with its plain white columns. Beyond that were the docks. Apollonia's tangle of streets led everywhere, and nowhere.

And I had nowhere to go.

Chapter 13

This ship was worse than the last, and I wasn't given a cabin of my own, no matter how small. Instead, the captain showed me to the cargo hold where a pile of filthy hay remained from the horses he'd delivered to Apollonia. At least I wasn't alone—there were plenty of ticks and fleas to keep me company.

The ship carried African red slipware pottery and crates of ivory, bound for Alexandria and from there to Constantinople. The captain hadn't wanted to take me—not that I could blame him, with my face rearranged as it was—and had gouged me on the fare, taking both of my pearl earrings. I'd have paid any price to get back to my daughter.

The boat creaked as we shoved away from Apollonia. This time I rejoiced to see the shore slip into the horizon. A few weeks and I'd be home.

Alone with my thoughts, I enjoyed my first respite from men since my early days in the Kynêgion. My days were spent on deck until I became brown as a slave, despite the goat hide awnings I lounged under. My bruises faded and my ribs slowly healed. I'd never rely on another man again—better to spend my days pressing olives or spinning wool, anything to stand on my own two feet.

Several days into the journey we made our first stop at Alexandria, the famed city of Alexander the Great, Marc Antony, and Cleopatra. We came in at dusk, drawn by the famed lighthouse astride the island of Pharos, its gleaming mirrors and fires a beacon amidst the orange-stained sky. The monument stretched to pierce the sky, the tallest structure I ever hoped to see. I strained to see the statue of Poseidon at its pinnacle, but the pagan god was hidden in the low purple clouds.

We passed close enough to read the inscription carved along the lighthouse base: *Sostratus of Cnidus, son of Dexiphanes, to the Gods protecting those upon the sea.* Sostratus had been the architect of the Pharos lighthouse, obviously not a humble man.

To have the power to create something for the ages—I wondered why all kings didn't leave a similar mark on this world. I would if I had that power.

The city showed no signs of settling in for the evening. A number of tavernas lined the dock, spilling yellow lamplight and drunken patrons into the streets.

The captain gave orders from the prow as we bobbed to the dock, the smell of salt and fish welcoming us to the ancient city. "Have you got the rest of the fare, missy?"

The man must have breathed too much salt air. "I'm paid through to Constantinople."

He laughed, revealing several chipped teeth. "Those eardrops got you to Alexandria, but not a whit farther. All the way to the capital costs another five *solidi*."

That was the same amount likely still hidden in the straw of my pallet in Pentapolis.

"No, that can't be—"

"I'll have to report you to the locals as a stowaway if you can't pay."

"But we had an agreement!"

"You got proof? A written contract?"

He knew I didn't. I struggled as two rather brawny rowers each took an arm and hauled me off the boat. "Sorry," one muttered as they deposited me on the dock.

The other scratched his head, but wouldn't look at me. "I'd give you five *solidi* if I had it. Maybe you can scrounge some up before sunrise when we shove off."

I'd been swindled, and it was my own fault, too. I was as likely to find five *solidi* as it was for angels to descend and offer to make me queen of paradise. I headed away from the docks toward the lights of town. There was a theater up the main road, but if the empty streets were anything to judge by, the show was still in progress.

An ugly brown monkey perched on the shoulder of one of the door-keepers, a man about my age in a blue tunica. The monkey was cracking walnuts and throwing the shells to the ground.

"Can you tell me if there's a faction of Blues here?" I asked the man. "I need their help."

He looked me over, popping a nut between his teeth. "There is, but you won't be able to see them until morning."

"By the dog," I muttered. By morning the ship would be gone.

He leaned against the wall, eyes roving over my crumpled stola. "What's a girl like you doing out here so late?" He glanced down the dark street. The monkey leaned forward to get a better look at me. "You're not out looking for trouble, are you?"

"Trouble always seems to find me."

"What's your price?"

"Excuse me?"

He rolled his eyes. "A pretty thing like you, alone at this time of night? What's your price?"

I almost told him to bugger off, but something seized my tongue instead. "Five *solidi*."

He whistled. "I think you've mistaken me for the Emperor."

"Men in Constantinople paid twice that for a night in my bed." I tried to keep the panic from creeping into my voice.

"Then perhaps you should return to the capital."

"Please—one *solidi*." Surely I could find five men to pay that much.

He pulled a single coin from the folds of his tunica. "I've got a *tremissis*."

I started to shake my head but stopped. It was better than nothing.

He was quick, although his monkey watched us with beady little eyes the entire time. I was able to find two more men after him, but by the time the sun rose, I had only four tarnished *tremissi* in my purse.

The captain laughed at me as dawn lifted the sun. "A horse pays a higher fare than that, missy. Good luck in Alexandria."

I spent two weeks catering to any man who would have me. I'd applied to the theater out of desperation, told the Master of the Stage of my position in Constantinople and my support of the Blues, but there were no positions open. He wasn't interested in Leda either—apparently the Patriarch in Alexandria was stricter about what went on in the theaters, and the stage master didn't want to chance anything so obscene.

And this morning I'd surprised myself by spewing the contents of my stomach all over the cobbles of the alley where I'd slept. A quick calculation told me my moon bloods were late by several weeks. My curses frightened off a little boy rummaging through a trash heap.

Hecebolus had gotten me pregnant before I'd even left Apollonia, despite all the potions I'd been forced to gag down. Everything I'd prayed for, all at the wrong time.

I couldn't very well tread the boards pregnant, nor did I have even half the fare I needed to get home. I trudged through the alley, stepping over heaps of filthy linen, some shifting and moaning as I passed. One reached out an open hand, but I had nothing to give.

Outside of the shadows, a gleaming white church faced the sea. If anyone could help me, it was probably God, despite the choice words I had for him.

The basilica was silent, save the beating of the waves on the shore outside. The altar towered on the far end of the nave, an island in a sea of ancient mosaics. The church must have been a pagan temple at one time—the floor mosaics contained a drunken Bacchus among his grapes, a leopard impaled by crows, and a curvaceous water nymph spearing a brown flounder. I shivered at the altar and fell to my knees, eyes closed and hands clasped before me. Without thinking, I began to move my lips in silent prayer. As always, there was no answer.

And then I cried. I wept at my humiliation, my stupidity, and having to sell myself again. I sobbed away the loss of my daughter and the child I now carried, who would be far better off raised by wolves. I sobbed until I was empty.

I'd given up my daughter and come all this way. For nothing.

Something shuffled behind me. I turned to see a black-robed prelate, eyes shiny and black as beetles on a face old enough to be my father's father's. I moved to stand, but he waved me to stay. "I don't wish to disturb you, Sister."

Sister. This priest would throw me from his church if he knew the stains on my soul.

I wiped my cheeks as he motioned me to the kneeler of a well-worn pew, its dark surface shiny from all the sinners who had begged for forgiveness. I smelled lemon as I sat and took a moment to realize it came from him. "I'm sorry. I'll go."

"That's not necessary." He tucked his hands inside his wide sleeves. "God helps those who ask for help."

I gave a strangled laugh. "God would be wise to abandon me."

"Never. Surely things are not so bad as they seem."

I snorted, but the priest's eyes only crinkled with kindness. "God has seen every sin under the sun. There's nothing you can do to surprise him."

I don't know what possessed me—probably some narcissistic urge to prove my story truly horrific—but I poured out the whole sordid tale to the priest, even admitting to the babe in my womb. To his credit, the man never flinched, although I'd have wagered my last *nummi* the story made his ears bleed.

It took him a moment to compose his question once I'd finished. "What is your name, child?"

I wasn't sure I'd heard right, but he looked at me expectantly. I swallowed. "Theodora."

"And how old are you, Theodora?"

"Sixteen."

He almost seemed to wince. "Well, Theodora, I am Severus."

"*The* Severus? The Patriarch of Antioch deposed by Emperor Justin?" I recalled talk of him at Justin's coronation.

"Better to lose my city than my head."

He had a point. "And you're a Monophysite?" That heresy had gotten Vitus into trouble with Uncle Asterious. It seemed to me that believing in Christ and saying your prayers were good enough.

Severus glanced at the magnificent bronze cross on the altar and sighed. "I believe Christ was divine, not human. Such a radical idea did not sit well with the Emperor's plan to reconcile with the Church of Rome." He spoke slowly, as if weighing each word before it passed his lips. "May I ask you a question, Theodora?"

"I believe we're past the niceties."

"Do you believe Christ died for your sins?"

"Of course."

"And can you recite the Ten Commandments?"

I smiled prettily. "In my sleep. My mother made sure all her children knew them." I ticked them off my fingers, ending with "Thou shalt not covet."

The priest nodded his approval. "And which of these commandments is most important?"

"For the sake of my immortal soul, I certainly hope adultery is toward the bottom."

His eyes widened—I thought for sure I'd be banished and damned to the fires of Gehenna—but then he gave a wry chuckle. "Well, it is seventh on the list."

A pigeon fluttered overhead, taking up its roost above a glittering mosaic of the Virgin. I stood and smoothed my rumpled stola. "Thank you for your time, Father."

He didn't rise, only folded his hands in his lap. "Where will you go now, Theodora?"

I rubbed the bridge of my nose. "I don't know." I expected him to offer some platitude—*God will always provide*—or some other useless drivel.

"Do you plan to keep the child?"

I thought of my pregnancy with Tasia. I knew now I'd been lucky Antonina's potion had failed. But how was I supposed to care for another child while still making my way back home to my daughter? "I want to, Father," I said, wiping my eyes on the back of my stained sleeve. "But I don't know how I'm going to manage."

"I know of an extra room in a convent nearby." He eyed my stomach. "The women there would let you stay, at least until the baby comes."

It was a generous offer, but I doubted it came from the goodness of his heart. I wouldn't be taken advantage of again. "What's in it for you?"

He started at the venom in my tone. "There's room for an extra hand keeping up the church."

I searched for any trace of hidden malice, but his eyes were warm. I supposed if I discovered any deceit on his part, I could always leave later. "I'd be a regular Saint Mary the Egyptian." She, too, had been a prostitute but became an ascetic on the banks of the River Jordan, living off the wilderness until she died and was buried by a lion. I gave a wry smile. "But I have no calling to take on an order."

"I don't expect you to become an ascetic." He returned the smile. "Or be buried by a lion." He gestured me toward the sunshine but stopped short of the door. "One more thing, Theodora, to put my mind at ease. Do you believe in the single or dual nature of Christ?"

The way he asked it made me wonder if my new room and position might hinge on my answer. "I've been a bit busy these past few years, Father. I truly haven't given the topic much thought."

"Well." He smiled so wide the wrinkles around his lips turned to deep crevasses. "Now you'll have plenty of time to do just that."

I stayed on with Severus as he proposed, donning an itchy black wool tunica and twisting my hair into a dark knot under an equally scratchy scarf. My hands bled with work and my knees callused over, but Severus' church was the cleanest in Egypt.

Once a week, usually on Saturday evenings, Severus lectured in convents and monasteries, and the occasional lavish villa of Alexandria's elite. His renown as the world's premier Monophysite theologian had only increased following his banishment from Antioch. Whereas once I might have followed him in the hopes of meeting some wealthy patron, now I tagged along only to fill my mind.

Severus was a patient teacher, allowing me to ask questions after each lecture and praising my quick thinking. We talked of everything— the lives of saints, the Holy Trinity, and Jesus' sacrifice on the cross. Sometimes our conversations strayed to the Empire's history, the stories of the old gods, and times of conquest. It seemed there wasn't anything Severus didn't know. I still wasn't sure if I believed as he did regarding God's true form, but I knew one thing: It was a miracle I'd found Severus when I did.

"You seem happier these days, Theodora," he said to me one rainy evening as we returned from a lecture, jumping from cobbles to curb to avoid the sluice of winter rainwater rushing down the street. "More content."

"I suppose I am." It was easy to be content with a warm bed and full belly, not to mention the lack of the constant pressure to please and keep a man.

"Good," Severus said. "God helps the helpless. He will happily lift your burdens, but only if you let him."

I'd have been happy to gift God with many of my burdens over the years if only he'd been there to take them. Yet it seemed I felt lighter with every day I stayed at the convent, more confident that I could do more than just survive in this life.

"I hope God has strong shoulders," I said.

"He does indeed." Severus chuckled, steering me under an awning to avoid the worst of the rain. "He does indeed."

Once, in my fifth month of pregnancy, I accompanied him for an afternoon visit to the anchorite hermits in the desert outside the city, praying with them while Severus granted the Sacrament. These ragged men and women lived off beetles and roots, sleeping in pagan tombs under blankets of sand, but their eyes blazed with the fervor of their worship. I wished I could be like them, but no matter how I searched, my heart never lit with the fire of God's divine love. I still felt abandoned by Christ, but along with a deeper understanding of what it meant to be a true Christian—and not just go through the motions as I had my whole life—I discovered a quiet affinity for Mary as my belly grew. I could understand the Virgin's sacrifice and motherhood more than a distant God who had ignored me most of my life. Instead of praying to Jesus as Severus suggested, I directed my prayers to Mary and felt a sort of peace fill me as I let out my tunica again and again. Yet the time after my lying-in stretched like a dark abyss when Severus might dispose of me, satisfied that he had done his duty to prevent me from destroying my child.

One late morning I felt a familiar pang as I'd swung my legs from under my hippo's belly after breaking my fast in the refectory.

"I wanted to join the sisters for prayers in a few minutes," I told the nun in the infirmary, a shriveled old woman ancient enough to have heard Jesus' sermon on the rock. The fine spring day was filled with birdsong and the buzz of the honeybees kept by the nuns. A good day for a birth, but I craved the quiet calm of settling into prayers with the sisters, the image of the Virgin smiling down on us. One never knew whether a birth would bring joy or sorrow—or death. "The pains are fast, but I'll be back as soon as I finish."

The nun gestured to a mattress, clean, but slumped in the middle after years of bearing the sick and dying. "I'm due for my afternoon nap. Let me check you now."

I supposed when I was her age I wouldn't let something as trivial as a child being born interrupt my nap either. I lay on my back and stared at the pile of woolen bandages I'd helped her cut a few days ago while she probed between my legs.

She chuckled and wiped her hands on a *mappa*. "The babe has a lovely head of thick dark hair."

"Excuse me?"

She pushed me down, her tongue pursed between gums toothless as a newborn. "A few minutes longer and you'd have dropped the poor mite on its head."

This time my child wasn't born in the filth of an alley among trampled fish heads and rotten vegetables, but in the warm cell of a Monophysite convent, caught by the scrubbed hands of a wimpled sister. I still screamed and begged God to let me die.

The old nun laid the squalling bundle of blood and wrinkled flesh on my deflated stomach. "Your son, Theodora. A perfect gift from God."

Ten tiny fingers with ten ragged fingernails and a head with a troubling conical shape, topped by a spike of black hair still tangled with vernix. He *was* a gift from God.

And he was all mine.

. . .

Severus came to see me the last day of my lying-in. I expected him to hover near the door and mumble his congratulations, but instead he plucked my son from his basket and tucked him to his chest.

"A sturdy lad," Severus said. "What have you decided to call him?" He gave a wide grin. "I don't suppose you considered Severus?"

I chuckled. "Too late, my friend. One of the sisters already suggested John."

"A sturdy name, too." Severus' eyes softened as John gave a wide yawn, showing off his pink gums. Severus patted my son on the back, but he didn't look at me. "And has his mother decided what she's to do now?"

I'd known this moment would come, but it still caught me off guard.

"I'll probably go to the Blues here in Alexandria, see if their network can help me get back to Constantinople." The Lord only knew what they would expect me to do for such a favor.

"I see." Severus tickled John's palm until my son's tiny fingers closed around Severus' thumb. "I thought you might stay here."

"With you?"

His eyes flicked to mine. "With the church."

I felt the reprimand. Before I'd given birth, I'd asked Severus why he'd never married.

"Why do you want to know?"

"I'm just curious," I had said. "I can't fathom why a man like you—talented, easy on the eyes, and too smart for his own good—doesn't have a plump wife and a house packed with children."

"Don't," he said.

"Don't what?"

"Don't do whatever it is you do with men," he said, opening his codex of the Gospels.

"I don't know what you mean."

He studied me, then sighed. "No, you probably don't. And that makes you even more dangerous." He caressed the codex when he closed it. "God has given you many gifts, Theodora, gifts that would make any man lucky to call you his wife. But"—he smiled—"I am too old for you. And I decided long ago never to marry. The church decreed a man of my rank must cast off his wife if he seeks to serve the Lord. I couldn't do that to any woman I loved."

"You are a noble man, Severus."

He smiled, sadly. "A man will give up much for love."

I thought of those words as I watched Severus with my son now. It seemed to me a woman would do much for love, too, most especially for her children. I thought of Mary, of her sacrifice as she watched Jesus on the cross. "I can't stay in Alexandria," I said. "I need to get back to Constantinople. To my daughter."

"Of course you do." Severus extracted his finger and ran his palm over John's spiky tuft of hair. "But I've seen great growth in you since you came, Theodora. You're no longer the frightened girl who showed up at my altar. And I have a feeling the young woman you've become would continue to flourish if you stayed at the convent a while longer. The invitation remains if you'd like to stay."

I reached out and squeezed his fingers—the first time I'd ever touched him. "Thank you. You're a good man, Severus of Pisidia."

His hand lingered under mine. "A selfish man, actually. I don't want to have to scrub the floors of the basilica myself." He made the sign of the cross over John and turned to go.

"Severus—"

"Yes?"

"I'd like to be baptized with John, this time with the Monophysite prayer. Could you arrange that?"

His eyes smiled. "It would be an honor."

The waters were cool and salty as Severus tipped me back into the baptismal pool. There was a moment of dark tranquility, silent as a womb before strong hands pulled me back into the air.

"Holy God,
Holy and mighty,
Holy and immortal,
Christ crucified for us."

A mosaic of Mary looked down on me as I chanted the Mono-physite prayer with Severus, then watched as he dipped John into the same waters. My red-faced son howled as if someone had dropped him. Just as Tasia had. She'd be two now.

Alexandria had given me a fresh start, purifying and healing me. Never again would I sell myself. I would find another way to survive— to live—for my children. And for myself.

Chapter 14

"Bird! Bird!" John squirmed to point at the gulls that screamed overhead, giggling as one swooped in front of our faces. I smoothed his hair, but it stubbornly stuck up in a sort of rhinoceros horn at the front of his head. Almost two years old now, he was big enough to walk, but I didn't want him getting trampled on the docks despite the ache in my shoulders from carrying him in his linen sling all morning.

"How long to Antioch?" Severus stood beside me in his black homespun, my woolen bag a lumpy brown puddle at his feet. This time I journeyed with a wooden rabbit Severus had carved for John when he was teething, a spare tunica for each of us, and a precious parchment copy of the Gospels that Severus had given me on my last name day. I was eighteen.

"A month, maybe more."

"Don't let the Blues harass you into doing anything you don't wish to," Severus said. He took something from his pocket and slipped it over my head.

I gasped at the heavy silver cross inlaid with amber, strung on a gold chain thin as a strand of hair. A mosquito was frozen in the center of the ancient stone.

"This must have cost a fortune." I moved to take it off, but Severus covered my fingers with his age-spotted hands.

"Turn it over."

Tiny words were etched into the back of the silver. *"Let love and faithfulness never leave you; bind them around your neck, write them on the tablet of your heart."*

"Proverbs 3:3." Severus pushed the black veil back from my shoulders, the movement of a proud father. "So you don't forget what's important."

I smiled through my tears even as he turned and stared at the ship he'd arranged to take me as far as Antioch. From there I would connect with the Blues to manage the rest of the way to Constantinople, although I still wasn't sure how I'd pay my way. My letters to Mother and Tasia had gone unanswered, as had two I'd sent to Antonina. I had been gone for a year before John was born, and then almost two more years in Alexandria. There had been no word from anyone since I'd left the Queen of Cities three years ago. I told myself they might have moved, but I feared what I might find upon my return.

Severus glanced at me, his lips in a hard line. "Write to me as soon as you're settled."

"Are you worried about me, Severus?" I tried to make my tone light, but he wasn't the only one who was worried. I was about to be alone as I'd never been before, with my son to care for.

"I'm not worried at all," Severus said. "Alexandria has made you strong. It's time for you to use that strength." It wasn't only the city that had tempered me. Severus had restored my faith in all that was good in the world. I owed him my life, maybe more.

"I'll write so often you'll soon hide from the post," I promised.

"Never." His eyes shone in the sun as he kissed his fingers and pressed them to John's forehead, so close I smelled the rosemary and lemon on his homespun. "May God keep you both."

The last of the freight had been loaded—we traveled not with fish this time, but with dusty crates of Egyptian grain—and the captain strummed his fingers on his beefy arm.

"Good-bye, John." Severus kissed the top of my son's head.

"Bye-bye." John waved, backward, still watching the gulls.

"Until we meet again, Severus." I kissed both his cheeks. "I love you."

His eyes widened at my words, and then he smiled. "As I do you, Theodora."

We stood on deck until Severus' form disappeared. Only then did the tears slip down my cheeks.

John snored softly in my arms as we jostled our way to Antioch's theater. I had felt like a leaf cast about in a storm since we'd left Alexandria, plagued by dreams of a great demon who would meet me in Constantinople, and I wondered every day at the possible folly of my decision. I desperately missed Severus and the security of my little cell in the convent.

I counted fifteen churches in Antioch and at least thirty tavernas, some gleaming with new façades and others a hodgepodge of ancient walls and fresh mortar. We passed the slave market with its river of naked bodies of every hue, plus two small theaters and a rowdy cockfight with the carcasses of several bloodied birds already strewn about the cobbles. Suddenly, the earth shuddered under my feet. People froze like ants in a summer shadow; then the ground stilled, and they continued their gossip and haggling as if nothing had happened. The crumpled skeletons of several buildings lay where the last quake had knocked them, their broken pillars like exposed ribs. A group of youths sat atop the rubble of an old church, tossing a skin of wine between them. Antioch was the hedonistic capital of the world, so often shaken by earthquakes that its citizens had learned to live for the moment and repent later. It wouldn't do for me to stay here long.

I expected to be shown to the manager upon entering the pillared building of the Blues' administration, but the slave ushered me into a room lined with codices and a few crumbling scrolls, the dusty scent the same as the cargo hold we'd just left. A woman sat with her back to me, her hair hidden under a blue scarf. The slave cleared his throat, and the scratching of her stylus stopped.

"An actress from Alexandria, *kyria*."

John chose that moment to lift his head, yawn, and grab one of the bronze hoops at my ear. It went straight into his mouth.

"Theodora?" The woman had turned around and set down her stylus. "Your customers would never recognize you in that costume."

I almost dropped my son.

I hadn't seen Macedonia since the night of the Medusa performance when I'd burst onstage for the first time. I wore my black wool tunica today, worthy of a postulant nun. Macedonia, however, shone like a peacock in mating season—a peacock with a taste for gold. Gold discs hung from her ears, knobs of the metal gleamed from her thumbs, and there were even gold ribbons threaded atop her veil.

"What are you doing here?" I said.

She chuckled. "I might ask you the same thing."

"We stopped on our way to Constantinople."

"I see you've been busy." She nodded at John. "Traveling with the boy's father?"

She was nothing if not straightforward. "No," I said. "Just the two of us."

"Children are a rather avoidable ailment, you know." Macedonia made a face at John that he found hilarious. "You've been gone from the capital for some time now."

"Almost three years. When did you leave?"

Macedonia gestured to a wooden stool as the slave reappeared with two glasses of watered wine and an amphora carved with frolicking satyrs. She smoothed the hair at her temples—still copper, but I thought I detected traces of henna there. "Almost a year ago. Whoring only lasts until our youth fades," she said. "I had to move on while I still had the chance."

It was hard to picture Macedonia, one of the most successful *scenicae* in Constantinople, scrambling for survival. She sipped her wine. "I made Justinian an offer he couldn't refuse."

"Justinian?" I recalled the man with the dark curls at Justin's coronation. I could easily picture Macedonia on his arm.

"He practically runs the Empire for his uncle," she said.

I shifted John to my other knee. "So, he became your patron?"

"In a manner of sorts. Justinian is an unusual man with unusual tastes." She looked up from the brim of her glass, took a long sip, and smiled. "I'm his spy."

I laughed. "No, really."

"It's the truth. I dance, too, to keep up pretenses. And then I report every filched coin, every rumor of misappropriated taxes to Justinian. Men like to talk after a romp between the sheets or a few too many drinks. I still prefer to listen." She gave me an odd look. "Speaking of—I heard about Hecebolus. It's unfortunate that things didn't work out between you two."

"The man is a prick."

She froze, her cup halfway to her lips. "Is?"

"He's probably thrown out several mistresses by now."

"You did fall off the ends of the Empire, didn't you?" Macedonia shook her head. "He married his mistress."

I almost spewed my wine all over John's head. He squirmed to be put down, oblivious to the news of his father.

"The one with the orange hair? Flacilla?"

Macedonia nodded. "At first I thought it might be you, but that's the one. He rewrote his will to leave her everything."

"His will?"

She stared, then laughed. "You really don't know, do you? Hecebolus is dead, Theodora. Rumor has it the mistress poisoned him after she got her red sandals."

By the dog. I could have had everything I'd wanted if only I'd used my brain. The flame-haired tramp had managed it, and all I'd managed to do was set their bed on fire. Although I had to admit that had almost been worth it.

"Well, I hope it was a long, painful death," I said. I hid my face from John, then stuck out my tongue, prompting a fit of giggles from him.

He pushed my palms to my face with his chubby hands. "Do it 'gain, Mama!"

I humored him, peeking out to look at Macedonia. "Did they have any children?"

"None that I'm aware of." Macedonia gestured toward John. "Is this one his?"

"Not that I could ever prove it."

"That's unfortunate. You might have challenged her for the estate."

I sent a silent prayer to the Virgin to calm my fury and stood, hefting John onto my hip. "It doesn't matter. I have to get back to Constantinople. To my daughter."

Macedonia shifted a few pieces of parchment on her desk and held one in front of her nose. Even her squint didn't mar her beauty. "There's a merchant headed to the capital this week for the Blues—I could probably arrange for you to accompany him."

"I'd owe you."

She smiled. "It seems to me you already do."

I thought back to her help persuading Hilarion to hire me—it seemed an eternity ago.

"What will you do when you get there?" she asked. "Go back to your Leda show?"

Easy money, especially with all the men who would flock to me afterward. It was beyond tempting, but I shook my head. "I need to learn a trade."

Macedonia poured herself another glass from the amphora. "You realize there are few trades open to women? You happen to be experienced in the most lucrative one of all."

"I have two children, Macedonia. It's time I started acting like a mother."

"So you're willing to be, say, a washerwoman?"

Reek of urine and become stooped and leathery before my time. God help me.

"If I have to."

"Either you're very brave or very stupid."

I grinned. "Perhaps both."

"Can you spin?"

"No, but I can learn."

"The Blues have a wool shop for stage costumes near the Kynêgion. They might have a place for you." She took up her stylus and a fresh sheet of parchment. "I'll write you a recommendation."

I wanted to kiss her. "You're a saint."

"Far from it."

John toddled over to a pile of costumes while she wrote. I set a gaudy gilded crown on his head, but he promptly replaced it with a woman's girdle set at a jaunty angle. Macedonia finally scattered sand over the ink, sifted the grains to the side, and shoved two sheets of paper to me.

"You can thank me anytime," Macedonia said. "I'm partial to gold."

The second missive was fraught with misspellings, but even once I'd deciphered her writing, it took a moment for her meaning to penetrate my brain.

"This is a letter recommending me to Justinian." I set the paper down and looked at her with wide eyes. "Have you lost your mind?"

Macedonia chuckled. "Probably. I'm sure he can use you in some sort of scheme."

It seemed she would know. I gestured to the letter. "But I haven't been to all these places. Egypt, yes. But Cyrenaica and the Holy Land?"

"A little exaggeration never hurt." She gave a slight smile. "Justinian may not be able to use you right away, but I guarantee he'll find something for you sooner or later. Prove you're not just another pretty face." She looked me over. "I'd be shocked if you last a week spinning."

I ignored that last comment. "When does the boat leave?"

"Boats are expensive. You'll be traveling in grand style."

"How's that?"

"The best donkey cart money can buy."

Chapter 15

For the record, there is no donkey cart worth traveling in that money can buy. I lost track of the days amidst the bump of the cart and the endless sea of brown and green, the fine grit that settled on our tongues and lashes. Only Cappadocia broke the monotony. Its valleys of rock chimneys hid churches and subterranean houses amidst rows of apricot trees and grapevines. I remembered John the Cappadocian, the man I'd rejected from Emperor Justin's dinner party. Camped beneath one of the largest phallic towers, I realized I'd not had a man in almost three years.

My bed was empty. I reminded myself that was how I wanted it to stay.

Constantinople, the Queen of Cities, shook the dust from her skirts to dance the day we arrived. The marble monuments still gleamed in the late-summer sun and garbage littered the streets, but the entire city surged toward the first hill. Men and women whirled on one another's arms, terra-cotta mugs of wine sloshing their golden liquid onto the cobbles of the *Mese*. A slave dressed in blue and gold stood on a balcony over a bakery and dropped warm loaves dotted with sesame seeds into greedy hands. A few buildings down, another slave threw a shimmering confetti of polished copper *nummi* to the street so that people scarcely had time to snatch the coins from the ground before more rained upon their heads.

I had no idea what had caused the revelry, but I didn't mind availing myself of the handouts. John sat wide-eyed in his sling on my hip as I tore some bread for him and slipped a few coins into my pocket.

"What's going on?" I shouted at a woman whose hair had come loose from her veil with all her bobbing to the cobbles.

She brushed the drab strands from her face and laughed, revealing a row of brown teeth to match the trace of mustache on her upper lip. "Justinian is celebrating his consulship."

"I thought Vitalian was consul."

The woman ducked and pushed more *nummi* into her bodice, her chest studded with the round imprint of scores of coins, like the nipples of a many-breasted Artemis. "Did you just crawl out from under a rock?" she asked. "The Emperor and Justinian had Vitalian executed."

That seemed to be a bad habit of theirs.

I turned to go, but the woman grabbed my arm, her eyes sparkling. "Don't miss the games at the Hippodrome—there will be lions and leopards from Axum, maybe even giraffes." She pinched John's chubby cheek. "Your little man will love it!"

I smiled my thanks, but it wasn't to the Hippodrome I went. Instead, I passed a dog baiting with several dead hounds and two more bloodied dogs in the ring to a building with a terrible list and a hideous red phoenix painted on its wall. It seemed strange that nothing had changed after my years away, a thought I found both comforting and disquieting.

Youths chased battered wagon wheels with sticks, and bent old crones lingered in doorways. I took the stairs to the top floor two at a time, John clinging to me with one little fist while clutching his now-soggy bread in the other. To the right of the doorway was a new addition, a tiny wooden *mezuzah*, the Jewish box containing verses from the Old Testament. It was probably another of Antonina's attempts to placate the world's many gods. Perhaps this time I might manage to persuade her of the truth of God. I knocked on the door.

No answer.

I pounded again. They had to be home, not lost in Justinian's ridiculous festivities. It had been so long and I'd come so far—

The door opened.

A man with a sharp nose peered at me, his tunica inside out and his feet bare. "Is Antonina here?" I asked. "Or Zenobia?"

He said something, not in Greek but some language I didn't recognize. I switched to Latin and asked again, but he only shrugged.

I stood on tiptoes and tried to look over his shoulder. "Antonina?"

The door opened wide with a moan. A woman with dark hair stood behind him, clutching a fringed green *paludamentum* to her otherwise-bare chest. Not Antonina. She said something in the same foreign language. I pushed the door open, ignoring the angry shout from the man. "Tasia? Mother?"

But the room no longer belonged to them. A bright yellow scarf covered the lone window, and the dishes and linens were in orderly stacks that neither Mother nor Antonina would have tolerated. Only the brown stain on the ceiling and the black cloud of mold on the wall proved this was the same room.

"Sorry." I held my hands up and backed away, jumping when the man slammed the door. Their muffled voices slipped through the cracks as I sat on the stair, unsure of what to do or where to go.

Dead. They must be dead.

"Theodora?" The door below me creaked open, and a familiar face poked out. It was Tasia's Jewish wet nurse, balancing a filthy baby on her hip. "I thought I recognized your voice."

"Esther!" I'd never been so happy to see a virtual stranger. "Where are Antonina and my mother?"

I held my breath, waiting for the bad news.

"Antonina married a while back." Esther bit her lip. "I think she moved somewhere near Marcian's Column."

I was so happy I could have kissed her. So I did, much to her surprise. "You're a saint!"

I fought my way back down the *Mese*, cursing Justinian and his worthless games all the way to Marcian's marble column with its bronze statue of the forgettable Emperor. My back ached—John was as heavy as a watermelon in his sling, a melon that squirmed and pulled my hair.

After I asked several shopkeepers, a hiccuping wine seller—of course it would be a wine seller who knew where they lived—pointed me down a deserted side street to a ground-floor apartment. Outside the door was a blue and white mosaic of two sandals in a sort of floor mat; it was quite a step up from the building I'd just left. I rapped the tongue of the bronze lion doorknocker.

A slave answered, one with broad shoulders and hair the color of sunshine.

"Is this the home of Antonina?"

"The *kyria* is out for the afternoon."

It must be terribly cold in Gehenna if Antonina owned slaves.

"I need to speak with her. Will she return after the games?"

"How much does she owe?" Coins jangled as the slave opened the purse at his hip.

"I'm not here to collect a debt. I just need to see her." I tried to peer past him. "Is Tasia here? Or Zenobia?"

The slave only cocked his head and closed the coin purse. "You may wait in the atrium if you'd like."

I wanted to see Antonina the moment she came down the street. She couldn't be much longer.

"I'll wait here."

And wait I did. I had to bundle John in his extra pair of clothes as the sun drooped below the buildings. Antonina's handsome slave brought us a tray of boiled vegetables and a crusty loaf of bread as John fussed, his hair sticking out in every direction, overdue for his nap and bored with the constant scenery of Antonina's alley. His eyes finally closed as children's shouts and squeals echoed down the street. A woman walked toward us surrounded by three children loping like gazelles and screeching like monkeys. As she came closer, I could make out another child flopped over her shoulder. The eldest—a boy of perhaps six with a gap where his front teeth should have been—wore Antonina's sharp nose and thin lips. The two girls holding hands and skipping might have been twins in their matching blue tunicas. Except—

The older girl wore a daisy tucked behind her ear, her mahogany hair a dark halo over a heart-shaped face and rosy cheeks. My heart stalled when she glanced at me. Her eyes were like a mirror.

"Tasia."

My daughter stopped skipping and looked to Antonina, the question clearly written in her eyes. She didn't know me.

Antonina's laugh bounced off the buildings. Her wooden cross had been replaced by one of hammered gold to match the thick bangles on her wrists. "By the gods! Look what the tide dragged in."

"Donkey cart, actually." I couldn't take my eyes off the little girl before me. Her mouth was smudged with something sticky—honey perhaps—and her hair had gone curly. But she was mine, more than my own heart or lungs.

"All of you demons get inside." Antonina swiped a stick from the boy's hand and waved it over their heads amidst their giggles. "Or I'll use this on your tails."

She laid a gentle hand on my daughter's shoulder as the others squealed and raced through the door. A slave girl rushed out to retrieve the baby from Antonina's arms. He started to fuss until the girl

177

pulled out a heavy breast. Men were all the same, no matter what their age.

"I heard you fell out with Hecebolus," Antonina said. "I figured you'd be back one of these days." She peered at John, his mouth open as he twitched in his sleep. "You sing like a bullfrog and dance like a drunk elephant, but you make pretty babies."

"At least I have one skill."

"Auntie Nina." Tasia laid a little hand on Antonina's dress. Relief washed over me—I might have died if she'd called Antonina her mother. "May I go inside, too?"

Antonina crouched next to her and looked at me, as if trying to decide something. I nodded. "Tasia, do you remember how I told you your mother had gone far away, but she'd be back for you one day?"

She nodded and peered at me. I knelt to look her in the eyes, forcing myself not to pull her into my arms. "I'm your mother, Tasia. And this is your brother. His name is John." I tilted him so she could see his face over the sling.

She smiled, revealing two perfect dimples. "He's little. I like his hair."

"He's very excited to meet his new big sister," I said.

I'd imagined this moment so many times; yet now I found I could scarcely speak. Antonina rescued me.

"Run inside and tell the slaves to pack you a trunk for tomorrow," she said. "We'll stay up all night—play games and tell stories, drink cherry juice and eat spoon sweets until our tummies hurt."

Tasia's little legs pumped to the door, but she stopped before ducking in. "Is it all right if I stop eating before my tummy hurts?"

"Of course, darling."

I dashed the tears from my eyes. "She's perfect. I don't know how I can ever thank you."

"She's a good girl," Antonina said. "Helps keep the others in line."

"That's quite the collection you have."

"Timothy wants a whole litter. I couldn't help but oblige him after he took in Photius and Tasia."

"Photius?"

She motioned me out of the alley and into the atrium. I recognized the old statue of Bes with his painted smile and Athena's wooden owl, his broken talon now repaired. Several new shrines had joined the collection: a pearl-studded cross with loaves of bread like an offering below the base, a golden statue of Apollo, and a flame burning in a hearth despite the warm night, probably dedicated to Hestia. Antonina shrugged her *paludamentum* into her blond slave's waiting arms. His fingers lingered on her skin for a moment longer than necessary, and she gave him a slow smile. I cleared my throat, and she glanced back at me. "Photius is my son from my days treading the boards. Before I met you."

"You never mentioned you had a son."

"I told you Petronia made sure I got rid of Perseus' baby. I only neglected to mention I'd had a child before that." She shrugged. "I couldn't bring myself to leave him at the gates. My mother's sister took him in." Antonina poured two glasses—not clay cups—from an amphora and handed one to me. "Timothy asked me to marry him just after you left. Kale was born in January."

I'd left with Hecebolus in July. I did the math. "And you call me an alley cat?"

"I always thought the gods wouldn't let me have any more children, but they seemed to think otherwise." Her eyes flicked to the slaves as she switched from Greek to Latin. "Although I'm hoping for a bit of a dry spell before the next baby." She walked to where the wet nurse suckled her youngest. "Zachariah here is almost a year old and looks passably enough like his father." Antonina's eyes followed her blond slave. "Hard to tell who that is sometimes."

"You're incorrigible."

She shrugged. "Timothy's off trading much of the time. My bed gets terribly cold."

I sipped the wine—it was a good vintage but didn't quite cover the bitter taste of my envy. "Is my mother here as well?"

Antonina set her glass down. "Oh, Theodora. Didn't you get my letters?" She was back to speaking Greek but crossed herself. "Your mother died after I married Timothy."

Almost three years ago.

"I didn't know." I sat down, clutching my silver and amber necklace as if to draw strength from the cross. I'd worried almost every day that something had happened to Tasia, but I'd never really considered my mother dying. It seemed strange that the woman who gave me life could die and I wouldn't even notice.

"How did it happen?"

"Too much poppy juice, I think. The wet nurse downstairs heard Tasia crying and sent me the message." Antonina sat next to me on the bench. "I made sure she was buried by your father. I slipped an amphora in with her—a good vintage, too."

"She'd appreciate that. Thank you." I owed Antonina more than I could ever repay her.

"Comito's back at the Kynêgion—I swear she's one of the longest running actresses in the history of the city. I'm sure she'd like to know you're back, but you should stay here tonight. Timothy's trading for silver in Chalcedon for the next few days, and there's a flat down the street for let. Timothy knows the landlord—I'll make sure you get a fair price."

"I owe you."

She waved her hand as if to dismiss the idea. "I'm sure you'll find a way to pay me back sometime. Speaking of—what do you plan to do now that you're here? The theater again?"

Macedonia's letters were in the bag at my hip. "I've got a few tricks up my sleeve."

"Better than up your skirts." She raised her glass to me. "You've got more lives than a one-eyed alley cat, Theodora. To your newest one—may you land on your feet!"

. . .

The next morning I took the children to visit Mother's grave. They watched with solemn faces as I tipped an amphora of good wine into the soil, but then they went off to play amongst the graves while I told her everything that had happened since I'd left.

"I'm sorry I wasn't here, Mother." At that moment John toddled after Tasia as she squealed and ducked behind a tree. I smiled and wiped my eyes with the back of my hand. "I wish you could have met my son."

I rented the room Antonina had suggested and traipsed through the debris of yesterday's festival on our way to the food market. A merchant with orange stains down his front used a cherry-sized bronze weight to measure a tiny terra-cotta jar of *garos* to go with the omelets I planned to make tonight.

"Who's that?" Tasia pointed at a woman's face etched onto a bronze weight the size of a melon.

I recognized the severe bird face, crown and earrings dripping with jewels, possibly the rubies I'd once seen. "Empress Lupicina. Pretty, isn't she?"

Tasia pulled a face, then covered it and looked at me with hesitant eyes. "Sort of."

I chuckled, and the merchant joined in. "They say she was lovely when she was young," he said. "But age hasn't agreed with the poor old girl."

My basket was only half full with an onion and four brown eggs, but with our new address we were also eligible for the city's bread tokens. Life was looking up, at least for now.

Tasia and John chased a scrawny tortoiseshell cat past stalls of pottery and copper urns—a magic cat according to Tasia because it had one green eye and one blue—while I rearranged our basket to fit the loaf of bread. Fat pigeons pecked at trampled cherries and apricots, green peas and lettuce, then took flight as two patricians floated past in a sedan, the feet of their slaves stopping all at once.

"Are you attending the *convivium* at the Palace of Hormisdas tonight?" The first was a portly old fellow and the second a pudgy man half his age, both clambering out of the sedan. Perhaps father and son.

I was about to turn down an alley to take a shortcut to our new flat, but the second man's words drifted to my ears, sweet as the music of an *aulos*.

"Justinian is always good for a party."

The first man snorted. "His consulship extravaganza cost the Imperial Treasury two hundred eighty-eight thousand gold *solidi*. I quiver to think what will happen to the Treasury should he manage to take his uncle's place on the throne."

The second man grimaced. "Or our taxes."

They turned away from the market—I was tempted to follow, but the children were wilting in the afternoon sun.

Justinian was hosting a party tonight.

And I had a letter of introduction. I only had to decide whether to use it.

Chapter 16

I drew far too many stares as I passed through the gates of the Palace of Hormisdas, compliments of my homespun and black scarf. A crow amongst swans. This was not the usual villa of Constantinople's upper crust—the granite palace was set back from the road behind straight rows of olive trees and lacked the shops on its front that some of the nobility rented to tradesmen and artisans. Justinian's sprawling villa had once been the residence of a Persian prince and possessed a breathtaking view of the sweep of the Sea of Marmara. I slipped between sedans as they jostled up the path, wishing I'd had the spare coin to hire a litter to keep the dust from my hem.

A troupe of female dancers—younger than I and dressed in scanty tunicas—flitted up toward the palace but diverged from the caravan of litters to the side of the house. I debated which to follow for a moment—it would be easy to slip back into my old life, but the weight of Macedonia's letter anchored me. I followed the cloud of perfumes wafting from the tide of nobility instead. A gaggle of patrician girls entered the palace with their mothers before being herded off to the *gynaeceum*; they were likely all virgins hoping for a chance to snare the consul and become the next Empress.

"I'm beginning to think Justinian will never take a wife," one of them said to her mother, retying a ribbon at her waist and plumping her breasts under her stola. "The man might as well be a monk for all the interest he pays us."

"Or worse." Another girl scratched her head with a single finger, a sign denoting an effeminate man, one worse than a eunuch.

The mother pulled a lock of dark hair from under her daughter's veil and curled it around her finger. "Of course Justinian will take a wife," she said. "Even if he doesn't care for her bed. And that lucky girl will receive a double boon—a crown and a husband who frequents her chamber only long enough to sire an heir on her."

No matter our class, we women all sold ourselves to men. The only difference was the manner in which we went about it.

Two portly patricians provided the perfect shelter up to Justinian's palace, and only a single elderly steward stood guard at the vestibule. I had almost passed by when he plucked me from the shadows like an errant child and deposited me before two colossal pink marble lions.

"We have enough dancers and poets. Come back next time for a proper interview." His voice was deep and heavily accented, Armenian from the sound of it. The steward was less grandfatherly upon closer inspection, although he approached that age, and while he was not a large man, the muscles snaking up his bare arms were thick and tanned. He wore a short beard twisted to a sharp point and already streaked with white, but his gold collar studded with rubies and the red cloak trimmed with gold told me he was a eunuch. He must have been gelded late in life.

"I'm not here to dance or recite poetry. I'm here for the *convivium*," I said.

"Only men are allowed."

"Justinian let you in, didn't he?"

One day I swore I was going to learn to control my tongue.

The eunuch glowered and crossed his arms. I caught a hint of his spicy perfume before he gave me a none-too-gentle push back into the night. "Plebian trash is not permitted in the Palace of Hormisdas."

The river of nobility stopped to raise their perfectly penciled brows. I gave them a look to freeze the Bosphorus and stood as tall as I could, but even on tiptoes I could still see up the eunuch's nose. "Better plebian trash than a barbarian half man."

His upper lip quivered like that of a guard dog. "In my country, children like you are left to perish on a windswept crag. It's a pity this Empire is so civilized."

Only the devil was going to stop me from seeing Justinian. I stood my ground, hands on hips. "I've been sent by an acquaintance of Justinian's. I demand to see him."

The eunuch threw his head back and laughed. I stomped my foot. "Listen to me, you imbecile. Macedonia of Antioch gave me a recommendation to see Justinian, and I'm not leaving until I see him." I shoved the parchment under his nose, Macedonia's tiny seal so close he might have inhaled it.

He laid his palm atop the letter and lowered it to his chest. "I don't care if God himself recommended you. This is not a taverna or a theater or a *lupinar*. Go back to where you belong."

I threw the parchment at him. The paper hit him square in the nose, and he jumped as if I'd scalded him with a pot of boiling water.

"Take that to your master, little man. Or wipe your ass with it." I turned and stormed down the stairs.

Five steps later I regretted the move, but I'd sooner cut out my tongue than apologize to that arrogant half man, even if he did have my letter of introduction to the future Emperor of Byzantium.

Instead, I cursed myself all the way home.

. . .

I wanted to gouge out my eyes with my spindle. My armpit ached from squeezing my distaff, and the constant scrape of wool had rubbed my fingers raw. All that, and my yarn scarcely resembled string. More like something a cat had hacked up.

It took exactly five days for the Mistress of the Wool House to demote me to drafting instead of spinning. I glowered at the silk workers, those lucky women and children chosen for their nimble fingers to unravel silk thread from Serinda and Persia, and then weave it into designs of lions and griffins. Instead, I sat all day with girls half my age, only to emerge at night like a pale moth, gossamer strands of blond fibers threaded in my hair, woven into my clothes, and clinging to my eyelashes.

It was an honest living, and I despised it.

I was more surprised than anyone when a rain-dampened messenger from the Palace of Hormisdas showed up at our front door one week after Justinian's *convivium*. The day was gray and dreary, so Antonina had brought the children over. Meowing, Tasia and Kale crawled around the floor, their tunicas hiked up to their hips and rags stuffed into the ropes at their waists as makeshift cat tails. Photius lay sprawled on his stomach, embellishing sketches of charcoal animals from Justinian's consular games at the Hippodrome.

"I presume one of you is Theodora?"

I set down the tiny bites of bread I was feeding John—his little cheeks were already puffed up like a squirrel's. "Depends on who's asking."

"Consul Justinian requests the presence of the famed actress Theodora at the Palace of Hormisdas tonight." The messenger turned on his heel and stalked down the creaky stairs, his duty complete. Justinian certainly didn't screen his servants based on their good manners.

I closed the door behind me, heart pounding in my ears. "Dear God."

Antonina gaped at me. "Since when do you consort with consuls?"

"I don't consort with them." I explained the letter from Macedonia all the way to pelting that snide eunuch with it. I tossed John in the air, earning a squeal of delight. "This is what I've been waiting for."

"Don't be a fool. You've been called to take your clothes off for his guests, not because Justinian plans to put you on the imperial payroll."

I stopped tossing John—I wanted to lob something else at Antonina. Preferably a brick.

"I doubt I'm his type."

"Who cares what his type is—women, boys, goats? All three at once?" She clapped her hands over her mouth, shoulders shaking with silent mirth. "No, I know. Geese!"

I looked to the heavens, but couldn't stop my smile as she gasped for breath through her laughter. "You really are foul—you know that?" I said.

"You have no idea." She dabbed her eyes with the corner of her *paludamentum*, then put on a mostly serious face. "Really, darling, all that matters is that Justinian is willing to make time for Constantinople's favorite actress."

"I'm done with all that. I need him to give me a position like he gave Macedonia."

Antonina flashed a wicked grin. "I'm sure he has all sorts of positions in mind for you."

I threw John's half-eaten loaf of bread at her.

I had no intention of sleeping with Justinian. He was a man, and like all men, he would toss me out with the evening's trash as soon as he tired of me. Antonina was probably right. It was a miracle I'd been summoned at all, especially after the little scene with that insufferable eunuch. Justinian probably wanted me to perform my Leda routine or something equally salacious.

Damn.

. . .

This time I wore a silk stola the color of ripe plums—one of Antonina's—to the Palace of Hormisdas. Its high neckline and wide sleeves were embroidered with tiny birds, so I looked perfectly respectable for once. Antonina had brushed my hair until it shone, then covered the dark knot at the nape of my neck with a matron's scarlet veil. I only hoped Justinian wouldn't notice my scuffed slippers.

It had stopped raining as I waved to the children and retraced my steps to the Palace of Hormisdas, careful to avoid the buckets of dirty rainwater the shopkeeps sluiced onto the cobbles. I was too slow to dodge one and ended up with a drenched foot. The merchant got an earful from me, but he only rolled his eyes.

The same ghastly eunuch stood guard as I approached the vestibule to the palace. This time the grounds were empty, not a single perfumed patrician in sight. I replayed the messenger's words in my mind to make sure I had the correct night.

"Welcome, Theodora." The eunuch stepped aside with a little bow, akin to a snake's slither in sand.

I thrust my chin out. "I was summoned by the consul. Where are the other guests?"

"You are the only guest."

"I don't understand." Only I did. Far too well.

"I delivered your letter and an account of your behavior to the consul last night, against my better judgment."

Perfect. Perhaps Justinian had summoned me to have me whipped for throwing things at his servants.

The eunuch chuckled. "Justinian was highly intrigued by a woman who spoke her mind so vehemently."

Right. All men appreciated women who spoke their minds.

"So there's no one else?" My stomach tied itself in knots worthy of any sailor, but I tried to keep my face a mask.

He smiled. "There's a Greek urn from the Golden Age in the atrium if you need to empty your stomach."

It was a wonder I'd ever been an actress. "Are you going to let me in or not?"

He swept me into the atrium with an exaggerated bow. A geometric mosaic stopped at the sunken step of the *impluvium*, full from the afternoon rains. A statue of Julius Caesar holding a map of the Empire stood astride a fountain, and there was indeed a massive Greek urn in one corner, something with a naked Heracles wrestling yet another monster. Definitely male décor. Torches lit a series of wall frescoes, the light quivering so the figures seemed to move. I recognized scenes from the Trojan War, noted the battle of Achilles and Hector, felt a pang as I remembered discussing the famed battle with Severus. How I wished he were here to guide me now.

"The consul is in the *triclinium*."

I followed the eunuch into the dining room, trying not to gape along the way. Hecebolus' villa in Apollonia could have fit in the Palace of Hormisdas several times; yet this lacked the garish opulence of Justin's villa. Not bad for the nephew of a swineherd.

Justinian reclined on one of three *lecti* pushed against the opposite walls. The future Emperor of Byzantium had a sharp nose and no longer wore the first beard of youth, but he was not so old that time had etched itself upon his face or dusted his temples with gray. I guessed him to be a few years shy of his fortieth year. Dark curls brushed his forehead, and underneath, his eyes were a mosaic of mahogany flecked with gold. And those eyes were watching me.

I dropped to my knees but didn't avert my gaze. A smile turned up the corner of his lips, and he gestured to a second couch. I tucked my feet under my hem as slaves marched in, carrying golden platters of oysters swimming in butter and topped with delicate dollops of salted gray mullet roe, doves on toast with quail eggs, and pale orange cantaloupe stuffed with minced lamb and rosemary. My stomach growled.

"Thank you for coming, Theodora," he said. "Your name means 'gift from God,' does it not?" His Greek wore an accent, but he was from Tauresium and had likely spoken Latin first. "Or a gift from the devil, if you hear Narses tell it."

The slave hovering at Justinian's elbow measured water into two silver goblets of golden wine. I almost wished for something stronger, but I was determined to keep my wits about me. "Narses, my lord? You mean that snake of a eunuch you've got guarding your palace?"

"Narses is my steward and a general of the Scholarii cavalry. No one has ever questioned his authority." He raised his brows. "Except you."

I shrugged. "He may have sacked Rome for all I care. He looks genteel, but his manners are worse than a Goth's."

Justinian laughed. "Precisely why he's guarding my front door." He scooped a spoonful of spices into his wine. "Macedonia writes highly of you as well." I recognized at Justinian's elbow the letter I'd used to pelt Narses.

"I'm surprised he deigned to deliver that to you."

"Honesty is a rare quality. Narses is under the impression it's one you have in abundance."

I set down the oyster I'd been about to crack open to save the future Emperor from watching me choke on shellfish.

"Macedonia wrote of your travels," he continued. "Cyrenaica, Egypt, the Levant. Anatolia."

I wasn't about to correct him about Macedonia's exaggerations.

His eyes gleamed in the torchlight. "I'd have to assemble twenty men to learn of all you've seen. And yet you've returned to Constantinople," Justinian said. "Why?"

Something stopped my tongue from telling him about Tasia. I shrugged. "It's home."

"And do you plan to return to the theater now that you're home?"

A silent slave refilled his glass. "I'm sure the Blues would be happy to reinstate their former star."

I covered the silver goblet with my hand before the slave could refill it. "I took up religion in Alexandria. I hope the capital will offer the opportunity to sustain myself without taking to the stage again."

Justinian set down his glass. "Your story grows more intriguing by the minute."

I briefly relayed my experiences with Severus while Justinian listened, his food growing cold on his plate. "So you are a born-again Monophysite," he said when I finished. "They are a group my uncle would like to see swept from the Empire."

"You can't keep banishing leaders of the religious opposition from the capital," I said, the words coming fast. "They only breed dissent in the footsteps left behind."

A shut mouth gathers no foot. Why did I never remember my mother's advice until it was too late?

Justinian stared at me as if I'd sprouted fins, then shook his head and rose from his couch. I waited for his order for Narses or someone armed with a freshly sharpened sword to mete out my punishment. Instead, he smiled, so slightly I might have imagined it. "You are a unique woman, Theodora."

"I'll take that as a compliment."

He chuckled, a deep, throaty sound. "I have more guests arriving at any moment, but I'd be pleased if you'd stay." He paused, then called over his shoulder, "As my guest."

I stood in the shadows as Justinian welcomed several well-dressed men into the *triclinium*, observing as he spoke to each of them as if greeting a long-lost friend. He gave a hearty laugh and clapped a handsome young man on the back, eliciting a low rumble of laughter from all his guests. Even surrounded by other men—presumably powerful ones—Justinian dominated the room with his sheer energy.

He arranged himself on his couch once again and gestured to its foot for me to sit. I perched on the edge and surveyed the ring of men as a slave offered a bronze bowl of rose water for them to dip their fingers.

They all inclined their heads in turn as Justinian made the introductions. General Belisarius wore a full beard and a general's silver belt, but he appeared to be no older than me; recently returned from his victory at Daras, he was acknowledged as one of the Empire's rising stars. His second-in-command, General Sittas—the one Justinian had laughed with—seemed even younger, with his smooth skin and soft lips. Justinian's legal counselor, Tribonium, wore fingers black with ink, and Peter of Thessalonica seemed a thin and quiet diplomat. Narses had joined us as well, although he remained standing. The last man recognized me before I did him. "Gods!" He clutched his heart. "Can it truly be? Theodora has returned at last to the Queen of Cities?"

John of Cappadocia. His dimpled chin was hidden under a dark beard, but otherwise he looked exactly the same. How different my life might be if I'd chosen him instead of Hecebolus at Justin's dinner party.

"Hello, John." I let him kiss my palm and press it to his cheek before he settled onto the *lectus* next to me.

"How long has Justinian had you hidden away here?"

The rest of the men had started to talk politics, but Justinian's eyes flicked occasionally in our direction. I had the feeling the man missed nothing.

"I've become newly acquainted with the consul tonight."

"Watch out for him." John leaned forward to whisper in my ear but caressed my knee instead. "He's a sneaky devil."

I turned my attention—and my knee—toward the rest of the conversation. "We were discussing Germanus," Justinian told me. His foot twitched.

"The Emperor's other nephew?" I knew little of Germanus other than his position as a potential heir.

John cracked open an oyster. "Germanus is a nonentity."

"We would prefer to avoid another debacle like we had last time the throne was vacated," Belisarius said. "We all agree Constantinople is for Justinian's succession. He's the obvious choice."

Tribonium took a dainty bite of partridge. "And we're not suggesting Justinian should take his uncle's place by anything other than natural means."

Their discussion was only borderline treason then.

"But we're unsure how the provinces feel," Peter said.

"Theodora is well traveled." Justinian scooped the seeds from a pomegranate with a tiny gold spoon too delicate for his large hands. "She's recently returned from Alexandria and a tour of Anatolia. I think only John here is as well-traveled as she."

That explained why Justinian had kept me around tonight. This was my chance to prove myself. "The people of the Empire couldn't care less about power struggles in the capital. They want only three things." I ticked them off on my fingers. "Food. Safety from invasion. And the freedom to worship the god they choose. Guarantee them those and they'll sing your praises to the Second Coming."

Narses spoke from the shadows. "A succinct evaluation."

Peter's thick brows knit together. "I don't believe your traipsing through the frontiers makes you an expert on religious or economic policy."

I shrugged. "How often have you traveled outside Anatolia?"

John chortled. "She's got you there, Peter."

Peter's ears flushed, and Justinian smiled into his wine.

"The first is easy," Justinian said. "The grain ships from Egypt are steady as the Nile itself. Belisarius is working on the second. It's the last that might prove difficult."

I snorted. "If a farmer wants to damn his soul to Gehenna, that's his choice. What does it matter to you if a man worships Zeus, or Yahweh, or Jesus? Or the Zoroastrian fire cult even, so long as he pays his taxes?"

The men looked at me in a sort of awed stupor, John with a morsel of partridge stopped halfway to his open mouth. Only Justinian continued to eat. He raised his cup to me, his expression indecipherable. "Something to think about."

The rest of the evening passed over a discussion of Justinian's planned legal reforms. I took Macedonia's advice and listened to the men, absorbing everything I could from them. Justinian planned to compile a codex of imperial edicts to streamline the Empire's centuries of convoluted laws, many of which contradicted one another. The city's new consul was nothing if not ambitious.

The night wore on until enough yawns prompted Justinian to stand, a sign of dismissal. The men all stood, oyster shells and partridge bones crunching underfoot, but I took Justinian's place, the fabric of his couch warm from his body. If he ordered me out, I'd be humiliated, but if not—

There were a few raised eyebrows, but the men all nodded in my direction before Justinian accompanied them to the atrium. Perhaps this was common behavior for Justinian. Yet I recalled Macedonia's comment and the women talking outside his palace. I'd heard no stories of mistresses, no gossip of illegitimate children hidden in villages across the Empire. Perhaps our future Emperor did follow in the footsteps of so many Emperors before him, preferring pretty boys and soldiers like General Sittas in his bed.

Justinian's voice carried as he bid farewell to his guests. This was my chance, but it was a huge gamble. My mouth went dry, and I suddenly wished I hadn't eaten so much.

I was still draped across Justinian's couch when he returned, two goblets of wine in hand. That was a good sign. He offered me one, his monogram impressed into the silver.

"Interesting company you keep," I said, raising the goblet to the empty seats.

Justinian sat across from me, his legs stretched out and arms reclined against the top of the couch. He sipped his wine. "Yourself included."

"Most especially."

He chuckled.

I moved my feet so our toes almost touched. "You need me. Those men are smart, but they don't know your Empire the way I do."

Slaves doffed the torches in the garden and disappeared while I waited for Justinian to answer. I found it difficult to believe the future Emperor was ever truly unattended, but it appeared we were alone amongst the perfume of potted rosebushes.

"What do you propose?"

"I find out what you need to know from places you can't get to. Make your life easier."

"Somehow I doubt you've ever made anyone's life easier, Theodora." He gave a low laugh and stood. "But I will think on your offer."

I'd bargained in the market enough to recognize his refusal. "Thank you for a most interesting evening." I caught a trace of his scent of mint and parchment, no hint of foreign perfume.

"Narses has ordered a sedan for you," he said. "May God keep you, Theodora."

I expected cold dismissal in his eyes, and so was surprised to find their warm depths smiling at me. Laughing, actually.

I bowed my head, feeling my cheeks flame with humiliation. "And may God keep you, Consul."

I stomped past the sedan at the entrance, refusing to accept charity from the man who'd just rejected me, and took what was certainly my last look at the interior of the palace. My skin prickled at Narses' gaze as I stalked down the dark path, trying to tuck myself into my *paludamentum* to ward off the shivering that had nothing to do with the evening chill.

I'd made a fool of myself, thinking Justinian would ask me to spy for him. I had nothing to offer a man like him.

My heart almost jumped out of my chest as a low voice rumbled behind the massive lion statues. "You are a dreadful woman."

John the Cappadocian straddled the farthest marble lion, a clutch of lavender crocus in his fist. A few still had roots clinging to bits of dark earth. He jumped down in one swift movement and offered the flowers to me with a crooked grin. "I've waited for you all my life."

I gave him a weak smile. "Somehow I doubt that."

"I think you enjoy toying with my heart. I was beside myself with the thought that Justinian might have snared you tonight. Or perhaps the other way around." He leaned forward like a gossiping fishwife, but I didn't react. "I have a better proposal for you."

"And what might that be?"

"Take up with me."

I pretended to sniff the blossoms. John was a little rough around the edges—Cappadocians were widely known as backwater rustics—but he seemed a good sort, at least easy on the eyes, even if a little soft around the middle. I had no wish to hurt him, or humiliate him as I'd just been.

"That part of my life is behind me, John."

He sighed. "It's never too late for love. I shall simply endeavor to change your mind." I noticed a second sedan waiting as he offered me his hand. "But for tonight at least let me take you home. The streets can be wicked at this hour."

"I can walk. Truly—"

He held up a hand. "No arguing. I won't have it on my conscience if you were attacked in some dark alley." He gave a mischievous smile. "Or tripped and fell into a puddle."

I smiled. It was a bit of a walk and I was exhausted. "All right."

"That's a girl." He handed me into the sedan and closed the door behind him. I settled onto the cushion, glad for the single seats facing each other.

I spared a last glance at the Palace of Hormisdas as we passed the palace gate. If I'd blinked, I'd have missed the dark outline of a man in the shadows. He ducked back into the warm light of Justinian's atrium, too quick for me to make out who it was.

I wanted to spy for the consul but couldn't even tell when I was being watched.

Justinian was right to dismiss me.

Chapter 17

Weeks passed.

John the Cappadocian sent a steady stream of notes extolling my beauty and stealing randy verses from Catallus that managed to make even me blush. I never replied but used the back of each to help Tasia sketch her letters, then let her crumple them into balls to kick back and forth with John. Several of the Cappadocian's messages were accompanied with jewelry—one offering a pair of tiny gleaming ruby earrings. Closer inspection showed the stones weren't really rubies but garnets. Perhaps the Cappadocian's finances hadn't changed much in the past three years.

Despite his pitiful attempts to court me, I felt my resistance chip away and wore my knees out praying to the Virgin for guidance. I wanted to keep the life I'd promised myself; yet my children were more important than any ideals I set for myself. My pitiful wage from the wool house would see us through with food on the table and a roof over our heads, but not much else. Tasia was almost old enough to start school, but the idea of a tutor was as likely as dining on suckling kid and wild gazelle each night. She would be lucky to attend the patriarchate's charity school when the leaves unfurled.

The Cappadocian started to look like a better alternative with each passing day.

I bundled the children off with Antonina's blond slave one morning, their noses pink and drippy from the cold. The little apartment was silent as I wrapped a wool scarf around my head and blew out the oil lamp, the room saved from black only by the murky light of a cloudy dawn. The brazier was cold since we shivered through the mornings to save on wood. Things would be easier come spring.

My hand was almost on the door when someone knocked. "I'm in a hurry today—"

I started to lambaste yet another of John the Cappadocian's slaves, but my mouth ceased to work. Justinian, dressed in plain brown wool, stood at my door, his breath curling like fog above him. "Hello, Theodora."

I think I managed to choke out a greeting.

"May I come in?"

Into my dark little hovel with no heat? "Of course, my lord."

"Please," he said. "Call me Justinian."

Thank God I had already emptied the night buckets out the window. I rubbed my trembling hands and warmed them with my breath. The oil in the lamp was still warm, but it took several tries to light before it sputtered unwillingly to life.

"How did you find me here?" I crossed my arms in front of me to stifle a shiver.

"Narses." His eyes swept over the shabby room. "You were on your way out?"

"To the wool house."

"May I?" He gestured to one of the chairs, fortunately not the shaky one with a leg shorter than the rest. The man wasn't huge, but he filled the room. "Do you enjoy spinning?"

"Not at all."

A smile flickered over his face—perhaps a trick of the light. "I won't take much of your time. I need to know people's reaction to the new tax collection in the city."

Probably best not to mention I knew nothing about the topic.

Justinian leaned forward, elbows on his knees. "The system is one I intend to implement across the Empire to increase revenues. The rates remain the same, but the taxes will be collected more efficiently."

"Resulting in more money for the Treasury."

"Precisely."

"From what I've seen, you're going to need all the money you can get."

He arched an eyebrow in my direction.

"Your consular games probably cost more than Anastasius and Justin ever spent in their entire reigns combined."

Justinian shrugged. "Octavian knew what he was doing with free bread, beer, and circuses. My uncle is a wise man, but he doesn't dream big. I do. And I need the people on my side if I'm to accomplish what I wish during my own reign."

"When will you need the information?"

"Within a week."

"Done." It wasn't spying on senators or prefects, but it was a start.

"Good. As you said, you can get honest answers from people I cannot." He stood to go. "Oh, and keep John out of this."

For a moment I thought he meant my son. "John?"

Justinian's eyes lost their warmth. I pitied the poor soul that fell on the wrong side of this man's temper. "The Cappadocian is in charge of the tax reforms. I believe you and he are well acquainted."

A hesitant knock stopped my response. "Someone from your entourage?" I asked.

I opened the door to see Tasia's bright hazel eyes, her cheeks round apples of pink. She peered behind me and bit her lip. "I heard voices, Mama."

So much for keeping my life secret.

I nudged her into the room, my hands on the frail wings of her shoulder blades. "Tasia, this is Consul Justinian. Justinian, this is Tasia." His name felt foreign on my tongue.

Tasia stared at the floor. "I am honored to meet you."

"Consul," I whispered.

"Consul," she repeated.

Justinian crouched before her. His eyes had warmed again, and lines crinkled at their edges. "And I am honored to meet you as well, Tasia."

I kissed her cheek. "Did you forget something, sweeting?"

She pointed to our pallet with its rumpled green blanket. "My doll. And Augustus Caesar. Auntie Nina said we'd have a party with them today."

"Go fetch them."

She returned with Anastasia's one-eyed doll and a brown wool sock with hog hair whiskers and two mismatched button eyes.

"That's a handsome cat you've got," Justinian said. I had no idea how he'd identified the brown lump as an animal, much less a cat. "Is he a good mouser?"

She looked at her cat, to me, and then to Justinian. "He's the best mouser ever."

"I'd expect so with a name like Augustus Caesar."

I gave her braid a little tug. "Tell Auntie Nina I may be a bit late today."

"Yes, Mama." She trundled down the stairwell, singing a song to Augustus Caesar. The day was growing stronger now, watery sun trying to nudge its way out of the clouds. I was terribly late. Justinian's sedan waited on the street—at least I assumed it was his, despite the lack of imperial insignia.

I felt him behind me. "I didn't realize you had a daughter."

"She's the reason I came back to Constantinople." I wished I hadn't said the words as soon as they were out of my mouth. It would be best if this man knew as little about me as possible.

"A good reason. Do you have any other children?"

"A son."

Something akin to dismay passed over Justinian's face, and the next words jumped unbidden from my lips. "But he died."

I don't know why I lied. Perhaps it was the urge to keep my life secret, or maybe I didn't want to disappoint Justinian. He stared at me for a moment, but then his expression relaxed and he crossed himself. "I'm sorry."

I stared at the frayed weft of the table weaving, wondering what was wrong with me. What kind of mother lied about the death of her child?

Justinian cleared his throat. "My sedan can take you to the wool house if you'd like."

That would set tongues wagging for at least a month.

I looked at him, startled at the warmth in his eyes. "No, thank you. I'll send a report to the Palace of Hormisdas within a week."

He walked down several steps, then stopped. "Deliver it yourself. And bring your daughter if you'd like."

I did not bring Tasia.

I left the children with Antonina and a story about spending extra hours at the wool house. Antonina raised her brows, but I didn't care if she believed me, so long as she didn't know what I was really up to.

I wore the plum-colored stola again, although Justinian had already seen me at my worst. I had finished his task in five days, so he wouldn't be expecting me.

The Palace of Hormisdas was quiet as Narses led me down the chilly corridors. We passed several closed chambers and were almost to the *triclinium* when a man emerged in the darkness before us.

"Theodora?"

An oil lamp illuminated John the Cappadocian, his sandy hair lit like a halo. "What are you doing here?"

I stifled a groan. The Cappadocian was the last person I wished to see. "Meeting Justinian."

He smiled at Narses. "I've just finished my meeting with the consul, but perhaps I can deliver this precious jewel to him?"

I struggled for a reason to ask Narses to stay, but the eunuch's expression contradicted the idea that I was a precious stone of any sort. He gave a stiff bow, and his lamplight disappeared around the corner.

I didn't relish lurking about Justinian's dark halls with John. "Shall we?"

John stepped so close to me that the flame from his lamp singed my arm. "I'm not good enough for Constantinople's fallen star?"

"Pardon me?"

"You reject me so you can take up with Justinian?" His lip wrinkled in a sneer.

"I have no intention of taking up with anyone." Least of all another man with a hidden temper—I'd had enough of those to last several lifetimes.

"Likely story." He glared at me through slitted eyes. "If you're not on your way to his bed, then why are you here?"

"That's really none of your business, now, is it?"

"Did you have a hand in my dismissal?"

No wonder he was in a black mood. I wondered why Justinian had dismissed him, but it was truly none of my business. And it certainly didn't excuse his pushing me around.

"In case you haven't noticed," I said, "I work at the wool house. I'm in no position to influence the hiring or firing of the consul's advisers."

A vein ticked in his throat. Then his hands fell to his sides. "I need you, Theodora." He pinned me between his arms, the wall cold against my back. The heat of his oil lamp fluttered too close to my face. "And you need me."

I needed him like I needed a hole in my skull.

"Unfortunately, I'm not available." I ducked out of his arms and around the corner, unable to breathe. His voice rang out behind me.

"That's what you think."

I drew a deep breath at his retreating footsteps. This was the sign I'd prayed for. I'd spend the rest of my life stinking of lanolin with the skin scoured from my hands before I took up with the Cappadocian.

"May I take you to the consul?"

Narses appeared from nowhere, hands clasped behind him. The man was silent as a cat before it pounced. I wondered how much he'd overheard.

"Please." I tried to look imperious—hard to do since Narses was a head taller than me. "And if you ever dump me on the Cappadocian again, I'll ask Justinian for what's left of your manhood."

Narses bared his teeth in what I hoped was a smile. "Follow me."

He didn't lead me to the *triclinium*, but to a cozy room at the opposite end of the palace, with a fire crackling in the brazier and a thick bear rug tossed over geometric swirls of mosaic. A water clock told the late hour, and a table large as a bed drooped under towers of scrolls and codices. Some of the open parchments revealed architectural schematics of great domed churches and what might have been aqueducts or triumphal arches.

"Theodora, what a pleasant surprise." Justinian set down his stylus. His fingers were stained black at the tips, and his thick hair seemed somewhat wilder than usual, if that was possible. Narses bent to whisper something in his ear, and Justinian's eyes flicked to me. There was a clumsy silence. I almost feared he'd send me away before he finally spoke. "Have you eaten?"

"Yes," I lied.

"I haven't. Send a tray," Justinian said to Narses. "And an amphora of wine." He gave a stiff smile and gestured me to a couch before the fire.

I ignored the chair and picked up one of the documents. "What are these?"

"Ideas. Dreams." There was a long pause. "I'd like to leave my imprint on the city one day."

Like Sostratus and the lighthouse at Alexandria. I turned the paper closest to me, a cruciform church with five domes. "The Church of the Holy Apostles?"

"I plan to tear it down. Save the crypts, of course, but replace the building with something worthy of its stature."

I recalled the crumbling church with its roost of pigeons and decades of droppings. "A worthy project." I gestured to another drawing, one of a building with a colossal dome. I stared at the scale, the tiny outline of a man sketched at the base of the structure. "Wouldn't something so massive collapse under its own weight?"

Justinian shrugged and smiled. "Far better to dare mighty things and fail mightily than to never dare at all, eh?"

The arrival of the food stopped me from saying more. No gilded plates of stuffed birds or platters of oysters this time, but crusty loaves of raisin bread, fresh crumbles of goat cheese flecked with sage, and terra-cotta bowls of dried plums and apricots. I filled an earthenware plate painted with a swirl of grape leaves, trying to work out a way to stuff my pockets for John and Tasia.

"I presume you have a report for me?" Justinian sat against the edge of his desk, balancing a plate with one hand. It occurred to me that the man amid the golden delicacies at that first dinner might not have been the true Justinian. Or perhaps the consul had more than one face.

I told him what I'd learned—that people grumbled about no longer being skipped on tax collections but were resigned to pay the full amount they owed.

"Excellent," he said. "Although the Emperor will refuse to implement all the reforms throughout the Empire. There's nothing further to be done until my uncle changes his mind."

I wondered if that meant Justinian would no longer require my services. If so, that might also explain why John the Cappadocian had been dismissed.

We talked a while longer—Justinian was interested in my opinion on a proposed law he wished to include in his compilation, one that would grant women more rights in divorce cases. The evening slipped away, marked by the gears and dials of the water clock. More than once, I swore I caught Justinian watching me. I was loath to leave the warmth of the room, or the consul's twinkling eyes, but I couldn't ignore the late hour forever.

"Thank you for the meal," I said, feeling my cheeks pink with the heat of the fire.

He offered me a hand and helped me to my feet. "Narses has a basket of the same for you to take home to Tasia."

Good thing I hadn't stuffed my stola with cheese. "You're too kind."

He gave a throaty chuckle, so low it was almost a growl. "I most certainly am not."

He reached up and touched a curl that had escaped my veil, his hand lingering. I knew the look in his eyes.

He wanted me. The future heir to the Empire wanted me.

We stood that way for a moment, so close the heat of him almost matched the warmth of the brazier at my back. My heart pounded, and my mouth felt stuffed with wool.

A choice.

I had sworn before the Virgin to keep myself pure. But the Virgin wasn't standing here, intoxicated by a man who treated me as an equal, who cared what I thought. A man who smelled of mint and something entirely male.

My hands stopped short of his chest, hesitating, but then I dared touch him, feeling the sharpness of his inhale with my hands. He groaned and his lips were on mine, a kiss heady as any wine. I pressed myself to him, surprised at the instant heat that spread through my body. I wanted to get rid of any space between us, to mold myself into his warmth.

Justinian pulled back and ran his hands through his hair so that it stuck out in all directions. "No."

The heat in my blood made it hard to think. I had two warring urges, to either throw something at him or tear the tunica from his body. Three years alone had apparently been too long.

"No?" My chest heaved and my cheeks burned. Justinian stepped away and poured himself a glass of wine. Unwatered.

"No," he repeated. He pressed a second cup into my hands. He smiled, a long, slow smile that almost undid me. "The men who have pursued you in the past were fools, Theodora. I'm no fool."

My entire body flamed with my mortification. I must have seen something else in his eyes, perhaps interest in the aberration of my life, but not desire. I set down the wine and smoothed the now-crumpled silk of my stola. "You may not be a fool, but you *are* an insufferable cad. And a pompous ass."

He grinned. "Is that the best you can do? I've been called worse."

"Fine. You're a miserable, curly headed, barbarian lout without the sense God gave a goat." I had a few other choice words for him but forced myself to bite my tongue.

"That's more like it."

I'd had enough humiliation for one night. "I presume I can still take the basket of food?"

Take it straight back to my cold bed, and perhaps go see a diviner of the black arts in the morning. I had a curse or two that I wouldn't mind putting on Justinian.

"Yes, you little imp—take the food."

Later, tucked between Tasia and John on our pallet, I realized the full extent of Justinian's scheming. He had already sacked John the Cappadocian and knew his uncle wouldn't expand the new tax system.

The man had known everything he'd needed about the tax collections. The sneaky bastard had never really needed me at all, yet he'd sought me out.

He wasn't a fool like the other men because he didn't plan to pursue me. Or was there some other reason? I didn't know what game Justinian was playing, but I had a feeling I hadn't seen the last of him.

I drifted to sleep with a smile on my face.

A forest of firewood was stacked outside our door the next day. Then came a wheel of cheese wrapped in goatskin large enough to feed a small army. A season's supply of olive oil made me snap at the children to stay away from the lamps lest we burn the entire building to the ground. The gifts were all anonymous, delivered in the dark of night, but there were really only two men who might have sent them.

The presents tapered off as a thin powder of snow dusted the roof of the Hagia Sophia and the Church of the Holy Apostles. I stifled a smile when a familiar sedan stopped before our building and a slave delivered a lidded basket with a message—my first note from Justinian.

Dear Theodora,

Forgive my presumption, but Narses discovered this little demon in the pantry. It reminds me of you, but I believe Tasia might enjoy it.

—J

The basket mewled. Inside, a scrawny patchwork kitten blinked its blue eyes. It was a pretty little thing except that it was missing half an ear.

I bit back a chortle of laughter as Tasia squealed.

"Do you have parchment?" I asked the messenger. He produced a fresh sheet, and I scribbled a response for him to deliver to his master.

Dear Justinian,

Thank you for the kitten. She'll taste wonderful made into sausage, especially with a little garlic and rosemary.

—Theodora

Tasia promptly named the stray Hippolyta, after the Amazon queen, convinced the little thing was a fierce warrior despite her torn ear. The little furball thoroughly entertained the children in our now-warm apartment all morning. Dusk had almost extinguished the day's meager light when Antonina arrived. Only her eyes were visible from her wool and squirrel skin wraps, which were dusted with tiny sparkling diamond flakes that melted as she stamped her feet.

"It's colder out there than tits on a bear. Sorry to arrive unannounced, but I swear I'm going to have to sell some of my children to a passing caravan."

There was a sharp gasp, and Tasia clutched Antonina's hand. "You can't sell them, Auntie Nina. I'd miss Kale and Photius."

Antonina smiled at me and gave Tasia a dramatic sigh. "I suppose I'll have to keep them then." She tweaked my daughter's nose. "But only for you, sweeting. Photius spent the morning coloring all over the frescoes in the *triclinium*—I wish that boy would play with swords instead of ruining the walls."

The kitten chose that moment to pounce on Antonina's toe as someone else knocked. Antonina shrieked, tripped over a chair, and stumbled back into her pile of furs as Tasia screamed. John, of course, mimicked his older sister.

A man stood outside, his arms wreathed in thick links of sausage still warm from the frying pan. "Are you Theodora?"

"I am."

"Where can I put this?"

I clamped my hands over my mouth, but the laugh escaped through my fingers. "On the table."

"What in the—" Antonina caught herself in front of the children. "First you house a demon rat—"

"Cat," Tasia corrected her.

"And now you've wiped the city out of Lucanian sausages?"

The sausages filled the room with the scent of cumin and peppercorn. Hippolyta swatted one with her paw and got smacked in the head as it swung back at her. The man handed me another piece of folded parchment.

I popped it open and palmed the seal before Antonina could see it.

Theodora,

Cat sausage tastes deplorable. Please accept these Lucanian sausages as a substitute.

—J

Antonina ripped the paper from my hands before I could stop her. "All right, who is he?"

"Who?"

"Don't even. Mountains of firewood, enough sausages to make you ill, and a suspicious sparkle in your eye. Who is trying to woo you with cured meat?"

"No one. Well, someone."

She sniffed the parchment. "Good quality. He's wealthy, isn't he?"

I thought of Justinian's palace, the fortune he'd spent on his games. "He's fairly well off."

She stepped closer to me and gestured with her eyes to where Tasia and John were playing hide-and-find with the kitten. "Have you told him about them?"

Some of the warmth fled from the room. "He met Tasia by accident one day. But not John." I didn't tell her I'd told Justinian my son had died. "Why?"

"I lost two patrons because of Photius." She caught my eye. "It's hard for men with money to reconcile themselves to a woman whose son would muck up the inheritance for their own sprats. That is, assuming he's not so decrepit he can't sire a brood of his own."

I did wonder on that for a moment. There was no doubt Justinian was pursuing me—and not a pretty soldier like Sittas—but at his age it did seem odd that he didn't already have any illegitimate children hidden away somewhere.

"I don't think this one has any designs to marry me," I said. It was against ancient law for any man of senatorial rank or higher to marry an actress. "But Timothy took in Photius."

Antonina pulled a knife from the box under the table and hacked the end off a sausage link. "Timothy is different. Do you know your man well enough to be sure how he'll react?"

I couldn't answer that.

"I thought not." She popped a piece of sausage in her mouth, licked her fingers, and took my face in her hands. "Enjoy your man, whoever he is. And enjoy his sausage"—she flashed another wide grin—"but guard your secrets."

Chapter 18

Antonina had to be wrong. And yet I couldn't summon the courage to tell Justinian the truth about my son, fearful he'd cast me off. Soon, I promised myself.

The snow melted, and Constantinople wore a shroud of brown when Justinian invited me on a tour of the city walls. He beamed like a proud papa as we passed the massive coiled chain that could be stretched across the Golden Horn to prevent foreign ships from invading, Constantine's red column with Christ's nail in his crown and priceless artifacts buried underneath, and the white vault of the Milion, the starting point for measuring all distances to the cities of the Empire. I'd seen these treasures before, but it was different seeing them with the man who would one day own them.

A sickle moon hung over the wooden roof of the Hagia Sophia, and the watchmen kept their eyes forward as Justinian and I sat on the ramparts of the city wall, legs almost touching and stale bread stuffed with mackerel in hand. Shadows from the flickering torches danced across Justinian's face as he stared in the direction of the Princes' Islands. He dipped the dried mallow leaves from his sandwich wrapper into the flame of a torch, letting them writhe in the heat so the shadows tangled with political graffiti scrawled upon the walls.

Now seemed a good time for a little test. I stood and swept imaginary crumbs from my stola. "So, I've been wondering—"

He released the leaves, red embers floating lazily in the cold air before blinking into the dark night. "Yes?"

"Do you send all your subjects mangy kittens and a season's supply of Lucanian sausages?"

"Only the vinegary ones who always say exactly what they think." He laughed. "I'll send more wood and oil if you run out before spring."

So all the gifts *had* been his. I had been mostly sure that Justinian had sent the other presents as well, but I thanked God that the Cappadocian wasn't my mysterious benefactor. I settled on the wall next to him and nudged him with my elbow. "I think you rather enjoy my vinegary self."

"That's only one in a long list of things I enjoy about you, Theodora."

There it was again—the same expression from the night we'd first kissed.

Justinian did want me. And I wanted him more than I'd ever wanted a man before. Yet—

"I thought you said the men who pursued me were fools." I tried to keep my voice light, but I still hadn't worked out Justinian's meaning that night.

"I'd thought that was obvious."

He bent his head and kissed me until I could scarcely think; yet somehow I managed to pull back and draw a shaky breath. "Enlighten me."

"They let you go. I won't make the same mistake."

His thumb caressed my lip, drawing out the moment as the waves slapped the shore below. He knew what he was doing to me. And I could tell he was enjoying every moment.

"This is your chance, Theodora. If there's anyone else—"

I almost laughed, but he was serious. I recalled the shadowy figure outside the Palace of Hormisdas that first night when I'd left with the Cappadocian, and Narses' whispers in Justinian's ear after John's demotion.

All this time he'd thought the Cappadocian was competition.

I kissed his palm and straddled him, not caring if I seemed wanton. "In case you haven't noticed, I rather enjoy the company of an ill-mannered nephew of a swineherd." I leaned down to whisper in his ear. "There is only you. And I want you. Now."

Something rumbled deep in his chest. "The watchmen would probably enjoy the show."

"I don't think I care."

His kiss was enough to make me hike up my stola right there, but he managed to pull me to my feet. We ran along the wall hand in hand, ducking into dark alcoves to taste each other, Justinian's lips on my neck and the swell of my breasts, his hands digging into the bones of my hips as I arched into him.

The ride through the city's deserted streets was exquisite torture. Narses took one look at us in the palace courtyard and snapped his fingers so the atrium was deserted when we entered. Shedding clothes up the marble stairs, Justinian let his teeth tease my nipples through the silk of my stola while my fingers struggled with the knot under his tunica. I finally pulled him on top of me.

"Here," I said, breathing into his ear as I wrapped my legs around him. "I need you now."

He laid me back against the cold stone steps, lifting me to meet him. His first thrust filled me so entirely I screamed in pleasure, clinging to him as further waves crashed over me until my body became too heavy to move.

Later, he carried me to his room and spread me on the bed, peeling off my stola and drawing out each caress as he traced the curve of my throat, the sweep of my collarbone, the naked hollows of my hips. He slipped into the wetness between my legs, and I arched against him.

I woke to the scratching of a pen on paper and the dim light of an oil lamp. Justinian sat at his desk, his wool robe open to show his bare chest.

I stretched lazily on the bed. "Don't you ever sleep?"

He chuckled and set down his pen, taking in my every curve. "Not very often."

I left the feathered mattress and padded over to him, sitting my bare backside on a letter to the bishop in Rome. I tugged open his robe to reveal the sparsely scattered hair that tapered to a dark line. "I think the pope can wait."

His lips trailed along my ribs, stopping to kiss the mole under my left breast and then lifting me onto his lap. "I think you're right."

I woke to dawn's rosy fingers creeping between the shutters. It took a moment to realize where I was, that the warmth I'd curled into during the night was not one of my children. I'd never woken next to a man before, but it was something I could grow accustomed to. Justinian's bare chest rose and fell, his face relaxed with sleep. He was a man it would be easy to love.

I shoved the thought away. Loving this man could only bring me ruin. I'd given Justinian my body, but not my heart. Never my heart. I'd learned that lesson too well already.

My borrowed stola made me shiver, my skin craving Justinian's warmth as I attempted to repin my hair before the gilded mirror.

"Where are you going?" Apparently Justinian excelled at faking sleep, his eyes still closed with one arm bent under his head.

"Home."

He rose from bed in one smooth movement, his body deliciously bare, and pushed the black rope of hair over my shoulder to kiss the nape of my neck. "Stay a little longer?"

Already my body started to react, that heat like wine flooding through my blood. "I can't."

I thought I caught a momentary flash of annoyance, but then his face relaxed. He looked at my reflection in the mirror. "Tasia."

I nodded.

He let my hair fall and wrapped his arms around my waist. "I'll have Narses set up a room for you."

My fingers fumbled with the cheap clasp on my brooch. "What?"

"He can arrange for your things to be brought over today."

"You want me to move here?"

"Unless you don't want to." Justinian took the brooch from my shaking hands and pinned it at my shoulder.

I managed to keep breathing. "You're too loose with your purse, temperamental as a goat, and smell like an inkpot. Why would I want to live with you?"

"Asks the woman with a temper like an ill-behaved mule." Justinian chuckled and stepped back as if to give me space. "It's your decision, Theodora, but as I said, I don't intend to let you go now that I've caught you. I'll bribe you with sausage to keep you here if I have to."

"And Tasia?"

"There's an old nursery that can be arranged for Tasia. And her mangy kitten. I'll hire tutors to teach her Ptolemy, Plato, and Aristotle—she'll receive an education worthy of a prince." Justinian tucked a curl behind my ear. "And I can help you arrange a good marriage for her when she's old enough."

A marriage for Tasia, but not for me. Antonina's warning filled my mind.

"I'm sorry she's not a boy."

"Why?"

I wanted to look away. "I'm sure you'd prefer I bring a son into your house."

Justinian looked at me so closely I was sure he could see the lie in my heart. "A son of yours would complicate matters."

"How so?"

"My succession is not entirely secure. I've arranged for the Emperor's other nephew, Germanus, to take up the magistrate of Thraciae so he's conveniently out of town when the question arises." He glanced at me, pausing as if choosing his words. "However, a son of yours would not be popular with the Senate."

"Because of who I was."

"No, because it would be best if the future line to the throne is straight." He splashed his face with water from a bronze basin and shrugged into a brown tunica. "I don't care about your past, Theodora. I plan to make you a powerful woman."

That piqued my interest, but I felt guilty for even contemplating the idea. "Powerful?"

"Beyond your wildest dreams." He kissed me, but my mind was so full I scarcely noticed. "I'll see you tonight."

My daughter's future secure. One of the Empire's most influential men in my bed. Yet how could I sacrifice one child for the other?

Chapter 19

"Who is he?" Antonina asked, arms akimbo. I'd rather be flayed alive than tell Antonina I was sleeping with the future Emperor. I didn't care to listen to a fresh tirade on my stupidity—I was well versed in the subject.

I hadn't gone straight home after leaving the Palace of Hormisdas, but I barely managed to duck into the Church of the Holy Apostles before I started sobbing. The sleeves and neck of my stola were drenched before I could lift my head long enough to look around. The Virgin stared at me from a delicate gold reliquary box set into the side chapel.

"How could you do this to me, Mary?" I wiped the snot from my nose as the tears started afresh. "What kind of mother has to choose between her children?" My raised voice brought a priest running, but one look at me sent him scuttling away.

I drew a ragged breath and crossed myself, glaring at the Virgin's serene face. She held the Christ Child on her lap, and both were lit with halos of divine light. God had sacrificed His Son, but so too had Mary lost her child. Surely she knew what path I should take. Leaving

Tasia had been hard enough, but now to abandon John? What kind of mother was I to even think of doing such a thing?

But perhaps my choice needn't be forever; I might be able to tell Justinian the truth later. Life threatened only never-ending drudgery for all of us if I rejected his offer, but it offered golden opportunities if I accepted him as my patron, even if it was only for a short time before he tired of me. A marriage for Tasia. Her education. The chance to live with one of the most intelligent, interesting men I'd ever met. I'd be able to send money to Antonina to pay for John's education. These were opportunities I'd be a fool to ignore.

"Am I making the right choice?" I searched Mary's face for an answer, but she continued to gaze at her Son, the smallest hint of a smile on her lips.

And so I made up my mind and left the church, hoping one day my son might forgive me.

I closed my trunk and glanced at Antonina. "You'll find out who he is soon enough." I motioned to John, and he toddled over, his rhinoceros horn of hair as spiky as ever. "Be a good boy for Auntie Nina, all right?"

My son was scarcely two—memories of me would shift like quicksilver and be easily replaced. He nodded, and I pulled him into my arms, covering his little face with kisses until he laughed and the tears slipped from my eyes. "You can send letters to my old address—they might take a few days to get to me." I'd sold one of the silver bangles the Cappadocian had sent this morning, accompanied with a letter telling me of his current travels. If he ever returned, I could claim I'd never received them. The money paid the landlord through the end of the year so I could exchange word with Antonina about John. And have a place to go when Justinian threw me out.

I took the other silver bangle from my arms and pressed it into Antonina's hands. "I'll send money as soon as I tell him—"

"John will be fine. It will probably take Timothy at least a month to realize he's even there. I might even be able to convince him he's forgotten siring the mite." She chuckled but fell serious when she saw my face. "Don't worry, Theodora. You came back for Tasia, didn't you, and look how well that turned out."

I made as hasty an exit as I could, sparing a kiss for my angel. My heart cried for him as it had when I'd left Tasia, but this time I wouldn't be at the ends of the earth, but in the same city as my son, securing his future.

At least that was what I told myself.

It poured one night a week later, spring thunder growling in the distance and the occasional flash of lightning streaking the sky to illuminate Justinian's chambers. I marveled at how perfectly our bodies fit together, how I could happily spend eternity wrapped in his arms.

I was less than amused when he sat up and shrugged a tunica over his head. I patted the empty space next to me. "Work will wait until tomorrow."

He held a hand out to me. "Come with me."

I sat up and pulled the sheet to my chin. "Where?"

"Outside."

"It's raining."

He chuckled. "You're afraid of a little lightning?"

"No. I'd just rather not get drenched."

"I promise to warm you up afterward."

I pursed my lips but slipped my wrinkled stola back over my head. "This had better be good."

The warm needles of rain made me gasp. Justinian covered me with his body, his breath warm on my ear. "You have no idea how happy you make me, Theodora."

"We can be happy inside." I tried to shield my eyes, but it was no use against the onslaught. Thunder rumbled in the distance. He clasped my hand to stop me from leaving, and pulled something from the pocket of his tunica. At first I couldn't quite make out what he held, it was so small, but then a flash of lightning illuminated the shape.

A gold ring with his insignia pressed into the metal.

I gasped, and for a moment the rain seemed to stop, the tapering droplets like fragments of stars slowly falling to earth.

"I commissioned a marriage belt in your size to match this," he said. The rain crashed down again so rivulets of water ran down his nose, his hair plastered to his head. "Will you marry me, Theodora?"

Impossible. This man couldn't possibly want to marry me. And then I remembered—

"Don't toy with me." I stepped out of his arms. "You couldn't marry me even if you wanted to. The law forbids it."

"In case you hadn't noticed, I'm in a fairly good position to change a law or two."

"Only the Emperor can overturn the law. And he may not want his heir marrying a woman like—"

"Like what?"

"Like me. I'm an actress, a pleb. I have a daughter—" My voice broke as I thought of my son. This man was offering me the world with an open heart, and I'd already deceived him.

Justinian caressed my wet cheek with one hand. "I don't care what anyone thinks. I love you, and I want to marry you."

I wanted to say yes, to throw caution to the sky and let myself fall in love with this man. To become his wife. But I could only shake my head.

"I'll say it again." He pulled me to him. "I want to marry you. I want you to sit beside me on the throne and tell me when I'm spending too much money, to grow old with you and bicker about what socks I'm to wear and which monuments to build to ourselves." He tipped my chin back so I could see his eyes, the edges glimmering with gold and rimmed with wet lashes. "I love you, and I want to spend the rest of my life with you."

I swallowed hard, glad for the rain that hid the tears streaming down my cheeks. There was another rumble of thunder as I spoke, one bittersweet word that might torment me for the rest of my days.

"Yes."

Justinian moved to sweep me into his arms, but I skittered away. "Under one condition."

"Anything."

"We tell no one until your uncle has given his consent." I held up my hand to stop his protest. "I won't jeopardize your position as heir."

"That's really your concern?"

One of many, but I nodded.

He kissed my knuckles. "Then I'll simply have to persuade my uncle to change the law."

My fingers closed around his, locking the ring in his fist. He'd keep his ring, and I'd keep my heart until possibility became reality.

Until then, it couldn't hurt to dream.

"They say you've bewitched the consul with black magic." Narses leaned against a table as slaves laid out a tray of cured ham and sweet melon to break my fast. I'd risen early, but Justinian had already gone, so I had spent the first rays of sunlight reading a letter from Antonina. She reported that John had fallen from the top of her stairway while playing King of the Mountain. He was fine, but Antonina had been there to kiss the goose egg on his head instead of me.

"If I knew black magic, I'd have used it years ago." I let the flame of an oil lamp devour the letter and ignored Narses' watchful eye. I was almost certain he knew of Justinian's proposal. I'd developed a grudging appreciation for the eunuch—he had thrown his lot in with me, so it only seemed fair.

A slave swept a vivid blue *paludamentum* around my shoulders and pinned it with a lapis bird perched on a gold needle. I let another slave massage my feet before stepping into calfskin slippers soft as butter.

Narses scrutinized me. "I'll arrange for Justinian to order some emeralds for tonight's dinner here with the Emperor."

I choked on air. "Dinner with the Emperor?"

He folded his arms in front of him, his face a mask. "Emperor Justin wishes to meet you. I'm sure you were informed of the dinner days ago."

I threw a slipper at him, but he dodged it. "You know you didn't tell me. Neither did Justinian."

Narses picked up the slipper and dangled it before me. "No point worrying you—we don't want you to come down with indigestion."

"Would that get me out of the meal?"

"I imagine not. The Emperor will be joined by Empress Lupicina and Justinian's sister, Vigilantia."

"May as well crucify me now." I sighed, then brightened. "Empress Lupicina comes from humble beginnings." That was putting it mildly for a barbarian whore who'd taken up with a swineherd before he bought the Emperor's diadem. "She can't look too far down her nose at me."

"If you say so." Narses reached into his pocket and retrieved an ivory box the size of a fig. "You'll want this."

"What is it?"

He pushed open the top to reveal an image of the Virgin Mary in flowing blue robes and surrounded by delicate gold filigree. "I believe you and I share an affinity for the Virgin."

I took the prayer box, marveling at the detail of Mary's face and wishing I could manage the same tranquility. My voice sounded like it hadn't been used in some time. "Thank you, Narses."

"You're welcome." He twisted the tip of his beard and gave a sardonic grin. "You need her help tonight far more than I do."

I glared, but he was right.

I prayed to the little icon of the Virgin in a hazy fog of incense, then spent the remainder of the afternoon preparing for dinner—bathed, plucked, massaged, and oiled like an Easter goose. My body shone like Cleopatra's before she met Marc Antony at Tarsus.

By the time Justinian entered my chambers, I was naked to allow the rose oil to absorb into my skin, and a silk stola the color of new leaves waited on my bed.

"Waiting for me, I see." Justinian twirled a strand of my hair around his finger, then kissed the thin black strand.

"What mischief have you been up to this afternoon?" I asked.

His smile told me he was clearly up to no good. "I had an important errand. You'll find out soon enough."

I let him continue down his path—his touch made me suddenly warm. "I spent my afternoon preparing for the Emperor."

"His heart might fail if you don't put some clothes on."

I shot Justinian a pointed look, and he cleared his throat. "I see Narses told you about tonight—"

"I haven't decided on your punishment yet." I kissed his nose and pointed to the waterfall of green silk cascading to the foot of my bed. Justinian fetched it and slipped the cool material over my head. "Don't worry—I plan to be magnificent."

I held my arms out for slaves to drape me with an emerald *chlamys* so long that its ends tickled the nose of a mosaic lion underfoot, then pinned pearls to the silk veil tucked over my hair. I had forgone the offer of Justinian's jewels—at my neck was only Severus' amber cross, but even my sandals were studded with pearls.

I could grow accustomed to such luxuries.

Justinian and I waited for our guests in the atrium as the horizon swallowed the sun. Tasia fidgeted next to me, her hair brushed until it matched the silk of her stola and a new gold cat brooch with emerald eyes pinned at her shoulder. I'd spoiled her with enough gifts and trinkets for more than two children since we'd moved into the palace. Trinkets and baubles couldn't make up for our lost years and her brother's absence, but it was a welcome change to be able to buy her whatever my heart desired.

Justinian's sister arrived first, her ebony sedan so tastefully carved it might have passed for a merchant's litter. Vigilantia took a slave's outstretched hand and stepped down, a female version of her brother with his thick mane of dark hair. A well-dressed boy with scuffed knees trailed behind her and skidded to a stop before Justinian with a succinct bow.

"Hello, Justin." Justinian ruffled the boy's hair and brandished a carved ivory soldier from his pocket. I felt a knife of grief that my son wasn't here, that Justinian wasn't able to talk to him as he did his nephew. "Your mother tells me you've been learning about military battles from the Golden Age. Which is your favorite?"

The boy's face lit with delight as he clutched the toy soldier. "Julius Caesar crossing the Rubicon."

"I like the Trojan War," Tasia piped up. "Especially the part with the Amazons."

"Both excellent battles." Justinian winked at Tasia and gave his nephew's shoulder a warm squeeze. "I believe this young lady has a fierce little patchwork lion as an accomplice, so watch out once you're inside."

"Yes, Uncle," Justin said.

Tasia gave a little grin and scampered inside, then stopped and ran back to me. She threw her arms around my hips. "I love you, Mama."

"I love you, too, sweet pea." My voice was husky as I kissed the top of her head.

A slave girl waited for Vigilantia to kiss her son's cheek, then herded the children off as Justin scrubbed away the imprint of his mother's hennaed lips with the sleeve of his tunica.

"Justinian." Vigilantia kissed his cheek and turned to me. No one would call the woman pretty with her thick neck and square jaw, but her face was kind. "You must be Theodora. You're a brave woman to take on all the family at once."

"Morituri te salutant," I said. *We who are about to die salute you.* It was the salute of condemned prisoners from the Golden Age.

Justinian choked and Vigilantia stared at me; then the jangling of the gold discs at her ears joined her laughter. "I like her, Brother. I only hope they don't eat her alive."

Justinian squeezed my hand. "I'd certainly prefer to save the slaves the mess on the mosaics."

"You'll be fine," Vigilantia said. "Our aunt believes Justinian walks on water."

Justinian chuckled into the cool air. "That's what I like my women to think." Vigilantia and I rolled our eyes at each other, then laughed, but the racket at the gate made my heart stutter. The royal entourage.

One hundred servants and slaves preceded the imperial sedan, blaring horns and tossing violet petals on the cobbles. Two slaves scrambled to open the doors of the gilded litter while more scurried to lay a carpet of new silk from the litter to where we waited. The Emperor emerged, the gold *torques* blindingly bright on his chest, followed by Empress Lupicina. Her plumage tonight was more gaudy than usual, a terrifying assortment of garnets, rubies, and carnelian that would have sent any self-respecting peacock into hiding.

Things fell apart from the start.

I shared Justinian's *lectus* as slaves labored to carry gilded trays to the roof so we could enjoy the view of the Sea of Marmara. The last of the sun's dying light turned the water to molten gold as pelicans swooped and dove into the harbor. I'd barely had time to peruse the menu this morning, but now I watched a parade of baked apricots oozing goat cheese and flecked with cinnamon, roast boar stomach stuffed with Lucanian sausages, and the delicacy of pale blue starling eggs served in their nests. Justinian served me himself, letting his fingers brush my hand every so often.

Vigilantia leaned toward me as the wine was measured and poured and more torches were lit. "I've never seen Justinian so besotted," she murmured into her cup. "It's about time my brother found a woman to match him."

I didn't have a chance to answer. Old Justin interrupted us as a slave cut a quivering bite of boar stomach, nibbled a piece from the point of his knife, and set the plate before the Emperor. "How do you like the Palace of Hormisdas, Theodora?"

Slaves presented golden plates of baked red mullet for each of us. I'd never have guessed I'd dine on fish like those from Justin's old pond, fattened on bread crumbs and tickled every day by slaves with nothing better to do.

The mullet's bones crunched between my teeth. "The palace is very comfortable," I said.

"Certainly more comfortable than a bench in a back room of the Kynêgion," Lupicina muttered under her breath, so loud we could all hear. Her husband squeezed her hand and sent me an apologetic look.

"As you would know," I said.

Lupicina sputtered, and Vigilantia grinned into her *mappa*.

"Try the boar." Justinian served the meat onto my plate as if he hadn't heard me, but I saw the smile tugging his lips. "It's delicious."

I'd anticipated trouble from the wrong corner. Vigilantia tried to draw the Empress into conversation about the recent chariot races, but Lupicina only pursed her lips and glowered at me over her starling eggs.

My mouth was full when a slave delivered a large blue silk bag to Justinian. He pushed it across the couch to me. I arched an eyebrow, but he only smiled. "Open it."

The bag itself was a gift, embroidered with gold clovers so tiny that sparrows might have stitched it. I gasped at what was inside.

Red sandals. The red sandals of a *kyria*.

I could barely speak. "You didn't."

Justinian shrugged, taking another bite of apricot as if he'd only handed me another helping of boar. "I delivered the parchment and lead seals proclaiming your elevation to the patrician class to the offices below the Hippodrome this afternoon."

So that was where he'd been.

"You can't do that!" Lupicina's face was red as the mullet on her plate. Vigilantia sat back on her *lectus* as if ready to enjoy a show.

The Emperor shifted on his couch as if sitting atop a bed of thorns. "Actually, my dear, it is well within a consul's jurisdiction to elevate any worthy citizen to the rank of patrician."

Justinian looked at his aunt rather matter-of-factly. "It seemed only fitting that I make Theodora a patrician. That way I can marry her."

I narrowly avoided spewing boar across the garden. Lupicina was not so restrained.

"You can't marry her," she screeched. "She's a whore!"

Her reaction was enough to make me want to shout my acceptance to Justinian's proposal from the palace rooftop.

Her husband patted her hand. "As were you, my dear."

It was no mean feat that the Emperor didn't keel over and die with the look Lupicina leveled at him. "There is a law," she said.

Justinian scowled. "An antiquated law that serves no purpose."

"A man of senatorial rank, including a consul, cannot marry an actress even if she does become a patrician," Lupicina said, and crossed her arms in front of her, looking smug. "It is forbidden."

Justinian leaned back on his couch. "That's why I'd like the Emperor to change the law."

His uncle swallowed hard. I didn't envy him, stuck like Odysseus between Scylla and Charybdis. He looked to me and tugged the droopy lobe of one of his giant ears. "Would you be amenable to such a marriage?"

Lupicina threw her linen *mappa* to the ground. "Of course she's amenable! Then she'll wear the purple once we're dead. I won't have it!"

I wished someone would shove the *mappa* down her throat. "I aim to serve the Empire and God." Justinian coughed into his fist to cover his laugh. He knew by now that I served no one. I looked only at him. "I'd be honored to marry Justinian."

Justinian's eyes softened, and he quietly slipped the gold ring over my third finger. Vigilantia gave a little squeal of glee, and Lupicina glared at us with lips sewn shut. Her joints creaked as she knelt before Justinian's couch, clutched her nephew's hand in her own, spotted and gnarled with age. "Justinian, you have your choice of any girl in the realm, certainly one blessed with modesty and chastity, a *young* woman still pert of breast with more years to give you the heir you deserve."

The dried-up hag thought me *old*. I was only nineteen.

"You promised your support of whomever I chose to marry," Justinian said.

Lupicina snorted. "I had no idea you'd choose a washed-up theater tart."

Justinian's eyes narrowed. "Theodora has already proven herself capable of bearing my children. Her daughter lives in my palace."

"Her daughter by another man!" Lupicina's spittle dotted Justinian's brown silk tunica. "She's a whore!"

Justinian flew to his feet, his shadow cloaking his aunt. "Theodora has maintained her grace and dignity despite her past misfortunes. God has blessed her."

Lupicina sniffed. "God's blessing or not, you shan't marry her and sully our family's good name."

"Our good name?" Justinian laughed. "You were a whore, and my uncle herded swine!"

The Emperor rose and cleared his throat. "I fear I've come down with a case of indigestion," he said, threading his wife's arm through his. "A shame as I was rather looking forward to the goat's cream with orchid pollen. We'll have to continue this lovely dinner another time."

Justinian, Vigilantia, and I bowed as etiquette demanded. Lupicina's purple hem sailed past, and I barely resisted the urge to stick my foot out. I was surprised when the Emperor paused to clasp my hand. "It was lovely to meet you again, my dear." I glanced up to see him watching Lupicina stalk away. "Unfortunately, I'm afraid I'll have to bow to the Empress' wishes. It's safer for all of us that way."

He followed after his wife, but my skin prickled at Justinian's next words.

"She'll pay for that."

Chapter 20

A nest of goldfinches hatched, fledged, and finally abandoned their perch outside my window as Justinian pressured his uncle to repeal the law, but to no avail. Winter etched a pale layer of lacy frost over the clutch of lonely twigs, and a single downy feather trembled in the chilly breeze. Behind the tree, a pillar of black smoke climbed into the blue sky, somewhere near Marcian's Column. The same direction as Antonina's flat. Another black snake of smoke emerged from its den in Blachernae and writhed upward.

I rushed my morning prayers and hurried to find Justinian, but I found Narses first. "What's burning?" I asked.

He beckoned me past several crates of chickens to the kitchen. His voice was almost drowned out by the crackle of the cooking fire and the squawks of the birds waiting for a slave to snap their necks. "The city burns. For you."

The way he said it made it sound almost poetic. Almost, but not quite. "What?"

"Justinian has ordered the Blues to be—" He seemed to search for the right word. "Disorderly."

"Where is he?"

"On the roof."

Narses called after me, but I ignored him. The cold air braced me as I burst onto the roof terrace. Men swarmed Justinian. The color of their tunicas branded them as Blues, but they might have marched straight from the barbarian frontiers—unkempt beards hung to their chests in the Persian fashion, and their long cloaks, baggy trousers, and knee-high boots were positively Hunnic. All wore lethal-looking swords tucked into their belts.

Justinian saw me and dismissed the men—some gazes lingered too long in my direction, but I looked down my nose at them.

"Narses tells me you're up to no good," I said, gesturing in the direction of the smoke. The plumes continued to grow—I only wondered what the fires consumed.

"Putting pressure on my uncle."

So Narses was right. This was for me.

"By giving the Blues your blessing to wreak havoc?"

Justinian looked out toward his handiwork. The smoke continued to curl like flags of death across the sky. "We've been patient long enough."

I had to know my son was safe. And Antonina and her children. "What are they burning?"

"Empty storehouses." Justinian caught my grimace. "No one will be hurt. This is only enough chaos for my uncle to relent." He tucked a stray curl behind my ear. "Are you offended at such violence?"

I watched the black columns eat the sky. "Will this get us what we want?"

"Almost certainly."

"Then I'm not offended."

Justinian chuckled. "I had a feeling you wouldn't be."

The riots continued for days, gaining momentum as it became apparent no punishment would be meted out—the Emperor and the

Sacred Palace were both strangely silent. Citizens barred their doors and markets closed as protection against the marauders. Not to be outdone by their sworn enemies, the Greens joined pillaging, so flags of smoke unfurled like goal markers on a *tzykanion* field each time one of the factions made a point.

"This has to stop," I told Justinian from my hands and knees, peering up from the blades of brown grass and dormant rosebushes. I'd lost Severus' silver and amber cross and was furious at myself for being so careless, but even more troubled at the possible omen of losing God's favor as the city around me burned. "If your uncle hasn't given in by now—"

"These things take time." He looked at the hazy sky as if divining a message from God.

"I heard talk of a woman who died yesterday." Another bad omen. "You said no one would die."

"She was traveling from Chrysopolis to the mainland with her husband when the partisans intercepted them. They boarded the ship and asked the wife to join them. She jumped into the Bosphorus instead."

"Because she thought the Blues would attack her."

Justinian's mouth was set in a firm line as he nodded.

I brushed the dirt from my hands. "I'd have slit their throats instead." Still, I felt a twinge of guilt. I wanted to marry Justinian, but the cost was high enough already.

"I don't doubt it." He helped me to my feet. "I have something for you." He pulled a delicate silver chain from his pocket, thin as a thread of silk. Hanging from the bottom was my amber cross.

"Where did you find it?" I moved to grab it, but he dangled it out of reach.

"Hanging from a rose branch." He held up his battered hands. "I had to comb through half the bushes before I found it."

I caught the familiar inscription as Justinian clasped the necklace around my neck.

Let love and faithfulness never leave you; bind them around your neck, write them on the tablet of your heart.

I loved this man, and I would be faithful to him until the end of my days. Despite my best intentions, he'd captured my heart.

"I don't deserve you," I said.

His fingers traced the silver chain, then dipped lower as his lips grazed my throat. My stola slipped from my shoulder just as Narses burst into the garden.

"Narses." Justinian's growl could have stopped a lion at twenty paces, but the eunuch only gave him a perfunctory bow.

"Empress Lupicina is dead," he said, straightening and crossing himself.

A flock of sparrows swarming a bare apricot tree took flight, leaving a blanket of cold silence over the garden.

"May God rest her soul." A look of triumph flickered over Justinian's face, so quick I doubted its existence. I shivered as I straightened my stola.

"How did the Empress die?" I asked.

Narses glanced at Justinian and back to me. "She was seized with a fit at dinner."

Neither of us spoke as Narses' steps echoed down the stairs, but then Justinian cleared his throat. "I must go to my uncle, offer my condolences."

"Of course." I'd half expected him to admit he'd had Lupicina strangled at the table or arranged a dash of wolfsbane to spice her dinner. I almost dared ask but swallowed the question.

"Be ready to leave within the hour," he said, his *paludamentum* billowing in the breeze.

I contemplated assuming the full regalia of grief—plucking out my hair and wearing a black stola torn by my own hands—but decided a black wool tunica and wearing my hair loose were sufficient. I made sure the tunica wasn't quite long enough to hide my red sandals Lupicina had so vehemently protested.

My teeth jarred as broad-shouldered slaves carried Justinian's sedan through the streets, the people parting like the Red Sea before Moses to let us through.

I'd envisioned my first visit to the Sacred Palace amongst some sort of celebration or feast day, perhaps even my wedding. Instead, a heavy silence enfolded the white marble like a tomb for the living, its colossal porphyry pillars swathed in black silk. At the Chalke, the huge main gate topped with a gilded domed chapel, massive bronze doors engraved with giant crosses swung open. Guards fell into line behind us as we trod over more gold than King Herod might have possessed. The exquisite mosaics depicted an elephant impaling a lion, a plebian mother breastfeeding her infant, and a trained monkey knocking figs from a tree with a stick. Stern-faced statues lined the reception halls, some reputedly able to predict the future. We passed a library of silent scribes laboring over manuscripts, likely copies of treaties and missives from foreign rulers, before stopping outside the throne room. The ebony doors were open, and inside under a canopy of leafy golden trees with birds of hammered gold sat the Emperor, two gilded lion statues at his feet. I knew from Justinian that the creatures were mechanical, brought to life through the power of hidden water wheels, but today the beasts were cold and lifeless despite the winter sunlight streaming through the clerestory windows. The Emperor glanced up at our approach, his cheeks streaked with dried riverbeds of tears. I felt no grief for Lupicina, but my eyes filled for Justin. We can't help whom we love.

"Justinian." The old man held out his hand as his rheumy eyes focused on me. "Theodora."

I bowed as Justinian kissed his uncle's ring. "We've come to offer our condolences."

"It was all so sudden. I keep expecting Lupicina to walk through the door and yell at me for being late for a meeting with my ministers. Or missing my bath." The old man's lower lip trembled. "I'm lost without her."

We spent the afternoon in the throne room, the movement of the patches of thin sunlight telling time as the Emperor regaled us with tales of his Empress. His voice grew younger when he recalled seeing her for the first time, and watching her win a tussle with another taverna maid for the pleasure of attending to an up-and-coming young general. It was easier to like this version of Lupicina, especially now that the glowering old version was being prepared for her imperial sarcophagus.

Justinian called for wool blankets and a fire in the brazier as the room grew chill. He played the attentive nephew, but I still wondered if he had been the instrument of his uncle's grief.

Finally, the horizon swallowed the sun, and the Emperor unfolded his ancient limbs to stand. "Thank you for listening to the rambles of an old man." He laid his hand first on my head and then on Justinian's. "I know we haven't all seen eye to eye lately."

"About that, Uncle." Justinian pulled a tiny codex from the folds of his robe. "I hoped you might be willing to sign this, to allow me a taste of the happiness you shared all these years."

The Emperor squinted to make out the text inside the leather covers. "I assume this seeks to abolish the old law forbidding you from marrying an actress?"

"You assume correctly."

"And if I won't sign?"

Justinian shrugged. "I can't be held responsible for what the Blues do next."

His uncle's lips almost disappeared, but then he looked to me. "Your betrothed doesn't fight fair."

Justinian cleared his throat. "Now might also be a good time to discuss our sharing the throne, Uncle."

The Emperor blew a puff of air between chapped lips. "You won't wear the purple until I'm moldering in my grave. Maybe not even then. This foolishness with the Blues—"

"Do you really want to follow in Anastasius' footsteps when you have the power to secure our dynasty right now?"

"I won't name you as my heir until I'm sure you're the best choice to succeed me. This recent—unpleasantness—has made me doubt your capabilities as ruler. Perhaps Germanus—"

"Germanus is a fool, and you well know it." Justinian's fingers thrummed against his knee. "I'm the best choice. My last impediment to the throne will be removed once Theodora and I are married."

I stared at Justinian.

Without a wife, Justinian would be seen as a risk to the Senate and the people, a man who didn't value family and without the potential for a legal heir. And as he'd said before, I'd already proven I was fertile.

I thought the man loved me. Wanted *me*. Instead, I was only a means to an end. Doubt pressed into my mind and made it difficult to think. Perhaps it might be best if we weren't allowed to marry—

"Give it to me." The Emperor waggled his fingers, and Justinian produced a wooden stylus and tiny bottle of ink. His uncle painstakingly scrawled four letters on the parchment. I recognized the single word from long ago. *LEGI.*

I had thought to feel overjoyed at realizing I could now marry Justinian, but I felt only a heavy numbness instead. Justinian wasn't the man I'd believed him to be this morning.

"I'm tired." The Emperor handed the stylus to Justinian and waved him away before beckoning to me. "Walk me to my bed, child."

"It would be an honor."

He glanced back at Justinian and pulled a sour face. "It's unfortunate I can't trade you for that nephew of mine." He shuffled along beside me, a decided drag to his left foot.

"Is your leg all right, Augustus?"

"You may as well call me Uncle." He harrumphed and patted my arm, his hand mottled with thick blue veins. "An old wound."

The smell of myrrh wafted from the chamber next to his—presumably Lupicina's. Her state funeral would be tomorrow morning, as quickly as possible to avoid decay.

"Augustus, may I ask how the Empress passed?"

His eyes snapped open and looked as if they might fill again.

"I'm sorry." I couldn't very well tell him my suspicions, but I needed to set my mind at ease about Justinian's involvement. "I was just curious."

"It was at dinner. Her stomach was upset, and she was tired. Halfway through the leek soup, she vomited. Then she couldn't breathe." He looked up at the bed hangings but closed his eyes. "She died in my arms."

Such symptoms might have been from an illness. Or poison. At least she wasn't alone when she passed. Not even Lupicina deserved to die alone.

I dared to lay my hand on his. "I'm sure having you there was a great comfort to her."

Eunuchs formed a circle around Justin so he could disrobe, and then I helped the Emperor into his massive bed and tucked thick cotton sheets under his legs. A eunuch pressed a steaming mug into his hands—poppy tea from the sweet smell of it.

"May God bless you with a restful sleep," I said.

"And may He bless you with many fruitful years." The Emperor's eyes had a hard time focusing. "I hope you know what you're getting into with my nephew. Justinian has always been fiercely loyal to those he loves, at least until he feels betrayed."

Justinian had used me as a stepping-stone to the throne, and I now suspected him of murdering the aunt who'd betrayed him. It seemed

I didn't really know the man I thought to marry. Nor did I know how he'd react when he realized that I, too, had betrayed him.

"A man must be forgiving," the Emperor continued, "especially to those he loves. I wish he'd found it in him to forgive his aunt before she—" Justin choked, and a tear leaked from the corner of his eye.

I dared touch the Emperor's cheek. "You should rest. The Empress wouldn't want you to mourn her passing."

Justin gave a wry chuckle. "Of course she would. Lupicina was nothing if not vain." Slaves released the silk bed curtains and doffed most of the oil lamps. Justin heaved a deep sigh and settled into his pillows. "Think about what I've said, Theodora. Great things may await you with Justinian. But so might great heartache."

Perhaps I should heed Justin's warning, before it was too late.

Chapter 21

Justinian didn't waste any time making good on his uncle's word—he planned to marry after the winter solstice, only a few weeks away. Our palace was overrun by day with milliners, bakers, and jewelers. I briefly toyed with the idea of taking his uncle's advice, of getting out with my heart mostly intact, to take the road to safety for the first time in my life.

But Justinian continued to dote on me, not to mention Tasia. Not only that, but I wanted to one day see my face on the bronze weights in the market, to feel the purple *chalmys* draped over my shoulders. I wanted to be Empress.

Then, one night Justinian didn't come to me.

I was alone in my apartments, the Gospels that Severus had given me forgotten in my lap as I dozed at my window. There was a terrible crick in my neck, and my oil lamp had burned out; yet a faint yellow glow bled from Justinian's window into the dark night.

I padded to the door between our chambers and listened. There was silence, and then I heard Justinian. And another voice. I'd learned my lesson from Hecebolus and could tolerate much from Justinian until I wore his wedding belt around my waist. Yet the thought of him with someone else gave me the urge to throw something terribly expensive. I promised myself not to light another bed on fire—that hadn't worked in my favor last time.

I pushed the door open, prepared for the worst. Justinian sat in his bed, unshaven and bare-chested with Narses and a bearded man in black robes at his side. None of the men looked happy to see me.

"Darling," Justinian said, "what are you still doing up?"

"I might ask you the same thing."

Narses gave me a minute shake of his head, then passed a finger before his lips in a gesture for my silence. "I'll help Theodora back to her rooms."

"It's all right," Justinian said. "She can stay. You should get some sleep, Narses. It's been a long night."

"I'm happy to stay until you no longer require my assistance," Narses said.

Justinian smiled. "I no longer require your assistance. Get some sleep."

Narses looked about to protest, then clamped his lips shut and bowed to Justinian. He paused as he swept past me. "Be nice," he growled.

"I'm always nice," I hissed.

He rolled his eyes and quietly shut the door.

"Saint Samson was seeing to my humors," Justinian told me. "It seems I have an imbalance of blood and yellow bile."

This I hadn't expected. I'd heard of Samson, Constantinople's legendary healer, but the fact that he'd been called for Justinian was more troubling than reassuring. "Is everything all right?"

"Everything is fine."

"You're a terrible liar."

He shrugged. "One of my few faults."

The saint tucked his wooly brown beard over his shoulder and packed up his trunk, but he paused to murmur to Justinian. I strained my ears and caught the words "blood in the seed."

The door closed, but the antiseptic scent of thyme and burdock remained. I perched next to Justinian on the bed. Even in this light he looked pale under the stubble on his jaw, his eyes glassy with fever. "Are you sure you're all right?"

"I'll be fine with the help of Saint Samson's herbs. Although I'm only allowed to eat chickpeas, dates, and pine kernels for the next two days." He grimaced and managed a weak smile, but then his face cracked and he sighed. "There's something else, Theodora."

I waited, trying not to wring my hands. I sat on them.

"My uncle had this same illness before he met Lupicina," Justinian said. "And I had it as a boy."

I stared at him blankly. "I'm not sure what you mean."

Justinian sighed and shifted in his bed. "As we all know, my aunt and uncle's union never bore fruit." He ran his hands through his hair, mussing the dark curls so they stuck out in all directions. The corner of his mouth quirked. "I was no saint before you, Theodora. There weren't many women, but there were enough."

Suddenly I understood and found myself desperately wishing I didn't. "But no children," I said.

"But no children. Samson claims it's a common pattern he's noticed with this illness."

"He told you that?"

"He told Narses," Justinian said. "Narses told me."

He covered my hands with his, his bronzed from the sun and stained with ink, mine pale as a summer flower and weighted down with his gold ring. "The fact of the matter, Theodora, is that I may never be able to give you a child."

The world grew dark, but I managed not to let terror overtake me. What use could Justinian have for me if not to conceive his heir?

"Can you still—" I withdrew my hands and made a little motion.

He gave a wry chuckle. "Don't worry. I'll still be chasing you around the bedchamber when you're seventy."

I laughed, but the sound was hollow. "Then it doesn't matter."

He sobered. "It matters to me."

Of course it did—he had to have an heir. The Sacred Palace contained a special room decorated in porphyry and hung with purple silk reserved specifically for imperial births. I wanted children born in the purple. "Is there any chance at all?"

His face clouded over. "I suppose it's possible."

But not likely. I almost wished he hadn't told me.

"Are you sure you still wish to marry me if—"

He grunted and tucked me into his arms, smelling of an herb garden. "You foolish little imp. What do I have to do to convince you that I love you?" He kissed my hair and tipped my chin up so I had to look at him. "Perhaps this is God's way of telling us the world is ill-prepared for the offspring from the likes of us."

I chuckled, although the sound came out strangled. "There might be something I can do to help."

"And what might that be?"

"There are ways to prevent pregnancies—I'm sure there are ways to encourage your seed to take root."

"Ways?"

"Herbs, potions." I said the last word slowly. Justinian had publicly condemned the black arts as consul, but I suspected he might be willing to indulge in them privately if it gave him a chance at a son. I smiled. "And, of course, different positions."

He raised his eyebrows and grinned so the corners of his eyes crinkled. "I like the sound of that last one."

"I thought you might." My tongue teased his in a long kiss. "Care to try one right now?"

He groaned, then winced. "I want to, I do, but—"

I pulled back. "When you're ready."

He crushed me to him. "God, but I love you, Theodora."

I still wasn't sure I believed him, but for this man, I was willing to take the chance. I laid my head on his shoulder and closed my eyes.

"And I love you."

I took the fertility tinctures Narses procured for me in the market—evening primrose and flaxseed oil, rabbit blood and goose fat. At first they made me gag, but I learned to hold my breath and gulp them down. More enjoyable were the variety of ways Justinian found to make love to me—each more creative than the next.

As a final effort, I traveled across the Bosphorus to visit a different saint in the hopes he might bless my womb. Saint Alypius was an ancient ascetic who had stood the past thirty years atop a lonely column, exposed to the elements amid the ruins of an old church. He was in the midst of prayers as I approached, arms outstretched like a cross of flesh and blood as the wind whipped the long white banners of his hair and beard. Behind him, the Bosphorus shone through a row of bleached and broken columns. Pilgrims claimed the sweet smell of paradise wafted from the saint, but the scent reminded me more of years of accumulated filth.

My attendants stood in the shade of a laurel tree as I waited for Alypius to finish his prayers, the wind and sun beating upon me. His voice was startling, smooth and rich with the cadence of youth: "Women are not allowed to approach the pillar. If we are worthy, we shall meet in the life to come."

Alypius had forbidden his own mother to visit him—the poor woman had died without seeing her son for almost three decades. I wasn't about to be repulsed by a monk in need of a bath. "I come to beg your help."

"Let me guess—you've come to beg Alypius to bless your womb." He eyed me as if I were vermin.

"Consul Justinian needs an heir."

A boy with scabbed knees and a wooden pail of frothy goat milk scampered up Alypius' pillar, presenting the ascetic with the milk and a piece of flat bread retrieved from his pocket. The little monkey clambered down, but I stopped him before he could disappear. Alypius stared down at us, crumbs falling from his mouth as a pigeon landed at his feet. "The One True God shall tend to this unworthy Empire."

That was all well and good, but not what I'd asked for. "It is imperative I give the consul an heir."

"Almighty God shall watch the Empire in victory and defeat."

The man was as helpful as a granite wall. "So you will not pray for us?"

"I have not prayed for a Monophysite in all my years on this earth," Alypius said. "I shall not endanger my soul by starting now, especially for one who sells the holy vessel of her body."

Anger pulsed at my temples, but I couldn't very well rage against a saint. I could, but I doubted Justinian or God would look kindly upon me—they were the only two men I cared about.

I pressed a silk pouch into the boy's hand. "Please give this to Saint Alypius." I'd asked Justinian for the gift before I'd left, thinking the saint might require some persuasion.

Alypius opened the bag and stared at me, then spilled the contents into his gnarled hand and looked at me as if I'd just offered him a bag of asps. Gold coins rained upon my head. "May your gift be damned as you are!"

I turned on my heel, walking over the tiny gold cobbles. "Keep the coins," I called over my shoulder. "Found a monastery or the like."

Cursed by a holy man. Yet another item to add to my list of accomplishments.

The morning of our marriage dawned clear and cold, and I awoke to find my monthly courses upon me. Not the most auspicious sign.

I spent the first moments of daylight writing a letter to Severus, something I hadn't done since Justinian began courting me, telling him of my marriage and asking for his blessing. Severus was the closest thing I had to a father, and I wished he could be at my wedding today. I set aside the letter and my morose thoughts as an army of giggling slave girls entered my chambers, armed with glistening silks, glittering jewels, and jars of pomade and perfumes.

Hours passed before they finally let me see myself in the mirror. My stola was a deep red, only one step from the imperial purple, embroidered with the letters of my *tablion*, and a thin hemp rope knotted at my waist for luck. The brooches on my shoulders glittered with rubies, and pearl earrings dripped from my ears to graze my shoulders. A saffron veil covered my hair, thin as a cobweb and dotted with tiny seed pearls like morning dew.

Imperial messengers had brought word of droughts in Palestine and floods in Ephesus, so we'd decided to curtail the extravagant wedding ceremony. Despite my elevation to the nobility, a number of patricians had voiced their concerns at the repeal of the old law. They'd looked down their long Roman noses and called me a leech, an opportunist, and a harlot. I'd heard worse. Narses had provided me with a list of their names—they'd soon find their taxes went up in direct proportion to their insults.

The people on the streets paused as my litter passed—Justinian had gone ahead of me, and quite a crowd had braved the chill of the morning. A fishwife with a swarm of filthy children stopped her brood and barked at them to bow, but one of the boys raised his grimy fist and yelled, *"Nika!"*

Victory.

No matter what color my sandals, I was a pleb like them, and one day I'd wear the purple. God did indeed work in strange ways.

I passed the twelve stone sheep outside the Hagia Sophia, one for each of the apostles, and spared a moment to pray to the Virgin.

"Bless this union," I whispered. "Let Justinian be faithful, and help me serve and obey him." I smiled into the clouds. "Although I won't fault you if that last request proves impossible."

Justinian waited for me at the altar, shrouded in the flickering light of hundreds of tiny oil lamps, and strikingly handsome in a black tunica woven with gold and silver thread. A gold mosaic of the Virgin and the Christ Child looked down on us with placid gazes as a handful of Justinian's friends and advisers looked on. Belisarius and Tribonium stood to the side of the altar with several of Justinian's other advisers, but I felt a pang of sadness to realize I had no family save Tasia to witness this happy day. Most of my family was buried outside the city walls, John was with Antonina, and Comito had chosen to ignore my presence in the city.

Justinian squeezed my hand as Patriarch Epiphanios—a new prelate chosen by the Emperor and not the corrupt windbag who'd once arrested me—recited Corinthians in flawless Greek.

"'Love suffers long and is kind. Love does not parade itself, is not arrogant or rude, does not seek its own, thinks no evil; does not rejoice in iniquity, but rejoices in the truth. Love bears all things, believes all things, hopes all things, endures all things.

"'Love does not fail.'"

Love does not fail.

I shoved away my doubts and worries about our marriage, of Emperor Justin's warning. My love would not fail Justinian. And he wouldn't fail me.

The Patriarch joined our hands together with a benevolent smile. "May God Almighty bless the love these two have found." He passed Justinian a gold and sardonyx chalice rimmed with depictions of Jesus and the twelve apostles and studded with rubies enough to feed the imperial army for a month. Justinian took a long draft and passed the wine to me. I touched my lips to the ghost of his, drinking the Sacrament as Justinian retrieved two thick gold rings from his pocket. Each was stamped with figures of saints, but Justinian's *tablion* flashed on the inside of mine before he slipped it on my finger. A quick glance revealed my insignia on the inside of his ring as well. I would wear his name and he mine until one of us was called to God.

Not for the first time that day, I blinked back the tears that stung my eyes. This day would have been impossible only a few short years ago; yet here I stood, red sandals on my feet, hands clasped with the man I couldn't help but love. Perhaps God had been watching over me after all.

We broke a loaf of crusty bread still warm from the oven and circled the altar together three times. Finally, Justinian traveled around me, reverently, draping my waist with a heavy gold wedding chain bearing traditional images of the Greek goddess of unity, Homonoia, with Christ blessing a marriage. The brush of his fingers on my hips and the burn in his eyes made me shiver with pleasure.

We were husband and wife. Now all that remained was for us to become Emperor and Empress.

We had two days and two nights of uninterrupted bliss. No business, although there wasn't much sleep either.

A slave laden with the imperial post was the first to pull us from our wedding bed. Most of the folded parchments were for Justinian, but three letters bore my name. I recognized the handwriting on all of them and scuttled to the window's ledge, as far from Justinian as I could manage.

My daughter Theodora,

I do hope this letter reaches you in time. Word just reached me of your impending marriage to the consul, and I wished to send you my warmest felicitations. May God and the Virgin shower your union with blessings.

Your father in Christ,
Severus of Pisidia

I could almost hear Severus' voice in my head as I reread the letter, like a warm blanket I could tuck myself into. I glanced at Justinian before opening the second message.

Dear Theodora,

Or should I address you as wife of the consul? Or Noblest Patrician? I admit I dropped Zachariah when I heard the news (fortunately not on his head—the child is already a bit daft; gets it from his father).

I wanted to be the first to offer my congratulations now that you outrank me, you little weasel. I thought to send a gift, but I doubt anything I could muster could compare to Justinian's sausage.

Good for you, darling!

Much love,
Antonina

Also, John adores the helmet and wooden sword you sent. The little monkey insists upon wearing them to bed.

"A letter from a friend?"

I dashed the tears from my eyes and folded Antonina's message, slipping it between the other letters. "My sister," I lied.

Justinian set down his parchment. "I didn't know you had a sister."

"Two, actually." I slipped both letters into my pocket. "My younger sister died when I was thirteen, and I've been estranged from my older sister, Comito, since I left Constantinople. She missed our wedding."

"I'm sorry." Justinian seemed about to say something else, but I looked away; I heard him break the seal on another parchment.

"There's been an earthquake in Antioch," he said. "The city is in rubble." He stared at the letter before him and ran his hands through his hair. "Macedonia reports thousands dead, including hundreds of penitents worshipping in a church that collapsed."

I crossed myself and sent a prayer to the Virgin to protect their souls. "The timing couldn't be worse."

Justinian sighed. "I know. I have to meet with the Emperor today."

"People already whisper that the drought and floods have been sent by God to punish the Empire." I took a deep breath. "Your uncle is too infirm to handle this."

"I can't push him too hard." Justinian paced the floor, Macedonia's letter forgotten on his desk. "But he needs to make me co-Emperor. Surely he must see that."

"Of course he does. He simply doesn't want to admit it." And he wasn't likely to listen to Justinian. I blocked Justinian's path, my hands akimbo. "I'll come with you."

Justinian shook his head, then stopped and looked at me as if with new eyes. "Perhaps you could make him see reason."

"He does like me."

Justinian chuckled. "Sometimes I think perhaps more than he likes me."

I shrugged. "I'm far more charming than you."

"You most certainly are, my little imp." He kissed my nose. "You could charm the devil straight out of Gehenna."

He threaded my arm through his, and we walked to our sedan, discussing possibilities for the rebuilding of Antioch, including a temporary remission of taxes and the construction of several hospitals, all while increasing Egyptian grain shipments to Palestine.

The last letter in my pocket would have to wait.

The stench from the Emperor's bedchamber almost doubled me over. Justin lay on his bed, his elephant ears empty of their usual earrings and his head bereft of its crown. A heavy wool blanket obscured his chest and arms. But not his foot.

The toes were black, the skin rotting into white bone. Pale blisters climbed up his leg, mottling the unnatural red of his flesh. Gray pus oozed from the wounds onto the silk sheets.

I almost heaved my morning meal into a Persian vase.

My fingernails bit into my palms as Justinian and I bowed. The stench clung to my nostrils and filled my mouth.

I didn't ask permission to throw the shutters open. The Emperor didn't object, but he turned away from the light, eyes screwed shut. It was no wonder he'd done nothing to help his Empire; soon our Emperor would join the souls of those who had perished in Antioch's quake.

Justinian stepped closer to the bed. "Uncle, how long have you been ill?"

Old Justin rolled over, his eyes still closed. "A few days. The rot in my foot spread quicker than anyone expected."

"What have your physicians recommended?"

"Poultices, but they're worthless as tits on a boar." The Emperor shivered. "And a fire in the brazier all the time—I can't seem to get warm."

I pulled a woolen blanket from a chest and covered him. His face was waxy, the mask of a man already dead.

"I fear God is punishing me for the bribes I used to take my throne," he said. "And my realm."

"I think God has more important things to worry about." I tucked the blanket over his feet. "But I'll pray to the Virgin for your recovery. Easter is coming—a time for new beginnings."

Justinian took the cue. "You need to focus on your recovery, Uncle."

The Emperor scowled and tried to sit up, but the effort was too much. "I am eighty years old—one does not recover at this age." I helped him lean forward to rearrange his pillows and smoothed the few hairs left on his head. His scalp burned with fever. "And so the vultures descend."

He was right—Justinian and I were vultures. But things might go awry if we didn't act now.

Justin sighed. "But I shall not be known as a feckless ruler who couldn't be troubled to settle the succession before I died. That's precisely why I adopted Justinian so many years ago." He grimaced. "It's difficult to swallow the idea that others are waiting for me to die."

Such a price seemed worth the purple mantle.

The Emperor took my hand in his—the bones felt like those of a frail bird—and laid it over Justinian's. "You shall rule when I'm gone."

I stared down at my hand atop Justinian's, wondering if he meant only his nephew or the two of us together. The very thought sent my heart pounding. Regardless, I'd be the most powerful woman in the world when my husband became Emperor.

"For now you must be content to share the purple with an old man." The Augustus sighed and shifted beneath the blankets. "I don't know how long I have before God calls me to him—your coronation should take place on Easter." He gave me a watery smile. "The time of new beginnings."

Less than two weeks.

Justinian cleared his throat. "With your blessing I'd like to assemble the Senate to approve measures to ease the hardships in Antioch and elsewhere. The Empire can't wait two weeks."

The Emperor fluttered his fingers in approval. Justinian waited for me by the door, but I waved him on. "You don't need my help to knock senators' heads together. I'll stay a while longer. If your uncle doesn't mind."

"Of course not, dear." Justin pursed his lips. "It's not as if you plan to poison me."

He spoke as if commenting about something as mundane as the

weather; yet I wondered if the Emperor shared my suspicions about Lupicina, suspicions I had yet to discount.

I ordered a juniper bath for the Emperor and wrapped his foot in honey poultices before seeing him to bed.

The Emperor muttered something after a few moments, but his chest rose and fell with the calm only sleep could bring. There was a stiff rustle in my pocket when I stood to leave. The third letter.

The cheap parchment was a water-stained page from the scriptures on one side, but a letter rife with misspellings on the other.

Dear Theodora,

The once-splendid city of Antioch is now a graveyard of rotting corpses. Everything I ownd is lost in the earthquake, so I am forcd to beg on the street lik the meenest pesant with only my body to sell.

I once helpd you and hope you'll return the favor. I herd of your marriage—pleese persuade Justinian to recall me to Constantinople. I cannot remain in this pit of hell another day.

—Macedonia

I wanted to recall her, to pluck her from the misery I knew all too well; yet something stalled my hand even as I set about writing the letter.

I was still unsure of Macedonia's relationship with Justinian before she moved to Antioch, and even barring that, she knew too much about me, about my son. I owed everything to her; yet I couldn't jeopardize my position now, not so close to Justinian's coronation.

I would recall her myself, but not until I saw the purple *chalmys* draped over Justinian's shoulders and the eagle scepter in his hands.

I had no choice. Macedonia would have to wait until after Easter.

Chapter 22

The sacred days leading to Easter are supposed to be a solitary time when it's forbidden to visit or even greet friends. Justinian fasted for two full days during Lent and lived on wild herbs dressed with vinegar and oil the rest of the season, but he forbade me to forgo food in the dwindling hope that I might become pregnant. We spent many of the silent days before that holy Sunday in prayer and contemplation at the Hagia Sophia, the Church of Holy Wisdom. Justinian would be crowned tomorrow, and I would strive to be an obedient and helpful wife, a proper consort to the Emperor.

God help me.

We prayed until tiny pins burrowed into my legs; yet I continued my prayers. I both dreaded and feared to reach so high. It only meant I had farther to fall.

I startled when Justinian cleared his throat next to me. His voice was low, but it jarred my ears after so long a silence. "I've recalled John the Cappadocian to court."

God couldn't even wait until the crown rested on my husband's head to test my obedience. I managed to keep my face calm, arching an eyebrow instead. "Really?"

Justinian continued to watch me. "I need him if I'm to finance my plans for the city. The man can squeeze money from a stone."

"One of his many talents, along with his debauchery and drunkenness."

Now Justinian arched an eyebrow.

"Surely you've heard the rumors," I said. "And you do know he's a pagan, don't you?" I was unsure if the rumors were true, but I didn't relish the prospect of the Cappadocian back at court. He'd been abruptly silent since the night of his dismissal, although I'd half expected him to continue his suit after I'd left him at the Palace of Hormisdas.

Justinian lifted my fingers to his lips. "If you were any other woman, I'd have John banished to Gibraltar."

"Is that an option?"

"You'll keep him in check." Justinian helped me to my feet. My legs were so stiff I almost stumbled. "And I have something else for you."

I shook my head, my veil skimming my shoulders. "No, thank you. Your gifts today leave much to be desired."

He pulled me to him to whisper in my ear. "Augusta Theodora has a nice ring to it, don't you think?"

"What?"

He grinned and brushed imaginary dust from his shoulder. "I'm not the only one being crowned tomorrow."

I couldn't speak. There had been thirty imperial wives since Constantine; but none had been given the purple with her husband, and only nine had gone on to become Empress with the title of Augusta. Justinian was giving me mine.

"I don't deserve such an honor."

His hands were heavy on my shoulders. "Of course you do. Where else can I get such honest counsel? Someone whose tongue doesn't slip with lies?"

Mary, help me. From the way he studied me, I feared for a moment he might unspool the secrets from my mind.

"Say yes, Theodora. Wear the purple and sit by my side." His eyes bored into mine, and he squeezed my hand as if he feared I might disappear. "For me."

Yet again, the promise of the future dangled before me. Anointed by the Patriarch, chosen by God, the Augusta was untouchable. Regardless of her sins.

Perhaps the Virgin moved my heart, knowing how I longed for my son. Mayhap she sought to use me to further the cause of religious reconciliation in the realm.

Or perhaps I simply relished the thought of such power, my name recorded for all eternity.

"I promise to prove myself worthy."

The purple in exchange for accepting the recall of the Cappadocian. It seemed a fair trade.

A lone man lifted a frail hand as our sedan passed the gates of the Sacred Palace on our way to the Hagia Sophia. The Emperor.

Too ill to attend, Justin would not be present at our coronation, but the entire Senate and council stood in attendance, dressed in stiffly pressed white tunicas and their hair pomaded. I remained in the shadows of the narthex as Justinian passed through the massive bronze doors reserved for the Emperor and the Patriarch. Six priests flanked Constantinople's city father, all seven holy men holding white candles so pure that no trace of smoke marred the sacred air. A table set before the altar held seven more candles, a terracotta jug of holy oil, and a plain basket of seven loaves of bread to symbolize the prosperity of Justinian's future reign and the seven sacraments. Patriarch

Epiphianos opened his gilded codex of the Gospels and recited Psalms, ending with an entreaty to Justinian. I didn't hear a word over the blood drumming in my ears.

The seven priests anointed Justinian with the sign of the cross in seven places—the backs of his hands, his palms, heart, lips, cheeks, eyes, and finally, his forehead. When they finished, Justinian kissed the priests' hands, the Gospel, and finally the ruby-encrusted cross on the altar. Epiphianos placed the Eastern diadem on Justinian's head and swept a thick purple *chalmys* over his shoulders to complete the transformation from man to Emperor.

Shouts of *"Nika!"* and "Flavius Petrus Sabbatius Justinianus Augustus!" shook plaster from the domes, but then the nave fell silent, and the faces of hundreds of senators and patricians swiveled toward the narthex.

It was my turn.

The double lines of the Emperor's honor guard formed two walls to guide me into the nave. Justinian waited for me at the altar with Epiphanios, a second crown in his hands.

My crown.

I walked slowly past Constantinople's nobility to allow them their first glimpse of their new Augusta, and to avoid tripping over my samite hem with its dainty clusters of shimmering seed pearls. If butterflies could sew, my stola would have been their creation.

To the right of the altar stood a knot of Justinian's closest advisers— Tribonium, General Belisarius, Sittas. And John the Cappadocian.

Tasia waited to the left of the altar, dressed like an exquisite doll and dripping with gold. Graceful as a swan, in her wide eyes and delicate bones she held the promise of the young woman she would soon become. She managed a timid smile as I winked at her.

I almost tripped as my gaze fell on another familiar face. Comito stood near the dais next to a frowning senator the size of a small hippo. Time had etched lines around her mouth like the finest spiderweb, and her blond hair was hidden under a green silk veil. She caught my eyes and gave a stiff bow of her head.

Across the aisle from my sister and almost hidden behind the Cappadocian was another woman I hadn't planned to see.

Macedonia.

It seemed she hadn't needed my assistance to make it back to the capital after all.

"I hope you don't mind," Justinian whispered once I joined him, glancing toward Comito. "I thought your sister should be here, so I had Narses track her."

"Thank you." I mouthed the words, touched at his thoughtfulness.

Epiphianos chanted and swung a censer back and forth, cloaking the air with the cloying scent of frankincense and myrrh. I swept to my knees in a rustle of silk, scarcely hearing the Gospel recited over my head. The purple *chalmys* was heavier than I expected as he draped it across my shoulders, a weight I would do my best to bear with dignity, no matter what the future held. The Patriarch fastened the cloak with a gold and amethyst cross before touching the crown in Justinian's hands.

"May God Almighty bless this woman, Theodora, wife of Justinian Augustus, with benevolence and wisdom while ruling this great Empire," Epiphanios said. "May her reign be just and fruitful."

Justinian placed the crown on my head. His hand was cool as his fingers threaded through mine. Constantinople's nobility fell before us like a wave, all heads bent in submission.

I was Empress. Augusta Theodora.

There was a breath of silence, and I caught Justinian's gaze, stealing a moment alone while all other eyes were hidden. I had hitched my star to his, for better or worse, and he to mine. His brows almost reached his crown, and I answered with a grin. The moment broke as we stepped from the altar, and the crowd's deafening cheers chased us down the middle of the Hagia Sophia and into the clean spring air.

Our first official act was to distribute newly minted coins to the poor outside the church and then make an appearance at the Kathisma gallery, the Emperor's special box in the Hippodrome. Justinian squeezed my hand as we stepped from the dark passageway into the giant amphitheater, open to the afternoon sky and filled with one hundred thousand of our subjects. They roared at the sight of us, a tapestry of our names and *"Nika!"* woven into the wind. Justinian and I made the sign of the cross over them and raised our arms for the games to begin.

I hadn't been to the Hippodrome since the sweltering afternoon Justin had been proclaimed Emperor. Then I had been nobody, but now I wore the Augusta's purple. I felt like an imposter but reminded myself I'd earned all of this. I'd certainly sacrificed enough to get here.

We were too far away to make out the carved base of the Egyptian obelisk and its image of Emperor Theodosius with eight chariots on the track and the Empire's damned enemies below, but the scene was reenacted before us as the charioteers took their places. Each circled the sandy track and saluted our royal box flying its purple pennants as they passed. They paused for the Blues' consul—a nod to the faction both Justinian and I favored—to step before the horses and hold up a gold sphere the size of an apple, one specially commissioned for these games. The horses snorted and threw their heads. The crowd fell silent as the sphere arced into the air, flashed in the sky like a small sun, and hit the ground.

The horses bolted. Tasia huddled her face in my lap as a Green chariot overturned on the last lap and its driver was trampled by the Blues. The charioteer didn't move, but a stain of crimson spread into the sands under his chest. A Blue in a fearsome bronze eagle helmet won and received the gold sphere that started the race straight from Justinian's hand. We settled in for the bearbaiting, hare chase, and display of acrobats, including a particularly lithe—and scantily clad— young woman who walked a rope perilously strung across the top of the arena. I knew how she felt.

Typically all women and children would be relegated to stand in the upper tiers of the Hippodrome, but for today, Justinian's sister joined General Belisarius, Sittas, and Tribonium with us in the Kathisma. John the Cappadocian was seated next to a little girl no more than five years old, Euphemia, his daughter. Rumor claimed the Cappadocian had fathered a clutch of bastard children all over the Empire, but this whey-faced girl was the only one he claimed. I watched him offer her honeyed cherries and toasted almonds, his whispers in her ears making her giggle. There was no mistaking she was John's daughter with her sand-colored hair and dimpled chin. Something else about her seemed familiar, but I couldn't quite place what it was. John ignored me, but that suited me perfectly.

Macedonia sat behind me, still turning heads despite the whisper of lines on her forehead and her glorious copper hair hidden beneath an embroidered blue veil. I'd offered her a position as my lady-in-waiting, and she already wore the golden girdle denoting her new position. It would be useful to have a woman about my court who could gather information where Narses and his eunuchs couldn't. Not only that, but I wasn't sure if she knew of my delay in recalling her. I owed her something, and I didn't want to be any further in her debt than I already was.

She waited until the men were engrossed in conversation, then leaned toward me. "Where's your son?"

I stared at the acrobat to avoid her eyes. "He died after we left Antioch."

Macedonia crossed herself. "I'm sorry. May he rest with God."

Comito sat down. My sister had always sparkled, but now she seemed like a drab river rock compared to the rest of us shining in our jewels. I clasped her hand, thankful she'd come today. "When are you going to join my court?"

"Never. I'd rather gouge my eyes out than live at court." The way she said it made me wonder if she really meant she'd never live at *my* court. Comito may have come to my coronation today, but the hardness in her eyes told me she might never truly forgive me.

I listened to my sister introduce herself to Vigilantia; they quickly fell to swapping tales of Justinian and me in our younger years, stories I'm sure we would both have preferred to remain buried. Such was the gift, and curse, of family.

Tasia's face blanched white as a spotted leopard tore a hare to pieces, the rabbit's blood blossoming onto the sand like the charioteer's had earlier. I thought of dismissing my daughter to bed, but soon the carnage would be replaced with dancers and more races. "Tasia," Sittas said, loud enough so Comito turned, too. I'd caught the dimpled young general's eyes on my sister, but Comito hadn't appeared to notice. "Do you know the story of Sisyphus? It's one of my favorite myths from the Golden Age."

The general relayed the story of the cursed king forced to roll a boulder up a hill for eternity. I'd never cared for the tale and was easily distracted by Justinian's discussion with Belisarius.

"The new laws will bar Jews and pagans from holding political office or serving in the military," Justinian said, taking an orange from the basket presented by a slave.

"Oh." I crossed my arms in front of my chest. "Is that all?"

"Their temples and property shall be confiscated and their meetings forbidden," he said. "I hope to persuade them to change their ways."

"Or leave the Empire," Belisarius added, grasping the hilt of his sword. "Perhaps they could use a little persuasion." Justinian loved Belisarius like a brother, but I failed to see the man's allure. The man thirsted for either blood or power, or both. Either way, I didn't trust him.

"That benefits no one," I said. "Levy a hearth tax, and leave them to worship in peace."

Justinian rubbed his chin. "Religious strife has divided the Empire for too long. I cannot reconquer the West if we don't reconcile these religious differences first. The Empire will be too large to handle such disagreements."

"What about the Monophysites?" I leaned forward, elbows on my knees. It was no secret that I'd been baptized a Monophysite in Egypt. "Shall you target them next?"

Belisarius coughed, and Justinian shifted in his seat. "I have no plans to do so."

"Not yet," I said.

"It seems our newly appointed Empress disagrees with your plan, Augustus." John the Cappadocian leaned back in his seat, peeling an orange and avoiding my eyes. "I cannot recall such a vociferous woman on the throne in all the Empire's history."

"I encourage Theodora to speak her mind," Justinian said, his eyes narrowing, "as I do with all my advisers."

John leaned toward Tribonium, speaking in a tone just loud enough for everyone in the box to hear. "I didn't realize a wife was meant to be an adviser."

I opened my mouth to give him a scolding, but Justinian's hand covered mine. "You would do well to remember Theodora is your anointed Augusta." He turned on his throne, giving John the insult of his back. "Belisarius, I'm sending you to Persia. It's time we trounced the fire-eaters once and for all."

I smiled to myself. It seemed John was no longer a favorite.

I prayed Justinian would remain in the capital and send Belisarius to the front to fight Persia. Widow's black didn't suit me.

"You seem to have the Emperor wrapped around that pretty little finger of yours," John whispered as he leaned forward to pick up a segment of orange he'd conveniently dropped. "Just like Hecebolus. We'll see how long that lasts once Justinian realizes the kind of woman you truly are. Empresses are easily unmade—just ask Claudia Octavia or Fausta."

Both Empresses had been killed by their husbands, one because she'd outlived her usefulness to the Emperor, and the other for possible deceit. I glanced at Justinian, laughing with Belisarius, and tried to imagine his ink-stained fingers signing my death warrant. I shook my head at the impossibility.

Yet surely neither Claudia Octavia nor Fausta believed her husband would have her wrists slit or order her suffocated in her bath.

I dared not turn around to confront John and make a scene, but forced myself to stare at the floor of the Hippodrome and listen to the men discuss preparations for war until the last acrobat finished her final performance.

War abroad, and a possible battle at home to keep my throne. This was a dangerous game I now played.

PART II

Empress

AD 530–548

The throne is a glorious sepulcher.

—ATTRIBUTED TO THEODORA IN
The Decline and Fall of the Roman Empire
BY EDWARD GIBBON

Chapter 23

Belisarius passed again under the Golden Gate's gilded elephants two years later, preening from his victory at the Battle of Dara and lording over the chests of gold he'd dragged back from Persia. Yet he had only crippled the Persians, not struck the deathblow to Kavadh's Empire, something Emperor Justin might have pointed out if he were still alive. The old Emperor had passed in his sleep months after our coronation, a blessed relief as his blood boiled from infection. Justinian and I ruled alone now.

Yet Belisarius acted as if he were Julius Caesar returning from Gaul. Few people knew that he had been challenged to single combat by the Persian commander before the battle, but like a coward, he'd sent a bath slave named Andreas in his stead. Belisarius was more Achilles than Hector, but Justinian refused to hear a word against him. Instead, he lauded him until the graffiti praising Belisarius on the city walls outnumbered the Emperor's.

The men closeted themselves to discuss plans for reconquering the Western Empire, starting with the ambitious scheme to retake Rome, although that was still a few years off. I'd spent most of my recent days drafting new legislation allowing women to seek divorce if their husbands beat them or committed adultery, and drawing up plans to adapt an old palace across the Bosphorus into a convent for reformed prostitutes. Today I decided to spend my afternoon in a different sort of reflection.

The Church of Sergius and Bacchus was incomplete, but already I loved the holy building. Every afternoon its net of pillars and columns trapped the last of the fleeting sunlight. One day the walls would be filled with gold mosaics and colorful frescoes, but for now lacy capitals held up plain marble walls carved with Greek inscriptions. It was a strangely delicate church for the two martyred Christian soldiers who were brutally tortured and beheaded. Justinian had dedicated the church after our coronation, but recently a new inscription had been added around the central nave.

> *May the One True God guard the rule of the unsleeping Augustus and increase the power of the God-crowned Theodora whose mind is bright with piety and whose unending toil lies in ceaseless efforts to nourish the destitute.*

There was a soft snort behind me. "Bright with piety? I recall a time when your mind rarely left the gutter."

Antonina's cheekbones were sharper than usual, and her hair hung loose to her shoulders. She was dressed in black. Terror seized my throat, making it difficult to breathe. "Is John all right?"

She fell to her knees beside me—my retinue was a respectful distance away, but I could scarcely make out her voice over the rush of blood in my ears. I would never forgive her, or myself, if something had happened to my son.

"John is fine. He got into a tussle after he broke Photius' new pens the other day—I swear that boy of mine thinks of nothing but sketching and sculpting. John ended up with a scratch on his temple.

The mark's going to leave a scar, but John's thrilled, of course, even though it's sort of shaped like a crescent moon. Although that's nothing compared to—"

I waited for her to finish, but she stared at the altar instead. "Compared to what?"

Her hands fluttered. "Nothing. Plato was right—of all the animals, the boy is the most unmanageable."

I didn't press the issue—my son was safe. "But you're in mourning."

"Yes, that." She sniffed and crossed herself. "The Weasel died."

"Oh."

Antonina snorted. "I see you're overwhelmed with sympathy for my plight."

"May Timothy the Weasel rest well with God." I crossed myself, searching her face for signs of grief, but they were well hidden, if they existed at all.

"Unfortunately, his recent investment of ivory went down with the ship. Along with him."

"Do you need money?" Justinian had recently granted me my own lands in Bithynia, ones rich with oil presses and vineyards. "Narses can arrange credit with a moneylender for you."

"For a while," Antonina said. "What I really need is a new man."

So much for mourning Timothy the Weasel.

"I wouldn't mind a rich one, possibly a patrician," she continued. "Perhaps you could recommend me to an eligible bachelor? I think I'd like a title this time."

Antonina prattled on about the qualities she preferred in her next husband—essentially an Adonis with a purse deeper than Justinian's and a little light in the brains category.

My grin stopped Antonina's tirade about her hypothetical husband's necessary sexual expertise. She frowned. "You look like you've just made a pact with the devil."

"I'm talking to you, aren't I?"

"Ha."

I rose from my knees, and she followed suit. "Would you be willing to provide delicate information on whichever man you marry?"

"Delicate information?" The flesh between Antonina's brows puckered. "I don't kiss and tell, if that's what you mean. Unless he's extraordinary."

"Political information."

"You want me to spy for you?" The creases between her brows deepened. "What do you take me for?"

"A practical woman who would enjoy a purse with more money than she could spend in ten lifetimes."

"It's hard to refuse when you put it like that." She straightened her *paludamentum*. "I'll tell you whatever you want, influence him however you need. So long as he's rich."

"Would Belisarius fit your bill?" Justinian already had plans to send the golden general abroad, but having someone keep an eye on him when he was in Constantinople would be invaluable. A man that talented couldn't be without ambitions. Possibly dangerous ambitions, considering the number of generals in history who had stolen the purple.

I swear Antonina actually wiped her mouth at the notion. "I bet he's a lion in bed."

"He could probably sire at least another ten mites on you."

She grimaced as if she'd bitten rotten cheese. "No more children—the last one almost killed me. Still might. But I'll be a blushing bride as soon as you arrange it."

"Belisarius is Orthodox. You'll have to be baptized a Christian."

Antonina gave a sly smile, fingering the cross around her neck. "I did that years ago."

I almost didn't hear. "I have to tell Justinian about John. I don't want Belisarius raising my son."

And I missed John. It killed me every time I saw a boy his age with a dirty face or hair desperately in need of a trim. He was my flesh and blood, but he would no longer recognize me if I passed him on the *Mese*. I would always wonder if I had made the right choice by leaving him.

"I doubt Belisarius will be around much," Antonina said.

"It doesn't matter. I should have told Justinian long ago." It was true; yet I could never muster the courage to tell Justinian I'd lied to him, to watch his trust in me crack and splinter.

To lose his love and be sent away, or worse.

Antonina's lip twitched. "What about Tasia? I hear you and Justinian have started fishing for eligible young men for her betrothal. I daresay the pool will dry up if Justinian divorces you before she's married."

Again the choice between my son and daughter. Yet Antonina had a point, and John was doing well with her, thriving even. Telling Justinian the truth would jeopardize Tasia's future, and my son might gain nothing. In fact, he could lose much if Justinian chose to divorce me. "Fine. I'll arrange some sort of event at the palace so you can come to court."

I kept secrets from Justinian, and now Belisarius would play father to my son.

I'd likely lose my head if either of them ever found out. Or worse.

Chapter 24

John the Cappadocian was a fiscal genius, so much so he could make money disappear straight into his own accounts.

"He's stealing from you." I stood before Justinian, arms akimbo as I prepared to do battle against his finance minister. It was long past midnight, but we were both still working. An army of flickering oil lamps lit Justinian's offices, so many that slaves had already had to refill them several times.

Justinian sighed. "John is pivotal to the success of my restoration of the Empire."

"You're not going to have an Empire to restore if you don't curb his excesses." In order to save more money for our foreign wars, the Cappadocian had cut the government subsidies for the imperial post, crucial to the farmers who relied on the public transportation for their crops and were now forced to carry them on their backs to Constantinople's markets, some from as far as Chalcedon. There were reports of unburied dead on the road, and many farmers refused to return to their fields, hoping for salvation in the city. Food was getting scarce. It wasn't only the plebs who despised the Cappadocian—the patricians were livid at the new tax rates that threatened to bleed them dry.

"The peace with the Persian Empire has cost more than anyone anticipated, and I can't afford not to pay their tribute," Justinian said. "I can't risk a war in the East while planning to conquer the West." I rued the day Belisarius had campaigned in Persia. The Persians had defeated him at Callinicum a year ago and now plundered our Treasury in return for the promise not to attack. I'd propose sending the ambitious general to them instead, would it not have widowed Antonina again.

Love, or lust, had been in the air. Antonina had married Belisarius, and Comito had married General Sittas shortly after. My sister had borne a pretty little girl with her mother's pale hair—Sophia—a scant seven months later. I had never seen my sister so happy, although I knew I'd never be able to induce her to come to court anymore.

"John's the best prefect I have." Justinian squinted at the dimly lit parchment before him. "I can't remove him."

"He's a drunkard and a pagan and a letch. No wife or virgin is safe from him."

Justinian gave me a wicked smile. "You were."

"I was neither wife nor virgin." I drummed my fingers on Justinian's desk. "The people are angry, patricians and plebs alike. They blame him for their problems."

"Let them. John has always been honest with me about his shortcomings."

"If you don't remove him, they'll soon blame you."

"Theodora, right now I have bigger problems to worry about than my corrupt treasurer." He shoved the parchment under my nose.

I read the letter from Carthage, written in Latin and stamped with the new Vandal king's seal. After the usual formalities, the usurper got straight down to business insulting Justinian.

To Flavius Petrus Sabbatius Justinianus Augustus, Emperor of the East,

As you may have heard, I have assumed the Vandal throne after the unfortunate death of my cousin.

I know you had dealings with Hilderic, but your long Roman nose should not stretch to Carthage. If you recall, the last Roman military expedition against my kingdom ended in utter disaster. The best Emperor is the one that minds his own business.

—Gelimer, King of the Vandals and Alans

"I had planned to use diplomacy with the old king to persuade North Africa back into the Empire." Justinian rubbed his nose. "Hilderic had even introduced coinage with my portrait. It's unfortunate Gelimer's sword was found in his back."

I held up the letter. "You can't let his insult go unpunished."

"Quite the contrary. I couldn't have asked for a better excuse to test Belisarius before I send him to Rome."

"And the Cappadocian?"

"I promise I'll speak to him."

Too little, too late. Within days the Hippodrome had become a cauldron of dissent, and violence spilled into the streets. Effigies of the Cappadocian burned there, and plays at the Kynêgion celebrating his execution became overnight sensations. Narses reported back to us on the nightly food riots and looting, mostly led by the Blues and the Greens against each other.

Justinian called the city prefect, Eudaemon the Pumpkin, to the Sacred Palace. The round-faced little man kept his eyes to the foot of Justinian's throne during the entire audience.

"Arrest anyone engaged in violence, regardless of his political affiliation," Justinian said. "This chaos must end immediately."

The Pumpkin followed his orders with great vigor, filling the jails to overflowing in only a few days. The prefect was colorblind, arresting Blues and Greens and sentencing seven of the main rabble-rousers to death.

Narses burst into my chambers the afternoon of the executions as I played a game of backgammon with Macedonia. I welcomed the interruption—Macedonia had almost borne off the last of her checkers, and I was about to lose a gammon. "You look like you've just come from battle."

Narses' chest heaved as he straightened to attention—sometimes I forgot the eunuch was twice my age. "Two of the criminals have fled the scaffolds and claimed asylum at the monastery of Saint Conon in Blachernae."

I set down the doubling cube and stood up. "How in God's name did that happen?"

"The knots on their nooses failed."

Macedonia started cleaning up the table. "The executioner is sympathetic to the rioters."

Narses barely glanced at her. My favorite eunuch didn't care for Antonina or Macedonia due to the women's low births and past occupations, and he found it easier to ignore their existence rather than acknowledge them. I'd once jested that he should then despise me, too, but he'd only heaved a great sigh as he locked away my jewels. "I could no more hate you than I could tell my lungs to cease breathing," he had said. "Even if my hands itch to throttle you most days."

"The criminals were saved by a mob," Narses said now, his eyes flicking in the direction of Blachernae. "The scaffold collapsed on the second attempt to hang them. The people claim it was a divine miracle."

I snorted. "If it was a miracle, then I'm the Virgin Mary."

"They want the men pardoned."

"Of course they do." I stood up. "Where's Justinian?"

"In his throne room—the Pumpkin came to tell him the news."

Eudaemon passed us on his way out of the throne room. Justinian barely glanced up from a large map of North Africa spread across an entire table, held down by four heavy gold orbs.

"You have to address the mob," I said. "Regardless of what happens to the criminals in Blachernae. This kind of revolt cannot be tolerated."

Justinian adjusted a string over Carthage, no doubt a point of possible invasion. "I've ordered a set of races at the Hippodrome for the ides of January. This will all blow over with a bout of games and free beer."

I hoped he was right, but just in case, I sent a message to Antonina on the ides to take the children to her Rufinianae estates and ordered my attendants out of the city, watching with a pang as Macedonia led Euphemia and Tasia to the waiting sedans. Now fifteen, my daughter possessed the slim curves of blossoming womanhood. Justinian and I would need to arrange her betrothal once things calmed down.

We emerged into the Kathisma of the Hippodrome swathed in purple and gold with a double guard behind us to watch the races. The herds of Blues and Greens joined together to appeal to Justinian before the chariots even took to the track. Their demands had grown—they commanded the release of the criminals, the removal of John the Cappadocian, and the repeal of all his taxes.

Justinian turned his back on them.

The crowd hurled epithets—I heard numerous shouts wishing Justinian's father had never been born—while the charioteers took their places and snapped their salutes. Scowling men slunk about the stands, and the horses careened around the track unnoticed. Our guards kept their hands on the hilts of their swords.

Justinian watched with the face of a statue, but I knew his eyes missed nothing. Winter's dark night threatened to fall by the time the final race concluded, but a new cheer filled the cold air instead of the usual cry to celebrate the victorious charioteer.

"Forever reign the Blues and Greens!"

Gooseflesh prickled my arms as I heard the two enemy factions joined together. Every spectator took up the cry until the roar likely carried beyond the city walls.

We retreated amidst our guards, and the heavy oak doors clanged shut behind us.

"Nika! Nika! Nika!"

Hurled like rocks, the victory cry followed us down the corridor. It wasn't difficult to guess whom the Blues and Greens had united against.

I waited until my heart had stopped pounding and we were safely ensconced in Justinian's chambers before speaking. "You must punish them. Now."

He paced before a huge window facing the Hippodrome. "There are tens of thousands of my people in there."

"I don't care how many there are. They're the rubbish of the city, and you're God's anointed Emperor. They cannot treat you like that."

"I will not punish them for my mistake. I should have reined in John the Cappadocian." Justinian's calm frightened me. He sniffed the air, his brows knit together. "Do you smell that?"

A faint orange glow lit the black sky in the window behind him. The numb taste of fear filled my mouth. "Holy Mother of God."

Flames licked the palace vestibule, sending slaves armed with wooden buckets scurrying into the Chalke courtyard. Our people had grievances, but they'd be damned to the fires of Gehenna for this rebellion. I'd make sure of it, provided we escaped unscathed.

Justinian shed his *chalmys* and fled the room before I could stop him, before he could see the rest of his city burned to ashes. I watched spellbound for what seemed like hours as fire shot up the Senate building and beyond it, the Church of Saint Eirene collapsed like kindling. Between them, the conflagration claimed their more magnificent victim.

"The Hagia Sophia," I moaned.

One of the city's oldest and most revered churches was engulfed in an inferno, the fire crackling as the wooden roof heaved a final sigh and collapsed, shaking the earth as it spewed fire and brimstone. Justinian returned too late to see, covered in soot and bringing the acrid scent of destruction and fear as the Baths of Zeuxippus joined the conflagration. Speechless, I clutched the balcony as we watched our city burn. It was only a matter of time before the palace itself became a target.

I recalled the woman who had jumped into the Bosphorus rather than be claimed by rebels before Justinian and I were married. I'd thought her a coward then, but now I understood her fear. Yet I had my children to live for. I wouldn't die without a fight.

"Augustus." My heart stuttered at the voice, but Narses spoke from the door, Belisarius next to him. "The rebels have set up their headquarters in the Hippodrome. They demand the Emperor grant their requests, or they have threatened further violence."

Justinian wiped his face with his purple *chalmys*, staining it with soot, and started pacing again. "Fine. Keep the Cappadocian in the palace. I'll reinstate him after this has all died down."

Narses didn't move.

"Is there more?" Justinian asked.

"There are rumbles in the Hippodrome of who would be best suited to assume the purple."

Justinian stopped pacing.

"Treason," I said.

"If the Emperor won't step down, the crowd plans to kill him." Narses seemed to speak only to me, imploring me with his eyes. If the rebels killed Justinian, I had no doubt what my fate would be.

Justinian held up a hand. "Who has been suggested to take the throne?"

"Probus was named first," Narses said. The old man was a nephew of the Emperor Anastasius. One of his sons had already expressed an interest in marrying Tasia. "But he has fled the city. The mob burned down his villa."

Better to lose his villa than his head.

"Who next?" Justinian asked. "Hypatius?"

Narses nodded.

Another nephew of Anastasius. I wished I could send the whole lot of them to hell.

"I can send men to retrieve Hypatius," Belisarius said. "It wouldn't be hard to arrange an accident before the mob claims him."

"Let them have him—it gives us a known target at least," Justinian said. "I want you to subdue the mob in the streets. Then we'll deal with the Hippodrome. No bloodshed." Justinian's face was hard as marble. "I am a Christian king. I shall not have my people's blood on my hands."

"You may not have a choice," I said.

"No blood," Justinian repeated to Belisarius. The general pressed his fist to his chest; then his footfalls disappeared down the corridor.

Blood was shed. Hours later, Narses recounted the story to the few of us still left in the palace. Clerics intent on saving holy relics from the flames of the Hagia Sophia watched Belisarius' men surround the crowd outside. The holy men tried to intervene to avoid violence between the two groups, but the troops saw them as rebel sympathizers. Soldiers beat the priests back at sword point, knocked them down, and trampled them into the cobbles. The mob pushed Belisarius and his men into the palace, then paraded the broken bodies of the clerics through the streets, limbs shattered and faces unrecognizable, evidence that Justinian was a heathen Emperor who murdered God's men with his own soldiers. The city was upside down—jails flung open, hospitals and churches lit afire, storehouses and shops looted, all accompanied by the occasional crash of a smoking building. Constantinople had become hell on earth.

"We are no longer safe." Justinian spoke before the few people left huddled within the walls—Belisarius, Sittas, John the Cappadocian, and Narses with his army of eunuchs. The imperial guards had abandoned the Sacred Palace, unsure of which side to gamble on. Even amongst the chaos, Justinian remained calm, his very presence filling the room. "I'm going to the Hippodrome as Anastasius did."

Years ago, Emperor Anastasius had appeared before a mob that threatened his throne without his crown or purple *chalmys* and invited the people to choose a new Emperor. Dumbstruck, the mob had returned home like sheep and allowed him to continue to rule until the ripe age of eighty-eight. Sometimes luck smiles on fools.

"History doesn't always repeat itself," I said.

"But it might." Justinian picked up his illuminated manuscript of the Gospels. "Will you come with me?"

His hand was cold as I squeezed it. "I'd follow you to Gehenna and back."

He gave a dead smile, his eyes empty. "That might not be a far cry from what I'm asking."

We left our crowns and purple robes on our thrones. Without them, we might have passed for any patrician and his wife. For a moment I wondered how life might have been if that were true. But I had never wanted an ordinary life. We had reached for power, and God had granted it. It was up to us to keep it.

The crowd took a long time to quiet as we arrived at the Kathisma from the deserted palace passageway, but finally it settled down to hear the Emperor speak. The night air was crisp, but my eyes stung with its smoke. It was difficult to believe our city was in flames outside the walls of the Hippodrome.

"Fellow Romans, I have only myself to blame for the crimes you have committed against me." Justinian's voice was clear, carried by the wind to the thousands gathered before us. "As such, there shall be no arrests so long as you return to your houses and peace returns to the Queen of Cities. Go home, and may God shower his blessings upon us all."

There was a moment of silence, and then the crowd erupted, hurling curses at him.

"Go hang yourself on a cross!"

"Donkey! Liar!"

With the hilt of his sword Belisarius beat back one man who was attempting to scale the imperial box and finally stabbed him through the ribs. There was a wet squelch as he withdrew the sword and wiped the shining blood on his tunica.

These were no sheep.

It was Justinian's power to draw people to him, eye to eye. He couldn't possibly convince a faceless mob of his right to rule. And he knew it.

A rush of blood filled my ears as we retreated, protected by a flotilla of Belisarius' soldiers as we fled the battlefield to the safety of our palace, quiet as a tomb.

"I'll order my soldiers to kill Hypatius," Belisarius said.

Fool—another rebel would only take his place. I tasted the copper of blood as I bit my tongue. I would stay in the shadows. For now.

Justinian's pacing was sure to wear a trench in the silk rug. "There would be ten men to replace him."

"And the troops may not act," Sittas said. "Roman guards are fickle when it comes to revolts." Caligula and Galba had learned that the hard way, their guards' swords the last thing they saw in this life.

Silence cloaked the room.

"Or we do as Zeno did." Justinian looked out the windows as he spoke, hands clasped behind his back, the city still ablaze.

My heart stopped beating. Emperor Zeno had fled Constantinople in disguise in the face of revolt, but he recovered his throne through the ineptitude of his replacement. The Senate flung open the gates of the city and almost begged him to take back his throne. That was unlikely to happen in our situation.

"I've contacts in Cappadocia and Antioch," John the Cappadocian said. I shot him a filthy glare—it was his fault we were in this mess to begin with.

The men bickered over possible destinations for the soon-to-be-deposed Emperor and his court—Dalmatia, Illyria, or Justinian's birth-place of Tauresium. They had already decided.

I stepped from the shadows and cleared my throat, feeling as if I were taking the stage at the Kynêgion again. "Some believe a woman ought not to assert herself against men, but the present crisis does not permit otherwise." The strength of my voice surprised me. "The present time is inopportune for flight, although it may bring safety. While we all must die one day, it is unendurable for an Emperor to become a fugitive. I hope to never be separated from this purple, and would rather die before others stop addressing me as Empress." I looked to Justinian and gestured toward the window with its view of the Sea of Marmara. "There is no difficulty if you wish to save yourself. We have much money, and there is the sea, the boats."

I looked about the golden atrium with its exquisite mosaics and golden frescoes, the empty thrones framed by purple silk curtains.

Purple. My purple.

I addressed Justinian alone now, my voice scarcely a whisper. "However, consider whether after you have reached that safety if you would gladly exchange it for death." I touched his purple *chalmys* draped over his throne. "As for myself, I believe the imperial purple is a good burial shroud."

The council didn't speak. John the Cappadocian glared, and the others appeared dumbstruck. My tongue was heavy with the acrid taste of fear. Justinian's skin was cold when he clasped my hand and squeezed it. I held my breath to hear what he would say, but his eyes sparked with life. "Then we stay. And fight."

The room erupted, but he bent to whisper in my ear. "I should have expected as much from you."

I managed a smile, recalling his words from long ago. "Someone once told me it's far better to dare mighty things and fail mightily than to never dare at all."

And we might fail mightily. But we wouldn't disappear to Dalmatia, branded cowards and failures with our tails between our legs.

One of Narses' eunuchs interrupted the melee with a poorly folded parchment missing its customary wax seal. The messenger whispered something in Narses' ear that made him smile, a fearsome sight. "It's from Hypatius. He was dragged from under his bed by the rebels and crowned with a gold necklace on the Emperor's throne in the Kathisma." He scanned the message. "But he requests an audience with the Augustus."

Justinian glanced at the paper but didn't touch it. "He's scared."

"Or he might be planning an attack from within," Belisarius said. "Enter the palace with the mob and murder all of us."

Justinian rubbed his face with one hand, black flecks of stubble on his cheeks. This revolt had aged him years instead of days. "Tell Hypatius you were unable to deliver the message—the Augusti had already fled."

My heart stalled. Of course I would follow Justinian if he changed his mind about fleeing, but he was only the nephew of a swineherd without the purple. And I was just a reformed whore.

"Take your eunuchs to the Hippodrome with gold from the Treasury," he continued to Narses. "Distribute the coins to the Blues with a warning to beware their new alliance. Remind them Hypatius' blood is Green—he'll favor that faction if he ascends the throne." A wry smile curled his lips. "Although he's not going to have a chance at my throne." He turned to Belisarius, his voice so quiet I could scarcely hear him. "Lead your corps through Deadman's Gate in the Hippodrome—a surprise attack should rout the rebels."

Belisarius and his men marched like a funeral procession as they left to carry out their orders. Justinian and I waited, ears straining and both of us jumping at the occasional crash of yet another collapsing building. This might be the last time we were alone together, the final moment of quiet before we were paraded before a mob to our deaths. Words wouldn't come, but I laid my head on his shoulder.

"I love you, Theodora," he said. "No matter what happens, my life has been full because of you."

I could only nod, my throat too tight to answer.

An hour passed until the wind carried the first screams of death to us and a blood-spattered imperial guard stormed through the door. A sword dripping with red hung from his hand. My knees gave way, but I managed to hold my head high, waiting for him to draw the blade against us. Instead, he used it to salute Justinian.

"General Belisarius sends word from the Hippodrome, Augustus," he said. "The Blues stormed from the Hippodrome after the Greens crowned Hypatius. The enemy was subdued by the imperial forces, and the General holds Hypatius to await the judgment of the Emperor."

We had won. Against all odds, we had triumphed. I could breathe again.

"I'll deal with Hypatius myself," Justinian said. The guard snapped his heels together and beat his fist into his chest armor once before retreating the way he'd come. Justinian crushed me to him. "You are truly a gift from God, Theodora. You saved my crown today."

"I told you I'd earn my purple." We embraced, my ear upon his steady heartbeat. I could have stayed there forever, but we had to face the reality of what we'd done. What I'd done.

We retraced our steps down the same imperial passageway we'd retreated down earlier in the night, emerging into the Kathisma to a sea of blood and bodies and the fetid smell of death. The entire floor of the Hippodrome and much of the stands were piled with corpses, the survivors already stripping the dead rebels of their shoes and emptying their pockets. There had been no clash of true battle—Belisarius' troops were professional soldiers girded with armor and equipped with broadswords and bronze shields. The rebels in the Hippodrome were craftsmen, farmers, and fishermen armed with stones and sticks. Now their bodies lay mounded upon the arena floor like freshly turned earth. One man lay at the foot of our box, arms flung wide over several corpses and legs curled into the mass of soft bodies beneath him. Lavender intestines poured from a gaping hole in his abdomen. Then his arm twitched, pulled by an invisible string. I vomited over the side of the Kathisma onto the body of another rebel.

Belisarius led a bound man to our box as I wiped my mouth. I hardly recognized Hypatius with the dried blood crusted into his snowy hair and the bruises blossoming up his jaw. Belisarius shoved him to his knees.

"You have betrayed us," Justinian said. "Just as we thought you might."

Hypatius crawled on hands and knees to kiss the hem of Justinian's *chalmys*. "I beg you for my life and that of my family. I sent a message to the palace to swear my fealty to your crown."

Justinian wore a mask worthy of any actor in the Kynêgion. "If you were so loyal, surely you might have stood up against the mob."

"They were deaf when I declared my loyalty to you," Hypatius sobbed, tears running down the deep creases in his cheeks. "The mob pulled me from under my bed—my wife tried to stop them, but she is only an old woman." He bowed his head to the floor, his body trembling. "Please spare me, Augustus. I am innocent!"

Justinian's mask slipped. He had known Hypatius well—they had run in similar political circles since Old Justin had become Emperor and promoted his nephew, despite Hypatius' being almost seventy.

"God has instructed us to be merciful in all things," Justinian said.

I laid a gentle hand on his arm. My voice was soft but didn't waver. "But not in this."

Hypatius looked at me with wide eyes glassy with fear. I had just saved my husband's throne. I hated what I had to do, but I couldn't allow Justinian to free the rebel figurehead only to face him in the future. This revolt had to be snuffed out so it couldn't blaze again.

"A traitor can never be trusted. Your new laws require the execution of all those who plot against the Emperor." I gestured to the carnage. "This cannot happen again."

Hypatius struggled to stand, but Belisarius slammed him back to his knees. "But I am innocent!"

Justinian's jaw tightened, but he motioned to the imperial guards. "Hold this man. His property shall be confiscated and his titles stripped from his family. He shall be executed at Sykae tomorrow and his body thrown to the sea."

A traitor's death.

I forced myself to remain impassive. Hypatius struggled against the guards, screaming his innocence. I didn't wish his family punished—after a suitable period his wealth would be returned to his widow and children. I laid a hand on his shoulder and whispered this in his ear. He looked at me with wet eyes, then sagged against his captors and let them lead him away without further struggle.

John of Cappadocia had been wrong. Emperors were not easily unmade.

And neither were Empresses.

Chapter 25

We walked through the rubble of our city the next day, swathed in heavy wool robes to ward off the winter chill. Slaves had begun to clear away the charred columns of the palace vestibule, but bits of ash still danced like gray moths in the cold air, and we had to watch our step to avoid glowing embers. The Senate continued to smolder, a black stub of a tooth, and behind it a greasy plume of smoke billowed into the cloudless sky—all that remained of the Hippodrome rebels. Nineteen senators had joined Hypatius on the execution platform that morning, and the Hippodrome would remain closed until Justinian decided otherwise. The ruins of our city looked as I imagined Rome had when the Vandals sacked it.

If only Justinian had listened to me before this all started and fired John the Cappadocian. Instead, John had already been reinstated, and he set upon the patricians to tap their fortunes for the state as penance for supporting the Nika uprising. I wished I'd found a way to sacrifice him to the crowd.

"This may be a blessing in disguise," Justinian said, picking his way over charred timbers. Frost clung to the pillars of the Hagia

Sophia, white lace over black as dark as pitch. His footsteps disturbed the gray ash to reveal the subdued sheen of the marble mosaic below.

I rubbed my eyes—I hadn't slept as the giant funeral pyre burned in the Hippodrome and Sunday's unholy night slipped into a new week. Instead, I'd prayed until my knees were bruised and my legs went numb. "How could this"—I gestured to the charred skeletons of the city's greatest treasures—"be a blessing?"

"A fresh start. Penance for our sins." He glanced at me, then into the vast expanse of gray above us. "My sins. We can fill the city with monuments to last to eternity, all for the glory of God." The clouds of our breath intermingled as Justinian helped me over a fallen pillar near the church's altar.

"The world would never forget us." I'd rather be remembered for our monuments than for yesterday's bloodshed.

"I can guarantee they'll never forget you, not after last night. Witness this moment for God," he called to the shivering slaves. "If I complete this temple, I will give thirty thousand gold pieces to the poor and helpless. This church shall stand for all eternity as a monument to the glory of God and the Empire. A crown for the Queen of Cities!" Justinian took a pickax from a slave and swung it to the ground, spewing fragments of snow and marble.

The only movement was the white puffs of air billowing from the slaves' lips. Then the men began to stomp, filling the air with the rumble of their feet. Would God be so easily fooled when we stood before him one day?

We walked back to the palace with red noses and pink cheeks while eunuchs followed behind with our litters. My husband raved about the gold mosaics of the Virgin and Christ Child that would fill the domes of the new Hagia Sophia, the porphyry columns he'd import from Egypt, and the relics he'd transfer to the city. My feet were stiff and cold through my leather slippers as we passed through the courtyard of the Baths of Zeuxippus, now a cemetery of statues, their broken limbs and naked torsos scattered through the trampled grasses. I picked up the sheared-off face of Julius Caesar, the same I'd admired the afternoon Comito and I had begged before the Greens. Lifetimes ago.

Another face lay nearby, that of Hypatia, the famed scholar murdered by a mob in Alexandria. I shuddered to think I might have shared her fate.

The wind whipped through my cloak, and I shivered. "We'll have to replace these."

"I intend to," Justinian said. "And I intend to do something else."

"What?"

"Actually, I've already done it." Justinian took the marble fragment from me. "I renamed the city of Anasartha today. It shall hereafter be known as Theodorias, in your honor."

I couldn't speak. The ashes of thirty thousand people floated in the air, and Justinian was naming cities after me.

He traced my cheek, eyes searching my face. "I'd have littered the map with Theodorias by now if I'd known that was the way to tame your tongue."

"I don't deserve anything."

He pulled me to him so close I could feel the warmth of his breath on the crown of my head. "Those people were traitors, Theodora."

"But their blood is on my hands."

"They made their choice. No one forced them to revolt."

I looked up at him. "Have you ever killed anyone? Before last night?"

His face clouded over. "What do you think?"

I didn't dare duck my eyes. "I once thought you ordered Lupicina's death."

There was silence. His heart seemed to have missed a beat. "And do you still believe that?"

"No." Only I wasn't sure that was true.

"Good." He stepped back, and I dared not flinch under his scrutiny. "I think some time outside the city might do you good. Perhaps a procession in Bithynia."

I didn't want Justinian to think I was fragile, that I couldn't face what we'd done, but the idea of leaving the city for a while held a certain appeal. An idea unfolded in my mind even as I spoke.

"Not right now," I said. It was too soon to flaunt ourselves, like throwing a party after a funeral. "But perhaps after Tasia's marriage."

"You want her married soon, don't you?"

I nodded. I needed to know my daughter was safe, especially with what I had planned.

"The procession will have to be extravagant," I said. "With elephants."

"I didn't realize you had an affinity for the beasts." Justinian's laughter startled the guards. "I promise it will be horrendously lavish."

"Good." I snuggled into his arm. "Won't the Cappadocian protest the expense?" I hoped he would.

"John won't object. He owes you his life."

I rather liked the idea that John was beholden to me. I could use that against him in the future.

"You'll come with me to Bithynia, won't you?"

I knew the answer before he spoke. There was no way he could leave the city anytime soon.

Justinian sighed. "Belisarius will be campaigning in Carthage—"

"And you have all your building projects to oversee." I sighed. "I'll miss you." It was true, but what I had planned couldn't happen if Justinian joined the procession. "I'll order Antonina to accompany me."

Justinian kissed the tip of my red nose. "Do as you like—you always do."

He had no idea.

Chapter 26

Macedonia walked with me among the orange groves of the monastery of Chalcedon, her musk perfume mingling with the citrus. This was our first stop since we'd left the Golden Gate, and I missed Tasia desperately; but I could hardly expect a married girl heavy with her first child to go on a royal procession through Bithynia. True to his word, Justinian had arranged Tasia's marriage to Flavius Anastasius Paulus, a distant relation of Emperor Anastasius' through his nephew Probus, the same man who'd fled the city in the face of the Nika riots. I'd cried tears of happiness at the wedding. Paulus was a soft-spoken consul, almost twice as old as Tasia's sixteen years, but kind and pleasant on the eyes. We all hoped for a boy, a grandson of my own blood who might one day sit upon the throne. I enjoyed the idea of my bloodline founding a new dynasty.

Shaggy-haired goats bleated as a tonsured monk herded them across the dusty path and away from a grove of brilliant sunflowers stretching their faces to the sun. White and brown wool that had not yet been woven into cloth hung in ropes between the trees to dry, and more of it lay in mounds on the dirt.

I plucked an orange from a tree as we walked downhill and peeled the rind in a single curled strip as the cicadas bickered around us. A child's laughter rang out, and I looked down the sun-spattered path to see Antonina strolling toward us, a tall young man I recognized as her godson Theodosius behind her balancing a chubby-cheeked infant with her mother's dark curls. Darting between them was a gangly boy, chasing a motley dog missing patches of fur.

Macedonia picked up my orange—I hadn't realized I'd dropped it. "Is that Antonina and Belisarius' child?" she asked.

"Yes." This wasn't a dream. The boy picked up a stick and threw it to the dog, his peals of laughter sending a black crow squawking into the sky. I took a deep breath, wishing for something to hold on to. I must have stumbled, because Macedonia grabbed me.

"Are you all right?"

"Fine," I said, thinking fast. "Perhaps the heat is getting to me."

She arched an eyebrow. The spring sunlight was still soft as a kiss, not yet the scorching glare of summer. "You're not pregnant, are you?"

"No chance of that."

"Well, you're white as milk. Maybe you should go inside?"

"I think I'll sit, for a moment," I said, unable to tear my eyes from the boy. "Perhaps you could get me a cup of barley water?"

"Of course." She led me to a patch of shade under an orange tree. "And maybe some sweet melon."

She could serve me wolfsbane and hemlock for all I cared. I just needed her to go.

Antonina waved to Macedonia and shooed the dog away, then walked toward me with my son at her side. John's hair curled at his temples, still damp from a recent bath, and almost entirely obscured the moon-shaped scar there. I saw myself in the point of his chin and the shape of his eyes.

John glanced up at Antonina, and she nodded her head. He bowed, a stiff little bend that made my eyes fill.

"Hello, John," I said. "I've heard much about you."

He shifted from one foot to the other. "I'm pleased to be introduced to Your Imperial Majesty."

Introduced. Imperial Majesty. My heart splintered as I thought of all the nights I'd cuddled his warm body to me in Egypt, the times he'd woken and I'd nursed him back to sleep, his little fingers curling into my breast.

Antonina took her daughter from her godson's arms. "I thought perhaps you might like to spend the evening with the Augusta?"

John's pale face and wide eyes spoke for him. My own son was terrified of me.

"Have you seen the traveling menagerie?" I didn't tell him he was the reason I'd plucked the beasts from their roles in the Kynêgion. "The giraffe has a penchant for raisin rolls dipped in honey. She's positively fat. And the elephant has a giant saddle if you'd like to ride him."

John smiled and let me thread my arm through his. That simple touch made me want to draw him into my arms and never let go. I looked back to Antonina and mouthed my thanks as she bowed.

The afternoon was a stolen moment of bliss I would treasure in the dark days ahead. I helped John feed carrots and turnips to the elephant and raisin bread to the giraffe, then watched him clamber onto the elephant's gilded saddle. In only a few years he'd be a man, but for now he was still a boy. I'd missed so much of his life—I didn't plan to miss any more.

When he finished tromping through the orange grove, I slipped Severus' cross from my neck as a slave helped him from the elephant. "I'd like you to have this," I said. "A reminder that you always have a friend in me."

His eyes widened. "Thank you, Augusta."

John shared my couch at the evening meal, and I served my son myself. I had no idea a boy could eat so much grilled goat with *garos* sauce.

A troupe from the capital performed *Ichneutae* by Sophocles, prancing about the monastery courtyard to act out baby Hermes inventing music. John's eyes drooped partway through, his head following so I felt the warm flutter of his breath on my skin. I let him linger until the play ended and almost objected when a slave woke him and helped him stumble to the empty monk's cell set up for Antonina's brood.

It had been a perfect day, but I was greedy for more. I would tell Justinian about my son when we returned to Constantinople. I'd saved his crown; he couldn't forsake me now.

A monk doffing the olive oil lamps pointed the way to Antonina's room across the courtyard, one with a mosaic of the Adoration of the Magi above the door. Onions dried on the porch and an old woman lay on the pallet outside, but she scrambled to her feet at my approach.

"Is your mistress within?"

"She's"—the slave avoided my eyes—"engaged at the moment."

"I need to speak with her."

The woman's gaze skittered back and forth, but she finally rapped on the door. There was a grunt followed by Antonina's muffled shout. "I told you I'm not to be disturbed."

"*Kyria*, the Augusta is here," the slave said. There were curses on the other side of the olive wood door before a young man emerged, his tunica hastily pinned and black hair rumpled from sleep—or from something else.

The tips of his ears flushed scarlet and he dropped to a bow, but not before I recognized him. Antonina had outdone herself this time, sleeping with her godson. "Get on with you, Theodosius," I said. "And don't let anyone else see you."

I shut the door behind me. The sheets on the monk's narrow bed were twisted, and the smell of sex filled the tiny cell. "What in God's name are you doing?"

Antonina was naked, the dark curls on her head matching those between her legs. She still possessed more curves than I did, but time had marked her with puckered white lines across her hips and the soft swell of her belly. "Jealousy doesn't become you, darling."

I kicked toward her the silk stola crumpled at my feet, but she ignored it. "I'm not jealous," I said. "I'm appalled. He's your godson!"

"Isn't it delicious? He has the stamina of an elephant."

I folded my arms in front of me, the better not to throttle her. "Need I remind you that you're married?"

"It wouldn't be as enjoyable if Belisarius knew." She sobered at the look on my face. "My husband is more demon than man. I gave him a daughter—I've more than done my duty." She pulled the stola over her head and smoothed the silk. "There were other pregnancies, too, but I lost them." She gave me a sideways glance. "Not on purpose."

All while I'd struggled to conceive Justinian's heir. A flood and a drought of blessings, all in the wrong places.

I crossed myself. "I'm sorry—I didn't know."

She shrugged. "Life is short. I intend to enjoy myself."

"You can't be serious."

Antonina laughed. "Theodora, darling, you can't stop me." She slipped her feet into red leather sandals, shoes she could wear only because I'd introduced her to Belisarius. She could take her chances, and I'd take mine.

"I'm going to tell Justinian the truth about John."

Antonina stopped, the laughter gone from her face. "You're willing to put our"—she at least had the decency to look chagrined at the slip—"your son in danger."

"What do you mean?"

"You and Justinian have had plenty of time to have a son, but there's been no hint of a child."

I nodded, not liking to hear the truth spoken aloud.

"Claim John now and you'll throw him into the ring with all the other men who believe Justinian might name them his heir. Like Belisarius."

"Belisarius aspires to be the next Emperor?"

"Belisarius is loyal to Justinian, barring the extra gold he siphons from his campaigns into his own accounts. And yes, he believes your husband might one day leave him the crown."

"But he wouldn't harm John."

Antonina shrugged. "I doubt it, but do you know Belisarius well enough to know for sure? I don't, and I'm married to him." She clasped my hands. "Please, Theodora. John is still a boy. I love him like my own—I couldn't bear for anything to happen to him."

Antonina's logic made me want to throw things at the stone wall of her cell, but I wasn't willing to put my son in danger. I desperately wanted John to come live in the Sacred Palace so I could watch him grow into a man instead of spying on him from afar. Had I known I might lose my son forever, I wondered if I might have chosen differently that day I'd left him with Antonina. But it was too late for second guesses.

Antonina, Macedonia, and I were enjoying the warm waters of Pythium's hot springs despite the sulfurous stench. The waters had wrought miraculous cures for many pilgrims in the past, and Saint Samson hoped they might help me conceive. I was under no such illusions.

I'd walked out to a startling blue sky to find Antonina and Macedonia already in the springs, one copper and one crow-black head bent together over cups of wine. My two closest friends had found an affinity for each other during our procession, and the three of us often stayed up too late into the night, reminiscing on our similar pasts and marveling at how far we'd come in life. They both looked up as I approached, and Antonina flushed into her cup.

"You two look like you're up to no good," I said, shedding my robe and stepping into the springs.

"Is there any other way to be?" Macedonia floated on her back, her still-glorious breasts bobbing like ripe melons above the surface. "We were just discussing my love life. Antonina thinks I should find a husband."

Antonina set down her cup. "I'd hate to see your bed stay empty."

"Who says it's empty?" Macedonia gave a sly smile. "The line to my bed may not be as long as it once was, but there are still men eager for my tricks. And I couldn't bear being tied to any one man for the rest of my life—how dull."

"Unless you really were tied." Antonina grinned. "That might be fun."

I splashed water at Antonina as a slave girl interrupted our swim to deliver a parchment bearing Belisarius' seal. The water from Antonina's fingers spread up the paper before she finished reading, and she bit her lower lip. "Belisarius is headed to Carthage before the harvest."

"I know. I had a letter from Justinian yesterday." It had been a letter full of praise for Belisarius, which I minded only a little, and also for John the Cappadocian and his ingenius tax reforms. The imperial coffers were filling even as Justinian emptied them to rebuild the city. I minded that quite a bit more.

Antonina frowned. "Belisarius doesn't sound too thrilled that Justinian is making him finance much of the excursion with his own funds."

"Funds pilfered from the Imperial Treasury." I might have let that slip to Justinian in my last letter.

Antonina laid the parchment on the water. The ink evaporated and floated in a murky cloud on the surface. "Belisarius recalled Theodosius to join him."

I waved the slaves away. "I thought you were going to be discreet."

"He couldn't possibly know—not even my slaves know." She bit her lip. "Not most of them anyway."

"Know about what?" Macedonia wrung out her hair, thin wisps of gray now woven into the bronze.

I looked to Antonina, but she only grinned. "I'm sleeping with my godson."

Macedonia lifted a brow. "Good for you."

I rolled my eyes. "You two are going to burn for eternity."

Antonina grinned. "We'll save you a spot, darling."

"Does Belisarius have any other reason to recall only Theodosius?" Macedonia asked.

"I don't know." Antonina stood, water pearling down her pale skin, following the trail of luminous blue veins down her hips and thighs. "I'm going with them."

"What?" I whirled on her as I wrapped a towel around my breasts. "Have you lost your mind?"

"It's the only way to keep my eye on both of them."

"You can't carry on with him in Carthage, not under Belisarius' nose."

"Of course she can," Macedonia said, perching on a rock like some sort of water nymph. "It'll be more fun that way."

"Now that you mention it," Antonina said, her grin showing off the tiny gap in her teeth, "this trip sounds absolutely delightful."

I heaved a sigh and rolled my eyes heavenward—it was no use arguing with them. "Don't come crying to me when your wicked little web gets ripped to shreds."

"Said one spider to another. Everyone has a talent, Theodora. Mine is getting people to do what I want." She grinned. "A talent we share, come to think of it."

She was right—better to be the puppeteer than the puppet. Although in this situation I felt more and more as if my strings were being pulled.

I'd been gone from Constantinople for only a few months, but it felt more like a year.

The *Greyhound* carried us across the Bosphorus, her sails pregnant with the late-summer breeze. Unsure when I'd see my son again, I swallowed hard as John was hustled into a litter with Antonina's other children. I waved away the imperial litter with its silk curtains to commandeer Antonina's ebony chariot, grimacing as she and Theodosius snapped shut the curtains of my litter behind them. I envied my friend's flush of romance, but I knew it would amount to little. Antonina was like a crow, easily distracted by anything shiny. Especially a pair of oiled biceps.

I was glad to be home. I'd missed my baths and codices, but most of all, I missed Justinian. My husband hadn't squandered time in my absence—it had been a year and a half since Nika, but the new walls of the Hagia Sophia already soared to a height to match the sky, looking down upon the rest of the city. We passed a new bronze statue of Justinian in the square of the Augusteum, tall enough to rival Constantine's. My husband looked like Achilles in his Persian military dress, sitting astride a giant warhorse. He held a globe topped with a cross in one hand while the other stretched out before him to the east as if to command some marauding horde of Persians to halt or the sun to rise. I expected Justinian would wait for me at the palace, but chips of pine and dried rosemary littered the cobbles and an imperial procession snaked its way to meet us, a man on a giant black horse at its front. I resisted the urge to spur the chariot to meet him—I'd let Justinian come to me instead.

It seemed to take an eternity before he reached us. Wordlessly, he pulled me from my borrowed chariot and onto the saddle in front of him. Tongues would wag, but I didn't care.

"God, but I missed you." He crushed me to him as the crowd cheered. "I forbid you to ever leave me for so long again."

"And I always obey my Emperor." I gave him a smile to rival Saint Pulcheria, although my impulses right then were far from virginal.

He gestured to the colossal statue. "What do you think of my latest project?"

I craned my neck. "It's a little small, don't you think?"

Justinian laughed and kept his arm around my waist as we started the slow procession home. "It's an ingenious invention. Wine actually flows from my feet on feast days."

"Of course it does," I said. "Because every Emperor should have a statue that pours wine from his boots."

"Probably not, but I don't care." He kissed my nose. "I've emptied my schedule for the entire day. This afternoon we can discuss your trip and my progress rebuilding the city."

"I cleared my afternoon, too." I gave him an impish grin. "But I don't plan to spend that time discussing much of anything."

The gold flecks in his eyes turned molten, and I felt the hardness of his desire. It had been a long summer apart—I'd have hiked up my stola and let him take me on that horse if I thought I could get away with it. He held me closer, and his thumb brushed the underside of my breast. "I knew you were a smart woman the moment I laid eyes on you."

"The smartest."

He threw back his head and laughed, the golden sound filling the square and making the crowds cheer even louder. "And the least humble."

I joined his laughter as he spurred his horse faster. It was good to be home.

Of course, that didn't last long.

Chapter 27

Ardent prayers and swinging censers had accompanied Belisarius' campaign to retake Africa from the Vandals. I watched until the last of the ninety-two *dromons* sailed from the Sea of Marmara and out of sight. Then there was nothing to do but wait.

There was no word for months. We were riding through the imperial hunting park one April morning, having already bagged a wild ass and two gazelles to serve to the visiting governor of Tarsus that night, when Narses delivered the first letters from Antonina. Delicate sunlight filtered through the budding leaves overhead, casting a puzzle of shadows on the three messages; one was a water-stained parchment, the second a crisp piece of vellum, and the third a thicker letter for Justinian bearing Belisarius' seal.

A hint of rose wafted from the parchment as I broke the seal of the first bedraggled message.

Most Serene Augusta,

I'm sure you've already heard about the great biscuit debacle. That wretched Cappadocian sent us to Carthage with biscuits already rancid with mold and water green with algae. By the time we discovered the spoiled bread, almost five hundred men had gone to meet their Maker. I had to load new supplies myself in Sicily, all while that filthy volcano belched smoke and threatened to kill us all. My nails will never be the same.

On a brighter note, my godson looks quite dashing in just his greaves and breastplate.

> *Your humble servant,*
> *Antonina*

Not for the first time, I wished John the Cappadocian had died at Nika. The first letter must have been waylaid for some time, but the second was already several months old.

Most Serene and Illustrious Augusta,

The men laid low by moldy biscuits and spoiled water shall not have died in vain.

My esteemed husband has routed the Vandals at the battle of Tricamarum. Gelimer, the imposter king, froze on the battlefield when he came upon the bloody body of his brother. Belisarius went on to take the city of Hippo, but Gelimer, a true coward, fled into the mountains. He didn't last long—Belisarius tracked down the heathen and, once surrounded, Gelimer asked for a lyre and a sponge to wash his eyes and beard when the soldiers took him. If it had been me, I'd have asked for a sword and fallen on it. But then, I'm only a foolish woman. Perhaps he'll enjoy being paraded on the streets of Constantinople and spat upon by our citizens.

> *Your humble servant,*
> *Antonina*

I set the letter upon my lap. It was so old that Antonina and Belisarius might appear in our harbor any day. "I suppose it's a good thing you added Conqueror of Africa to your list of titles months ago," I told my husband.

Justinian rolled up the parchment from Belisarius and grinned. "I am nothing if not efficient."

"And yet John the Cappadocian almost sabotaged the entire campaign."

"He made a mistake. A huge one, but a mistake nonetheless."

"The man is a miser, except when it comes to his wine and women."

Justinian rubbed his temple with one hand, the other still on his reins. "I know. Yet, without him, I could never finance the rebuilding. The Hagia Sophia alone cost an Emperor's ransom."

"Justinian." I practically growled his name.

"I'll deal with John."

"I'll send for him."

"That's not necess—"

Not giving Justinian a chance to defend the miserable excuse for a man, I motioned for Narses, who was patiently waiting near a cluster of blossoming purple Judas trees. "I don't care if the Cappadocian is in bed with ten of his whores. Truss him like a hog and drag him here if you have to."

I'd swear Narses smiled at the thought. "You'll have him before the sun sets."

"I'm not sure what John did to earn your spite," Justinian said on our way back. The slaves had already hauled away the gazelle and wild ass, so we let our horses walk as we retraced our path toward the city.

"The man is incompetent," I said. "He almost cost you your crown, yet you coddle him like a lapdog."

"This was not his finest hour." Justinian ran one hand through his hair, still thick even now that he was nearing fifty. "But Belisarius still carried the day. He's a damn fine general. I plan to reward him upon his return."

"Aren't the spoils of war reward enough?" Belisarius was quickly becoming the most popular man in the Empire, and he commanded the entire military of the Empire. One only had to look to Rome's history to see how that story often ended.

Justinian scratched his chin as if he hadn't heard me. "Perhaps something akin to the triumphs of the Golden Age."

I snorted. "There hasn't been a Roman triumph for a general in more than five hundred years."

"Not since Octavian gave one to Balbus for his campaign in Africa." Justinian's eyes lit. "Another opportunity for history to remember us."

It was almost tempting. "Except Belisarius will be the star of the show."

Justinian frowned. "Belisarius can parade through the streets with Gelimer and the Vandal treasures, but he'll bow to me in the end. I sent him to Carthage—this is *my* victory." He crossed his arms. "This triumph will be remembered to eternity."

Eternity was a long time—I'd settle for here and now.

Later that night, Narses announced a rather disheveled John the Cappadocian into our throne room. His sandy hair was thinner, and a web of tiny red lines radiated from every direction over his nose and the pores of his cheeks, the mask of a man who enjoyed his wine too much. He gave a perfunctory bow. "I seek to serve the Augusti."

Justinian cleared his throat. "We need to address the issue of the supplies you sent to the front. They were less than adequate."

That was a colossal understatement. "The grain was moldy and the water spoiled," I said. "Your poor preparation caused the deaths of more than five hundred men."

John had the decency to look troubled. "An unfortunate oversight."

"Is it not your job to oversee the purchase of supplies for the imperial troops?"

John gifted me with a placating smile. "It is impossible for me to inspect every weapon, every greave, and each barrel of biscuits. Belisarius should have checked the grain before setting sail." He paused, then added as if in afterthought, "Augusta."

The man had gall.

"And yet you require the same impossibility from Belisarius?" I asked.

John shrugged. "Were not they his men who died?"

I leaned forward from my throne, my tone murderous. "I should have let the mob have you at Nika."

A smile flickered over his face so fast I might have imagined it. He bowed his head. "And I should have told the Emperor the truth of our relationship long ago."

My fingernails dug into the arms of my throne. "What do you mean?"

"Our affair before you left for Pentapolis. And our son, the one you've hidden all these years. The boy you named after me."

Time seemed to slow as I stared at the Cappadocian, a smug look on his face. He knew. I didn't know how, but somehow this lying, shifty bastard had discovered my secret. And he was going to ruin me with these lies.

Justinian seemed more shocked than me, his brow furrowed in disbelief. I remembered Emperor Justin's warning all those years ago.

Justinian has always been fiercely loyal to those he loves, at least until he feels betrayed.

I panicked, words jumping from my mouth before I could stop them. "You're mad."

"Theodora."

"How dare you use my name." I wanted nothing more than to cut out John's tongue, to lock him in a cell below the palace and make him beg for forgiveness as the whip flayed the skin from his back.

"Augusta." John tutted under his breath. "Do you deny leaving with me after the *skolion* hosted by Emperor Justin?"

"No, but—"

"That I pursued you after you returned from Egypt, but you kept our son secret so you could pursue other, more illustrious"—his eyes flicked to Justinian—"more powerful, men?"

"That's a lie!" I leapt from my throne, my fingers itching to claw the Cappadocian's face, my entire body trembling with fury and terror. Justinian might cast me off if I didn't control myself, or worse, divorce me. I'd lose the one man in this world who ever truly loved me. Somehow I managed not to fall to my knees and beg Justinian to believe me, but instead sneered at the Cappadocian. "He's deranged, trying to denounce me with these lies."

"Enough." Justinian's tone was frigid, his face paler than usual. "I don't know where this slander came from, John, but you shall swear the imperial oath so we can be sure that your incompetence at Carthage won't happen again. And that you shall not speak another ill word against your anointed Augusta."

I watched with little satisfaction as John the Cappadocian bent to his knees. I'd have kicked him in the face if Justinian hadn't been here, or more likely, run him through with a sword.

John's gaze on me was as cold and dark as a winter's night. "I swear on the One True God that I shall faithfully serve our divinely chosen Augusti, Justinian and Theodora—"

The man's words were the now-common verse, created after Nika, and recited by all those given a position by the crown. Special adviser to Justinian, the Cappadocian had been spared making the oath. Until now.

"If I should fail them," John continued, "may I suffer forevermore—"

God could take care of forever—I'd just hasten John's appearance to the fires of Gehenna.

"May I suffer the burdens of Job, the leprosy of Simon, and the fate of Lot's wife, and may I undergo the full punishment allowed by the mercy of the Augusti and Almighty God."

Except in John's case there would be no mercy.

"Who did you tell?"

"No one, I swear!"

My fingernails dug into Antonina's soft flesh as I searched her brown eyes for traces of deceit. She shook me off with a glare and rubbed the angry red welts on her arm. "Welcome back to you, too," she muttered, stalking to her window. "Gods, Theodora, do you really think I'd tell anyone after all these years? What would I gain from doing something so stupid?"

I'd already racked my mind for that answer and come up empty. Antonina had almost as much to lose as I did if Justinian and Belisarius discovered that John the Cappadocian had spoken the truth.

"I don't know," I said, collapsing into a chair across from her rumpled bed. I hadn't managed much sleep in the weeks since the scene with John the Cappadocian, instead lying awake in my cold bed while listening to Justinian pace the corridors. Finally, we'd received word that Belisarius' ships had docked. Once dawn broke, I'd slipped away to Antonina's villa—passing Belisarius' entourage on the *Mese*—and promptly evicted a naked Theodosius from the morning light streaming onto her bed.

"But he knows, Antonina," I said. "He told Justinian everything."

"Did Justinian believe him?"

"No. I don't know." I picked a loose thread on the arm of the chair, almost glad I didn't know Justinian's mind. "I don't think so."

She pulled me to my feet. "Justinian is a good man, Theodora, and he loves you more than he probably should. He's not going to listen to John's blather."

"He might." I swallowed a sob, feeling the terror I'd held at bay creeping in. "I can't lose him, Antonina. I just can't."

"You're not going to." She shook my shoulders once, none too gently. "Listen to me. The Cappadocian has no proof. And even if he did, do you honestly think Justinian wouldn't forgive you?"

"I don't know." I drew a ragged breath and forced myself to think rationally, no mean feat for my exhaustion-riddled mind. I ran a shaky hand over my hair, straightening my silk veil. "Maybe you're right."

"Did you ever doubt it?"

I snorted and managed a weak smile. "Thank you for bringing me to my senses."

"Don't mention it. In case you hadn't noticed, I'm rather fond of you." She kissed both my cheeks. "Actually, I'm more fond of the snarky, sarcastic Empress. I could do without the waterlogged wife who kicks handsome young studs from my bed before the sun has had a chance to rise."

"The sun's been up for hours."

She glanced at the window and shrugged. "Perhaps. But I still plan to pull my godson back into bed once you leave."

Which she planned to do quite soon, judging from the way she was ushering me toward the door.

"Just don't get caught." I hugged her, inhaling the scent of a rose garden in full bloom. "And I'm rather fond of you, too."

"I know, darling."

I passed Theodosius on my way out and heard the door shut, followed by Antonina's lusty squeal. I hadn't wanted to suspect her of telling the Cappadocian, but she was the only person I could think of who might have spilled my secret.

So now the question remained: If not Antonina, then who?

Cheers heralded Belisarius' triumph long before the horns blared in the newly reopened Hippodrome. The entire city had turned out for a celebration to rival that of Octavian when he conquered Egypt. Imperial wine flowed through the streets, and clay bread tokens stamped with the image of Michael the Archangel had been distributed to each household in the city. We'd hired every fire-eater, puppeteer, and actress in the capital and surrounding countryside to entertain the waiting masses. The dull roar of the crowd grew to wild screams as the Vandal treasure poured through the gates of the Hippodrome.

An unarmed regiment of Belisarius' men marched onto the track with wreaths upon their heads, followed by slaves bearing painted frescoes of the vanquished cities of Hippo and Carthage. Baskets of gold ingots stacked an arm's length high whetted the crowd's appetite, along with a train of gold and silver, trunks and litters containing the metals in every form imaginable—goblets, crowns, diadems, necklaces. Then came one of the greatest treasures on earth—the silver menorah from the Temple of Solomon in Jerusalem, seized by the Vandals during the sack of Rome almost eighty years earlier.

Followed by his family and dressed in imperial purple, Gelimer shuffled behind his lost treasure, hands and feet bound in heavy silver chains. His shoulders slumped like Atlas as the crowd hurled vulgarities at him.

"*Canis!*"

"*Fur!* You deserve to hang!"

"*Prospice tibi—ut Gallia, tu quoque in tres partes dividareis!*"

I cringed at the last one—Gelimer might be a dog and a thief, but I had no wish to watch him divided into three parts. Cleopatra had the right idea—I'd welcome death rather than face such humiliation.

The crowd chanted Belisarius' name as he entered the arena on a gilded chariot drawn by four perfectly matched chestnut stallions, a mirror of the bronze Triumphal Quadriga at the entrance of the Hippodrome. The gleaming laurel wreath on his brow matched his gold armor, too close to a crown for my liking. He frowned each time the ancient slave at his side whispered in his ear; occasionally he even tried to brush him away. I had insisted on following the old tradition of keeping a slave in his chariot to whisper the adage, "You are merely a man." Unfortunately, it seemed likely Belisarius might forget that piece of advice with everyone hollering his name.

Familiar faces soon followed—Sittas, Antonina, and Procopius of Caesaria, a beady-eyed historian with a face like a monkey who accompanied Belisarius to record the victory for all posterity. John the Cappadocian was there as well, despite my prayers that he be impaled by a Vandal sword.

The Cappadocian passed me on his way to join the line of advisers behind Justinian. He smiled, but his hand was tight on my arm. "I need to speak with you. Alone."

I smiled as if he had just complimented me on the embroidery on my new stola, glad Antonina had chosen that moment to distract Justinian. I'd sent her a message last night outlining my plan to her. "The Sunken Palace," I said to John. "Tonight."

He released my arm, and I had to force myself not to rub the spot where his hand had been. I refused to give the man the satisfaction of knowing he'd rattled me. I still wasn't sleeping well and had yet to determine how he'd discovered John. I planned to make him pay, and soon.

Belisarius leapt from his chariot and prodded Gelimer with his sword into the Kathisma. The crowd fell silent. The Vandal king fell to his knees, lanky ropes of filthy hair hiding his eyes. The man's life hung in the balance, but Justinian planned to exile him to estates in Galatia since the Vandals wanted nothing to do with their cowardly former king.

Justinian stepped forward and wrapped Gelimer's purple *chalmys* around his fist. His voice boomed into the silent stands. "Gelimer, usurper of our African kingdom of Carthage, you have been bested by mighty Rome and the Emperor whom God anointed with the true purple. You are neither imperial nor Roman." With that he yanked the purple robe from Gelimer's shoulders and spat at the ground before him.

The former king raised his head and dared look Justinian in the face. "'Vanity of vanities,'" he said. "'All is vanity.'"

The line from Ecclesiates was a reminder of failure, but he was the failure, not us. Perhaps Gelimer needed to spend some time chained beneath the palace before he moved to Galatia to enjoy his retirement.

Justinian looked at Belisarius—the general still stood straight as a granite pillar, his massive silver general's belt gleaming brightly. It took him a moment to realize why the Emperor was staring at him, but then he slowly joined Gelimer on his knees. His helmet shielded his face so I could only guess at his humiliation. Both Antonina and Narses had informed me of all the Vandal gold he'd managed to siphon into his own accounts; the obscene wealth he had confiscated would buy his loyalty for now.

At least I hoped so.

The damp air made my arms prickle with gooseflesh as I left the last light of dusk behind me. The Sunken Palace wasn't a palace at all, but an unfinished cistern tucked almost under the Hagia Sophia. Slaves bowed as I descended the stairs into the cavern and emerged into a dark forest of mismatched marble columns lit by sputtering oil torches. Dust and the sound of chisels filled the air. My leather boots did little to keep out the ankle-high water.

I almost forgot why I was here as I gaped at the upside-down colossal head of Medusa, a column stretching from her neck to the ceiling.

The cistern's columns had all been commandeered from pagan temples throughout the Empire. Two contained the witch's head, one left upside down and the other sideways to ward off the evil eye. I waded into the water that lapped at her hair and touched the cool granite of her face. Carp swam lazily at my feet, unconcerned with the gorgon or Empress in their pond.

A slave hammered a column etched with a Hen's Eye and swirls of what appeared to be tears, or peacock feathers, pouring down the stone. The man's mouth formed a perfect O to see me, and he dropped his chisel, his hair covered in white dust like finely milled flour as he struggled to bow.

I continued through the maze of columns alone when someone touched my arm, almost a caress.

The Cappadocian held up his hands and motioned me to be silent. Suddenly I wished I hadn't left my guards at the entrance, although they probably wouldn't have made a difference. John was a trusted member of Justinian's inner circle and would likely have to pull a knife on me before they'd move against him. I trembled to think what Justinian would think if he discovered that I'd come here alone to meet the Cappadocian.

"What do you want?" I asked.

"That's hardly how you should greet your faithful servant, don't you think?"

"You've never served me. You're a lying, conniving fraud, and I don't know where you came up with those lies—"

"Hardly lies when I have proof of the living, breathing son you never mentioned to your husband, our illustrious Emperor."

Ice coursed through my veins. I had to continue to test him, to find out how much he knew. "You are mistaken, Prefect. God has seen fit to bless me with a daughter, but no living sons."

He pretended to inspect a column. "Yet I know you had a son after you took up with Hecebolus."

"And he died while he was still a child."

"Don't lie, Theodora—it doesn't become you. The boy's been hidden under Antonina's roof all these years. She's such a slut, no one would notice an addition to her herd of brats." His lips curled in a slow smile. "Everyone saw you leave with me that night at Justin's." I moved to escape, but his fingers closed around my arm. "I'm sure the

Emperor would be thrilled to know that you and I shared a rather spectacular night together that resulted in your illegitimate son."

I wanted to punch the smug look off his face. "You already tried to tell him those lies. He doesn't believe you."

"Will Justinian believe me after I describe every freckle on your magnificent body?" His fingers brushed the ribs under my breast. "About the mole under your left breast? How you screamed my name and begged me for more?"

I clenched my fists to keep my hands from shaking. I'd let John kiss me that night at Justin's, allowed him to almost undress me before Hecebolus interrupted us. Justinian would think I'd lied to him about my relationship with the Cappadocian. John's lies would transform his love into hate.

"Why didn't you just tell him all that in the throne room?"

John rubbed the cleft in his chin. "There is a price for my silence. I could probably be persuaded to keep our little secret in return for the revenues of your lands in Bithynia."

Even though I was dressed in purple with a golden crown on my head and red sandals on my feet, men still extorted me. It felt like being back in the tiny cabin on board the *Naiad*, Wart leering over me.

"You'd blackmail your Empress?"

"You could have had me, but your choices have brought us to this point, Augusta, not mine. I have a daughter to care for, to ensure she has a proper dowry."

"You have plenty of money."

John shrugged. "Easily gained, easily lost."

I glared at him. "I should have made sure you dangled from the gallows with Hypatius."

He reached out to touch my cheek, but I slapped his hand away. He chuckled. "Still a hellcat, even when cornered. You decide how much this secret is worth." He walked past me toward the dim light of the entrance but turned before he got too close to the guards. "And don't think of sending one of your nasty little eunuchs after me. I have a nice bundle of proof of your transgressions that would quickly be found if my body washed up in the Bosphorus."

Frozen with rage and terror, I watched him disappear up the stairs. I didn't know if he spoke the truth about the proof, but I couldn't risk it. Not yet.

I'd find a way to destroy John the Cappadocian if it was the last thing I did.

I was glad Justinian was still in his offices when I returned to the palace. I sent a yawning eunuch for Narses, but one of his guards told me he'd left court and might not return for several weeks. I needed Antonina to keep an eye on Belisarius, and her disappearance from Constantinople would alert John the Cappadocian of my plan. There was only one other person I could trust with this mission. I wrote a letter while I waited, the first of several.

Macedonia bowed as a eunuch announced her, but I didn't have time for such niceties. "I need you to take my son to Alexandria."

"Your son? With Hecebolus?" She blinked. "I thought your son died after you left Antioch."

"That's what I told you, and Justinian," I said, still writing, "but Antonina's been hiding him all this time."

"So Justinian would put you on the throne?" Her tone was soft, not accusatory.

"That, and for John's protection. For my daughter." There had been so many reasons at the time, but now they all bled together.

She gave a great exhale and sat down hard. "So I'm to take your son to Alexandria?" I was ordering her to the ends of the earth.

"John the Cappadocian knows about him. He threatened me at the Sunken Palace tonight."

"So your son isn't safe." She perched on the edge of the carved olive wood stool. "Neither are you, for that matter."

"I'll worry about that later." I was already working on a way to tell Justinian without his banishing me to a rock in the Mediterranean. "I don't know if the Cappadocian would try anything with the boy, but I can't chance it."

"I'll leave immediately."

I handed her a folded piece of vellum, fine in quality but lacking my imperial seal. "Give this to Antonina."

"May I?"

I nodded—Macedonia should know what she was getting into.

She raised her brows as she read. "So the boy is to study with Severus of Alexandria."

I nodded. "I've already sent another letter ahead to warn Severus." In actuality, I'd asked him to bear witness to the true date of John's birth so I could tell Justinian the truth. I'd kept up correspondence with Severus since my marriage—I was reasonably sure he'd help me. I handed a second letter to Macedonia. "This will explain everything to the Patriarch. Make sure John wears my silver cross—it will prove your claim to Severus."

Macedonia stood and smoothed her stola. "I hope this works, for your sake."

"It will."

It had to.

Chapter 28

Darkness cloaked me behind an ebony screen, a clutch of guards and the secret passageway to the palace's Horse Courtyard at my back. It was the dead of night, yet the sound of hammers and chisels filled the air of the Hagia Sophia.

I pressed my hand to my eyelid to stop its incessant twitching. I'd seen Saint Samson about the problem a few days ago, but he believed I only needed more rest. That might be true—I doubted I'd pulled together more than a few hours of sleep since Macedonia had left. There had been no word from her, and Justinian had sent John the Cappadocian to Antioch to deal with the tax collection, but I'd been steadily funneling money into his accounts and would continue to do so until I received confirmation of my story from Severus. Then I could go after the Cappadocian.

I peered through a gap in the screen, watching laborers struggle to raise one of the columns from Ephesus' famed Temple of Artemis. Justinian had reached out to all corners of the Empire to gather a meadow of colored columns: Greek powdered white marble, Egyptian porphyry, and green marble from Thessaly, all to beautify what would become God's most glorious church. Even more impressive, he'd also twisted arms and spent a fortune on bribes to bring together a host of holy relics for the new Hagia Sophia including the Virgin's cloak, the table from the Last Supper, and fragments of the Golgotha cross.

My husband handed out coins to the workmen, their smiles glinting in the lamplight almost as brightly as the gold they slipped into their pockets. Justinian often came here to watch the progress of this, the crown jewel of his rebuilding. He would hide behind the screen and then emerge to pass out generous rewards to the hardest workers, but since the laborers never knew when they were being observed, the men were always soaked with sweat. This time he beckoned me out from behind the screen. I ignored the workers' furtive glances as he pressed a sack of coins into my hands.

"Is there no gold left for them to excavate from the foundations?" I divided the newly minted *solidi* amongst the workers' callused hands. Justinian's first trick had been to hide gold amongst the rubble of the old church to encourage them to dig faster.

He chuckled. "That ran out long ago. But it served its purpose—we're already ahead of schedule."

"Your church will be magnificent."

His hand caressed the small of my back. "God has also answered my prayers to retake Rome. The Mediterranean shall soon be a Roman lake once more."

It was a stain on Justinian's reign—on all Byzantine Emperors since Odoacer deposed Romulus Augustulus—that the city of Rome wasn't ruled by Rome, but instead by an Ostrogoth king who posed as a Roman viceroy. Justinian had long awaited an excuse to invade, especially since the hand of the Ostrogoth king was light upon Roman backs. The Roman people might not mind being reabsorbed into the Empire, but they weren't interested in paying our heavier taxes. It would be less than ideal to reconquer our people only to have them revolt against John the Cappadocian's taxes.

"What is this miracle?" I asked.

"Queen Amalasuntha has asked for my help retaking her throne."

"That didn't take long." Amalasuntha's husband, the Ostrogoth king, had recently died and left his lovely young queen a widow. "I was under the impression Amalasuntha was content to act as regent until her son comes of age."

Justinian shook his head, his face dark. "The patricians killed her son, and her cousin seized the throne."

We crossed ourselves, my mood suddenly dark. Amalasuntha's son would have been close to John's age. "So our imperial army marches again," I said.

Justinian nodded. "Just as soon as I can convince the Sardinians to revolt against the Ostrogoths."

"A diversionary tactic." I touched his toe with my sandal. "You sneaky devil."

"Always." He smiled, then strummed his fingers against his arm— the man couldn't think if he was sitting still. "I can't trust this campaign to anyone but Belisarius."

"So he can have another triumph?" I pursed my lips. "Antonina tells me of the company he keeps these days—senators, consuls, the Patriarch. Do you want to share the purple with your general?"

"Belisarius is a soldier. He prefers his armor to the purple."

"So he'll politely decline when the widowed queen offers him the Ostrogoth throne?" Justinian might not realize it, but Belisarius would have ample reason to divorce Antonina if he discovered her affair with Theodosius. Then he could march into Rome and accept Amalasuntha's hand and kingdom on a golden platter.

Justinian turned his back to me, pretending to survey a column inscribed with his monogram. "It will be difficult for him to take Amalasuntha's throne when she's under my protection."

"An ocean away."

"No," he said slowly. "She'll be here."

"What?" I stopped dead. "Amalasuntha is coming here?"

Justinian glanced back at me. "Amalasuntha is a fugitive. I have offered her asylum."

Amalasuntha was rumored to be as cunning as Julius Caesar and as mercurial as Caligula. And as beautiful as Cleopatra. I didn't want her within a hundred miles of my court, or my husband. I had John the Cappadocian to deal with—I couldn't fight wars on two fronts.

I gave Justinian my most glittering smile. "I look forward to greeting the great Ostrogoth queen."

And sending her back to Rome fast enough to make her lovely little head spin.

Crosses of palm fronds decorated the throne room the Sunday before Easter, the pillars draped with gold and green silk banners and the mosaics strewn with violet petals. Justinian had walked to the Church of the Holy Apostles at dawn, leading the donkey on which the Patriarch rode. I was glad he was gone when a messenger appeared with a letter for me from Alexandria. I expected Severus' familiar script, but I opened the parchment to find it blotted with ink and blurred with what may have been tears.

Most Honored Augusta,

It is with a heavy heart that I must inform you that Severus, Patriarch of Antioch, has passed to God. The prelate fell ill some months ago and rid himself of all his worldly possessions in order to spend his final days amongst the anchorite hermits. They say he passed peacefully in his sleep, a smile on his face in the tomb of an ancient pagan pharaoh.

Yours in God,
Sister Mary of the Cross

I wept for Severus, wishing I'd been able to see my old friend again, but I shed more than a few tears for myself. With Severus gone, no one knew the truth of John's birth, and Sister Mary hadn't mentioned the arrival of Macedonia and my son. They might have been blown off course along the journey, or lost in a storm. Or worse. Even if they'd arrived after Severus' death, I now had no proof to verify my claims against those of the Cappadocian.

Slaves had applied cool lavender cream to my face to erase the signs of my grief, and now I stood in the throne room with Justinian to begin the annual payment of our court officials, forcing myself not to dwell on this morning's bad news. My stomach rumbled—we'd feasted two days ago, but Lazarus Saturday began a new fast, and we still had the Holy Week before we'd truly be able to eat again. Everyone might have been on edge had it not been for the tables laden with bags of coins surrounding us.

Justinian faced the court but glanced at me from the corner of his eyes. "You look stunning today."

I'd dressed carefully before receiving the letter from Alexandria, choosing a deep purple stola edged with red flowers and a crimson *paludamentum*. A net of rubies and amethysts covered my veil and matched the gems in Justinian's crown. I marveled for a moment at the man by my side. Lines radiated from the corners of his eyes, and strands of gray whispered at his temples, but he was still as hale and handsome as the day I'd met him.

I bumped my hip to his, the tiny movement hidden from prying eyes by the table before us. "You don't look too bad yourself."

A slave struggled to lift one of the largest moneybags, and Justinian pretended to read the name stamped on the burlap. "Narses! One thousand *solidi*."

Narses had only just returned from his long trip away from court. He stepped out of the crowd and onto the dais, hefting the sack onto his shoulder. I draped four cloaks of honor over his free arm, all silk woven with glittering samite. "Not bad for an ill-tempered eunuch from Armenia," I said, giving him a cheeky grin.

He inclined his head toward me, a smile in his eyes. "I believe I've earned twice this for serving a stubborn chit from the stage of the Kynêgion."

"I don't know how you've managed all this time." I rolled my eyes. "I'll be sure to put in a recommendation for your raise."

He chuckled and somehow managed a bow. "Augusta."

Justinian called Belisarius next, but the bronze doors swung open before he could award the general's massive sack of coins. A harried-looking slave cleared his throat and banged his eagle staff on the ground. "Amalasuntha, Queen of the Ostrogoths!"

Rumor of the woman's beauty didn't do her justice. Amalasuntha's cheekbones were chiseled to perfection, her lips full and red as an open rose. Stunning in a green and gold stola, she strode into the throne room, the crowd of courtiers parting before her like the Red Sea. The gauzy silk veil made the thick blond braids coiled around her ears sparkle, and a heavy gold crown studded with emeralds matched the earrings hanging to her shoulders.

Justinian stepped forward to greet her, and I forced myself to do the same. She halted before us but did not bow.

"Augustus." Her full lips curved into a smile to reveal white and perfectly straight teeth. She stepped up onto the dais and clasped my hands. "Theodora."

The move caught me by surprise, but her smile didn't extend to her eyes; it was more the cold stare of a lioness stalking its prey.

"Amalasuntha." My voice dripped with honey. "We didn't expect you until after Easter."

"The seas were obliging, especially for this time of year," she said. "I'm sorry to interrupt your festivities, but I simply couldn't wait."

"We were seeing to the annual payment of our officials." Justinian gestured to an ebony chair next to his throne. "Perhaps you might join us?"

He may as well have offered her my throne. I scarcely managed to keep my smile as she settled in near my husband, feeling her eyes on my back as the assembled courtiers ogled the famous beauty. We were halfway done when a familiar face surfaced in the crowd, one I hadn't seen in months.

Macedonia inclined her head toward the bronze doors and wove her way out of the throne room. I thanked God to see her safe, grateful my earlier worries had been unfounded. It would be some time before we finished here, but this couldn't wait.

I moaned and swayed on my feet. Justinian looked up from the grinning *illustris* he was clapping on the back. "Are you all right?"

I pressed fingertips to my temples. "A little light-headed."

The line of patricians squirmed to see what had slowed the payments. Justinian's brows knit together. "No wonder, with standing so long on an empty stomach. You need to eat."

My hand fluttered. "I'm fine. I think I might take a walk—some fresh air might help."

I'd barely made it a step when Amalasuntha's voice purred behind me. "Might I take the Augusta's place? I've never had a head for figures, but surely I could help. I may even learn something from you, Brother."

I froze to see the Ostrogoth queen's rather large breasts brush Justinian's arm. *Brother*, indeed. Yet Macedonia waited for me, with news of my son.

I forced myself to keep walking. I'd deal with the Ostrogoth tramp later.

Macedonia stood against the wall outside the throne room, but I led her to a little courtyard garden with a large lion fountain that would mask our voices. I gestured her to a red marble bench littered with apple blossom petals. She didn't sit.

"How is John?"

She bit her lip, fingers plucking her sleeve. "It was a difficult crossing, Augusta."

"It's been longer than I expected. I worried you might have run into bad weather—"

"The weather was fine."

But something wasn't fine. The numb taste of fear filled my mouth, but I prattled on. "How did John settle in with Severus? Does he miss Antonina and his siblings?"

"John is dead."

I couldn't move, but then my legs collapsed beneath me.

"No." My pearl eardrops slapped my neck. "That's not possible."

Macedonia sank to the ground at my side and touched my hand. "It was the pox. He fell ill at sea and took to his bed with the rash, but there was nothing we could do." Her eyes shone with tears. "He was buried at sea off the coast of Pelusium. I wanted to save the amber cross to bring back to you, but the captain insisted we bury everything he'd touched to stop the contagion from spreading."

"No." The word turned into a moan, followed by sobs so strong I could scarcely pull air into my lungs. "No!"

An ocean grave. I couldn't hope to visit him, even in death. I beat my head into the dirt and grass, keening in the fresh spring air as birds chirped and butterflies danced overhead.

My son was dead. He had forgotten me, and now he was forever lost to me. Because of me. First my sister Anastasia, and now I was responsible for the death of another child. My child. Stains on my soul.

I don't know how I got to my apartments, but Justinian came that night through the doors that led straight from his rooms to my bedchamber. Dirt was still caked under my nails, crushed blades of fresh green grass clutched in my hands. I'd stopped crying to stare at the wall from under the thick blankets on my bed.

"What's wrong, my little imp?" He brushed hair from my clammy brows and touched my damp feather pillow. "Are you ill?"

I closed my eyes. "Only a headache."

"I'll send Saint Samson to you." His lips grazed the place where his fingers had touched my brow. "Rest and feel better."

I had caused my son's death. I would never feel better again.

John is dead.

Three words had changed my world.

I wanted to set up a shrine to my son, but there was nothing I could even hold in my hands that he had once touched. Nothing but memories, and those weren't enough. He was gone from this earth, transient as a gust of wind.

I dismissed the slaves who came to dress me several mornings later, letting grief and guilt take turns pummeling me until my tears might have been wrung from the pillows. Narses entered and held the door open for the slave departing with my untouched dinner tray from the night before.

His eyes flickered with surprise to see me abed, still dressed in the same purple stola I'd worn on Palm Sunday. "You need to get up."

"Leave me alone." My voice sounded rusty, cracked with disuse.

Instead, he opened the curtains, making me wince to see the happy sunlight. "I thought you might wish to know Queen Amalasuntha has requested an audience with the Emperor."

I rolled over, giving him my back. "I'm sure she has."

"A private audience. In his chambers."

That made me sit up. "When?"

"An hour ago."

I stuffed my feet into slippers and shoved the hair from my swollen eyes. "And you're only telling me this now?"

"She was only just admitted into Justinian's chambers." He frowned. "Are you all right, Augusta?"

"Fine," I lied.

I tried the doors that led from my room to Justinian's. Locked.

Two Scholarii brandished shields and spears outside my husband's private apartments. I opened my mouth to berate them to move aside, but the doors swung open and Amalasuntha tumbled out, cheeks flushed and hair becomingly mussed. Her eyes flicked over my loose hair and the rumpled stola I'd worn since the day she arrived. Her lips curved up in a cunning smile. "Well, hello, Theodora."

I stepped so close she stumbled back. "What in God's name were you doing in my husband's chambers, Amalasuntha?"

Fear flickered in her eyes, but then her fingers fluttered to the neckline of her stola. "Whatever are you insinuating?"

"Don't play stupid. You know exactly what I'm insinuating."

Her smile deepened. "I had a proposal for your husband. One he couldn't refuse."

"Stay away from my husband, you filthy tramp."

"Tramp?" Her sneer revealed those perfect white teeth. I wanted to punch them out of her mouth. "This, coming from a known whore rumored to have hidden an illegitimate son from the Emperor all these years?"

That deflated my anger. My voice was smaller this time. "You don't know what you're talking about."

"We'll see about that." She sidestepped me but turned back after only a few steps. "In case you were curious, your husband was very amenable to my suggestions. Justinian is quite a man."

White-hot fury surged over me again, but I remained rooted to the spot as she smoothed her hair and sauntered down the corridor. The doors opened for a second time.

"Theodora?" Justinian's tunica was open at the chest, and his hair was wilder than normal. I imagined that foul woman running her fingers through his dark curls, her lips kissing the thin trail of black hair that tapered to his navel. My knees threatened to buckle. "I thought I heard your voice," he said. "Are you feeling better?"

I swayed on my feet. I'd always had Justinian's love and trust, had known he'd always been faithful. Until now.

Justinian led me to a polished ebony chair inside, and he set about rearranging papers on his desk. Over his shoulder in the next room, the silk hangings of his bed were drawn to reveal a tangle of sheets. "I've agreed to send Belisarius to assist Amalasuntha in Rome. She's a very persuasive woman."

I was numb but managed a nod. "I'm sure she is."

He set down his papers. "You look terrible, Theodora. I want you to rest. Amalasuntha can take your place at the Easter festivities this week."

"No, I—"

"I insist." He ushered me toward the little side door, kissed my forehead, and unlocked the door. "Don't worry about anything. Rest and get better."

I didn't have a chance to protest before the door shut behind me. A key turned in the lock.

I'd lost everything.

Chapter 29

"You look like hell, Theodora."

I didn't argue with Antonina—my mirror had obliged me with the ugly truth this morning. She didn't look too well herself, her loose hair whipping in the sea breeze and dressed in black for the public mourning of her son.

Our son.

We had just come from a banquet in the Sacred Palace's Hall of Nineteen Couches. The ceiling had opened, and mechanical cranks lowered gilded trays of honeyed fruit and other delicacies onto the tables, eliciting childlike gasps of pleasure from Amalasuntha. I gritted my teeth as she grasped Justinian's hand while an acrobat balanced a ribboned pole on his forehead and two young men clambered up to perform tricks on the top. All this had been ordered for the Ostrogoth queen, a celebration to see her off to Rome. I hoped her ship would sink along the way.

"Justinian's sleeping with her," I said now, watching Justinian talk to Amalasuntha on the docks, their heads almost touching. Two ships floated behind them, one to carry Amalasuntha to Rome and another to carry Belisarius and all the accoutrements of war.

"No." Antonina surveyed my husband and shook her head. "I've never seen a man dote on a woman like Justinian does you."

"I caught her leaving his chambers."

"That's it?"

I thought of Amalasuntha's tousled hair and Justinian's bare chest. The knot of sheets on his bed. "There was more."

She waited for me to continue, but forcing myself to say what I'd seen out loud would make it far too real. "Well, I doubt it's what you thought it was," she said. "Although you really couldn't blame Justinian for straying, given the way you look."

"I don't care how I look. Our son is dead."

"I'm so sorry, Theodora." Antonina's voice was so quiet I'd barely heard her.

"I know," I said. "I'm sorry, too."

The words felt hollow. Antonina squeezed my hand, her rose perfume mixing with the salty sea breeze. "You have to keep on living, even when all you want to do is die."

Over on the dock, Amalasuntha surveyed the parting gifts Justinian had given her, including chests of gold and several purple cloaks. She squealed with excitement at a ruby-studded chalice of sardonyx and enamel decorated with representations of the twelve apostles. It was the chalice Justinian and I had drunk from at our wedding.

I'd always thought death a single event, but over the past weeks I'd discovered it was possible to die a thousand little deaths. Soon there would be nothing left of me for the angels—or the devil—to claim.

Amalasuntha kissed Justinian's cheeks, her hands lingering over his as the breeze played with her cloak. She whispered something in his ear and blinked hard, despite the gray clouds shrouding the sun.

Belisarius saluted Justinian. "Next time we meet, I shall bring you

Rome." His voice was loud enough for everyone on the docks to hear. The little man next to him yelled at a slave carrying a crate of parchment and pens. He was Procopius, the historian sent along again to record Belisarius' triumphant campaign for all posterity. I still thought the man resembled a monkey.

Justinian clapped Belisarius on the arm and Amalasuntha boarded her ship, trailed by her entourage.

"Are you sure you want to go with him again?" I asked Antonina, nodding toward Belisarius.

"I couldn't possibly let him sail all the way to Rome with that harlot." Antonina scowled, but then I saw the true reason she wished to travel with the army. Her golden godson emerged from the crowd and took his place beside Belisarius, taller and more handsome than I remembered. She at least had the decency to blush. "Belisarius asked Theodosius to accompany him."

"Don't let him find out about the two of you." The old advice was a feeble attempt to ward off the possible coup I feared from Belisarius. I found I no longer cared much what happened to Justinian's crown.

I saw Antonina's son Photius then, looking very much like his mother, but dressed in a fierce scowl along with his new military uniform. "Photius is joining you?"

"He's not pleased about it either. He'd rather apprentice himself to a fresco artist. Or a sculptor, if he had to," Antonina said. "He'll get over it soon enough."

The rest of the officers were filing onto the waiting ship. "Write to me?" I asked her. The days ahead promised to be bleak—I hoped Antonina's letters and news of her intrigues would keep me sane.

"I'll send you all the latest gossip." She kissed me on the cheek, but I stiffened to see Justinian striding toward us. "Talk to him, Theodora. Your husband is a good man."

Instead, I turned on my heel and walked away.

. . .

"A letter from Antonina." Narses offered me the parchment as if it were a dead rat.

I let it dangle there for a moment, then swiped it with a roll of my eyes. "I've never understood your low opinion of Antonina. I'd have thought she'd have grown on you by now."

His upper lip curled, and he brushed his hands as if to rid them of contagion. "Antonina is the lowborn daughter of a whore and a charioteer who has managed to hoodwink a line of men using her sexual wiles. She's a crass and filthy pagan with a sharp tongue, hardly company fit for the likes of the Augusti."

"Well, if that's all." I borrowed the knife from his belt and used it to slice Antonina's seal from the letter. "It almost sounds like you've just described me."

He crossed his arms. "You are not a pagan, and you have managed to rise above your birth because you have an uncommon mind. And, despite my best intentions, I've grown accustomed to your sharp tongue." He cleared his throat, and his features softened. "That said, Augusta, you haven't been yourself lately. If there's anything I can do to help—"

He dared squeeze my shoulder, and for a moment I almost told him everything, wanting to unburden myself. But I was Empress.

I handed back his knife. "Thank you, Narses." I managed a wan smile. "This will pass. And then you'll have to deal with my sharp tongue once again."

"I look forward to it, Augusta." Narses bowed and walked off, all business once again.

My smile fell as I read Antonina's letter.

Dearest Augusta,

I write bearing the best of news. Amalasuntha is dead. She betrayed us by arriving first in Rome and persuading her

cousin to offer her a joint rule. To celebrate their new rela-
tionship, he gave her a lovely amethyst and pearl necklace, and
she gifted him a sardonyx chalice decorated with the twelve
apostles. Their new arrangement would have put Belisarius in
a bit of a quandary, but fortunately the cousin quickly rem-
edied his grievous error and used the amethyst necklace to
strangle the dear girl in her sleep. I really think you and Jus-
tinian should consider nominating him for some sort of award.

The path for conquest is wide open. Your husband will
soon be the sole ruler of Rome—he couldn't have planned it
better himself.

—Antonina

I wanted answers and I wanted them now, no matter how they might kill me. I shoved open the doors to Justinian's chambers and kicked them shut behind me, both relieved and terrified to see my husband at his desk.

"Did you have a hand in this?" I stormed to Justinian and shook the paper in front of him, but he barely glanced up from the schematics of the Hagia Sophia's colossal dome to scan the letter. We'd scarcely spoken since Amalasuntha's entourage had departed, not for lack of trying on his part, but because I could barely stand to look at him. To make matters worse, Justinian had invited John the Cappadocian back to the capital, although I had yet to see him. Eventually, Justinian had given up until we acted like charged magnets, one of us pushing the other away so we never shared the same room.

Justinian gave me a wary look. "Actually, some people think you may have had a hand in Amalasuntha's death."

"Me? That's absurd."

"Is it?" Justinian's eyes were hooded. "You certainly made it plain that you didn't care for her while she was here."

Of course I didn't care for her. And while I almost entertained Antonina's idea of rewarding Amalasuntha's cousin, I hadn't ordered her murder. At least not yet.

Justinian sighed. "Do you honestly think I'd send Amalasuntha back to Rome, knowing her cousin would offer her the crown and then kill her?"

"I don't know what to think. Did you send your lover with Belisarius to help you conquer Rome, or did you have her killed?"

He set down the plans. "My lover? Is that why you've been acting this way?"

"I practically caught you in the act."

He exhaled and tipped his chair back, running hands through his hair. "That day in my chambers—that's what you thought?"

"What was I supposed to think? That you two looked like you'd just tumbled out of bed because you'd been arguing?"

"Actually, that's not far from the truth." He stood up and paced before his desk. "Amalasuntha did propose we, er . . . further our relationship." His cheeks flushed. "She was quite convinced that I'd be lucky to have her, and she was rather put out when I refused."

"And I'm supposed to believe that?" And yet I wanted to so badly.

He clasped my hands. "I've loved you from the first moment I saw you, Theodora. I moved heaven and earth to marry you. What do I have to do to prove that love?"

I sniffed and blinked, pulling my hands back. "So you didn't have her murdered?"

A muscle ticked in his jaw. "I love you, Theodora," he said, "but you do test my limits. I did not have Amalasuntha murdered. Nor did I have my aunt murdered as you once believed. I have never plotted anyone's murder."

I searched his eyes, but they were bare. I'd never felt more alone than these past few weeks without Justinian. I needed him like I needed air in my lungs and blood in my veins.

"I believe you."

"Good," he said, his hand cupping my face. "I've missed you, Theodora."

"I missed you, too." I buried my face in his shoulder, my dry eyes managing to find the last of their tears. "I love you."

I was broken, but perhaps my love for Justinian would heal me.

Dawn raised her rosy head over the Queen of Cities when a scrawny messenger was ushered into the royal box at the imperial *tzykanion* grounds a few months later. The sport had been imported from the Persians decades ago, one of the only useful contributions the fire-eaters had made to civilization.

Justinian cantered over on his black horse, the net at the end of his stick trembling over his head like a war pennant. The courtiers watched the leather ball as they waited for the Emperor, their horses eyeing the tufts of grass at the edge of the field. "What is it, boy?"

The runner fell to one knee and bowed his head. "The Goths in Ravenna have offered General Belisarius peace to end the siege on their city and all of Italy." He glanced at Justinian and a tremor traveled up his thin frame. "They've offered him their crown."

Justinian's fist tightened on the horn of his saddle. "And what did he say?"

The youth swallowed again, his eyes on the grass. "I don't know, Augustus. That was the entire message relayed by the last herald."

By now Belisarius might have traded his silver general's belt for a king's crown of gold. Justinian bellowed a curse, and the messenger scuttled from sight. I called him back, forcing him to wait until I'd written a hasty letter to Antonina, commanding her to explain what had happened.

Word spread about the debacle in Italy—Narses' spies reported many in Constantinople believed the calamity was related to the bearded star that had recently streaked the sky. Yet it remained to be seen whether Belisarius would betray us and we'd soon have to send another force to conquer the conqueror. Finally a response came from Antonina.

Most August Augusta,

Thank the gods I wasn't around when the runner brought you the news that the Goths offered Belisarius their crown. I certainly hope you didn't run the poor messenger through.

I've warned you Belisarius is nothing if not devious. He pretended to accept (I won't say he wasn't sorely tempted by the offer), and the Goths threw open the gates of Ravenna, conveniently allowing him to arrest Vitiges and the Gothic patricians waiting inside. Then my husband made a public proclamation that he followed only Emperor Justinian, leaving the women of Ravenna to spit and hurl obscenities at their idiot men.

Now you and Justinian can cease plotting creative ways to destroy Belisarius. (I know you too well—don't try to deny it!)

Your faithful servant,
Antonina

Also, a personal reward for persuading Belisarius his head looked best attached and without a crown would be much appreciated. The Goths do have an obscene amount of gold that would look lovely melted down into a new necklace or two.

I gave a wry chuckle—Antonina called me an alley cat, but she was like a scorpion, always waiting in the shadows until the best moment to strike. Justinian received confirmation of his general's loyalty that same day and summoned Belisarius back to Constantinople, although he could have stomped through the rest of northern Italy all the way to the Alps.

Vitiges and his wife arrived in Constantinople dressed in heavy silver chains instead of their stolen purple. But this time there was no triumph for Belisarius. Instead, I suggested a mosaic commemorating Belisarius' victory in the Sacred Palace—the gold-studded work of art was almost finished by the time they arrived in the Sea of Marmara. Justinian ordered the ships anchored outside the harbor until night fell to avoid any sort of spontaneous triumph by the people. We weren't taking any chances.

Plus, another public slight to Belisarius fit my latest plan to perfection.

I sent Narses to escort Antonina from her villa before the sun had risen. He muttered something about fetching filthy pagans under his breath but stalked off to do my bidding. Antonina arrived in a foul mood as the sparrows began to chirp.

"I'll have you know I was in bed when that demon of a eunuch summoned me," she said, straightening from her bow.

"With Theodosius, no doubt."

Antonina shrugged and yawned into the back of her hand. "I needed to relax after being imprisoned in the harbor all day by your brute of a husband."

"That was my idea, actually." I ignored the glare that flickered over her face. "Belisarius still doesn't know about you and Theodosius?"

She plucked a peacock feather from an alabaster vase, twirling it under her nose. "He came upon us in Rome. Theodosius was caught with his trousers down—literally. I told him my godson was helping me bury the most precious of our plunder so the Emperor would never discover them." She gave a catlike grin. "It's amazing what a tunica can hide."

Belisarius was no fool. What game did he play that he'd allow his wife to cuckold him? Perhaps he didn't care what his wife did, so long as she ran his household and her affairs remained secret. "I need to pull you from Theodosius for a rather delicate job."

"I'm all ears, darling."

"It's time to rid the Empire of John the Cappadocian."

"I've always thought you should have fed him to the rioters at Nika."

"Now is the chance to rectify that egregious error."

She perked up. "Perhaps this was worth getting out of bed."

"Which side will Belisarius take?"

"Whichever side I tell him to." I frowned, but she sat up straighter, the peacock feather forgotten as she leaned forward on her elbows to inspect her perfect manicure. "He's still furious at John for the spoiled supplies in the Carthage campaign."

"I need you to convince the Cappadocian that you and Belisarius want to overthrow Justinian and me."

Antonina's elbows slipped. "You want us to commit treason?"

"It's not treason if you're acting at my behest. I'll sign an affidavit if you want. You convince John to act against us, and I convince Justinian to execute him after he's caught in the act."

Antonina shook her head. "The Cappadocian hates me almost as much as he hates you. He won't believe me."

"Your husband was formally snubbed after returning victorious from conquering Rome."

"About that," Antonina drawled, "you may want to stay away from Belisarius. He figured that was your idea, and he's fit to be tied."

"Precisely. He could have been Emperor, but instead he received a slap in the face."

"And a mosaic." Antonina rolled her eyes.

"A very expensive mosaic."

"In *your* palace. I should have known you were up to something when they wouldn't let us off our ships."

"Perhaps Belisarius is tired of campaigning without reward? When this is over, you'll find an unimaginable sum mysteriously funneled into your accounts."

"How unimaginable?"

"Beyond your wildest dreams."

Antonina grinned. "Music to my ears."

"Good. Go through John's daughter, Euphemia." I sometimes doubted John had sired the girl at all—such a sweet apple couldn't have fallen so far from such a twisted, poisonous tree. "She visits the public baths once a month to hand out bread tokens to the infirm and elderly," I said.

"A regular saint." Antonina pulled a sour face. "Probably still a virgin, too. Does she go to the baths alone?"

"Usually with Macedonia. They're rather close."

"Do you think Euphemia's old enough to influence her father? I'd need him to meet with me. Privately."

"She's eighteen," I said. "Old enough to think she knows everything and young enough to understand very little."

Antonina rose. "That's one of the benefits of being old hags now—we really do know everything."

Old. I had turned forty in March. Fortunately, Macedonia had given my slaves an excellent hair tonic recipe of lead oxide and slaked lime. The stuff smelled worse than a latrina, but the strands of gray had disappeared as if by magic.

"Convince her you need her father's help—a palace insider—to topple Justinian once and for all. Tempt her with the thought of all the poor people she could help with her father on the throne."

"Leave everything to me. You just worry about how much of John's wealth you're going to send my way." She gave a wicked smile. "His estates in Prusa are particularly lovely." She sauntered off, and I sat back to wait, eager to serve the Cappadocian's head to Justinian on a gilded platter.

. . .

It had taken my lust for revenge and the love for my remaining family to pull me from the abyss of grief for my son. Reconciled with Justinian, I invited Tasia to the palace, pulling her away from the peace of her seaside villa across the Bosphorus. I needed to be close to her, to drink up her happiness with her husband, Paulus, and her son, and know that at least I had done something right in this life in seeing her happily settled.

My grandson, Athanasius, was at the age of missing teeth with a rabid fascination for reptiles and a healthy disgust for girls. I quizzed him on his Latin version of the *Song of Ilium* when Macedonia entered with a letter that smelled like a bouquet of roses, its seal still intact.

"A messenger just arrived with this," she said. "He said it was urgent."

Tasia peered at the seal from over her needlework, an intricate camel and lion design for one of Paulus' tunicas. I took pride in the fact that she was quite talented with a needle and thread, although she certainly hadn't learned the skill from me. "How is Auntie Nina these days?" she asked.

"Up to her old tricks, as usual." I smiled and broke the wax seal. I hoped Antonina had been up to a few new tricks as well.

> *Most Supreme and Exalted Augusta,*
>
> *Our mutual friend has agreed to meet at my Rufinianae villa this evening for a lovely dinner of oysters in garlic, swordfish with an apricot glaze, and dormice pounded with pepper and almonds. A menu fit for a last meal, don't you think?*
> *Belisarius and I shall endeavor to serve the imperial throne in all ways.*
>
> *Your faithful servant,*
> *Antonina*

Narses answered my summons immediately.

"John the Cappadocian is on his way to Belisarius' villa at Rufinianae," I said. "Take a contingent of imperial guards with you, but don't let him see you. Arrest the traitor the instant he mentions Justinian's throne."

Narses gave a frightening grin and snapped his fingers at several of the guards stationed at the door.

I'd have John in my clutches in mere hours. Revenge would be sweet.

"What's going on, Mother?" Tasia set down her sewing as I sent a messenger to fetch Justinian.

"John the Cappadocian is about to walk into a trap."

"What do you mean?"

I explained the plot to her, but she only pursed her lips, reminding me of my mother. "It seems to me you and John the Cappadocian are mirror images of each other." She bowed as Justinian entered and gifted my husband with a sunny smile as she collected her son.

"You don't need to leave," Justinian said, kissing her on the forehead. "I've only come to spend time with my girls and this young man." He ruffled Athanasius' hair, and the boy beamed, clutching the *Song of Ilium* to his chest.

"We'll join you for dinner," Tasia said. "Mother received important news—we'd only be in the way right now."

More like the cross fire.

Athanasius gave Justinian a solemn bow. He was the closest male relative Justinian possessed—one day this little man might wear the purple. I opened my arms to him and squeezed him tight.

"Have your mother come to dinner early, all right? I promise I'll have the Emperor teach you how to spar before the soup is served. Perhaps I'll even join in."

Athanasius' eyes grew round, but Tasia steered him away by the shoulder. "The Empress excels at sparring," I heard her say once they were almost outside. "She's made it her life work."

Justinian wrapped his arm around my waist. "What news deprives me of my daughter and grandson?"

His words made it difficult to swallow. For a moment I wondered again what would have happened if I'd told him of my son, if he might have accepted John as easily as he'd done Tasia. I wouldn't think of that now.

"John the Cappadocian is about to betray you."

He sighed. "Enough, Theodora. You've suspected John and Belisarius for years and all for naught."

"I set him up." Not waiting for him to protest, I explained the entire plot I'd set into motion. It took an eternity for him to respond.

"And Antonina offered to help you out of the goodness of her heart?"

"More like the goodness of her pocketbook."

"And John is headed to Rufinianae now?"

"As we speak."

Justinian stood perfectly still. "Then we shall wait for Narses to return with him—if he does betray me, that is."

I would bet my favorite racehorse that John the Cappadocian wouldn't bat an eye at Antonina's request, but I bit my tongue.

Justinian patted my shoulder, not looking at me. "Send for me the instant Narses returns."

I had almost worn a trench in the silk carpet when Narses appeared, a storm worthy of Zeus on his face.

"What happened?" I asked. "Where's John?"

"We waited until he intimated his wish for the throne, then sprang to arrest him. His own guard protected him as he fled." Narses glowered and held out a creamy piece of vellum. "We found this left behind."

The letter was written in a hurried hand, but the remnants of Justinian's imperial seal still clung to the crumpled page. My own husband had circumvented me to protect the man who sought to destroy me. I sat down, hard, and balled the paper in my fist before throwing it into the fire and watching the parchment writhe until the flames consumed it.

"John fled to the monastery of Saint Conon," Narses said. "He's claimed sanctuary."

Saint Conon was the same monastery the criminals had sought before the Nika riots. Laughter rose in the back of my throat—Narses looked at me as if I'd lost my mind.

"John is a pagan," I said. "Sanctuary doesn't apply to infidels. Drag him from the altar if you have to. I want him dead by daybreak."

"Do not follow that order."

Justinian strode into the room, his purple *chalmys* billowing behind him. "Bring John to me."

"So you can pardon him as you wished with Hypatius?" I sharpened my voice. "John is a traitor who has plotted your overthrow. He must die."

Justinian ignored me. "Bring John here, Narses. See that he's not harmed."

My temples throbbed, but I clenched my teeth until Narses was out of earshot. "You are a fool."

"And you are obsessed with this vendetta." Justinian's face thundered with rage. "I will not have more blood on my hands. John has served me faithfully for more than a decade—"

"He's a debauched, lying thief!"

Justinian grasped me hard by the shoulders. It was the only time he had ever laid a hand on me in anger, but I leapt back, scorched.

He held up his hands. "I will not order John's death, and neither shall you." His eyes narrowed. "You've gone too far this time, Theodora—you cannot fault a man for trying to grasp the treasure you've dangled before him."

"The same treasure Belisarius recently resisted."

Justinian gave a hollow laugh. "And yet you faulted him for even that at the time. John is only a man—infallible and imperfect."

"As are you."

Justinian tensed. "Perhaps, but I am God's anointed king here on earth."

"Only because I saved your crown."

It was the first time I'd held Nika over Justinian's head. I almost wished I could take the words back.

"And that is why I shall not punish you for going against my wishes in this." His voice was the same as the one he used in his throne room—imperious and haughty. "I've trusted you, and you've betrayed that very same trust."

I had betrayed him, but not in this. My husband had forgiven Hypatius, Belisarius, and now the Cappadocian, but I'd betrayed him by revealing John the Cappadocian for the traitor he truly was?

It took every shred of my willpower not to slap him. "I shall take my leave of you then—you may send my messages to my palace in Hieron. I shan't trouble you anymore." I turned on my heel and stormed from the room, waiting for my husband to call me back.

There was only silence.

Chapter 30

The glare from the waves made me squint under the shade of my silk awning, the languid smell of salt and decay floating in the heat. Earlier in the day a slave had claimed to have caught sight of Porphyry, the legendary whale that occasionally overturned boats in the Sea of Marmara to feed on hapless sailors. There were a few people I wouldn't mind feeding to the giant beast, my husband included.

Only the narrow strait of the Bosphorus separated Justinian and me, and the distance wasn't so great that he couldn't send for me. All day long vessels skipped over the waves like water bugs, plying the blue garland of water between the two continents and bringing me news of Belisarius' latest foray into Persia. And yet there was still no word from my husband.

I was adrift here in Hieron, occupying my hours counting fishing boats bobbing past coastal caves as I trekked to the thermal baths and stalked the small palace grounds. I recommended the sea breezes and Hieron's healing waters to patricians who came to my palace to beg favors, some of whom clustered outside my tent even now. They helped me keep up the charade that things were as they should be when in truth my world had spiraled out of control long ago.

I kicked off my calfskin slippers and walked into the sea foam, the warm sand slipping between my toes.

"Would you like me to walk with you, Augusta?" Macedonia fanned herself, looking like a wilted rose in the sun.

"I'm fine." I dismissed her with a flick of my wrist, suddenly annoyed at all the damp slaves and courtiers awaiting my every whim. "You may all return to the palace."

I meandered the lonely stretch of beach with only my thoughts to keep me company. A black and yellow snakebird impaled a silver fish with its beak and took flight, the fish writhing in vain for freedom as the bird soared in careless circles toward the clouds.

The beach was long and my legs were tired when I finally returned to my tent, only to find that a messenger in imperial livery waited outside. Justinian had finally come to his senses. I had to force myself not to run and snatch the purple vellum from the boy's hands.

I spared a glance at the opposite shore as I broke Justinian's seal, glad to know I'd soon be returning. There was nothing in Hieron for me.

John the Cappadocian's wealth has been confiscated. I have exiled him to Cyzicus, where, after he shall be known as Brother Augustus.

Your faithful husband,
Justinian

The silver ink mocked me. No salutation. No apology. No invitation to return to the palace.

I was still furious with Justinian, but I'd be a liar to claim I didn't miss him. Life without my husband had gone gray, one day blending into the next. I needed him.

"Is there no other message?" I turned to ask the servant, but he had already gone, not even instructed to remain for a reply. I gave a mangled curse and crumpled the paper in my fist before hurtling it into the sea. The little ball bobbed in the waves, staining them with a cloud of purple. The irony of John's new name did not escape me—the man who had reached for the Emperor's crown would now be known by the Emperor's title. Exiled, but still alive, he had escaped relatively unscathed yet again.

I didn't have long to ponder Justinian's lenient sentence or his neglect at asking for my return to the Sacred Palace. A sedan carried by four of the finest-looking slaves I'd ever seen lumbered into view, complete with a full cadre of female attendants. Antonina descended from her litter and gave such a wail that the slaves scattered. She collapsed at my feet in a puddle of silks, her hair wild and her normally flawless complexion splotchy as a freshly plucked hen.

I waved everyone away and helped her to a stool under my tent. Her performance was worthy of a tragic death, but I knew better. "I take it all is not well, Antonina?"

She took a deep breath, but more tears poured down her cheeks. "Photius betrayed me."

Antonina's eldest son had campaigned in Carthage and Ravenna with Belisarius, but he remained in the capital now as his stepfather fought in Persia once more. He had been sketching the sails of *dromons* last I saw him.

"The ungrateful cur told Belisarius of my affair with Theodosius in front of all his generals!" She buried her face in her hands, and her shoulders heaved with less-than-silent sobs. Antonina had always excelled at tragedy.

"How did Photius find out?"

"I don't know." The blubbering began afresh. "Someone must be spying on me."

More like someone had finally decided not to turn a blind eye.

I patted her on the shoulder. "Darling, you had to know Belisarius would find out sooner or later." I'd gambled on the former and was truly shocked the scandal hadn't broken until now.

Antonina's face emerged from her hands, the red blotches darker than before. "But my own flesh and blood betrayed me! He only wants to ensure I don't disinherit him in favor of Theodosius."

Photius had learned the art of manipulation from one of the masters, but now likely wasn't the best time to point out that Antonina's own son had outsmarted her. She wiped her nose on the back of her sleeve, leaving a line of snot like a slug's trail on the lemon silk.

"And now Belisarius has threatened to cast you off?" I offered a linen towel to dry her face.

"Belisarius says he loves me. Exceedingly. He swore vengeance on Theodosius instead." Her chin trembled. "I don't even know where he is—Photius captured Theodosius and has him hidden somewhere." She laughed, a deranged sight as the tears started anew. I doubted she'd shed half so many tears for her first husband, and poor Timothy the Weasel had had to die for those. Theodosius still lived, although he might wish for death after Photius finished with him.

"And Theodosius' wealth?"

"Confiscated." She blew her nose so loudly that a flock of seabirds scattered from the shore. "I curse the day I conceived the ungrateful whelp! Belisarius has me under surveillance while he fights the Persians, but I can't live without Theodosius." She fell to her knees and grasped my hands between her damp ones. "Help me, Theodora."

This drama was worthy of Sophocles. "Your husband is one of the most powerful men in the Empire. I don't know what I can do."

She clutched my hands, her eyes wild. "Please. I helped you take down John the Cappadocian. You're my only hope."

I hesitated, then beckoned for one of the courtiers who'd slunk back outside my tent. I really needed Narses, but he was back in the

Sacred Palace with Justinian. The youth who came forward, Areobindus, was a recent addition to my court, recommended by Macedonia. He had the body of an ancient god with chiseled features that reminded me of busts of a young Alexander the Great. "Go to Narses. Tell him I want Photius brought to me."

Areobindus repeated the message and walked off, his tunica pushed by the breeze to reveal the outline of his legs. Antonina licked her lips. "I see why you keep that one around. He reminds me of Theodosius." She sniffed, and her lip trembled again.

I had to bite my lip to keep from laughing. "I'll find Theodosius for you."

I only hoped he was still in one piece.

Photius proved difficult to find, and meanwhile Belisarius decided not to pursue the Persians past the river Tigris. Rumor had it Antonina's infidelity had completely unmanned her husband, but I knew from Narses that he was negotiating a truce.

Yet that was practically all I knew, still cut off here in Hieron. I watched with great fascination as Areobindus sliced a ripe peach to break my fast, the juices dripping down his long fingers. There was a steady patter of rain outside, but my room smelled like an orchard on a sunny day. Antonina had returned to her Rufinianae estate, and Macedonia had left after asking permission to revisit the monastery in Chalcedon. I was lonely here in Hieron.

"Would you like me to taste it first?" Areobindus asked. A single dark curl fell onto his forehead as he set the peach before me. I resisted the urge to push the hair back.

"No, thank you." I enjoyed the burst of summer on my tongue as a slave delivered several letters on a golden tray. I'd received nary a word from Justinian since his brief message about John and refused to take up my pen to write to him, although the other night I'd written him a long and plaintive letter begging him to take me back. I'd woken the next morning with it plastered under my face and promptly relegated it to the flame of an oil lamp.

I searched for Justinian's seal in vain and set aside a letter from Antonina with a sigh. I didn't have to open it to know what it said. Belisarius had stepped up the surveillance of his wife, so she rarely left their villa across the Bosphorus. There had been a steady stream of missives since her last visit, all imploring me to find Theodosius before her heart withered and died. I knew how she felt, but instead, I suggested she take up weaving or beekeeping. Anything to get her mind off Theodosius.

The rest of the letters were tedious, save one message from Tasia to tell me she wished to apprentice Athanasius to a monastery so he could study theology. I'd prefer to arrange the boy's betrothal, finding him a suitable girl who might wear my crown after Justinian and I were cold in our tombs. Yet there was plenty of time for that—Justinian wasn't yet sixty and I was only forty. There was also Comito's daughter, Sophia, who might bring the Empire its next Emperor by marriage. All this needed to be discussed with Justinian, but that was difficult as I was no longer on speaking terms with my husband.

The letter from Antonina still waited after I'd returned from the thermal baths and my prayers at chapel that night. The light rain had grown to a thunderstorm, but then it died as night fell. The moon was full as a ripe melon, and its white light spilled into my room. I sighed and took the letter to bed.

The crisp paper sliced my thumb as I opened it. I pressed the cut to my lips and tasted blood as I read the single line.

I found the spy.

I sent for Areobindus and woke two slaves sleeping at my door. Yawning, they dressed me in a black stola and wrapped my hair under a dark silk scarf.

Areobindus arrived fully dressed, looking as if he'd been waiting for my summons. I murmured instructions in his ear, unaware of my hand on his arm until I felt the guards' eyes on me. Antonina's message had best be true or she'd receive more than an earful.

We slipped across the Bosphorus like thieves, the water still as black glass as the oars of our little boat floated up and down like lazy drag-onfly wings. A plain curtained litter waited on the other side. I didn't care for anyone to report back to Justinian that I'd reentered the city.

The streets were deserted and the Rufinianae house and grounds dark, but Antonina met me in the atrium, silent save for the occasional drip of water from the roof into the *impluvium*. She waved me inside with one hand, the other holding a sputtering oil lamp that scarcely cast any light. However, it was enough to make out that the dark stain up her bodice was no shadow. She motioned to Areobindus. "He stays."

Antonina could have undone me long ago—she wasn't about to have me murdered. Areobindus fell back at my nod, but his stormy expression told me he wasn't pleased.

"Follow me."

We traipsed silently through the dark maze of rooms and out the kitchens, then back into the clean night air. I followed Antonina's haloed outline beyond the towered well house to a storehouse tucked behind a modest grove of olive trees, its doorway so low I had to duck. My eyes took a moment to adjust to the black of the room, but the aromas of pepper, cardamom, and cloves mingled with those of a fall day's damp earth and decay. I had no idea why Antonina had dragged me here. Perhaps her mind had finally come unhinged.

A larger oil lamp sputtered to life in Antonina's hands. Then I saw her.

The edges of the room came into focus so I could make out a woman against the far wall, chin on her chest as if she were sleeping. Or dead. Then I caught the scent of her musk perfume.

"Macedonia?" Her right eye was swollen shut and her lip torn, her hands and feet bound with thin ropes that had cut into her skin and now melded into the bloody flesh. A black stain stretched from her brow to her nose. I struggled to help her stand but discovered too late the length of rope along her neck, tied tight to an amphora of wine as tall as I was. I whirled on Antonina. "What have you done to her?"

Antonina spat at Macedonia. The fob of spittle lodged on my friend's tangled copper hair, once so beautiful. "Less than she deserved. The woman is a traitor."

"She has been faithful to me for more than twenty years!"

Macedonia moaned, and a fresh trickle of blood slipped from her lips, black ink on her pale skin. Her good eye opened but lolled about its socket. This woman had saved my life countless times. Without her I'd likely still be on the stage, or worse, a pox-ridden whore found dead in an alley one morning. Macedonia would never betray me.

"I'm getting you out of here." I worked the rope around her neck, but it was slick with fresh blood. Macedonia groaned again, an animal moan that made my flesh prickle. I finally worked the rope free, ignoring the sticky wetness on my palms. "Can you walk?"

"No, she can't walk," Antonina said. "She can't talk either."

"What do you mean, she can't talk?"

"I cut out her tongue."

Antonina let out a little yelp of surprise as I slammed her into a bag of onions and tried to claw at her face. She managed to shove me off to scramble to Macedonia, but my fingernails had skin and blood under them.

"She's a traitor." Antonina yanked a handful of Macedonia's matted bronze curls and kicked her outstretched thigh, but the half-conscious woman barely flinched. "She told Photius about Theodosius and me so she could get a cut of his inheritance!"

"She only spoke the truth!" My eyes fell on a rusty scythe hanging on the far wall—I could certainly make it there before Antonina realized what I intended.

I heard the tears in Antonina's next words before I saw them gleaming in her eyes. "She had our son killed."

"What?"

"Macedonia has been spying for John the Cappadocian ever since she returned from Antioch after the earthquake," Antonina said. "They've been lovers all these years. You gave our son to her, and she had him killed, all on the Cappadocian's orders."

"I don't believe it. How could she possibly know about John?" The awful realization blossomed in my mind. "When did you tell her? It was in Bithynia, wasn't it? I asked you if you'd told her, and you said no." My fingernails bit into my palms. "You lied to me."

Tears poured down Antonina's cheeks. "I'm so sorry, Theodora. I'd take it back if I could, all of it. I'd had too much wine that afternoon in the hot springs, and it just tumbled out. I never thought she'd turn traitor and use the information against you. Against us."

"It's you who's the traitor, not Macedonia." Lunging toward the far wall, I yanked down the scythe and whirled on Antonina.

"You want to kill me?" Her voice was hysterical. "Go ahead! But I think you should hear the truth before you run me through."

"I don't want to hear another word from your filthy, lying mouth," I said, the scythe trembling in my hands.

"Why do you think Macedonia is so close to Euphemia? She's the girl's mother." Antonina jerked her head toward Macedonia. "I imagine she and the Cappadocian kept their relationship secret so she could continue to spy on you."

I could scarcely breathe. I'd always wondered what caused the abrupt end of John's pursuit of me. The dates matched—Euphemia would have been born while Macedonia was in Antioch, before the earthquake and while the Cappadocian had been exiled before I married Justinian. Euphemia's pert little nose, her mannerisms—they were familiar because they were Macedonia's.

I didn't realize I had sat down until the splinters from the crate dug into my legs. The scythe dangled from my hands. I stared at Macedonia as my mind fought to make sense of Antonina's words. "Are you sure?"

Macedonia moaned and Antonina took a hesitant step toward her, then tugged her ropes tighter when she realized I wasn't going to stab her. "Photius kindly gave her permission to take whatever she liked from his mother's house. I caught her sneaking out of my villa, making off with a hefty bag of jewels. After a little persuasion, she told me she was headed for Cyzicus."

John of Cappadocia had been banished to Cyzicus.

I'd send spies there to torture John the Cappadocian, Justinian be damned. I sank into the earth beside Macedonia, my eyes clamped shut as I pressed my fist into my mouth and tasted the film of dirt.

I would kill Macedonia, dragging out her endless torture until she begged for death's mercy. Let her watch her own lifeblood leak away as an ox-hide whip scourged her back. Such a death would be generous for so much evil. I drew a ragged breath into my lungs and forced my eyes open.

I expected to see her grinning while I hoped to see her crying with remorse, but instead, Macedonia's finger trailed haphazardly in the earth, a frothy foam of pink on her lips in the lamplight. There was a pattern to her design in the dirt. Words.

Not dead.

I heaved her to her feet, almost choking the last bit of life out of her before letting her fall back to the ground. "Who's not dead?"

An eternity passed before her finger moved again.

John.

"Of course the Cappadocian is still alive." Antonina gave an impatient sigh. The scythe dragged on the ground behind her.

Macedonia's hand was ice in mine.

"My son. Do you mean my son?"

Her eye focused for a moment, and I shuddered at the naked hatred there. I'd surpassed her, abandoned her, and banished her patron, the father of her only child. She nodded.

"You can't trust her." Antonina stood over us, scythe in hand.

"Please," I said. "Where is he?"

A gush of blood dribbled over Macedonia's lips as she was seized by a coughing fit so strong I feared death would claim her right then. Her lone pupil rolled wildly, and then her eye squeezed shut. Her finger trailed in the earth once more.

Two symbols. Letters.

H C

"What does that mean?" Antonina sounded as confused as I felt.

"I don't understand." I pressed Macedonia's finger to the dirt, but her hand didn't move. I begged. I bargained away my jewels, my estates, but still she didn't move. I slammed my fist into the ground, hot tears coursing down my cheeks before Antonina laid a gentle hand on my shoulder.

"It's no use, Theodora. She's gone."

Macedonia's eye was unseeing, shiny as Charon's obol before the coin was placed in the mouth of the deceased. She would keep her secret forever between bloody lips. There was only one person who might be able to tell me where my son was. And I intended to find him.

The riddle of Macedonia's symbols remained a mystery. I scarcely slept, imagining my son chained to some dungeon of the Cappadocian's making, or worse. When I did sleep, it was only to see Macedonia beckoning me, her empty mouth dripping blood with the letters *H* and *C* carved into her cheeks. I wasn't sure which nightmare I preferred.

I dispatched Narses to Cyzicus to retrieve the Cappadocian, giving him explicit instructions that I wanted John breathing, but he was free to use any other means necessary to bring him to Hieron. There was news that plague had reared its head in Egypt, but without Narses I couldn't be sure if the reports were true or simply rumors. I'd had only a single delivery from him in weeks, one I cared little about but knew would interest Antonina.

She arrived swathed in black, her face pale as parchment. "Any word on John?"

We had an unspoken agreement not to discuss the night in the storehouse. I couldn't bring myself to punish Antonina for her betrayal either, knowing I carried a fair share of the blame for all that had happened. Instead, we both awaited the return of our son.

I shook my head and handed her a bowl of dried apricots. "Black really isn't your color."

"Don't mock me." She turned her nose up at the apricots. "I'm in mourning for Theodosius."

"I didn't realize he was dead."

"He might as well be. Life is no longer worth living. I might keel over and die."

"So long as you don't make a mess on my carpets," I said. She dabbed her eyes, but I opened a door to an empty side room and glanced inside. "I may have something to cheer you."

"Nothing shall ever cheer me again. Except obscenely large jewels, but I doubt Belisarius will shower me with gems after all this."

"You're in luck. I acquired a rare pearl yesterday, like one never seen before." I chuckled as her eyes lit up. "Would you care to see it?"

"Anything to take my mind off my sorrows," she said. "Although it best be hideously large."

I held the door open, taking secret pleasure in Antonina's blotchy face—the woman was far too melodramatic. Her hands flew to her mouth as a man emerged, and for the first time ever I saw my friend struck speechless. Theodosius was thinner and wore a broken nose and several fresh scars from his sojourn in an abandoned cellar on Photius' meager estates. Yet he might have been much worse had Narses not found him when he did. Antonina catapulted herself into her lover's arms, wailing into his shoulder.

Theodosius cleared his throat, my friend tight in his embrace and love written clearly in his eyes. "Thank you, Augusta."

Antonina clung to Theodosius with one hand and mopped her tears with the other. "You are my savior, Theodora. You're all that is good and kind."

I doubted anyone had ever called me good or kind before. Embarrassed to witness such a private reunion, I closed the door behind me and tried to ignore the stab of loneliness in my own heart.

Macedonia's riddle haunted me.

I sketched out the possibilities yet again in the dirt of the garden, ignoring the honeybees as they landed on the red and purple Kalanit blossoms at my elbow. Perhaps they weren't letters, but symbols—a bridge and the swell of a pregnant belly. Or an intersection and a curved street.

Or perhaps they were the trick of a dying woman bent on revenge, a final betrayal meant to torment me to the end of my days. I was utterly alone in Hieron, having had no word from Justinian and only a single letter from Antonina since her reunion with Theodosius. The letter gushed with so much happiness I could scarcely finish reading it.

Someone cleared his throat, and I stamped out the symbols in the dirt. Areobindus held a steaming tray of food, and a slave with a large wooden box stood behind him. I waved away the soup—garlic and leek from the smell of it—and took a glass of watered wine, intent on the dirt before me.

Areobindus didn't move.

I set down the stick I'd been using to trace letters and rubbed my scratchy eyes. "May I help you?"

"You need to eat, Augusta. And I think something in the box might prove a pleasant diversion." His smile would have made a younger woman weak in the knees.

I opened my mouth to dismiss him, but my temples ached. Perhaps a break might help clear my mind.

I snagged a poppy seed roll from the tray and gestured to the crate. "Shall I open it?" He stepped back, barely able to keep a straight face.

I lifted the lid and groaned.

The slate-colored puppy yipped and peered out of the box, its ears flopping over as it gave me a quizzical look.

"The last thing I need is a greyhound."

Areobindus picked up a stick. "You'll break his heart if you reject him now. I've already told him how lucky he is to have the Empress as a mistress." He tossed the stick, and the dog catapulted from the crate. Its back legs slid out from under it on the turn so it skidded into a rosebush. I couldn't help but laugh as it launched itself back toward us.

"Does this little demon have a name?"

He shrugged. "I've been calling him Cyr, but I'm sure he wouldn't mind a name of the Empress' choosing."

"Cyr it is."

He threw the stick again, but it splashed into a tiled pond of goldfish. Cyr swerved to a halt at the edge. He touched his foot to the water and looked back at us, whimpering. Areobindus grinned. "You weren't supposed to realize he was a daisy until later."

He gamboled back with the dog and was about to throw the now-dripping stick again when I gasped and clutched my throat.

"Where did you get that?"

He looked behind him. "Get what?"

"That." A silver cross hung round his neck. It must have been tucked into his tunica until he bent down to pick up the stick.

Amber inlaid in silver, with a mosquito frozen in the center.

I grabbed the cross and twisted it to see the words etched into the back.

Let love and faithfulness never leave you; bind them around your neck, write them on the tablet of your heart.

I dropped the cross and stumbled back as if scalded, knocking my chair to the ground. "Who gave you that?"

Areobindus touched the cross. "You wouldn't believe me if I told you."

"I'll have the skin flayed from your back if you don't tell me."

He dropped the stick, and Cyr loped away with it. "You gave it to me."

I couldn't move. For a moment I couldn't breathe.

"In Bithynia," he said. "Don't you remember? The day I rode the elephant and we fed the giraffes. I was known as John then."

I shook my head, violently. "That's not possible. That cross was lost long ago."

"I've worn it every day since you gave it to me." He knelt before me, clasping my hands in his. "I'd have told you sooner, but I feared your reaction. I thought it best to let you find out on your own."

I pushed his hair back to see the white scar on his temple, the shape of a young moon. A gift from Photius years ago for stealing his pens.

Suddenly Macedonia's message seemed perfectly clear—*HC*, but missing the middle letter. *Hic.* Here.

"How is this possible?"

His gaze fell. "I'd rather not say. I have no wish to be sent away from court."

"Tell me now. I have a right to know."

"John the Cappadocian is my father." He bowed his head as if waiting an executioner's blade.

I almost laughed aloud. "John the Cappadocian is not your father."

"It is the unfortunate truth. I lived with General Belisarius for many years, but then my true father claimed me."

"Why didn't you come to court with Euphemia?"

He flushed. "I'm only one of my father's many bastard children, and not his favored daughter. I despised life in Prusa, but I changed my name with the belief that it might be safe to approach your court in Hieron now that my father has been banished. He forbade me to ever come to court."

For fear I might recognize my own son. John had stolen him from me and raised him to believe the lies he had threatened to tell Justinian.

"You are my son. I am your mother, but the Cappadocian is not your father."

His face hardened. "Don't toy with me, Augusta."

"I gave that cross to my son. And sent him away with Macedonia to protect him from John the Cappadocian. I was told you died on the journey, but they must have kept you hidden in Prusa instead."

"I don't understand. If that's true—," Areobindus said, breaking off, and I could tell from the look on his face that he didn't believe it was. "If that's true," he continued, "then who is my real father?"

I thought of Hecebolus, not wishing him on any child. "It doesn't matter. He's dead now."

"It matters to me." Cyr pushed his muzzle into Areobindus' hands, but my son didn't notice. His face was so anguished, I had to resist the urge to pull him into my arms, to stroke his hair and tell him everything would be all right.

"Your father was my patron for a time," I said. "A governor of Pentapolis. He cast me off before I realized I carried you. And then he died."

"This doesn't make any sense." He ran shaky hands over his face. "Why did you send me to live with Belisarius and Antonina? And how did I end up with John the Cappadocian?"

So many questions. And none of the answers made me seem anything but a demon.

"I never told Justinian I had a son."

He stepped back and looked at me with horror. "You sacrificed me."

I grasped his hands, desperate not to lose him again. "I planned to tell him, but by then it was too late. I sent you to live with Antonina so you'd be safe, but the Cappadocian discovered you. He was using you to blackmail me."

"All while he lied to me, made me believe he was my father." He pulled his hands from mine, then ran them through his hair in a gesture so like Justinian's my heart almost broke. "What will you do now?"

I searched his eyes for the answer he hoped to hear. A boy's eyes on a grown man. My son, returned from the dead. There was only one answer.

"I'll do what I should have done long ago. Tell Justinian the truth."

"What will he do?"

"Justinian will forgive me. And he will accept you as his son." I spoke with a certainty I didn't feel. "One day, you may be Emperor. Until then, you shall assume the position of my chief steward."

It was unheard of for an ungelded man to assume such a position, and Areobindus was not only a man, but also young and pleasant to the eyes. Rumors would fly, but since when had I cared about such things?

I wrote to Justinian that night, unable to sleep, and asked for him to come to Hieron. It took three days for him to find the decency to send a reply, one so cold I could hear his disdain in my head as I scanned the parchment.

Dear Theodora,

I received your invitation, but I am far too busy to leave the Sacred Palace for a pleasure cruise to Hieron. My eyes and ears tell me you are enjoying your holiday—it must be a relief to abandon your responsibilities for a time.

Justinian

I held the vellum over the dancing flame of an olive oil lamp, watching the fire consume Justinian's words. If his tone was this frigid before I told him of Areobindus and my duplicity, then I could scarcely imagine how he'd react to my confession. But it didn't matter.

I had hoped Justinian would throw open the Golden Gate to usher me back to the Sacred Palace as he had years ago upon my return from Bithynia, but I would take my chances and make my way home uninvited. I ordered my slaves to pack my trunks for departure the next morning.

I did not know death would stall our reunion.

Chapter 31

"Augusta, wake up."

An oil lamp illuminated Areobindus' face, framed by my bed curtains with the evidence of hasty packing behind him, half-full trunks and an explosion of silks and shoes. I had finally ordered my slaves to their pallets sometime after midnight and managed to find sleep myself shortly after, despite much tossing on my feather mattress. Only a crisis would prompt anyone to wake me at so ungodly an hour.

"What's wrong?" I rubbed my eyes and pulled myself to sit. Cyr blinked from the foot of the bed and pushed his muzzle into Areobindus' hand.

"Reports of plague." He covered his mouth with a square of linen and pressed another to my nose, a bouquet of rosemary, bay, and vervain to ward off the sickness.

"Here?" I crossed myself as my feet hit the cool mosaic floor.

"In the capital. Confirmed yesterday, probably carried by an Egyptian grain ship—the *Alexander*. Most of the crew is already dead. The Virgin's icon has been paraded about the walls, but people in the city are dying."

I crossed myself, and Areobindus followed suit. "What about the Sacred Palace?"

His voice could scarcely be heard behind his linen. "The Emperor has ordered everyone to stay indoors." His eyes flicked to mine. "Including us."

I was trapped in a cage of my own making, quarantined from my own palace. But Justinian was still alive. That was all that mattered.

I waited until the door closed behind Areobindus, then sank to my knees, dropping my posy to clasp my hands before me. "Mary full of grace." My eyes flickered toward the heavens, but then I squeezed them shut. "Please protect Justinian from this plague. Keep my love safe."

Plague raged through Constantinople and spilled into Hieron while my husband barred the gates and locked the doors to the city. I paid an Emperor's ransom to the man collecting the dead to travel to Tasia's villa and find out how they fared, but he returned empty-handed. Their gates were locked, the villa empty of both the living and the dead. Tasia was a smart girl—I prayed they'd managed to escape to the country in time.

We had enough food in Hieron to last a few weeks, but messages shouted up the walls informed us that death's appetite was far from sated. Ten thousand people a day died, so many that their graves couldn't be dug fast enough. I watched from the window as a wagon made its way to gather more bodies, already creaking under its heavy load. A young girl lay atop the mountain of corpses, her black hair cascading in a waterfall over the tangle of white limbs and waxy faces. I let the curtain fall.

Easter neared, and with it, the fifteenth anniversary of our coronation, but there would be no games, no plays to celebrate our longevity on the throne. Nothing but black.

My eyes shut out the plague, but my other senses were not so lucky.

The bronze doors to my palace were barred; yet someone pounded from without for the better part of the day. The horizon had swallowed the sun by the time silence fell. I awoke that night to the smell of fire. It was Nika resurrected, the same stench after the riots as the bodies of non-Christians burned. I'd heard of the mass graves nearby in Sykae, and I knew there weren't enough people living to bury the dead.

My palace was a fragile bubble of safety, but every bubble must burst.

I passed two kitchen slaves on my way to prayer one cloudy morning. A fire roared in the hearth and sprigs of dried rosemary and thyme hung from the rafters. The girls' words stopped me dead.

"—Stricken with plague, too. What'll the Empress do when she discovers it?"

The slave yelped to see me in the doorway and dropped the mound of dough she'd been kneading. The other almost missed cleaving off the head of a speckled chicken to strike her own fingers instead. She cursed, and the knife struck again. The head rolled off the table, and blood poured to the ground.

Plague here, in my palace. God couldn't be so cruel. "Who is stricken?"

The girl turned as pale as her bread dough.

"Tell me, or I shall cast you into the street." Whoever was ill, I would send the victim to a physician in the city—they couldn't stay here and infect the rest of my household, including my son. The girl's lips knit together, and her friend studied the dead chicken.

I heaved a sigh. "I'll have the name beaten out of you if I must. We can't risk contagion."

A tear slid through the streaks of flour on her cheek. "It's not here, Augusta."

Her friend pulled feathers from the headless bird and let them fall to the ground. She wiped the hair from her eyes, leaving a smear of wet blood across her forehead. The first slave fiddled with the dough.

"We heard from the cook's son who heard from the Master of the Horses"—she looked at me with wide eyes—"there are reports of plague in the Sacred Palace. And the Emperor's taken to the streets."

I worked to swallow, glad for the table's support as my bones turned to water. "He's mad."

"No one knows if the Emperor is stricken." The girl mistook me—some of those taken with fever in the early stages of the illness wandered the streets, raving lunacy and threatening to kill themselves. Justinian was never sick, at least not since his early illness that had robbed us of children. Plague might carry away half the population, but Justinian would find a way to outsmart death. He had to.

The slave trembled. "That's all I know, Augusta. I'm sorry—I'll do extra penance for listening to such gossip."

I left the girl begging me not to have her beaten. Plenty of patricians surrounded Justinian in the Sacred Palace, many of whom would have been happy to attend his funeral. He needed those who were loyal to him, but I was all the way across the Bosphorus.

I flung open the doors to my empty chamber and rifled through the freshly packed chests, searching for my traveling cloak. Bent over a particularly large trunk, I almost hit my head when someone cleared his throat behind me.

"What are you doing?" Areobindus had stepped inside the threshold, but barely.

"I'm going to the Sacred Palace," I said. "Now."

"It's not safe."

Since when did I care about safety? God would watch over me now as He always had—playing it safe had cost me almost everything.

"Everyone else shall stay here." I'd swim if I had to.

"I'll come with you." A loaf of moldy bread hung suspended from the arch over Areobindus' head. It was believed the bread captured the miasmas in the air, but it only served to make my chambers stink like mold. "You'll need someone to row you across the Bosphorus."

"Absolutely not. It's too dangerous."

"I'm a grown man who can make decisions for himself," he said. "I'm going with you."

"No, you're not." I might lose Justinian—although I refused to think on that now. I couldn't bear the thought of losing my son, too.

Areobindus crossed his arms in front of his chest. "I'm going, and there's nothing you can do to stop me."

"Please," I said, feeling the hysteria rising in my throat. "I don't know what I'll find at the palace—"

"You're not going to lose me." He clasped my hands. "No matter what you find in the palace, I promise I'm not going anywhere."

I turned without answering, wincing to hear my son's steps follow me.

I drew my wool cloak closer to ward off the chill of the rain once we were outside. No boats darted over the gray waves of the Bosphorus—none had for almost a week—but Areobindus found an abandoned skiff to carry us across the water, little better than a child's toy and ready to sink at the slightest breeze.

My son handed me to my seat as the rain picked up and soaked through to my skin. I didn't mind—the wet chill reminded me I was still alive. Areobindus arranged the oars, then threw off the ropes. The boat slipped into the embrace of the dark water. The Bosphorus was patient today and allowed us easy passage despite the rain. I watched another boat embark from the opposite shore, its deck piled high, but then stop and a man use a long pole to tip his cargo into the sea.

Bodies.

They fell like giant white spiders. The man was still at work as we bobbed past, and the stench of rot and decay hit us, conjured from the depths of Gehenna. I'd left my posy in my haste and buried my nose in my cloak, breathing in the damp wool as we passed the walls of Sykae.

Areobindus glanced at me and then at the towers that punctuated Sykae's walls, his nose pressed into a square of white linen. "The city started storing bodies in the towers—there's nowhere else to bury them."

The corpses of Constantinople clung to my nostrils. It was too much to bear—I heaved the contents of my stomach over the side of the skiff. Areobindus kept his eyes averted as I dragged the back of my hand over my mouth.

The air should have rung with barked orders to slaves unloading ships and the cries of shopkeepers hawking their wares under awnings along the city walls. Instead, rotting melons lay in abandoned stalls, and the Baths of Zeuxippus watched over the bedraggled Queen of Cities, the bathing pools drained of the dangerous waters believed to spread contagion. My own pale marble face stared down at me from atop a porphyry column in the empty courtyard, a gift from Justinian years ago. We passed the old wool house where I'd once worked, now transformed into a hospital, and heard the death rattles of the hundreds of dying souls within. A piece of parchment tumbled down the cobbles in the breeze, an advertisement for a performance of *Antigone* set for a few days hence, a tragedy that would likely never play with most of the actors and audience dead in their beds. We covered our mouths with our cloaks as we passed through streets filled with ghosts, a forest of black slashes on the doors of those stricken with plague. The doors of those not afflicted were barred to shut out plague demons.

We were within the shadow of the Sacred Palace when a gaunt old man lurched into our path. He grabbed my arm and twisted it, and I cried out at the spasm of pain as he stumbled to the cobbles. His fever-glazed eyes bored into me, a giant black bubo like a rotten apricot bursting from his neck. I stared wide-eyed at the hand on my arm, the ragged fingernails edged with dirt and pale, knobby knuckles.

"Unhand the Empress." Areobindus shoved the man away.

I ignored the lance of pain in my shoulder to bend over the man.

He had already exposed me with his touch, and soon I would be at my husband's deathbed. If God—or a demon—chose to call me to Him now, so be it.

"May God rest your weary soul." I squeezed the man's hand, his flesh like parchment over bones so brittle they felt ready to snap in half.

He coughed, a bloody gurgle, and closed his eyes. His trial was almost over, but mine had only begun.

The guard posts at the bottom of the Chalke were empty, but someone looked down on us from the chapel atop the gate, a black head against the gray sky.

"The palace is closed, you fools," he hollered, his voice muffled. "Go back to where you came from."

"How dare you? Do you not know who this is?" Areobindus bristled like a peacock but stopped at my hand on his arm.

"Open the gate for the Empress," I said. "Now."

"Augusta?" the guard sputtered. "But you should be in Hieron— it's not safe here."

"Yet I'm already here." I tried to keep my voice level. "Open the gate."

There was scrambling from the other side, and a few moments later the massive hinges groaned and the thick bronze doors crept open. The guard bowed as I entered, one hand over his heaving chest—he was probably hoping I wouldn't impale him—and the other clutching a posy of herbs to his nose. His face still bore the pocks of youth, yet he appeared to be the lone guard on duty. Heaven help us if the Empire was threatened now.

"My apologies, Augusta."

I passed under the dome of the Chalke, watched by glittering eyes from the mosaic I'd ordered to commemorate Belisarius' campaign in Rome. It depicted the Senate, Belisarius, Justinian, and me, all celebrating victory over the Gothic and Vandal kings. Lifetimes ago.

I scanned the courtyard, its fountains barren and walkways empty. A stack of bodies filled one corner, arms and legs splayed among heads and torsos. A fly landed on my arm, and I slapped it without thinking. Its iridescent wings came away on my palm. I shuddered, not wanting to think of what it had touched before me. Justinian's massive balcony loomed at the far end of the courtyard, and I waited a moment, half hoping to see him emerge. "Where is the Emperor this hour?"

The guard snapped to attention. "In his apartments."

"At least he's not still out in the streets."

The guard stared straight ahead. "The Emperor did take to the streets to rally the people, but that was before he fell ill."

No. Not Justinian. His empty balcony mocked me now.

I might be too late, too late to apologize, to tell Justinian the truth. Too late to tell him how much I loved him.

My sandals slapped over the cobbles as I ran. Slaves huddled in doorways reached out as I passed, but I vaulted the stairs two at a time. Weary guards slouched outside Justinian's chambers while a flock of black-robed patricians rustled at my approach. Carrion crows, all of them. I forced myself to slow and keep my head high as I passed, but one barred my way at the doors.

"Augusta," he said. "You cannot go in there. The Emperor—"

I held up my hand to stop him. "I am well aware of the situation."

"You would expose your most sacred person to the bad air within." A physician crossed his arms in front of him. "We cannot allow that."

"Get out of my way before I permanently relocate you below the palace."

The physician blanched and removed his cap to wipe the few hairs on his head. "As you wish, Augusta." He pressed a fresh sachet of herbs into my palm. "Take this."

I breathed in the now-familiar tang of rosemary and vervain, my hand on the door as blood pounded in my ears. "Is he very bad?"

The physician had the decency to look me in the eye. "A saint has already said his last rites. I think he's been waiting for you."

I managed to keep the tears at bay until I was inside. An Emperor's death chamber was usually crowded with witnesses, but Justinian's bed curtains were drawn and the room was dark save for a fire in the brazier. A portly physician stood sentinel at the bedside.

My husband lay in the same wide bed as his uncle when he'd lost his battle with death, but Emperor Justin had been an old man with his wife and family waiting to greet him on the other side. Justinian wasn't yet sixty. I needed him here.

I drew a curtain but let it drop with a gasp as the shaft of light fell on Justinian. His face wore the waxy mask of death, but the skin on his neck was a violent shade of red, an angry black bubo under his right ear.

"There is another on his leg," the physician said.

"Holy Mother," I moaned. "Help him. For the love of God, help him."

I put my hand on Justinian's forehead and was shocked to feel the fire of Hephaestus' furnace under his skin. His fingers looked charred, black as if covered in soot.

"Bring me hot water." I wiped my forehead and banked the fire. "And linens."

The physician cleared his throat. "Water transmits the sickness, Augusta."

"My husband is already ill."

"The Emperor's life is in God's hands. There is nothing more to do but pray."

God helps the helpless.

I recalled Severus' advice from long ago. Justinian was certainly helpless now, but I wasn't. I would save my husband or die trying.

I pushed my sleeves to my elbows. If the physician wouldn't fetch the water, I'd get it myself. "You are dismissed."

"You should remove yourself from the palace. The Empire shall need someone near the throne in case—"

That didn't bear thinking about.

"Get out. I'll care for him myself."

The physician opened his mouth several times, then sputtered and stormed off. I was alone, and I had no idea what to do. Justinian couldn't die; I wouldn't allow it.

Areobindus stepped inside and closed the door behind him. "What can I do?"

I drew a ragged breath. "I need hot water. And willow bark and a set of heavy needles. Bronze, not ivory."

"Needles?"

"To lance his buboes."

My son grimaced, a look I probably reflected back at him, but he hurried off. I fell to my knees and prayed to the Virgin not to take Justinian before I had the chance to make things right. To tell him how much his love had meant to me.

I lost track of time. Day turned to night and night to an eternity of darkness. My hands shook as I lanced the bubo on Justinian's neck, but he screamed in his unconsciousness, the cry of a dying animal so heart wrenching I couldn't bring myself to touch the blain on his leg.

"I'm sorry," I cried through my tears. "For everything."

I washed Justinian's fevered limbs, massaged his blackened hands, and begged him to fight for his life. Unconscious, he still managed to vomit, his frail body racked with convulsions, but I bathed him and cleaned his sheets. Areobindus always hovered nearby, and for that I was thankful.

Justinian woke once, eyes wide and skin burning as he kicked off the damp sheets. An incoherent stream of garbled Latin flowed from his lips. Then he closed his eyes and was still. I feared that might be the last time I'd see his eyes, their mosaic of cinnamon flecked with gold.

I awoke disoriented to a gentle tap on my shoulder, asleep in my chair with my head on Justinian's mattress. I straightened slowly and winced at the crick in my neck. Justinian's illness would rob me of my youth, but I would gladly barter that and more for his life.

I expected Areobindus, but Narses hovered over me instead. His face glowed white as a skull. I grasped Justinian's hand, dreading the cold I might find having settled in his skin, but his fingers felt like the flames of Gehenna. I exhaled, feeling the stench and filth of the room on my skin and in my mouth.

I wiped my brow and sat back in my chair. "News from Cyzicus?"

He shook his head. "The Cappadocian has disappeared, but I'll find him." He scanned Justinian's prone form. The Emperor who never slept lay like a man in his coffin. "How is he?"

"Unchanged," I said. The bubo on Justinian's thigh was the size of my fist now, the skin around it peeling away like an asp shedding its skin. I would know by next sunset whether I would emerge from this chamber dressed in purple or swathed in black. I doubted whether I possessed the strength to survive Justinian's passing.

"The generals of the realm are taking measures to secure the throne," Narses said. "Amongst themselves, of course."

"What if he recovers?"

"Justinian hasn't named an heir. The generals have taken it upon themselves to choose his successor for him."

My husband struggled for his life while his men plotted to steal his throne. A forgotten emotion, rage, pushed through my grief and terror.

"They've chosen Belisarius, haven't they?"

"They've done everything short of crowning him and draping him in purple."

"Justinian isn't dead yet." I slammed my fist into the arm of my chair and felt the impact echo up my bones. "This is treason!"

I'd always known Belisarius couldn't be trusted. The general despised me and was unlikely simply to exile me after his humiliation. I could claim sanctuary and become a nun, but the discovery of my living son, a possible heir for Justinian, would prove a huge obstacle in Belisarius' path to the throne. I could remarry and put a man of my own choosing on the throne, but the very idea repulsed me. If Justinian died, I would join him before Belisarius could reenter the city.

There was no reason to surrender now, not with the fight yet to come.

"The Emperor might still survive," Narses said, but he didn't believe the lie any more than I did. Only a miracle saved a soul from plague, and Justinian had already been granted more than his share of miracles.

"And if he does, we must be ready to punish the traitor." I paced the room. "I may have heard a rumor that Belisarius claimed he'd never accept another despot like Justinian as Emperor." Words were powerful weapons, ones that could be twisted to suit my own needs.

Narses' lips curled back in a smile stolen from the devil. "Indeed. It's difficult to tell precisely what was said from such a distance."

"Such treason demands Belisarius be invited back to Constantinople."

"He will refuse. The fighting has stopped as the officers try to keep the men isolated to avoid the plague. They cannot even receive supplies—there are reports of men eating their horses."

"He will come if he thinks Justinian is already dead."

"And if the Emperor doesn't survive?"

I would forgive Narses' treason as the same question filled my mind. I shrugged. "Then we will have invited him to the capital to seize the throne."

Although I didn't plan to be around if it came to that.

I didn't have to wait long to learn Belisarius' mind on the subject. Had his letter been from anyone else, I might have burned it for fear of contagion. I wished after I read it that I had.

Theodora,

It is with great sorrow that I heard of Justinian's illness and with a heavy heart that I assume the mantle he leaves behind. You are his widow and as such, I cannot allow you to continue your rule. I offer you two options. First, you may take orders and live cloistered among the women of God for the remainder of your life. Second, you may choose to join your husband.

I trust you will have made your decision by the time I've reached the Golden Gate.

—Belisarius, General of the East and the West

The Empire held its breath as the fields lay fallow and the markets empty. I ordered invocations as the final black sores on Justinian's body burst, weeping their putrid contents as my eyes burned with hot tears and my husband moaned in merciful unconsciousness.

I washed his blains of their blood and pus, and bathed his shrunken body, dressing the blisters with compresses of lavender and chamomile, the scent of spring in a deathbed. The herbs helped with minor kitchen burns and scarring, but Justinian's skin appeared as if he'd emerged from an inferno. Yet I didn't know what else to do.

I crawled into bed next to Justinian, tucked myself into his fiery heat, and held him tight. Whether he woke or not, he would not be alone.

My body shook, and I wept hot tears for the man I was about to lose, for the lost days I could have spent in his arms instead of in my cold bed in Hieron. I'd have done anything at that moment to take his place.

I meant to stay awake, but exhaustion pulled me into the abyss of sleep. When I woke, the sun's golden glow warmed the cracks in the shutters. I was nestled next to Justinian with my head still on his chest. His skin was cool for the first time in days.

I scrambled to feel for his breath, but his fingers were woven into my hair. He looked at me with bloodshot eyes sunken deep in their sockets.

Open. His eyes were open.

"Thanks be to God," I cried out in relief. My hand lingered on his clammy brow as I kissed his cheeks. "If you ever scare me like that again, I will murder you myself."

Justinian winced as he tried to sit up. "It feels like you already did." His voice creaked like an ancient hinge.

I moved to rise, but he grasped my arm. "Stay. Please."

I did as I was told, sending prayers to the Virgin to thank her for her mercy. Hot tears streamed down my cheeks to catch like diamonds in the dark hair lightly scattered on Justinian's chest.

"I'd have fallen ill months ago if I'd known this was what it would take to bring you home," Justinian whispered.

I mock-punched his side but burrowed closer to him, filling my lungs with the scent of lavender. And life.

"You didn't fall ill?" he asked.

"The devil protects his own."

"That explains why I'm still alive." He winced and his lips tightened. "How many dead?"

I thought to lie, but he'd soon learn the truth. "Some say ten thousand a day. It's too early to tell."

He gave a mangled exhale and squeezed his eyes shut. I'd have to spoon-feed Justinian bits of information over the next few days. There was so much to tell.

Belisarius. Areobindus.

We lay together as the light gained strength. I was loath to announce the miracle of his recovery and share him with the Empire, but finally I had to rise—Justinian wanted water, and his bandages needed changing.

Areobindus startled when I opened the door, the late sunlight from Justinian's windows streaming into the hall. He glanced to the imperial bed and then back to me, hand raised to cross himself. "The Emperor?"

"Has recovered through the grace of God." The words felt like a glorious hymn. "The city needs to know of the miracle."

Precious few recovered from plague, but God's anointed Emperor would survive. It wasn't the devil that protected him, no matter what Justinian claimed.

I found a boiling pot of fish broth in the kitchen and fixed a tray with two bowls. Almost half the kitchen slaves had perished during the time I'd been cloistered in Justinian's sickroom, as had much of the palace, courtiers and slaves alike. I hadn't the heart to verify the claim that the pile of bodies in the courtyard now reached the height of the palace walls.

A trickle of broth slipped from the corner of Justinian's lips into the beard that now covered his jaw as Narses and Areobindus were announced. Cyr wove his way through my son's legs—the dog had grown since I'd seen him last. I wiped my husband's chin and gave them a look of warning.

"Narses." Justinian inclined his head. "And who is this?"

"Areobindus," I said. "My steward."

"I see." Justinian's tone was suddenly frigid.

"Augustus." Narses gave a deep bow. "The Queen of Cities gives thanks for your recovery."

"What is the state of the Empire?"

Not even a brush with death would coerce my husband to rest. I took away the soup and mixed his wine and water with my back turned, adding a healthy dose of valerian. I'd tie him to his bed if I had to.

"The fields are deserted. It's estimated the plague claimed half the population of the Empire," Narses said. "There are reports of sickness from Alexandria to Persia."

Justinian perked up at the mention of Persia, but he glowered in the direction of my son as he sipped his wine. "So the fire-eaters must face this as well."

"The war is at a standstill," Narses said. "General Belisarius has been recalled to the capital."

"Recalled? Why?" Justinian looked to Narses, but I gave a minute shake of my head. Word of Belisarius' treachery might kill him.

"He wished to see to the well-being of his family," Narses continued smoothly. "Plague has been reported at his villa in Rufinianae."

"No." My hand fluttered to my mouth. "Antonina and her daughter? Are they stricken?"

"I have not heard of Belisarius' wife or child, Augusta."

"Find out. Please."

Narses' lip curled—he'd probably consider the plague a fair exchange if it claimed Antonina—but gave a terse nod and bowed again. His eyes crinkled with a smile for Justinian. "It is good to see you well, Augustus."

He backed from the room as Areobindus bowed to me. "Is there anything else I can bring you, Augusta?"

Justinian shoved his goblet to my chest so fast his wine splashed onto my lap. I wiped the front of my stola with a frown, but I might be surly, too, if I'd almost died of plague. The valerian should soon hasten him to sleep.

"I require nothing," I said. "Thank you."

Cyr bounded after Areobindus—he might be my dog in name, but I knew whom the beast truly loved. The door had scarcely closed when Justinian grabbed my wrist, surprising me with his strength. "How dare you." His growl was at odds with his gaunt face and bandaged neck. "Bring him to my sickbed and flaunt him under my nose."

He knew.

I glanced to the door, heart pounding like eagle's wings. He must have known before he fell ill. This was the moment I'd dreaded for so many years, but now the hideous truth was exposed. Justinian would exile me to the ends of the Empire, or worse. And I deserved it all.

He followed my gaze with a glare that could have obliterated every village in the Empire. The floor was hard under my knees, and while I yearned to take his hand—now the hands of an old man—his grip remained viselike on my wrist. "I'm sorry," I said. "So, so sorry."

"So it's true."

The fire in his eyes banked and his shoulders slumped as he looked everywhere but my face. He released my wrist. "Go to him then," he said. "And be happy."

"What?"

"You cannot have us both, Theodora. There can only be one man in your life and in your bed."

"My bed? What are you talking about?"

Realization blossomed in my mind and I laughed, first a chortle, but then tears streamed down my face and my ribs could scarcely contain my breath.

Anger brought welcome color to Justinian's cheeks, and he banged his fist on a pillow as if it were his throne, sending puffs of white feathers to drift in the air like snowflakes. "You dare mock me?" Gold sparks flared in his eyes, but I scrambled up to his bed and covered his face with kisses, his cheeks, nose, and chin. He stared at me as if I were mad.

"You fool. Areobindus is not my lover." I could scarcely get the words out. "He's my son."

"But I thought—" Justinian stared at me. "Your son? How is that possible?"

So much for spoon-feeding him.

I took a deep breath and spilled the entire story, sparing no detail as the horizon swallowed the sun and an orchestra of crickets welcomed the night.

My conscience was finally clean, come what might.

Justinian looked older than his fifty-eight years by the time I finished. He rubbed his temples—I could see the weight of the valerian in his eyes.

"I had reports of a young man you were taken with in Hieron, that you'd made him your steward. I should have known better."

"I have always been faithful to you." I dragged my eyes to his. "Can you forgive me?"

"I wish you had told me long ago." He kissed my palm, letting it linger on his lips. "I understand why you hid the truth, but things might have been so different—"

Justinian cleared his throat, looking at the stars through the window as he stroked my palm. "And you're positive Areobindus is your son? He couldn't be lying?"

"He has my cross and the scar from his fight with Photius. He remembers the procession to Bithynia. There's no doubt he's my son." I wanted to smooth the wrinkles from his eyes. "You need to sleep. We can discuss more of this tomorrow."

Not to mention Belisarius.

"I love you, Theodora. No matter what."

"I love you, too. Rest well." I unfolded my legs to fluff his pillow and snuffed out the oil lamp at his bedside. I craved several hours of uninterrupted sleep in my own bed, my thoughts no longer plagued by an uncertain future.

I opened the door and almost ran into Narses, his hand raised to knock, a contingent of Scholarii guards behind him. "The Emperor sleeps," I said. "Whatever it is will have to wait until morning."

"Antonina and her daughter are in good health, untouched by the illness." He looked almost disappointed at the news. "She sent this for you."

I tore into the vellum, uncaring whether the paper carried plague.

Theodora,

> *Praise be to God that Justinian has recovered. I've been holed up here in Rufinianae without a word, but Narses told me of my husband's treachery. Your crown is far too gaudy for my tastes, and I'd prefer you kept it on your head.*
>
> *You've already gifted me with more favors than I deserve, but I have one more to beg of you. Belisarius deserves death, but I beg you to be magnanimous. After all, we both know I look horrific in black.*

> *Yours,*
> *Antonina*

Belisarius deserved death, but he'd been lenient with Antonina when her treachery was revealed. Perhaps I might be creative with his punishment.

"Thank you." I waited for Narses to leave, but he didn't move. "Is that all?"

"Belisarius docked this evening and awaits your pleasure in your receiving room." He folded his hands behind him. "He believes the Emperor to be in a grave state."

Sleep would have to wait.

I found Belisarius fiddling with the ties on my silk curtains, a picture of life and vitality while my husband looked as if God still might claim him. "I'm disappointed, Theodora," he said. "You haven't taken either of my recent suggestions."

I gave him a silky smile. "Unfortunately, I'm not fit for a nunnery. And your other option—" I pretended to shudder.

He stroked his beard. "Well, we can't have you underfoot while I am crowned."

"Perhaps you can tell Justinian that yourself."

The smug smile fell from his face. "The Emperor lives?"

"Through the grace of God."

Belisarius swallowed hard. We both knew his fate.

"But I was only planning. . . . The Empire must have an heir."

"And it will. Unfortunately, that won't be you." I snapped my fingers for Narses and his guards. "Your new accommodations await below the palace."

"You'd let me live?"

"Perhaps. You'll have plenty of time to think on your treason while you await my judgment."

Belisarius unsheathed his sword and stiffly handed it to the guards before Narses escorted him to the depths of the palace. He could share a dark cell next to Photius.

Belisarius would remain below the palace until I forgot about him and rats ate his bones. Or until I broke him in half.

Chapter 32

The plague abated, but Justinian's bones still rattled when he coughed, and he could scarcely rise from his bed without his knees knocking together. He was already troubled with a kingdom decimated by plague and a distinct lack of tax revenues that made the current Persian campaign especially problematic. But I could no longer put off telling him of Belisarius.

"I cannot believe Belisarius would deceive me so."

I rinsed the bronze blade to shave away the fresh stubble on his jaw and forced myself not to speak. Justinian sat for a long moment, half his face lathered with sheep tallow and the other smooth with a fresh sheen of olive oil. A tiny trickle of blood marred his throat where I'd nicked him on his Adam's apple.

I dabbed a towel at the cut. "He cannot go unpunished."

"You'd have him killed, wouldn't you?"

"But you would not."

Justinian tilted his chin so I could finish. "Belisarius is a good man. Misguided, perhaps, but I will not have his blood on my hands."

"Of course." The sarcasm dripped from my voice. "Plotting for your throne and asking me to commit suicide certainly deserve a gentle response."

He inspected my handiwork in a bronze mirror and yanked the towel from his neck. "Now is not the time to execute Belisarius. Plague bodies are washing up in the Bosphorus, and we need him to deal with Persia. And possibly Italy again in a few years."

I hated how logical my husband could be sometimes.

"Find a nice rock in the Aegean to banish him to." I was willing to go along with Justinian's leniency, but only because I had another plan for Belisarius. "Even Antonina agrees he's overstepped his bounds this time."

"You two are as ruthless as Scylla and Charybdis."

I didn't relish the comparison to the sea monsters, but I let it go. "At least strip him of his belt. Show everyone you no longer favor the traitor."

Justinian kissed my hand, twining his fingers with mine. I could see how much this cost him and wished I could lighten his burden. "You're right."

"I'm always right," I said. "It's one of my better qualities. Speaking of which—"

"What are you up to now?" Justinian smiled, but his eyes looked heavy. Yet I had to broach the subject.

"You must name an heir. Nothing like this could happen again if the succession was secure."

"And I'm sure you have a candidate in mind."

"Several, actually."

His eyebrow arched.

"Antonina and Belisarius' daughter would make a good match for Athanasius. A betrothal between their daughter and Tasia's son would bind Belisarius to us through family so he'd be less tempted to play this little game again. And Vigilantia's son, Justin, would make a good pair with Comito's daughter, Sophia." My eyes flicked to him. "And then there's Areobindus."

Justinian frowned. "I'm hesitant to name a man I've scarcely met as my heir."

"He's my son."

Justinian kissed my forehead. "My darling little imp, I just cheated death. I have no intention of dying anytime soon. Be patient and everything will fall into place."

I'd be patient, but that didn't mean I had to like it.

"Release Belisarius to the custody of his wife and write a letter telling him of his demotion," Justinian said.

"You won't see him?"

"Not yet."

"As you wish." I kissed his forehead and let my hand trace the outline of his jaw before giving him a long, slow kiss. I breathed in the smell of the tallow on his skin and his usual scent of mint. I would never take this man for granted again.

He groaned. "Get out now, or I might have to rouse myself to chase you around the bed."

We both knew that wasn't going to happen, but the heat in his eyes was reassuring.

"Is that a promise or a threat?"

His eyes lit with the spark I'd so missed. "Both. Now go and let me sleep."

I gave a mock bow and sashayed from the room. I felt ten years younger with my conscience clean and Justinian on the mend. And I would take Justinian's plan for Belisarius one step further.

Back in my chambers, I ordered Belisarius' release and retrieved a fresh sheet of vellum, choosing a warm patch of sunlight on the balcony to put the final nail in the general's coffin. I wondered if Belisarius would be waiting at his villa for a summons, or worse, the footsteps of an imperial assassin. The tables were turned, and I intended to remain on this side of the game. Fear could be a powerful weapon.

My pen scratched the paper as birds twittered outside my window. I chose my words carefully, praying to the Virgin that this would be the last time I would have to protect my throne and my husband's.

To the Honorable Belisarius, General of the West and East,

You are well aware of your offense against us. However, as I am greatly indebted to Antonina, I have decided to dismiss all charges against you and give her your life.

From this day forth, you may be confident concerning both your personal safety and property, but we shall know your attitude from how you treat your wife.

—Theodora Augusta

Now Belisarius would owe not only me, but Antonina, too, for the very air he breathed. The man who had vanquished Africa and Rome would be beholden to two women.

While I waited for a reply, slaves scrubbed me with lavender salts and massaged my skin with olive oil so pure it looked like water in its jar. My scalp stung with the scrubbing, but my hair shone like ebony, although my nose and eyes burned with the lead oxide and slaked lime that I'd used in my hair to mask the feathers of silver at my temples.

I waited all day, but there was no response from Rufinianae. I was not a patient woman. The afternoon was chilly, as if summer dared not show her face in a city still sunk in mourning. A few people hurried in the streets, but the atmosphere was that of a house after a funeral.

Even Antonina's villa at Rufinianae seemed sedate as Areobindus and I approached the deserted entrance in our sedans. Antonina emerged as we stepped from our litters, an ancient slave out of breath behind her.

"Forgive my tardiness, Augusta," she said as she straightened. "Plague claimed my former herald, and Basil here is still learning."

I smiled at the slave as Antonina led us inside—the poor man would attain sainthood by the time he finished serving my friend.

We settled among the silk cushions of the *triclinium*, a room so lavishly appointed that a visitor to the city might have mistaken it for the Royal Treasury, but only if the Royal Treasury contained chartreuse silk curtains and a life-sized ivory statue of a grinning baboon with gilded nipples. Antonina's shrines to the gods were absent, likely a result of Belisarius' orthodoxy, but Areobindus gaped at a randy mosaic of nymphs and satyrs on the ceiling, one that could have made the madam of any *lupinar* blush. There was even a tree of life, complete with erect phalluses hanging from the branches.

"How does Theodosius fare?" I asked.

Antonina fiddled with her curls—they had taken on a rather flagrant reddish hue. "He's well, glad he no longer has to hide while Belisarius is in the capital." She chuckled. "After your letter to Belisarius, I think Theodosius and I could be caught *in flagrante delicto* in the Hippodrome and Belisarius wouldn't protest."

That was hardly my intent when composing the letter to her husband, but so be it. "So he received my message?"

"The poor man thought you had sent an assassin to kill him. He actually kissed my feet for saving his life and swore he'd be my slave for the rest of our lives."

The man had a passion for life, but what shade of life without his belt? For a moment I pitied Belisarius, for all he had been and never would be again.

Antonina turned her attention to Areobindus, still standing at the door. Her brows rose to the flames of her hair. "And who is this fine young patrician?"

I motioned him forward, my heart in my throat. "This is Areo-bindus, or as you knew him, John."

Antonina's gaze flew to mine.

I touched the amber cross at his throat. "He had this."

Antonina barely glanced at the necklace, her gaze intent on Areo-bindus' temple. Her fingers fluttered to her mouth. "And the scar. I suppose Photius was good for something."

I cringed at her callousness toward her own son. Photius was still imprisoned below the palace, in a secret cell so dark that night and day were indistinguishable. I would let him escape at a later date and perhaps encourage him to become a monk.

Antonina circled my son. "And where have you been hiding all this time?"

"He was secreted away to Arabia after Macedonia first lied about his death."

I expected Antonina to fling her arms open or burst into tears, but she did neither.

"And the scar on your back?" Resuming her place amid the cushions, she sat straight, hands folded demurely in her lap, but her lips pressed into a thin line.

"What scar?" Areobindus looked as puzzled as I felt.

Antonina ignored him and addressed me instead. "Photius took Timothy's bronze seal to John's back shortly after Timothy died."

"I don't understand," I said. "A seal wouldn't leave a scar."

She looked at Areobindus. "Do you remember what he did?"

He shook his head. "Perhaps I was too young?"

"He heated it in the fire first. The metal was still red when I came in and found you screaming."

"This is ridiculous," I said. "You never told me—"

"I almost did, the day I came to you in mourning for Timothy, but

I feared you'd take him back. I needed the money with all those mouths to feed."

"None of this would have happened if you'd let me tell Justinian."

"No one has ever *let* you do anything, Theodora." She kept her eyes on Areobindus. "It's a simple insignia, just a letter *T* the size of my thumbnail. Surely you don't mind showing us to verify your story." She glanced at me. "Macedonia wouldn't have known about the mark, although she might have set this imposter up with everything else."

I stormed past her and yanked my son by the arm. "We're leaving."

Antonina grabbed my wrist. "I know you want to believe he's your son. Ask Photius if you don't believe me."

I shook her off and released Areobindus. "Show her," I said. "Take off your tunica and show her the scar."

His face drained of blood.

"Show her!" The sound of ripping seams echoed through the *triclinium* as I tore the neck of his tunica, but he covered my hand and slowly lifted what remained of the fabric over his head, his eyes like an old man's. Then he turned. My eyes searched for any scar, any blemish, but his skin was smooth as bronze, unmarred by man or nature.

"You filthy lying whore." I turned on Antonina. "Who put you up to this? That bastard from Cappadocia? Your husband?" I gasped. "Was it Justinian?"

Antonina grabbed my shoulders and shook me. "Your son is dead."

I slapped her so hard that she staggered back, hand raised to her cheek as fire raged through my palm. "This lie will cost you your head."

Once we were out of earshot from Antonina, I whirled to face Areobindus. "Tell me she's lying."

My son's face shared the same pallor as someone stricken with plague. "Of course she's lying. I spoke only the truth. I am your son."

I searched his expression for any hint of a lie, but there was nothing. Of course, I scarcely knew this man before me, even if he was my son. "I hope so, for your sake."

My teeth chattered as our litters ran down the *Mese*, Areobindus' bearers struggling to keep up with mine. I wanted to send the assassin Belisarius had feared to crucify Antonina, but the rational part of my mind gained ground with each step. I needed to verify her story with Photius. I'd send Antonina to rot in prison with her son if he knew nothing of her story. And if he did—

I wouldn't think on that now.

Photius would deny his mother's wild tale. Antonina must stand to gain something from all this. I just wasn't sure what.

The prison smelled of terror and years of filth and decay. Those who dwelt here in the dark were half dead, awaiting hell. I barked Photius' name to the warden, a swarthy man whose ruddy complexion belied his time spent away from the sun.

He led me past Belisarius' now-empty cell and used a giant key shaped like a lion to unlock a dented bronze door. Antonina's eldest son was crammed in a corner, chin resting on his knees. The light from the warden's oil lamp illuminated graceful charcoal ships sketched on every bit of the rough stone walls—mostly military *dromons*, their curved prows headed to battle.

"Our resident artist," the guard said. "I'll be outside the door."

Photius scarcely looked capable of swatting a fly, but I remained near the entrance. His nose was broken, and there were gaps in his teeth as he smiled, but I recognized Antonina in the curve of his lips and the stubborn set of his jaw. He squinted at me through blood-shot eyes.

"I'd bow," Photius said, "but my legs no longer obey me."

"You have information I want," I said. "Your honesty in the matter could purchase your freedom. If you lie, I'll find new ways to make you wish for death."

Photius licked his flaked lips. "I'm listening."

"You have several siblings, correct?"

"My mother excelled at spreading her legs for all sorts of men."

"And if I needed to identify the brats in your mother's brood?"

Photius thought for a moment, then rambled off a list of height, hair color, moles, and warts belonging to Antonina's herd of children, but with no mention of John.

"Is that all? What about another boy who didn't share your blood?"

"The stray? John?"

My heart leapt. For a desperate moment I considered leaving with the truth unsaid, of returning to life as it had been before Antonina's revelation. "What did he look like?"

Photius gave me a strange look. "He died after he left us. Gangly thing—plain enough—dark hair and a snub little nose. I drew him once."

"No distinguishing features?"

"A scar on his temple, shaped like a sickle moon." Photius smiled. "I gave it to him. And another on his back."

No. Antonina couldn't be right.

"What did it look like?"

"A little *T* for Timothy. My father's seal." Photius struggled against his chains as I turned on my heel. "Where are you going? You said I'd go free if I talked!"

Photius' screams of rage chased me into the corridor. Areobindus was gone.

I ordered Narses to find him, but the imposter had disappeared, a fact that caused me to swear and break numerous priceless vases.

"Find him," I told Narses, "if it's the last thing you do."

"Augusta." The artist shook his brush at me, the giant brown caterpillar of his brows creeping from one temple to the other as precious pearls of blue paint splattered from his brush to the floor. I hoped the slaves could scrub the mess from the mosaic when this torture was over.

I shook the golden chalice I held in his direction. "It's not possible to hold still all afternoon."

The little man peered out the window. "The sun has scarcely risen, Augusta." He gave a long-suffering sigh. "The portrait is almost complete if only you wouldn't move."

Easier said than done. For two weeks now, I had stood motionless in a pose of imperial majesty, dressed in a stola embroidered in gold with the three Magi and weighted down by a monstrous headdress encrusted with enough pearls and gems to buy off Persia for an entire year. My image was slated to join Justinian's in a massive mosaic for the Basilica of San Vitale in Ravenna and this artist would provide my portrait to the Master of Mosaics. Justinian and I would be frozen in *tesserae* in a distant church, surrounded by our glittering retinues of priests, attendants, soldiers, and eunuchs. Even once our earthly bodies had turned to dust, we would never truly die.

Fortunately, Narses saved me by striding into the room, travel stained and grim faced. Cyr raised his head but whimpered and lay back down when he realized the visitor wasn't Areobindus.

I dismissed the artist, forcing myself to wait to speak until the door had closed behind him.

"Where is he?" I wanted to cut Areobindus' tongue from his mouth and flay the skin from his back.

"Areobindus is dead," Narses said.

"Dead? Or murdered?"

"Murdered, unless he managed to stab himself in the back," Narses said. "I traced him to a seedy taverna in Cyzicus, but no one had seen him in a few days. I inspected his room and found him on the floor, along with several rats availing themselves of his corpse. He'd been dead awhile."

Cyzicus. John the Cappadocian was in Cyzicus.

"The innkeeper was willing to talk after I greased his palm,"

Narses continued. "The bishop of Cyzicus met with Areobindus downstairs and broke bread with him. There was an argument, and Areobindus was upset. Then the bishop said he would take care of things."

"Arrest the bishop. Torture him until he talks."

"Too late. The bishop was found dead the day I arrived in Cyzicus, strangled in his bed."

"John the Cappadocian served the bishop."

"There's no evidence against him," Narses said. "It was common knowledge throughout the town that the bishop and John hated each other, but I couldn't find one scintilla of evidence to prove his involvement in either death."

"I want him," I said. "Preferably alive."

"You have him." Narses gave a slow grin, the one that always made my flesh prickle. "The Cappadocian is a coward; he was on a ship bound for Alexandria." He opened and closed his fist. "It took some persuasion to change his destination, but I've relocated him to Photius' old cell."

I'd released Photius a few days ago and paid for his passage to Jerusalem. The boy would make a good monk, perhaps designing frescoes for churches in the Holy Land. I had yet to tell Antonina that I'd freed her son. And that she was right about Areobindus.

John the Cappadocian had found a way to torture me all the way from Cyzicus. I swore to be equally creative with the miserable piece of offal under my own roof.

I retraced my steps to the tiny closet of a cell tucked into the dimmest recesses of the prison. A monk's tonsure ringed John's shaved skull, but otherwise he seemed haughty and arrogant as always. He wasn't broken like Macedonia or Photius—I'd have bet on his spitting at me if not for the horsehair gag across his mouth. As it was, he leaned against the moldering wall with its charcoal ships, one eye almost swollen shut and the other laughing at me as if I were the one shackled in my own filth.

"I know all about Areobindus," I said. "How you and the bishop set him up to get to me." John flinched as I yanked down his gag.

"And now you've come to kill me." His voice rasped like that of one long ill.

"No." I tightened my fingers around the whip in my hand. "I've come to hear you beg for mercy."

"You set me up, you and that whore Antonina."

"You killed my son!" The whip cracked and sliced the soft flesh of his shoulder, a trickle of blood red as poppies slipping to his chest.

John gave a sharp hiss and bowed his head as if awaiting an executioner's ax. "I only arranged for Macedonia to bring him to me in Caesarea. I knew Justinian would pay dear for the release of your son."

I doubted whether Justinian would have believed I even had a son, not if the story came from the Cappadocian.

"So did he truly die of the pox? Or did you kill him?" The whip trembled in my hand.

"Macedonia spoke the truth. The boy fell ill of a pox and died a few days after the ship left Constantinople. I never meant him any harm."

I'd expected the truth to bring some sense of peace, but instead I felt only a vast emptiness. My son was truly dead.

"You kidnapped him to use against me. Only a coward would use a child in such a vile manner."

John's chin tilted up in defiance. "And only a coward would cut out a woman's tongue and have the rest of her chopped into tiny pieces and thrown into the sea. Neither you nor Antonina is worth the dirt Macedonia walked upon."

"Death was too kind a punishment for Macedonia."

"She would have been true to you, but you abandoned her after the earthquake. You left her starving and destitute, living amongst the rubble in Antioch, so she was almost dead when I met her the second time, struggling to provide for our daughter. I didn't even know the girl existed until then. Euphemia is the only thing that's good and pure in this wretched world. I was a fool to abandon her mother the first time."

"So you brought Macedonia to my court. To spy on me."

"You humiliated me." John's cheeks burned under the crusted blood and filth. "And sought to destroy me. I was content to blackmail you, but then John died and you set me up for treason. You punished Euphemia for my sins."

I thought of his daughter, disgraced by her father's treason and now penniless. A pariah in the Queen of Cities, she had no hope of making a suitable marriage without her father's wealth. The girl was no better off than I'd been at her age, despite being raised amongst the silks and splendor of court. "I never wished her harm. What about the bishop? Areobindus? Did they just happen to be in your way?"

"The bishop and I used Areobindus—he was a foundling left at the monastery as a boy, one with a convenient scar on his temple and willing to deceive you into believing that he was your long-lost son. Macedonia gave him the cross and the memories of his trip to Bithynia to prove his story. He was to be my revenge on you, my puppet on the throne after Justinian's death."

"And after I discovered the truth, the bishop feared Areobindus might use the failed plot to blackmail both of you."

John nodded. "Areobindus was naïve, not stupid. But the bishop had much to lose."

"So you killed him?"

John shrugged. "One of us had to die."

So he was responsible at least for that murder. Yet I no longer cared.

I straightened to find the mantle of old age settled on my shoulders.

I was weary of hatred and revenge; I didn't want them to rule my life any longer.

"A ship shall take you to Antinoopolis. I never want to see you again." The city clung to the ends of the Empire, two hundred miles south of Alexandria, named by Emperor Hadrian to honor his lover. "You shall take only the cloak on your back. All your remaining property shall be confiscated—"

Were it not for John's chains, he might have murdered me then and there. "You have condemned Euphemia—"

"And be transferred to your daughter," I said. "But she shall forfeit every *nummi* should you set foot beyond Antinoopolis' boundary markers while I still live. Do you understand?"

John slumped against the wall, his chains slack. "I understand."

I forced myself to turn and walk calmly from the cell, ensuring that John's last view of me was my purple *chalmys*. My heart nearly jumped from my chest as someone touched my arm in the dark corridor. Justinian stood there, his face swathed in shadows.

"How much did you hear?" I asked.

"Almost everything," he said, his hands open at his sides as if he couldn't bear to touch me. He ran his hands over his face and appeared more haggard than I'd ever seen him. I'd finally lost him.

"This isn't how things were supposed to happen," he said. "This is all my fault."

"What?"

"I knew about your son, Theodora." His voice cracked. "You denied John the Cappadocian's claims after we reprimanded him for the Carthage campaign, but I sent Narses to investigate. He discovered the truth."

I'd first thought to send my son to Alexandria with Narses, but he'd been gone from court—now I knew he'd been on Justinian's errand—so I'd sent Macedonia instead. I'd delivered my son to the enemy without even realizing it.

Justinian tried to pace the tiny corridor, unable or unwilling to meet my eyes. "John tried to ransom the boy after you sent him to Alexandria, but Narses knew your son had died. I didn't know how you'd react if I knew, and I couldn't bear the idea that you might leave me." He stopped pacing and reached out to touch me, but I didn't move. His arm dropped back to his side. "I failed you. I'll understand if you can't forgive me."

I couldn't think. I'd worried all these years that my husband might cast me off, that he would despise me for my deceit, for my failings. Yet all this time he'd feared the same.

The whole situation would have been laughable if it hadn't been so sad. I wanted to scream at him, to rail against him for the part he'd played, but he was no more guilty than I. Less so, in fact. Sometimes it took us poor wretches far too long to realize God's blessings. And despite everything that had happened, I knew I had indeed been blessed by having Justinian in my life.

I'd held grudges close to my heart all my life, but this man had always loved me, despite my many failings, and often because of them. I could not judge him.

Unable to speak, I held out my hand for his, needing him to anchor me as he always had. The soft wool of his tunica scratched my cheek as I laid my head on his shoulder, glad he couldn't see the tears that slipped from my eyes and thankful for the strength of his arms around me. "I forgive you."

His arms bound me to him. "I love you, Theodora. More than you'll ever know."

His words undid me.

I sobbed into his tunica then, clinging to him and weeping for the years we'd lost, all the time we'd squandered by doubting each other. He crushed me to him as if he feared he might lose me again.

Finally I lifted my head with a shuddering breath and wiped the tears from my swollen eyes, still tasting their salt on my lips. I was shocked to see tears glistening on his cheeks. I brushed them away with my thumb and clasped his face between my hands. "You stupid, foolish man," I managed to choke out. "I love you, Justinian. Forever and always."

I had forgiven so many people: Justinian, Antonina, and the Cappadocian. Perhaps one day I might learn to forgive myself.

Chapter 33

"Are you sure you're well enough to attend the wedding?"

Tasia handed me a fresh clutch of mint leaves as a slave wrinkled his nose and carried away my chamber pot. My daughter was statuesque in a mahogany stola with a *paludamentum* the same shade and luster as polished pearls, her hair tucked under a veil heavily embellished with gold.

The wedding of Comito's daughter, Sophia, would have been a welcome thought were it not for the ever-present gnaw of pain in my stomach. The saint I'd seen in secret a few weeks ago had informed me I had an imbalance of black bile, but he believed it might right itself if left alone. He'd offered me drafts of poppy juice, but I refused to spend what might be my last days in a fog. Yet my appetite had deserted me, and my waist thickened, hidden now beneath the mahogany silk stola embroidered at the hem with my monogram. My monthly bleedings had ceased ages ago, so I knew these symptoms did not herald the quickening of my womb, barren as the sands of Cappadocia.

I wiped my mouth on a silk *mappa* and felt my stomach settle with the mint. I missed Antonina, but she was off in Rome keeping an eye on Belisarius as he attempted to subdue the latest Ostrogoth uprising. I regretted that she wouldn't be at my side when the time came, but we'd already said our good-byes, although I doubted she had realized it at the time.

"Are you sure that's how it's done?" I'd asked. The imperial gardens were drenched in sunshine, and I'd chuckled as Antonina stabbed a needle into a silk belt for Belisarius. She and her husband had resolved most of their differences after Theodosius' death from illness a few years ago, and they had settled into a mostly amicable partnership.

"We are old women now," Antonina said, not bothering to look up at me. The tip of her tongue showed between her teeth as she yanked the thread through the fabric, producing an impressive knot. "It's high time we started acting like it."

"I just turned forty-five," I said. "That's hardly as ancient as you make us out to be."

"One foot in the grave," she said.

Little did she know.

I traced the line of sunlight on my stola and breathed in the delicate fragrance of the white and purple Nazareth irises Justinian had recently had planted for me and the heavy scent of Antonina's rose perfume. I would miss both precious smells. "We've had a good run, you and I, haven't we?"

Her lips curled in a smile, and she glanced up, likely ready with some sarcastic quip. Instead, her smile fell at the look on my face. She set her sewing in her lap. "The best, darling."

"I'll miss you," I said.

She cocked an eyebrow at me and resumed her sewing, although her eyes darted back to me. "Don't go soft on me," she said. "Belisarius and I won't be gone in Rome too long this time."

"I know." I pulled myself to stand, hiding the effort it took, and walked slowly toward her, dropping a kiss on her scarlet hair. "I love you, Antonina."

She took my hand and covered it with hers, the veins like a web of rivers on an old map. No matter what I said, somehow time had managed to sneak up and take us unawares. "I love you, too, darling. Even if we have tried to kill each other."

"More than once."

She chuckled and patted my hand. "More than once."

A few days later I'd watched the *dromons* slip into the Bosphorus again, knowing I wouldn't live to see her return.

Now the blood and green bile in my vomit this morning were a hint from God to finish the rest of my business before I ran out of time.

I held out a hand to Tasia, and she helped me find my feet. "I'll be fine," I said.

"You look like death on legs. I can't believe you've kept the Emperor in the dark this long."

I fluttered my fingers and took Tasia's arm. "Justinian has enough to deal with, with Totila and the rest of the Ostrogoths in Rome. I don't care to trouble him."

My daughter exhaled a puff of air. "You've never troubled that man. He loves you as much as he did the day he married you. More now, I think."

Justinian waited for me at the passage to the Hagia Sophia. The glow of gold beckoned from the other end, a promise of paradise.

"You'd best go join your aunt, Tasia." I gave her a stern look and walked straight as I could to take Justinian's arm, glad I'd worn black silk gloves to cover my mottled fingers, a fresh sign of the disease spreading through my body. I leaned my head on Justinian's shoulder to watch Tasia walk away. Whatever else I had done in this life, I was proud of my daughter. And proud of the man I'd married. I didn't deserve either of them, but I had done my best the past years to make it up to them.

I smiled but clenched my teeth as a fresh wave of pain slashed at my abdomen. "A momentous wedding."

"Indeed," Justinian said. "I shall be able to die a happy man after today."

The mosaics of the Hagia Sophia shimmered like a sweep of golden sky at sunset over our heads as we emerged from the tunnel, the letters of my *tablion* forever intertwined with Justinian's on the forest of white marble columns. Four feathered seraphims observed the imperial ceremony from their lofty perches on the pendentives while patricians watched from the gallery behind us and their women peered down from the balconies. The dome itself seemed to float in the air, lit by God's own light. Eight years ago, before the plague and the debacle over my son, Justinian had walked into his newly finished church and grasped my hand, muttering the words, "Solomon, I have eclipsed you."

Now that divine light shone down on my niece and her betrothed while the sweet voices of a *castrati* choir reached toward the heavens.

And almost a lifetime ago I had entered a less-ornate church on this same spot, been draped in purple, and felt the imperial diadem placed on my brow. Since then, I had done many things I wasn't proud of, and I would shortly have to answer to God for many of them. I had been tempered by my past, made all the stronger for it, and managed to reign successfully alongside my husband. Yet soon all my accomplishments would be only memories, carried by the people I'd loved. They were my greatest accomplishment, and not realizing that sooner was my greatest failure.

I smiled at Sophia and then at her mother. Comito's lovely golden hair was now a stunning cascade of snowy white, but her eyes shone with tears as she beamed at her daughter. General Sittas had passed to

God a number of years ago, but Justinian stood in his stead to give my niece to his own nephew, Justin, Vigilantia's son. Through our siblings, Justinian and I would found a dynasty.

Sophia smiled shyly through her saffron veil as Justin broke bread with her before the silver altar, their fingers brushing and ensuring fertility and happy years to come. My niece promised to obey her new husband, prompting a wink at me from Justinian. Obedience was highly overrated.

I sent a silent prayer to the Virgin for their happy marriage and a string of children and grandchildren to fill their laps as they grew old together. My prayer was almost finished when a stab of pain in my stomach threatened to double me over.

I bit my lip to keep from crying out as Justin circled Sophia and clasped the gold wedding belt—the same one I'd worn to my own wedding—around her tiny waist. Justinian caught my eye, but I looked away. With this marriage I had completed all my earthly tasks, ensuring Justinian the heir I'd never given him.

The liturgy finished, and the Patriarch of Constantinople blessed the bride and groom as they knelt before the altar surrounded by their circle of family. I bowed my head over clasped hands, my prayers changing from wishes for Sophia to begging the Virgin to see me to the end of the ceremony. I could no longer control my breath, struggling for air one moment and panting like a dog the next.

Justinian touched my elbow. "Are you all right?" More than once I had feared life without him; yet it was I who was going to leave him behind.

"Fine," I said through gritted teeth. "I hope they have a peaceful life together."

"Then I'll have to demote Justin and exile them from Constantinople. Perhaps Sophia would like to be a fishwife in Gallia." Justinian chuckled, and the Patriarch gave us a sharp glance, at least as sharp as one could give the Augusti.

I shivered, mostly a guise so I could clutch Justinian's arm. The room was too cold, but a white-hot iron of pain stabbed my navel. My knees buckled, and I sank into the swirl of mosaic, curling into the fire in my abdomen with a curse.

"Theodora?" Justinian's voice was frantic, and I felt him crouched at my side, but I could only pant through the pain. Breathing seemed to bury the knives deeper into my abdomen.

Not now. I wasn't ready to go yet.

Strong arms lifted me, and I could barely make out Justinian's tight face.

"You told me you were eating." His tone was firm, but he looked more frightened than he had during Nika. "You weigh less than a bird."

I'd not been able to eat anything more than fish broth for weeks, but I had kept the fact hidden under the drapes of my stolas. "Cyr's been enjoying all the extra food." I closed my eyes again. "He's fat as a hog."

"Call the physicians to meet us in the Augusta's chambers." Justinian held me close, as if he feared I might evaporate in his arms.

"It's too late for that." I opened my eyes as the pain retreated, waiting for it to return with reinforcements, an enemy intent on conquest. I would not fight.

Sophia trailed wide-eyed with her mother and bridegroom as Justinian carried me over the threshold of my apartments and laid me upon my bed, taking off my veil to brush the damp hair from my forehead. I barely managed to swallow my cries as the flames of Gehenna licked my stomach.

Slaves flitted across my rooms, rushing to and fro with ewers of water and stacks of linens. I waved away the familiar saint with his bag of foul-smelling potions and worthless poultices. "I am dying," I said, surprised at how small my voice sounded. "Go away." The physician whispered in Justinian's ear, and my husband gave a terse nod, his lips a tight line. I hadn't much time.

Across the room, tiny oil lamps sputtered in a golden shrine, a silver and amber cross shining with the lights of the flames. My son waited for me.

I clasped Sophia's pale hand to her husband's bronze one as the slaves retreated from the room. "Love each other."

Justin kissed her hand. "We will," he said.

Sophia blinked and nodded. "Just like you and the Emperor."

Comito took their place, brushing my brow with her hand, now speckled with age spots. "You always had to make a scene, didn't you?"

I smiled to cover a wince of pain, but doubted I fooled anyone. "An exit is more important than an entrance," I said.

"Go easy," Comito said, kissing my forehead. "And rest well."

Justinian shut the door behind them and slipped to my bedside. We were alone. He sat on the mattress and stroked my hair. "We could have traveled to Bithynia," he said. "Taken the waters or consulted astrologers."

I pulled his hand to my lips, a Herculean effort. "It wouldn't have made a difference."

In twenty-seven years I had seen him cry only once, but now tears slipped down his cheeks unchecked. "You can't die. I forbid it."

"Since when have I ever obeyed?" I curled into myself as the barrage began anew.

"You are a brave woman, Theodora." Justinian's breath was warm on my ear, grounding me to this life. "And I've loved you all the more for it."

"I love you." I pushed the words past gritted teeth, grasping his hand in a vain attempt to shield my body from the onslaught. I squeezed his hand and forced my eyes to stay open, wanting to take the image of his eyes as my last gift from this world. Flecks of gold in a mosaic of brown, larger now through his tears.

Then, just as I had done when I feared plague would claim him, Justinian climbed into my bed, fitting my body to his. He would shepherd me to greet my son and the rest of my family; he would usher me into the unknown.

And I would wait for him.

Epilogue

Narses ducked to avoid the lace of cobwebs draped across the stone arch to the crypt of the Church of the Holy Apostles. The sweat and sea spray from the voyage from Italy still covered him, but his mind refused to believe what his eyes had already seen. The Sacred Palace had greeted his ships on the way to the Harbor of Eleutherious, but the sun of the Empire was draped in black. Such a display meant only one thing—Justinian was dead.

Seventeen years ago, Narses had watched through bleary eyes as Theodora's body was lowered into her porphyry sarcophagus and tucked into the mausoleum below this church to join the bodies of Constantine, Theodosius, and Ariadne. An imperial purple shroud had draped her body, just as she'd requested so many years ago during the Nika riots, but even in death her chin had still seemed tilted in defiance. Theodora would never let something as trifling as death get the best of her. And yet her death almost got the best of her husband. Justinian had locked himself in her apartments with Theodora's body until Narses threatened to break down the door. The Emperor's back was stooped and his hair had gone white when he finally emerged, just in time for the funeral. Narses recalled the ceremony, the city draped with black and the air choked with incense as the entire court came to pay homage to their Empress.

"No woman should hold such power," one patrician had muttered during the funeral mass. "Justinian's Empire was like one upside-down with her on the throne, with only demons wearing crowns."

"I hope she burns for eternity," another had replied—the historian Procopius. Theodora had been right in comparing him to a monkey.

Theodora wouldn't burn—the devil wouldn't wish to deal with a woman who could outsmart him. Narses touched the foot of her sarcophagus, reverently, like a lover. And he *had* loved her—it was impossible for any man not to love her or hate her, such was her power. The woman was not without fault, but it was beyond doubt that the Lord had made her to match men. Yet few men had ever wielded such power so well as Theodora.

Narses had feared Justinian might have wandered aimlessly without his wife, but if anything, the Emperor had lived the remaining years as if for both of them, even six years ago at the age of seventy-six going so far as to direct the battle outside Constantinople when the Kutrigur Huns attacked. And Justinian had never remarried—any other woman would have been a pale shadow in comparison to Theodora. Instead, the Emperor wore the gold wedding band inscribed with her name until the day he died, where it almost certainly still remained.

Narses lit a lamp, the burning oil overpowering the musty smell of death. Only the sound of his sword bumping against his creaking hip broke the silence of the tomb. Justinian's gleaming sarcophagus sat in the middle of the dusty mausoleum, a marble statue of the Emperor in repose on the top. Narses didn't kneel—surely Justinian would excuse his lack of decorum if it meant an old man might not rise again—and placed the flickering lamp on the cold stone.

"Rest well, Augustus," he said. He lingered for only a moment before moving to the purple and gold sarcophagus at Justinian's right. Dried Nazareth irises lay atop Theodora's sarcophagus, their rare petals scattered about the floor. Justinian's final gift to her—he had made no secret that he had visited her tomb every week since her death and always left an iris for her.

"Rest well, Augusta." Narses leaned on his cane to kiss the cold marble. "And wherever you are now, try not to cause too much trouble."

AUTHOR'S NOTE

The majority of events and title of this book are borrowed from the work of Procopius of Caesarea, the primary historian during Justinian's reign. While Procopius lauded Justinian's accomplishments in his official works, *History of the Wars* and *Buildings*, he also wrote another unofficial account of Justinian's reign, *The Secret History*, which was understandably kept hidden during his life and only rediscovered in 1623 in the Vatican Library. It is from this work that we learn of Theodora's early life on Constantinople's stage and how she met Justinian and eventually became Empress of the late Roman—or Byzantine as it is called in modern times—Empire. Procopius used *The Secret History* to malign both Theodora and Justinian (among others); it was he who recorded that Theodora would sleep with her fellow party-goers and their servants—up to thirty men in one night—and still not satisfy her lust. Procopius also called Justinian a demon and claimed the Emperor's head would temporarily disappear from his body while he paced his throne room, only to magically reappear. (It may be wise to take much of Procopius' vitriol with a hefty dose of salt.)

Most events and all the major characters in this book are a

reflection of the historical record, with a few twists. Theodora really did perform the salacious *Leda and the Swan* routine, follow Hecebolus to Pentapolis before he threw her out (although he almost certainly never slept with Comito), and contend with Empress Euphemia (whose name I kept as Lupicina, her name before becoming Empress, so as not to confuse her with Euphemia, John of Cappadocia's daughter). Theodora turned the tide at Nika with her famous speech to Justinian and essentially ran the Empire while he was ill with bubonic plague, including dealing with Belisarius' attempt to become the next Emperor. I am deeply indebted to H. B. Dewing's translation of *History of the Wars* and Richard Atwater's translation of *The Secret History* for their insight into these subjects. However, due to the many years covered in the novel, I elected to start off Theodora's story at a more mature age than what Procopius recorded. In truth, Theodora was less than seven years old when she begged before the Greens and not much older when her mother put her on the stage.

There were also several characters from history that I merged in the story. *The Secret History* alludes to a mysterious son named John who was abandoned by Theodora, but who returned to the capital as a grown man to meet his mother. Theodora supposedly feared Justinian would discover the truth of her illegitimate son, so John was sent away with one of her servants, never to be seen or heard from again. Procopius also mentions an attractive young man named Areobindus who served as Theodora's steward and who disappeared after displeasing Theodora. While it is extremely unlikely that the two disappearances were connected in reality, the idea of Theodora sacrificing her son, only to lose him a second time, captured my imagination early on while I was researching her life.

There are two Macedonias mentioned by Procopius, one a dancer in Antioch who wrote a letter introducing Theodora to Justinian, and the other a servant of Antonina's who leaked information about her mistress' affair with Theodosius. Antonina promptly cut out the servant's tongue, chopped the rest of her into tiny bits, and threw them into the sea. It didn't seem much of a stretch to combine the two women into a single, doomed character.

In the interest of clarity, I took the liberty of blending several religious figures from history. Both Severus and Timothy, the Patriarch of Alexandria, left their stamp on Theodora's religious beliefs during her stay in the Egyptian city. Only Severus plays a role in the novel, but he carries many of Timothy's traits, including his visits to the anchorite hermits living in the Egyptian desert. And while there was no single known stylite perched on a marble column during Theodora's reign, there were many stylite monks in the surrounding years, the most colorful of whom were Saint Alypius and two Saint Simeons (the Elder and the Younger). Theodora did ask a ninety-year-old ascetic monk, Saint Sabas, to pray for her to conceive Justinian's heir and was rebuffed due to her Monophysite beliefs, but Saint Sabas was not a stylite.

The scenes between Theodora and Amalasuntha are entirely products of my imagination. Amalasuntha did write to Justinian to receive his protection (and provide a perfect excuse for him to finally invade and reconquer Italy), but there is no evidence that she ever visited Constantinople. However, Procopius recorded rumors that Theodora arranged Amalasuntha's murder from afar, so I couldn't resist the firestorm that would inevitably occur by pitting the two powerful women against each other face-to-face.

Theodora had many enemies, including Belisarius, whom she never trusted. She managed to convince her husband to suspect him as well, especially after he was offered the crown in Ravenna. The rivalry between Theodora and John the Cappadocian was well recorded by Procopius, although I doubt her supposed son factored into their hatred for each other. The mob at Nika did call for John the Cappadocian's removal (along with Justinian's other unpopular minister, Tribonium), and it was Antonina and Theodora who finally brought him down, using his daughter to convince him that Antonina and Belisarius sought to topple Justinian's throne. He was finally exiled after being suspected of the murder of the bishop of Cyzicus, but he was recalled to Constantinople after Theodora's death.

I imagine Theodora as a woman of passion. She despised and punished those she saw as a threat to her or her husband, but she rewarded those who were loyal. She and Antonina enjoyed a lifelong friendship that ended only with Theodora's death, and Theodora and Justinian shared a deep love, one never questioned by their contemporaries or modern historians. I hope that I have been faithful to her character.

I first came across Theodora's story while teaching world history, a subject rife with accounts of bloody wars and the accomplishments of well-known men. The rather scant textbook chapter on the Byzantine Empire included Constantine's vision at the Battle of Milvian Bridge, iconoclasts, and a lonely sentence about an actress-turned-Empress who saved her husband's throne. This, of course, was a reference to Theodora's speech during the Nika revolt. Since then, I have sought out several forgotten women in history, including an Egyptian pharaoh and the wife and daughters of Genghis Khan, determined to breathe new life into their fascinating life stories.

My sincere thanks go out to everyone who had a hand in this manuscript, and there are many. I am immensely grateful to Renee Yancy and Jade Timms for slogging through an early draft—no mean feat—and I owe a huge thank-you to Vicki Tremper and Amalia Dillin for their comments and suggestions. Gary Corby, an expert on all things historical and writing related, has been a good friend and sounding board since this novel's inception. Also to my super-agent, Marlene Stringer, and my amazing editor, Ellen Edwards, both of whom deserve some sort of monument for all their work on this novel. Finally, thank you to Elizabeth Bistrow, Jane Steele, and Maryellen O'Boyle at NAL for helping to bring this book to life.

And finally, to Stephen and Isabella. Thank you for gamely putting up with being dragged to obscure historical sites (usually at midday in the height of summer) and ignoring my random scribblings (often about beheadings or ancient birth control) left scattered on scraps of paper around the house.

I love you both.

Further Reading on the Byzantine Empire

FICTION

Bradshaw, Gillian. *Imperial Purple*. New York: Houghton Mifflin: 1988.

Perry, Anne. *The Sheen on the Silk*. New York: Ballantine Books, 2010.

Reed, Mary, and Eric Mayer. *One for Sorrow*. Scottsdale: Poisoned Pen Press, 1999.

Waugh, Evelyn. *Helena*. Chicago: Loyola Press, 1950.

NONFICTION

Brownsworth, Lars. *Lost to the West: The Forgotten Byzantine Empire That Rescued Civilization*. New York: Three Rivers Press, 2009.

Cesaretti, Paolo. *Theodora: Empress of Byzantium*. New York: Vendome, 2001.

Dauphin, Claudine. *Brothels, Baths & Babes: Prostitution in the Byzantine Holy Land*. Classics Ireland Volume 3, 1996.

Gibbon, Edward. *The Decline and Fall of the Roman Empire*. New York: Tess Press, 1963.

Herrin, Judith. *Byzantium: The Surprising Life of a Medieval Empire*. Princeton: Princeton University Press, 2007.

van Millingen, Alexander. *Byzantine Churches in Constantinople*. London: MacMillan & Co., 1912.

Procopius. *History of the Wars*, translated by H. B. Dewing. Cambridge: Harvard University Press, 1914.

Procopius. *The Secret History*, translated by Richard Atwater. Ann Arbor: University of Michigan Press, 1961.

Rosen, William. *Justinian's Flea: The First Great Plague and the End of the Roman Empire.* New York: Penguin Books, 2007.

Photo by Katherine Schmeling Photography

Stephanie Thornton is a writer and history teacher who has been obsessed with infamous women from ancient history since she was twelve. She lives with her husband and daughter in Alaska, where she is at work on her next novel.

THE SECRET HISTORY

A NOVEL OF EMPRESS THEODORA

STEPHANIE THORNTON

A CONVERSATION WITH STEPHANIE THORNTON

Q. This is the first novel in a series you plan about the "forgotten women of history." Can you tell us what you mean by that phrase and what inspired you to embark on this ambitious project? What about Theodora convinced you that her story had to be told first?

A. Our history books tend to focus on men, and while there are a handful of famous (or infamous) women who have been written about many times—Cleopatra, Isabella of Castile, and Anne Boleyn, to name a few—it's the stories of extraordinary women that few people have ever heard of who most intrigue me.

A single sentence in a history book, about Theodora's involvement in the Nika revolt, originally brought her to my attention while I was teaching world history. After reading Procopius' *The Secret History*, an unauthorized first-person account of Justinian's reign, I realized that there had to be more to her story than the ancient historian allowed for. Theodora was a flesh-and-blood woman, not,

I suspected, the lusty demoness that Procopius described. I was fortunate to be able to travel to modern-day Istanbul and see Theodora's monogram in the Hagia Sophia, read the inscription about her piety in the Church of Saints Sergius and Bacchus, and ogle the gorgeous Sacred Palace mosaics upon which she might have once walked. I knew then that I simply had to write her story.

Q. Why did Procopius hate Justinian and Theodora so much? What other historical record has come down through the ages to complete our current understanding of Justinian's reign? And are Justinian and Theodora regarded favorably by historians today?

A. Other Byzantine writers such as John the Lydian left us histories and records about Justinian's administration, but *The Secret History* is the only major primary source we have about Theodora's early life. While the book was intended to be published after Justinian's death for obvious reasons, historians are unsure why Procopius wrote such a scathing account. Perhaps he felt slighted at being left out of the imperial circle of power. In any case, it is this book that tells us most of what we know about Theodora. Later writers such as Edward Gibbon and Cesare Baronio mention Theodora, but she is often cast as a sort of notorious *femme fatale*. More sympathetic biographies have come to light in recent years, including the excellent biography by Paolo Cesaretti, *Theodora: Empress of Byzantium*. Modern historians tend to view Justinian as the last truly Roman Emperor before the advent of the Middle Ages, and his reign as the height of the Byzantine Empire, which began its long decline after the plague and his death.

Q. I know very little about Constantinople in the fifth century AD, which seems so distant and different from our own time. Can you recap the history of Constantinople in a nutshell, to explain why this city above all others became the new center of the waning Roman Empire?

A. Constantinople started out as Byzantion, a small trading town perfectly situated at the joining of the Black and Aegean seas. However, after Constantine the Great won the Battle of Milvian Bridge in AD 312, and with it the Roman Emperor's throne, he decided to found a new capital. That distant little trading town seemed the ideal place to remove himself from Rome's decay, effectively splitting the Empire into East and West. People from all corners of the Empire flocked to the new capital of Constantinople—pagans and Christians alike—and when Italian Rome fell in AD 476, Constantinople became the only capital left standing.

Q. Theodora's rise from pauper to Empress of an Empire, before the age of twenty-five, remains an extraordinary achievement. How do you account for it? And was the social order of the time really as flexible as her rise suggests?

A. Theodora's rags-to-riches story wasn't typical for the majority of the population at the time. If you were born to a poor family in sixth-century Constantinople, you would likely die in a similar situation a few decades later. However, for a lucky few, it was possible to climb from the gutters to the palace. Emperor Justin really did start out as a swineherd who traveled to Constantinople with only a few crackers in his pocket. However, as was typical in Rome, military men were often perfectly poised to seize the throne when it became available, and Justinian's uncle, Justin, managed to bribe his way into power, bringing his barbarian, prostitute-turned-wife, Lupicina, with him.

As an unmarried mother with a murky history, Theodora experienced an even more impressive rise because she managed to become Empress based on her wits and a fair bit of luck. Macedonia's letter of introduction to Justinian, his infatuation with her, and Empress Lupicina's death all combined to allow her extraordinary ascent to power.

Q. The women at this time seem to be completely dependent on men for their financial security. Did they truly have no options outside of marriage, prostitution, or the convent?

A. There were few professions available to most Byzantine women of Theodora's time. Upper-class women were expected to remain fairly sequestered in the *gynaeceum*, or women's quarters, of their homes, so women at the bottom rungs of society actually had more freedom than their patrician counterparts. Regardless of social stature, marriage was the surest bet for putting food on the table and a roof over their heads. The wife was seen as the head of the household and, depending on her class, she might work in the fields alongside her husband or run the family shop. Fortunately, Byzantium's literate society ensured that many girls could read and write, but that in no way guaranteed their financial success. Some women became prostitutes, often sold into the world's oldest profession by families eager to rid themselves of an extra mouth to feed. A very few other women became washerwomen, innkeepers, nuns, or midwives. Still, compared to modern standards, a Byzantine woman's prospects were fairly circumscribed.

Q. Can you tell us more about Severus, the deposed Patriarch of Antioch, and the Monophysites? How significant were differing religious beliefs during this time in fomenting social and political unrest?

A. Severus was one of the eminent theologians of Theodora's age and a staunch Monophysite. This religious minority believed that Christ had only one divine nature, as opposed to the more prevalent belief of Christ's dual human and divine natures. This was a hot topic in sixth-century Byzantium, and Emperors (and Empresses) often chose sides in this debate. (Justinian typically sided with the Dyophysites and Theodora with the Monophysites.) In fact, Severus was appointed Patriarch of Antioch by the pro-Monophysite Emperor Anastasius, but he was deposed when Emperor Justin sought a reconciliation with Rome and needed to rid himself of the heretical Monophysites. Luckily for Theodora, Severus ended up in Alexandria where he had a profound influence on her life.

Q. Despite the wide acceptance of Christianity, this period seems incredibly violent, with blood sports offered as public entertainment. Can you help us make sense of that?

A. Fortunately for the Byzantines, their culture wasn't nearly as bloody as that of their Roman predecessors. Early Byzantine Emperors did continue the Roman tradition of bread and circuses, supplementing the people's diet with grain from Egypt and offering a fairly constant schedule of games and chariot races at the Hippodrome. Gladiatorial games like those held in the Colosseum were on the decline after Constantine outlawed them in AD 325, but hunts of wild beasts were often staged, and the halftime entertainment might include a bearbaiting like the one Theodora witnessed.

However, it's also interesting to realize that in some respects the ancient Byzantines would have considered our society even more violent than theirs. For example, Byzantine law typically preferred to blind even the worst criminals or cut out their tongues rather than order an execution. Most modern legal systems would deem that cruel and unusual punishment, but the Byzantines would have seen such disfigurement as being kinder than capital punishment.

Q. We're told that the plague killed off half the population of the Empire—a loss that is inconceivable to us today. Do we have any idea of how many people actually died? How did the towns and cities continue to function with such a massive loss of life? And do we have a sense of the long-lasting consequences of the trauma?

A. The trauma of Justinian's Plague on the Byzantine Empire cannot be stressed enough. Procopius recorded that the bubonic plague raged in Constantinople for four months and that ten thousand people died per day during the peak of the disease. The city eventually ran out of places to bury the dead and resorted to tearing the roofs from the towers along the Sykae walls and filling them with bodies. The Empire's loss of roughly twenty million people meant a sharp drop in tax revenues and production, a critical and utterly practical problem for Justinian as he could no longer finance his wars and massive building programs. His reign might have ushered in a second Roman golden age, but after the plague of AD 542, the Byzantine Empire instead began its long, painful decline.

Q. Did your research suggest that Theodora and Justinian were true soul mates, and their romance one for the ages? What do you think Justinian saw in her that convinced him to marry her, and make her an Empress?

A. Theodora and Justinian had a romance to rival many of the most famous love stories in history, and theirs certainly had a happier ending than the likes of Antony and Cleopatra or Napoleon and Josephine! Procopius recorded that when Justinian first saw Theodora, he fell violently in love with her and that after he made her his mistress, she seemed the "sweetest thing in the world." Justinian might have had any woman in the Empire, but it was Theodora he chose and essentially fought his aunt and uncle to marry. Theodora was an attractive, well-traveled, intelligent woman who wasn't afraid to speak her mind, and in those qualities Justinian recognized his future Empress. After her death, he chose not to remarry, remaining a widower for seventeen years. I like to think he remained alone because he knew no other woman could replace Theodora.

Q. Theodora and Justinian had no children of their own, but they forged many marriages that they hoped would secure their continuing dynasty. Were they successful? And what happened to the other major historical characters—Antonina, Belisarius, John the Cappadocian, etc.?

A. Theodora and Justinian did manage to continue the dynasty, but it was extremely short-lived. Sophia and her husband, Justin II, ruled after Justinian's death, but Justin suffered numerous mental breakdowns and finally went mad. His successor, Tiberius II Constantine, was a military man and not related to the family, although Sophia proposed marriage to him and was rebuffed.

Antonina was sent back to Constantinople to seek more men for Belisarius' latest foray into Italy, but returned to a city in mourning for Theodora and instead convinced Justinian to recall her husband. The last mention of her by Procopius involves her breaking up a marriage between her daughter, Joannina, and Theodora's nephew, Anastasius. Nothing is known of her death.

Belisarius was sent to fight several more of Justinian's wars, but he remained a diminished man after his belittlement at the hands of Theodora and Antonina. He died in AD 565, only eight months before Justinian.

John the Cappadocian continued to oversee tax affairs in Antinoopolis, although Theodora attempted and failed several times to bring him to trial. Justinian recalled John to Constantinople after her death, but he never returned to political power.

Q. What would you most like readers to take away from the novel?

A. I hope readers appreciate Theodora's ferocious tenacity throughout her struggles. Regardless of her situation—being thrown out by her sister, abandoned by Hecebolus at the ends of the earth, or facing an angry mob that wanted to kill her and her husband—Theodora never gave up. I think that's an important lesson. You never know what you can achieve so long as you never stop trying.

Q. This is your first published novel. Can you tell us a little bit about your journey as a writer so far?

A. I've dabbled in writing stories since I was in third grade, but I realized my passion for storytelling while teaching history. I began my first novel about Hatshepsut, a female pharaoh who stole the crown from her stepson and ushered in Egypt's golden age, in 2008, but I set it aside to write *The Secret History* because I simply couldn't get Theodora's story out of my head. Teaching history is a great complement to writing historical fiction—I get the best of both worlds, playing with primary sources by day and writing fiction at night.

Q. What can we anticipate from you in the future?

A. I've moved from the alleys of Constantinople back to the sands of Egypt for my next novel about Hatshepsut. I'm currently at work on my third novel, about the Mongolian wife and daughters of Genghis Khan, the greatest conqueror the world has ever known.

QUESTIONS FOR DISCUSSION

1. What did you enjoy most about *The Secret History*? Who is your favorite character?

2. What do you think of Theodora? What do you see as her greatest strengths and flaws? When does she win your admiration and when does she earn your disapproval?

3. What role does luck play in Theodora's life?

4. Is Theodora a good mother? Is Antonina a better one?

5. Discuss the friendship between Theodora and Antonina. Is theirs the kind of friendship you hope to have? When do they save each other? When do they betray each other?

6. When Macedonia pleads for Theodora's help after an earthquake leaves her destitute, Theodora deliberately decides not to help. Discuss why she makes this choice and how it comes to haunt her. Would you have done the same?

7. What do you think makes Theodora and Justinian's marriage so successful?

8. Justinian is a dedicated ruler. Is he an effective one? Discuss the tactics he uses to acquire and retain power. Do they interfere with his ability to rule wisely?

9. Can you imagine living in Constantinople in the sixth century AD? What kind of life do you think you would have there? What would you most like and most dislike about living in that time and place?

10. Plague had a devastating effect on the Byzantine Empire. Discuss what you imagine the world of today would be like if half the population was suddenly wiped out by illness.

11. Have you traveled to any of the places mentioned in the novel, in particular to Istanbul, the current name for the city that was once Constantinople? How do the places you experienced compare to the way they're described in the book?

12. What do you hope to remember about this novel?

The gods erred that day. Or perhaps they were simply cruel.

It was the season of *Akhet*, and the Nile swelled with Isis' tears and the rich dark silt that would feed the barley and emmer wheat during the cool months of *Peret*. Hatshepsut and her sister sat as rigid as statues at the bow of the royal skiff, shaded from Re's heat by a thin awning of spotted goat hide. The slaves' ostrich wing fans kept the lazy flies at bay but served only to rearrange the heat. A trickle of sweat snuck down Hatshepsut's back and her scalp itched under her wig. Sandalwood oars tipped with gold spread like glittering dragonfly wings behind them as slaves rowed to the steady beat of the drums.

"You fidget like a sparrow." Neferubity laid a hand on Hatshepsut's leg, her nails graceful half-moons and her hands painted with intricate swirls of henna. The paint on Hatshepsut's hands was already smudged and her nails ragged from constant biting.

"A sparrow would be able to fly from this boat." Hatshepsut rubbed the ears of the black dog curled at her feet and scanned the river. This hippo hunt had seemed a good idea until she realized she wasn't to wield a spear or even a bow to hunt the brown cranes soaring overhead. Not that it mattered—the courtiers from the Pharaoh's court in the boats ahead were making so much noise, most of the animals had probably fled to the desert of the Red Lands by now.

Rekhyt lined the banks of the river, mostly farmers looking like they'd just been dug from the Nile's black mud and fishermen struggling not to upset their boats as they bowed to the Great Royal Wife and the rest of Egypt's court. Bare-breasted women looked up from pounding linens upon the rocks and fell to their knees in the murky water, drenching the linen sheaths they'd tucked between their legs. A naked girl ran along the bank, her braided youth lock flapping as she laughed like a hyena. Hatshepsut wished she could do the same instead of being trapped in this boat wearing a wig that scratched like Ammit's claws. She leaned over the edge of the boat and waved at the girl. *"Ankh, udja, seneb!"*

Life, prosperity, and health.

Neferubity chuckled next to her. "You won't have any life left if Mother hears you yelling like a *rekhyt*." The bells at the ends of her braided wig tinkled as she smiled and shook her head.

"What Mother doesn't know can't hurt her," Hatshepsut said. "Or me."

"I see you're wearing your new necklace. It suits you."

Hatshepsut touched the gold-and-jasper pendant of Sekhmet, the goddess of war and hunting, a gift from Neferubity for her last naming day. "I thought I might speak to Father when he returns. Perhaps I might serve Sekhmet in her temple."

Neferubity laughed. "Even the lion goddess might not be able to keep you from trouble, little sister."

The boats continued their languid procession until Hatshepsut thought she might jump overboard to escape the boredom. Fortunately, the furious rattle of *sistrums* and men yelling upriver interrupted her plans.

"They found a hippo." Growing a shade paler, Neferubity pursed her lips, but Hatshepsut jumped atop their bench, sending the little skiff bobbing. The sleek black dog at her feet whimpered, straining on his leash.

"Hush, Iwiw." Hatshepsut knew how he felt.

Their boat crept closer, confirming Neferubity's guess. A hippo calf with rolls of fat ringing its neck shaded itself in a papyrus grove at an island's edge, its gray skin shiny in the sun. Several boats ahead, Imhotep—the ancient vizier in charge of the government during the Pharaoh's long campaign in Canaan—stood and nocked an arrow onto his bow. Next to him, glimmering with gold, sat Ahmose, Hatshepsut's mother and Egypt's Great Royal Wife. The courtiers and nobles fell silent as Imhotep let the arrow fly. He aimed too high. The wooden shaft arced into the reeds, sending a black-and-white ibis screeching into the blue sky. The little river cow honked his outrage at the disturbance, then splashed clumsily into the Nile and disappeared into the murky waters with a wiggle of his gray rump.

Neferubity joined the polite clapping, but Hatshepsut glared into the reeds and scratched her scalp. Would her mother notice if she dropped her wig into the Nile? "I'd have hit that hippo from fifty paces," she declared.

It wasn't bragging because it was true. Neferubity kissed Hatshepsut's temple, smiling fondly as she smoothed her sister's wig. "I'm sure the hippo is glad you weren't behind the bow."

They glided forward, passing the crushed grasses that bore the indent of the river cow's body. Ahead, slaves pulled the first boats of the expedition onshore. There the nobility would enjoy a meal under baobab trees and linen awnings before returning to the capital.

"Perhaps we'll sight a hippo on the return," Imhotep speculated, loud enough for the meager breeze to carry his words. Hatshepsut snorted. The old man would need the blessings of the nine great gods to shoot a sleeping elephant at twenty paces.

She twisted on her bench. "Pull to the side here."

Neferubity glanced at the bank of the island, one that would connect to the shore when Isis' tears receded, and shook her head. The golden disks at her ears flashed with Re's light. "I'm not dumb, little sister."

"You have two choices, Neferubity." Hatshepsut crossed her arms and gave a honeyed smile. "We can either pull to the bank so I can relieve myself in seclusion, or I can do so in front of the entire court of Egypt."

Neferubity studied her for a moment, then heaved a sigh. "We should probably keep your bad manners hidden from the Nubian ambassador for as long as possible."

Hatshepsut shot her a grin. "I'll be right back." In one movement she swiped a stick from the bench of the head rower. The elm shaft, unpolished and lacking balance, was a poor substitute for her own spears, but it would do.

"Hatshepsut!" Neferubity shrieked as Hatshepsut splashed into the Nile, sending the little boat swaying. Iwiw barked and leapt after her, his rope leash trailing in the mud. They tore through the papyrus grove, the bushy fronds at the top of the reeds quivering with the breath of the gods. The river was alive, the drone of flies and the waves lapping at the shore marred only by the occasional shriek of laughter from the courtiers upriver. Great Royal Wife Ahmose surely would have noticed their absence by now. And she undoubtedly wasn't happy about it.

Mud squelched between Hatshepsut's toes, ruining her gilded sandals. She kicked them off onto a low table of rock. Her mother was going to have her head for ruining them, but she'd worry about that later. She'd have preferred to strip everything off and dive into the river glinting through the reeds, but she settled for tucking the hem of her skirt into its beaded sash. With any luck, the slaves would be packing up by the time they arrived upriver.

Hatshepsut stilled, forcing her breath to slow until her chest scarcely moved. A white egret pecked at the mud under a slender baobab tree on the opposite shore. It was a difficult shot from such a distance, but worth it. She crept closer, out of the reeds, wondering briefly where Iwiw had gone. Muttering a prayer to Sekhmet, the lion goddess and Egypt's greatest hunter, Hatshepsut lifted the stick, every muscle tensed to send it flying.

"Hatshepsut! Where are you?"

The egret flapped its glorious wings, then launched into the air, soaring away from Hatshepsut.

"Sekhmet's breath!" Hatshepsut stomped, spattering freckles of mud up her white sheath.

Neferubity grabbed her arm and pulled her to an open swath cut through the sedge grass, higher up the bank than the swamp Hatshepsut had trudged through. A sheen of sweat pearled on her sister's upper lip and a pile of dried hippo dung swarmed with flies near her feet, but otherwise Neferubity might have been on her way to a royal banquet. She grabbed the hunting stick and hesitated, glaring as if ready to hit Hatshepsut over the head with it. Instead, she tossed it into the reeds. "You would try Thoth's patience."

"I almost had that egret."

Her sister ignored her. "I don't care if you almost took down a whole pride of lions. Mother is going to kill us."

"Not us." Hatshepsut looked down at her dirty sheath and the mud up to her knees. "Just me."

Neferubity chuckled and released Hatshepsut's arm. "I'll wear my best sheath to your funeral. Let's go before anyone else falls victim to our mother's wrath."

"I need to get my sandals."

"Nice try, little sister."

"Mother will never believe I fell out of the boat if I don't have my sandals," Hatshepsut called over her shoulder, tromping through the swamp before Neferubity could argue.

The sandals lay on the rock where she'd left them, coated with a thick crust of dried brown mud. Iwiw jumped out of the reeds, the hair on his neck on end and his teeth bared. Hatshepsut stepped forward and he snapped at her.

"Iwiw! Heel."

But his lip only quivered and he continued to growl, a low sound of warning. Beyond the dog a menacing gray hulk rose out of the river and trudged through the reeds. Her heart stopped.

A river bull.

His thick hide was cracked with scars from prior fights with other bulls, some healed and others freshly pink. The thick hairs on his snout bristled in the air and he flicked his ears, his black eyes like shiny beetles. More dangerous than any lion, the hippo could easily gore her with his tusks, leaving her body mangled and her *ka* unable to pass to the Field of Reeds.

Hatshepsut held her breath and tried to back up, but the gods were against her. The beast glared straight at her, then bellowed, his giant yellow tusks ripping through the air. The breeze had carried her scent to him.

The world seemed to slow, the gods cursing Hatshepsut and her body turning to granite. The river bull galloped up the bank, reeds snapping and mud flying. Anubis stalked Hatshepsut, a foul smell filling her nostrils and her body going cold as the jackal-headed god reached into her heart to steal her *ka*.

Someone screamed.

Something hard slammed into her shoulder and the world went black. She opened her eyes to a scene worse than Ammit devouring the emaciated bodies of the damned on the Lake of Fire. Neferubity lay facedown, splayed in the mud where Hatshepsut had stood just moments before. The hippo reared up with a roar; then his colossal jaws scooped into the mud and snapped shut, crushing her sister's thigh in its pink maw. Neferubity screamed, the sound searing itself into Hatshepsut's mind, and the river bull jerked its head to and fro. Neferubity lurched in the air like a drunken dancer.

The hippo bellowed and Neferubity went flying, crashing into a clump of papyrus and mud. The monster stopped still, leveling a yellow stare at Hatshepsut. Then he snorted and lumbered off, disappearing into the river with scarcely a sound.

Panicked screams far in the distance broke the gods' curse. Time hurtled forward and the world snapped back into focus.

"Help! For the love of Amun, someone help!" Hatshepsut raced to Neferubity, tripping into the mud at her side. Her sister was curled up like a newborn babe, her right leg bent at a painful angle and the jagged white edge of bone poking out of the maimed flesh. Neferubity gave a tortured cry when Hatshepsut touched her ribs.

"Everything's going to be all right." Hatshepsut wiped the mud from her sister's eyes and took her hand, alarmed by the slackness of her grip. Neferubity's wig was askew and coated with brown slime, her eyes screwed tight against the pain. She opened her mouth as if to speak, but only gurgled, a froth of red blood streaming down the mud on her cheeks to feed the earth below.

"Help is coming," Hatshepsut said, clutching Neferubity's hand as if to keep her sister's *ka* from flying away. Blood poured from her leg, pools of red like broken wings in the mud. The crushed papyrus reeds trembled and the foul stench of death returned. Anubis circled her sister now—Hatshepsut could almost make out his yellow eyes among the reeds. "You have to hold on."

Neferubity's chest heaved and her lungs rattled, the blood seeming to seep out of her body from all directions even as she gasped for breath. Her nails dug into Hatshepsut's palm for a fleeting moment, as if she might cling to this life. But Anubis was too strong; he had her sister tight in his jaws and refused to release such a prize as the Pharaoh's eldest daughter.

Neferubity blinked but her eyes were unfocused, her voice less than a whisper. "I'll watch you from the Field of Reeds, Hatshepsut." More blood trickled from her lips. "Make me proud."

Hatshepsut shook her head, the braids of her wig slapping her cheeks. "Don't say that. You'll be here watching me ruin everything I touch."

"Neferubity?" Their mother's voice trembled, barely penetrating Hatshepsut's mind.

The nobility had arrived, their wide eyes ringed with kohl and mouths slack with shock. Ahmose rushed past the courtiers and stumbled into the mud next to Hatshepsut. "Neferubity!"

But it was too late. Neferubity looked beyond Hatshepsut, her blank eyes already staring at Ma'at's scales in the afterworld. Their mother gave a mangled sob, drawing the body of her eldest daughter to her chest and silently rocking back and forth as tears streamed down her face. The courtiers on the shore wailed, the women clawing at their hair and breasts in the traditional display of mourning.

Hatshepsut stood and stumbled away, watching the whisper of her sister's *ka* depart her body. She stared at Neferubity's footsteps in the mud, evidence that she had been alive only moments ago, the imprint of her own body where Neferubity had shoved her from the hippo's path.

Anubis had claimed the wrong sister.